A FED SPIRIT

A NOVEL

To Wanid,
With gratitude,
Loretta, as Erma

ERMA CLARE

A Fed Spirit
Copyright © 2022 by Erma Clare

This is a work of fiction. Any characters, businesses, places, events, and incidents are either the products of the author's imagination or used in a fictitious manner. Any resemblance to actual persons, living or dead, or actual events is purely coincidental.

Printed in the United States of America

Paperback ISBN: 978-1-958714-59-1
Ebook ISBN: 978-1-958714-60-7
Library of Congress Control Number: 2022949349

CHICAGO-NEWYORK-PARIS-ROME

Muse Literary
3319 N. Cicero Avenue
Chicago IL 60641-9998

In memory of my sister, Marie.

AUTHOR'S NOTE

Dear Readers,

Thank you very much for your interest in *A Fed Spirit*.

When I was no longer an employee of the Federal Reserve System and thinking about what came next, I sought to combine a love for fictional stories with a passion for a broader public understanding of the Fed. The idea for *A Fed Spirit* was born from the recognition that not enough of the Fed's public information meets people where they are.

Though I offer an insider's view, the characters' days are based on publicly-available information. I used news articles, documents made public through the Freedom of Information Act, Congresspersons' communications with the Fed, Fed job descriptions from various recruiting sites, economists' social media sites, reports from the Government Accountability Office, and more. Most important was information from the Fed's websites. External events were selected for their relevance to the fictional tale and may be approximately true. All information was modified to serve the fictional story.

Though I was prohibited from taking a public partisan position for most of my life, I acknowledged my respect for those elected officials who comprehend our laws and regulations, follow the rule of law, and seek change through legal paths consistent with our democracy. If *A Fed Spirit* feels partisan, please consider my lens.

My hope is that *A Fed Spirit* will inspire your curiosity about the Fed and that it might serve as a gateway to reading a news article here or there, perusing the Fed's resources, or even tapping the wealth of experts' nonfiction. But with caution to avoid those who, intentionally and unintentionally, mistake the Fed's complexity for some grand conspiracy. At the end of the day, the Fed is just a bunch of people doing their jobs in an organization with a very lofty mission that touches all of us.

Wishing you a fair job when you want one and moderate prices.

TABLE OF CONTENTS

LUCY

Your willingness to trust those you've never met is both a wonder and a fright.

I've been among some of those you've trusted since I died, here, in a Federal Reserve Bank, in 1915.

I'd come to see Mr. Myers. He was my boss during the months I worked here as a Secretary and a friend afterwards. Ever enthralled by his role in opening this Federal Reserve Bank the November before, he'd written an essay about the Fed Bank's promises and challenges for my new baby's commonplace book.

Creating commonplace books for our babies was a tradition in my family. Three-quarters was filled at the baby's birth with all sorts of information, while one-quarter was filled when the child's interests emerged.

I'd brought the commonplace book with me that day and am certain it is that book that's held me here rather than anything to do with this Fed Bank. However, as time's gone on and I've wished for meaning of my inexplicable existence, I've suspected such meaning would have to do with this Fed Bank.

Though I first sought inspiration in the tale of Mr. Jacob Marley, who dragged his chains and frightened Scrooge into sharing his money, I've no flair for drama nor the willingness to frighten others. But finally, it is your willingness to trust that inspired my search.

Your trust is a wondrously powerful enabler of the evolution of your financial system.

First, there was trade. When the shoemaker and bread baker first decided they would trust one another's skills and trade shoes and bread, each gained some time. The shoemaker might have used his found time for leisure, the bread baker to make cake.

Then, the use of money emerged to facilitate trade. A dentist wanting a quart of strawberries and a strawberry farmer with a toothache would no longer need to find one another. But using money assumed trust, since you probably wouldn't exchange your labor for money if you didn't trust the money could be traded for what you needed or wanted.

Societies define what serves as money. First, and most importantly, it must be a medium of exchange. The dollar you use to buy a quart of strawberries must be the same dollar that the grocer or farmer wants. Second, it must be a standard of value. The dollar in your pocket can be traded for no more or less than the dollar in your neighbor's pocket. Third, it must be a reasonable store of value. The dollar in your pocket today can be traded for not too much more or less than the dollar that might be in your pocket a year from now. These requirements came about by trial and error, some of which are memorialized through slang, such as calling a dollar a "buck" as a legacy of when deerskins served as money.

The dollar in use, the Federal Reserve Note, has been around a bit over a hundred years. Each Note is signed by the Treasurer of the United States and the Secretary of the Treasury. Though few think about what "Federal Reserve Note" means or who those people are, most using the Notes trust they mostly meet the three requirements of money.

Most of you trust commercial banks enough to store your money as electronic bits of information and you trust in the bits' convertibility back to dollars. That trust is so important that the Federal Deposit Insurance Corporation puts the full faith and credit of the U.S. government behind those commercial banks, to a limit.

The Treasury, the Fed System, and the FDIC are all creatures of Congress, so there's another layer of trust.

It is ironic that the only trust a Federal Reserve Note calls for is trust in God and it's only done so since 1957. I don't think God worries much about our money. When I was alive and reliant on money, I didn't pray to God about it, though I did for purchasing power. I believe God gave humans free will and it's those humans with free will who decide our means of trade. I don't think there's much use in trying to divert an accountability for money to God.

Though money enters most everyone's thoughts for at least a few seconds each day, those thoughts take the form of wondering can a boss be trusted to pay a fair wage, a bank be trusted to maintain working ATMs, or one of the myriad other pesky intermediaries be trusted to exercise their free will in an ethical and moral way. Those thoughts are not likely to include wondering about the folks in the layers described above.

Even if they occasionally do, few have the time to distill speeches and meeting minutes that describe the Federal Reserve's Federal Open Market Committee's decisions about interest rates. And those who purport to do it for others cannot always be trusted to put aside their own agenda.

Of course, there are some for whom that trust is the subject of their life's work, either by concern for it or the search for opportunities to exploit it. But who among those can be trusted.

In the late 1980s, then U.S. President Ronald Reagan brought the Russian proverb, "Trust, but verify," to the U.S. lexicon. How would one even begin to verify the financial system?

I lack the answer but believe a starting place might be appreciating how the trusted become so. This tale is about imaginary staff in a Fed Bank's Research Department in 2018 and 2019. You trust their real-life counterparts by virtue of your reliance on dollars.

Most everything written in the Fed System carries a disclaimer. A sure sign I've been here too long is that here are mine.

I don't know if I skip time or time skips me, but sometimes, I'm not here. I don't go anywhere else, I'm just not. So this spun-up story has as many holes as Swiss cheese. I think that's acceptable, since you're meant to be left with more questions than answers, and if you find that an irritant, I'll remind you that some of our philosophers framed wisdom in knowing what you don't know.

Regardless of whether it's spun-up or accounted-for truth, the representation of one Research Department in one Federal Reserve Bank has no more power to describe the Federal Reserve System than does one cookie describe a bakery with a dozen cookies that are small or large with chips or nuts or none, a dozen cupcakes with and without cream in the middle with a little or a lot of toppings, a dozen muffins each with different berries or nuts and some with and some without a crumble topping, a dozen donuts frosted in a rainbow of colors and chocolate and some with sprinkles, a few gluten-free or sugar-free items, and a many-tiered wedding cake embellished with sparkly sugar and figurines and seven types of frosting and flowers from both a greenhouse and a backyard. At least as long as that one cookie hasn't, say, been served after falling in mop water.

Finally, I apologize, but some acronyms, not as many as the staff use, but some, are needed to describe the complex structure of the Federal Reserve System. Whether an organization should have a structure so complex it requires acronyms is outside of the scope of this story.

RD	Research Department
DOR	Director of Research
Fed Bank	Federal Reserve Bank
BOD	Board of Directors of a Federal Reserve Bank
BOG	Board of Governors
RBOPS	Reserve Bank Operations and Payments Systems
FOMC	Federal Open Market Committee
Fed System	Federal Reserve System

My name is Lucy. Come. I'll introduce you to the staff.

A New President ~ 10/1/2018

The PhD charged into Stella's office on Thursday morning. "I read your email. With all due respect, Stella, you don't understand economics."

Stella looked up from the memo she'd been reading. "Good morning. At your level, no, but gosh, at some level I hope I do. You're here about your grant?" Her smile vanished. "I do understand this Bank's policies and won't let us run afoul of ethics. You can't take a grant that tops up your Fed salary for work the Fed's already paying you to do. We'll figure out some other way."

The PhD glanced toward the doorway when Wendell, his Group Head, interrupted. "Winning a prestigious grant is a big deal for his career and is good for this Department. Don't create obstacles."

After Stella rattled off a couple policies, the PhD bristled and claimed the policies didn't apply to researchers.

"They do though."

Wendell tried bullying. "I think you might be overinterpreting there. On purpose."

She offered, "How about if we get a second opinion from our lawyers? If you'll forward an electronic copy of the grant paperwork, I'll attach it to the invite."

The PhD shook his head, shuffled his feet, and pleaded, "Wendell?"

"Go ahead and give it to her. Change is coming. Let's go."

In the hallway but not yet out of Stella's earshot, Wendell told the PhD, "She's so damn dogged."

Stella picked up the memo she'd been reading before the PhD arrived but instead gazed out the doorway, so lost in thought she didn't feel the hoop earring she loosened when she pushed her hair behind her ear. The public service role she'd reveled in for years was fraught by what felt to her as the tipping of the RD away from its core responsibility for managing the supply of money and credit in the economy.

At the sound of her desk phone, she shook her head as if to clear it and turned to reach for the speakerphone button, catching her mug of tea with her elbow. Her expression when she saw the earring and mug together on the floor belied the cheery tone with which she greeted her colleague.

Her colleague asked, "You've seen it?"

There was no need for either to name the memo. Each in charge of the administration of a Fed Bank's RD, they were two of twelve among a few people on the planet to appreciate the seemingly innocuous memo for the sea change it was. Authored by staff in RBOPS, the Reserve Bank Operations Division at the Board of Governors (BOG) of the Federal Reserve System, it was addressed to the Presidents of the Fed Banks, copied to the Fed Banks' Directors of Research, and described first-ever budget targets for the Fed Banks' spending on monetary policy.

Such a memo would be business as usual most everywhere else. But here, the memo nudged some of the many lines of independence that have grown out of lines drawn in 1914.

The 1914 lines ensured geographical independence in the then-new Fed System's monetary policy by scattering twelve Fed Banks across the country, independent from one another and separate from a Washington, D.C., Office. That independence was intended to prevent agricultural and other regional economic issues from being swept away in national averaging and remains dear to Fed Bank Presidents and RDs. It's expressed in many ways, including an independence in spending.

Some of you may know about the Fed System's independence from Congress and the U.S. President. Independence defined in 1913 by politicians who knew some of their successors would cast aside long-term monetary health of the U.S. if it would get them reelected. For example, when a U.S. President wants to lower interest rates to goose asset prices, especially stock prices, even though the low rates will cause hardship for seniors who live on savings. That independence from political influence is crucial and is emulated in other countries.

This is not about that budgetary independence.

Stella and her colleague were talking about a next level down where independence in decisions about spending was claimed along the original lines of the geographical decentralization. Not budgetary independence from politicians, but budgetary independence from other Fed Banks and the BOG.

Over the years, Fed Banks' Officers have created a spiderweb of such internal independence lines. Though Stella and her peers believe the web a work of grace and beauty, I'd liken it to an abandoned spiderweb after a hailstorm. Either way, they and I will wonder whether the memo might be the broom to knock it down.

Stella's colleague said her Director of Research (DOR) thought the memo might just be a shot across the bow. "But he's afraid if the

Board tells us how much we can spend, next they'll say to use their FOMC stuff, and we'd all end up at the same recommendation for interest rates, and defeat the purpose of the independent Fed Banks. We call foul."

Stella said, "Interesting. We can't call foul. Not where we sit on that spending chart."

Stella's colleague sheepishly added that she and her DOR had wondered whether Stella's Fed Bank had drawn this wrath of RBOPS on to all of them. He'd heard, all the way across the country, that some unhappy local Business Economists had taken to calling Stella's Fed Bank the "Fed University."

Business Economists focus on interpreting the current economy rather than a theoretical economy and often hold just one or two masters' degrees instead of a PhD. Their connections with Fed Banks were symbiotic but challenging to initiate as PhDs replaced the RD's Business Economists.

As her colleague spoke, Stella ran her finger around the rim of her pink mug, checking for chips. When she turned it upside down over the trash to empty a few drips, she smiled at the black cat face on its bottom.

The mug was a gift from her sister. During an expansion of her flower shop, Nora had asked Stella about popular office mugs. After Stella shared the RD's use of mugs to display one's academic pedigree, Nora sent this mug with a note telling Stella not to be that way.

Stella said, "I've heard the Fed University label too. They aren't wrong. I wondered whether some of those locals would reach out to our Board of Directors and tell them it's been too long since we had a President who wasn't a PhD. I'd never say it to anyone here, but I'm glad there's pushback. As a taxpayer, not as Fed staff. Anyway, we'll find out soon."

"That's right, you're getting a new President. You know, some of us were talking here about Christine Blasey Ford on Friday, how much courage she has. And if there was someone in the background like that for a candidate for Federal Reserve Bank President, she'd never know because the public doesn't even know who's being considered. And if there was someone in the background of a nominee for Fed Board Governor, would she think it was worth the risk. Not just because Governors are not lifetime appointments but because maybe the Governor role isn't perceived as requiring morality the way the Supreme Court roles do."

Stella's face had fallen at the mention of Kavanaugh's Senate hearings and when she didn't respond, her colleague continued. "I know we're not supposed to talk politics, but theoretically."

Finally, Stella said, "No, that's not it at all. Your question is really interesting. To imagine a member of the non-Fed-watching public wanting to have input feels so pie-in-the-sky, but it shouldn't. At least for Governors. But Blasey Ford's sacrifice is huge. Listening to her really gutted me." Stella hesitated but then spoke quickly. "And I can't be gutted here today so how about your ski plans for this year."

The two discovered their mutual interest when each began a ski trip at the close of one winter meeting of their Fed System committee at the Denver Branch of the Kansas City Fed Bank, but now laughed over a shared fear that they'd crossed an age when it had become unsafe to jump on skis once a year to fly down a mountain.

Stella confessed she'd already looked up local cross-country ski paths as a substitute.

After they hung up, Stella wetted a paper towel with bottled water and blotted a spot on her black wool skirt where tea had splashed. Then she turned to her expansive wooden desk and carefully pushed a pile of papers to the side in order to restore the space allotted the mug.

Each of the RD's Officers had one of the decades-old desks on which they piled paper, ignoring the Facilities Department's pleas to adopt a new standard which prioritized informal meeting space over a surface for paper.

Paper included research papers, articles, and presentations thought essential though not so essential that they justified file space or filing time. Enough paper to cause a first-time visitor to gaze with speculation and inevitably ask had the piles ever fallen. And the anecdote shared, with humor, was when a previous DOR had stopped in a PhD's office, leaned on a pile, and fell when the pile gave way. Unhurt and a paper-dependent PhD himself, the DOR appreciated the humor even as the guilty pile was restored and elsewhere piles continued to grow, excused as the nature of PhDs.

Except for Stella's desk, which, also in humor, was called out as without excuse since she had no PhD, the only Officer in the RD without one. She was also the only female Officer in the RD.

After she'd reinserted her earring and finished cleaning up the tea, she rose to investigate an increasingly loud conversation outside her door.

Several PhDs debated the probability of their favorite, David, the current DOR, being named the Fed Bank's President and the possibilities if he wasn't. David had earned the PhDs' favor by pushing the RD's culture as close as it could get to academia and the PhDs' salaries as high as he thought possible.

The PhDs' conversation bounced to bemoaning the timing of the turnover. During the 2008-2009 financial crisis, when the public's criticism and Congress' scrutiny of the Fed System were high, it had become de rigueur to promote DORs to fill open Presidents' spots and avoid the risk of an unknown external candidate. But the crisis had fallen from memory and the Fed System had lost its place as the most-hated public institution and so, the PhDs said, there was no telling who David's competition might be, plus one couldn't count on the Fed Bank's Board of Directors (BOD) making a rational choice.

One PhD said, "Who even are our Board of Directors now," and when he noticed Stella, "You must know something."

Another said, "Ah, she won't tell us anything anyway."

Focused on what Stella knew, the PhDs didn't see David's approach or course reversal.

Winnie, Executive Assistant to David and Stella, looked up as David slunk past. A few seconds later, she opened his door a crack and whispered. "David? A Director called."

"You can come in. I talked to him. Get Stella. Then get Wendell, tell him ten minutes. And tell the E-Floor I'm not going to dinner."

Winnie's mouth twitched though no words came out. Missing an Officer dinner or any event with the BOD generally carried a large penalty.

Knowing what she was thinking, David said, "I'm not. What are they going to do to me? Shut the door on your way out, would you?"

After she left, he plopped into his chair and leaned back, rubbing the few hairs at the front of his balding head as he glared around his office. In keeping with his DOR predecessors, he was the sole exception among his peers on this Fed Bank's Executive Committee in having an office away from the thick-carpeted and art-laden Executive Floor, or "E-Floor." To his would-be E-Floor neighbors, this was explained by a need for the DOR to be always privy to the PhDs' hallway debates. To his actual neighbors in the RD, it was explained by a desire to avoid the conversations of the "head bureaucrats." Both were true.

As he began a second look, his glare turned to a grimace and his eyes rested on the signs of wear and tear in the office. A decade earlier, when he'd moved into this office and was offered changes in the style of the lavish E-Floor, he reported his wife took care of such things at home and referred the Facilities staff to Winnie and Stella. Winnie had no changes and Stella shrugged in wonder at having been asked. And when Michael, the DOR before David, was offered changes, he too declined, claiming consideration of taxpayers. In this moment, David looked as if he were blaming the state of his office for the bad news he'd received.

He was looking at the empty space on the floor where his briefcase usually sat when Stella knocked. As she opened the door, he'd found the briefcase atop his desk, and said, "Found it."

Had Winnie not warned her, Stella would've been surprised by his countenance.

He repeated what he'd told Winnie about dinner but asked Stella to run interference in interactions she might have yet that day. Though only the E-Floor Officers and David were invited to dinner with the Fed Bank's BOD, the rest of the Officers knew the new President would be announced there. Any news of David's absence would enter the grapevine and travel quickly, be correctly read as he didn't get the promotion, and blossom into speculation about all sorts of things in the RD.

The decades-long tenures of many of the Fed Bank's staff supported a strong and speedy grapevine. Stella, one of the long-tenured staff, was distanced from the grapevine by virtue of being in the RD but connected to it peripherally in meetings most days. David valued her connections and willingness to articulate why, warts and all, the RD was important and the PhDs were different-in-a-good-way whenever news of either hummed through the grapevine.

Stella hesitated for a couple seconds, uncertain of what interference she'd be running, before agreeing.

With his coat on, briefcase in hand, he dialed Wendell's extension. "Are you coming?"

Wendell stepped in seconds later, his finger stuck in his mouth feeling around for food. Hired on years earlier at the same time, the two were friends. "What's up? You can't have heard yet, the Directors don't meet until four."

"They might tell the candidates first, you think?"

Wendell's head reared back in surprise at David's sarcasm. "Okay then. You are President, right?"

"Shut the door." David waited until Wendell sat. "They gave it to Michael."

Wendell often adopted a fake expression of surprise while he processed whether he ought to express joy or sorrow and he did that now. For that second, his head extended and jaw dropped as he asked, "Michael?"

"That's what I said."

Wendell's head snapped back and his jaw shut and grew rigid, his lips barely moving. "Not happening. Not you, it's me."

David seemed calmer and waved his hand in dismissal, as if Wendell's anger had drawn from his own. "Neither you nor I are going to be President. I was supposed to meet with a reporter at two. The one who wrote that article about rates and governance that got the Governors in a tizzy. Winnie will bring her to your office. I'm leaving."

"Can't someone else do that? I don't have time." He looked slyly from the side. "Can't Stella do that too?"

Wendell didn't really think Stella should meet with the reporter. He was just needling David about some business that had occurred the week before. Since Wendell had been on vacation, Stella had replaced him at a meeting of one of the Fed Bank's internal committees. Following the meeting, the committee's Chair asked David to permanently replace Wendell with Stella or send Stella too as Stella's experience of day to day operations was more valuable to them than a "ten- thousand-foot economic view."

Finding humor in the idea that anyone would willingly trade a PhD economist's input for a non-PhD's, David told Wendell so.

Wendell was embarrassed and offended and within just a couple days, he'd asked David how Stella's research paper was going though she didn't do research, whether she could talk at a conference on inflation though she was not an economist, and now this. Stella never learned about any of it, and David told the committee's Chair that Stella was already too busy.

In this conversation, David snapped, "Don't be an idiot. Winnie will bring the reporter to your office unless you find someone else."

David left then, after mumbling goodnight to Winnie without mentioning the reporter.

Elsewhere in the Fed Bank, there was excitement and dread among staff who viewed the Fed Bank's President as a CEO. Conversations supplanted meeting agendas and elevators slowed as doors were held while those exiting concluded their thoughts. Those conversations and thoughts had little overlap with those of the RD.

And neither had overlap with the conversations outside the Fed Bank. Regional bankers may wonder whether the President will feel a responsibility to the Fed Bank's role in supervising commercial banks. Community groups are concerned with the President in his role as a member of FOMC, where he, along with the other eleven Fed Bank Presidents and seven Governors at the BOG, will decide the course of policies that impact prices and employment in their communities. Those are just two examples.

That these singular views of the role of a Fed Bank President form is not a surprise. The role is always evolving in response to demands put upon it. The varied views bring to my mind the parable of the six blind men and the elephant.

One blind man feels the trunk and thinks the elephant is a snake. Another feels the ear and thinks the elephant is a magic carpet. Without seeing the elephant in its glory, each man thinks it's only what he touches. Only together can they find the truth.

Those who know the full role of a Fed Bank President include staff who have need or interest. And Fed Watchers and some reporters. And some members of Congress.

One is Senator Elizabeth Warren. In April, she criticized the appointment of John Williams to President of the New York Fed Bank. He'd already been a Fed Bank President, but in San Francisco. Warren's statement read, "The Fed's Board of Governors and the New York Fed should go out of their way to solicit and consider public input when selecting a new president who will have so much influence over interest rates and Wall Street supervision - instead, they turned the process over to a handful of private individuals and ignored calls to choose one of many qualified alternatives who might have brought a new perspective."

The reporter excused Wendell's tardiness when she asked, "I'm sure you're busy getting ready for a new President. Is that why David's unavailable?"

He made a sound between a snort and a laugh as he jumped at an out from the meeting. "Um. I can't talk about the President if that's why you're here. We could delay this."

While she reached in her bag, he noted her navy bankers' suit.

"No need." She slid a card and a few pages across the table. "I'm here because your Washington bosses didn't like my article, though it hardly feels like punishment to get the face time that I was refused a few months ago. By the way, what a wonderful building. The Great Hall is so majestic."

I wished she'd seen the original Great Hall in its glory, before the renovations that stripped the original light marble from the walls and floor, made it into paperweights for staff, and replaced it with dark-toned marble. So dark that staff referred to the space as a mausoleum until sconces were added in a pretense at lightening it. Now, years later, if staff refer to the space at all, it's usually in the context of the caution with which one crosses it when weather is wet.

Or when, from time to time, they ask one another, "Did you see the flowers?"

HR places flowers in the Great Hall to announce the death of an active employee. So many of the long-tenured staff know one another that the flowers often draw shock and tears, especially when noticed by half-awake commuters. Stella and a few of her team have committed to one another, should one die in service, the others will take and toss the flowers.

Wendell focused on the tattoo under the reporter's ponytail, as if its presence justified the snark with which he said, "You're here about architecture."

Their meeting went downhill from there.

The reporter asked a question about the role of Fed Banks' BODs in setting the Discount Rate, a rate charged on loans made by the Fed Banks to commercial banks that was calculated by adding a premium to the FOMC's Fed Funds target rate. The latter is the rate that's always in the news. "I know some of the Directors are bankers and others are from utilities or pharmaceuticals or what have you. With respect to the Directors who are bankers, why would they get to set the rate at which their banks might borrow from you?"

"Well, there's a formula for the last ten or so years."

"But then why do you continue to pay the Directors to discuss it and — "

"My time's up."

The reporter sputtered as Wendell left to tell Winnie to escort the reporter out. All visitors were escorted out, except for those who held economics PhDs. The latter were trusted, according to Stella and

David, because the cost of alienating a Fed Bank could destroy their careers.

Wendell went straight to Stella's office. "You worked in Discount Window, didn't you?"

"No, Reserves."

"Do you know why Directors still meet about the Discount Rate? Someone told me it's set by a formula now."

"Yeah, I think it is set at Fed Funds plus a premium. But I don't know about the Directors. Maybe because we persist in our fear that Congress will open up the Federal Reserve Act and play politics with us. Worse than they already do."

"The meetings are in the Act?"

"Yes. You know, I wonder how many politicians would be wary of ticking off Directors anyway. The Boards of Directors are made up of people who'd generally have strong political leanings."

"Huh. Do you know anybody in Discount Window?"

"Yeah, but I'd recommend talking to Ted. He's the formal liaison from Research on the Directors' Discount Rate calls."

Staff who work in the Fed Bank's Discount Window area lead the calls with the BOD but include a PhD to ensure Directors' questions about the economy can be answered on the spot.

"Is he the new red-haired Regional guy?"

"Yes."

Wendell returned to his office and spent a couple minutes looking up the Discount Rate and Ted. Then he emailed Public Relations to report he lacked the time to teach the reporter the basics.

They responded quickly with an apology.

After he read their email, he nodded his head and switched computers to work on a research paper.

That evening, I left the RD for the first time in years. I'd thought the world of Michael during his time here as DOR and looked forward to the announcement he'd become President of the Fed Bank. Dinner was downstairs in the Conference Center, catered by the Fed Bank's in-house catering vendor.

Michael ate no more than two bites from each course. Though he allowed his wineglass filled for show, he drank water. Once the servers began trading the dinner plates for dessert, he asked the Chair of the BOD for a minute.

Away from the table, Michael said, "I heard about David."

"Ah, news here does travel fast. I just saw the email on my way over. We chose you, unanimously. We were going to tell you in the morning that he'd been on our short list but he resigned from his Director of Research job about an hour after we told him he didn't get President. An outsized reaction, I'd say."

Michael laughed. "That's an understatement. He doesn't have a job yet so he must be pretty angry. My worry is the staff. Taking the job away from the economists' favorite won't set well, and some will probably follow him even though I hired them when I was here." Michael's eyebrows rose as he half-laughed. "But. A President will have a tough time at FOMC if they don't have the committed support of their PhDs. Let David have it."

"Well — "

"Really. I'm honored to have been chosen, but I decline. I'd been waffling a bit anyway. I've been doing good work since I left the Fed and would have been sorry to have left it unfinished."

"All right. I've gotten on the bad side of some of them myself by questioning their never-ending assumptions. Not getting you is a miss for the Fed System though. I'll let the Governors know when I leave here." The Director placed his left hand on Michael's upper arm and shook Michael's hand.

When the attendees finished their dessert, the Chair of the BOD walked to the podium and said there would be no announcement after all.

On Friday morning, Stella was reading emails and drinking tea when Winnie stopped in on her way to her cube.

"Good morning, Winnie. Look at you, dry as a bone with that umbrella."

The two laughed. Both Winnie and Stella were relatively short. Stella, who used a mini umbrella, once asked Winnie how she managed her golf umbrella on a crowded rush-hour sidewalk. They were different that way. Stella worried about poking someone's eye with her umbrella, and Winnie worried about arriving at work dry.

"Oooh, today's the day, Stella. Who do you think it will be?" Winnie took a sip of her Starbucks. "I still don't understand who's picking him with all of the emails and calls. David asked Frank about some old Goldman guy change in New York. Do you know what that was about?" Frank was the First Vice President, or First VP, of this Fed Bank, second-in-command to the President.

During the 2008-2009 financial crisis, Stephen Friedman was Chair of the NY Fed Bank's BOD while he was also a member of Goldman Sachs' Board of Directors. When he was first appointed at the NY Fed Bank, Goldman Sachs was an investment bank, so he was eligible to join the Fed Bank's BOD as a representative of the public's interests, rather than as a representative of commercial banks' interests. But as the crisis unfolded, Goldman Sachs organized a commercial bank to gain access to the NY Fed Bank's Discount Window. Though Friedman had become a commercial banker, he retained his Fed Bank BOD designation as a representative of the public interest. Even as he bought up Goldman Sachs stock.

Friedman's tangle of conflicts created an urgency that brought light to the degree on which the Fed System relied on an honor system with the commercial bankers who serve on Fed Banks' BODs and drove a change to the Federal Reserve Act.

At the time I'm writing this story, the commercial bankers who are selected by their peers to represent their own and their peers' commercial banking interests on the Fed Bank's BOD no longer have a say in picking Fed Bank Presidents.

Though Winnie's eyes were glazing over, Stella couldn't stop herself from finishing. Stella reveled in the Fed System's history and finds the rare substantive changes to it fascinating.

"Okay, Win, last thing, for completeness. I expect some day we won't have Directors, at least not ones who approve Officer promotions and oversee us. Otherwise, I don't know why David would have asked Frank about it unless he thought one of our Directors had some conflict or if he wondered exactly who was picking our President."

"Stella, I've always told you the truth. I don't want to pretend."

Stella's brow furrowed. "Right, me too, and no, don't pretend."

"I don't know if I should talk about this, but David got President."

Stella's thoughts popped out in excitement. "Really? Then I really don't understand why Friedman came up. But wow. The economists will be so relieved. Oh Winnie, he must be so excited. He seemed so down yesterday. Is it public knowledge?"

"No, no. Not yet. The Bankwide email and external press release go out at 9:00 a.m. But Stella, I didn't understand something else in Frank's email to David, after the thing about the Friedman guy."

Stella eyes squinted in caution. "Do you want to tell me?"

"He said congratulations, and that he was sorry that David missed dinner but understood the first news must have been tough. Then he said he hoped David didn't get whiplash from the changes over the last twenty-four hours. Do you know what they meant?"

"I don't know, Win." Stella looked concerned. "Do you think David didn't get it at first?"

"Kind of. But then how did he get it?"

"I don't know, Win. Wow, though, I'm so happy for him and yay for the Bank."

Winnie said, "Me too," as she threw away her coffee cup and shook the drops from her umbrella before continuing on to her cube.

David could barely contain his giddiness as he called out greetings on the way to his office. He dropped his briefcase in its usual place and headed right back out to a meeting with the BOD Chair. When he returned, Winnie followed him into his office, eager to talk with him. He brushed her off and headed for Wendell's office, closing the door behind him.

In addition to the usual furniture found in all of the RD's Officers' offices, Wendell's had a four-person meeting table and chairs that were castoff from a long-retired SVP's E-Floor office. Since Wendell had moved into this office nine years earlier, he relegated the guest chairs, three of the four chairs at the table, and half of the table-top as surfaces upon which to stack paper, despite empty space on his bookshelves.

David perched on the small round table between the guest chairs. "Can you believe it?"

"Well, sure. That was a stupid idea to offer the job to Michael. Congrats."

"I don't think I would have punted the way Michael did if I'd been in his shoes."

"Why would anyone? So, what's the plan?"

"Transition's officially started. Is word out in the department?" David looked at his watch, seeing that it was 9:10 a.m., and added, "I guess it's still early up here."

Wendell asked, "So, when's my announcement?"

David pulled a face. "The Directors asked how I'd replace myself. We'll go through an interview process."

Wendell frowned and rolled his eyes.

David then added, "For show. You'll get to be Director of Research. We really should call a Director of Research by something other than Director since the Board is Directors. If the Board of Governors had a Board of Directors, they wouldn't call us Directors of Research."

"Who cares so long as I'm it."

Next, David went to Stella's office.

"I heard. Congratulations, David. All the grapevines are running positive, I think the Bank really needed this. Even those who don't know you are saying this is good change."

"I'm pretty excited. I'm sorry I couldn't let you know sooner. You're probably behind the grapevine's positive thoughts. Thank you."

"Everyone's coming back from breakfast so word's spreading quick. The dream job of a macroeconomist. It's pretty cool."

"Yeah." He let out a breath. "It is a dream job. Not just of macro guys. Any economist."

"Are your kids excited?"

"I should have made them come on one of the Take Your Kids to Work Days when they were younger like you used to tell me. They'll think being interviewed by the newspaper is pretty neat, but they have no idea what my new job is about. Or the Fed. I'll have to fix that."

They talked about how his wife managed him during the interview process and how tough it had been to be interviewed and judged by non-PhDs.

His habit was to tilt his head down and look up when he was saying things he knew were controversial, and he did that now.

"Wendell will get my job here in Research. We have to go through the show of a search like they did for President but won't let it go too long – a few weeks tops."

Mid-afternoon, Winnie came into Stella's office and shut the door. After she took a seat, she pulled over a dish of Silver Tops and slowly unwrapped one. "Everybody at lunch was asking about David. New Head of our Fed Family." She saw Stella's cringe. "I know you hate that."

Stella laughed. "I do. We're not a family, though I'll grant there's a certain spirit here. Before I forget, I have vacation tomorrow."

"What are you going to do?"

"No big plans, just a dinner tomorrow night with old friends from college. I want to be on time."

Winnie set down a partially unwrapped chocolate and stilled her hands. "Okay. Stella, did David tell you about Wendell?"

"Yeah. You too?"

"Yeah. Do you think he'll keep me?"

"I'm sure, Win. He'll change things a bit, but you're in. Your work for me is about three-quarters of your time anyway." Stella began unwrapping a Silver Top. "He's a tough one to figure though. He's always suspicious of something. We'll get through this. David won't let anything go way out of whack."

"Promise?"

With certainty, Stella said, "Promise."

A Rabbit Hole:
Home Economics

As a child, I visited my grandparents' farm and enjoyed tea parties with my grandmother, most often in the sitting room she called her library. But when the weather was right, we followed a path through their lavender field, stopping along the way to peek into the rabbits' dens, and held tea on a bridge my grandfather had long before built across a creek.

A few times, our tea was styled after the Mad Hatter's from my grandmother's favorite childhood tale, *Alice's Adventures in Wonderland,* and we discussed rabbit holes, time, and created nonsensical questions.

"Rabbit hole" is particularly suited to describe some musings of my lived life.

I tripped into one after watching Wendell pore over the organizational charts of the other eleven Fed Banks' RDs. I wondered about his interest since each RD has a similar core.

Macroeconomics is the study of the economy as a whole, including how monetary policy affects the economy. The PhDs in this Group play a critical role in preparing the President for FOMC meetings, where he will discuss and, if it's his turn, vote on national monetary policy.

Regional economics in a Fed Bank studies its "Region" or "District," as defined by the lines of geographical decentralization I mentioned earlier. Since those lines were drawn according to the distribution of politics, population, capital, and trade routes in the U.S. in 1914, there's several Fed Banks up the East Coast, two in Missouri, but one in San Francisco whose District includes the entire West Coast and Hawaii. The Chicago Fed District includes parts of Illinois, Indiana, Michigan, and Wisconsin, and all of Iowa, where I'm from. While other functions of the Fed Banks moved beyond the geographical lines to redivide their work along strategic lines, the RDs have shied away, citing their role in preparing their Fed Bank's President to present the economic conditions of their Region to his FOMC colleagues. For example, this President might discuss the auto industry in Detroit.

Finance, or financial economics, is the study of banking and markets. Banks and some markets play a critical role in transmitting FOMC's monetary policy decisions to the economy.

Microeconomics is the study of individuals and firms. Early on, the microeconomics studied here was limited to questions about how monetary policy affects consumers and vice versa. But now, at this Fed Bank, microeconomics has expanded to include any issue concerning any person who is, might be, was, or depends on a person who works. The breadth of research is tremendous, including studies such as *Health Capital and the Prenatal Environment: The Effect of Ramadan Observance During Pregnancy* and *Prenatal Sex Selection and Girls' Well-Being: Evidence from India.*

None of his charts mentioned home economics, my own field of study, and one I'm certain could have been quite useful to you if it had evolved without gender bias.

My studies were dear to me.

As a child, I loved the winter evenings when my family joined near our fireplace to read books. And I was grateful that, just as I was learning to read, Mr. Andrew Carnegie established his philanthropy and funded a library in my town with his steel fortune. That library quickly became my favorite place away from home.

My second favorite place was school. I loved my studies, and as I progressed through high school, I wished for college. I couldn't assume I would go though. My older brother had just become the first member of our family to finish high school.

But in the end of my third year, I was surprised and grateful to learn my parents had saved some of my tuition and my brothers agreed they'd take up my chores.

I was immediately at home when I arrived at Iowa State University. My dormitory was the school's first for women and we residents became fast friends. I was enrolled in Home Economics in the Ladies Course, a curriculum already well-established after its creation in 1871 by Mary Beaumont Welch, a member of the faculty whose husband was the University's first President. He'd supported her work, so much that he said, "We offer, then, to the young women from time to time, shall resort to this College, a scope for scientific progress and research as unlimited and free as that which we offer to the other sex."

In my years there, Home Economics gained stature and was recognized by the creation of a University Division of Home Economics. And by the time I graduated in 1914, a graduate level program was available. I was excited for the existence of the latter, though it wasn't for me.

I was moving to Chicago to be with my husband, Everett, who was beginning his last year at Northwestern University's law school. My studies well-prepared me for my job here as a Secretary. I could have easily slipped into the role of my Manager, Mr. Myers, but that wasn't the way things were then. Anyway, my job here was intended only as a steppingstone to Everett's and my return to Iowa to open a commercial bank to serve farmers, where I would certainly have used my studies.

Though there were no stepping stones once I died, my education was still of use.

Several years of sorrow passed before I took interest in the work of the RD. Though I wished forever that if I must linger, it would have been near my family, since not, this was as good a place as any other. My mind's been occupied and challenged as I've watched the work evolve.

Sometimes, I wonder how I'd have fared here without my economics background and recalled my graduation day in 1914 when my grandmother told me my education was the only thing I'd have that no one could take from me. How true that has turned out. I'd been able to successfully follow most of the PhDs' work for decades, especially studies that absorbed home economics, up until some of the profession adopted high math as its language. Otherwise, I would have been terribly bored.

Once, a few of the current PhDs laughed when a visiting PhD suggested value in home economics. That was when I realized I could, if I felt an injustice deeply, kick. Not so hard to draw a bruise but enough to make the recipient jerk and look.

I once peeked over the shoulder of one of those PhDs after he opened his profession's website, Economic Job Market Rumors, or EJMR. An anonymous poster wrote in 2015, that "Actually, home ec was good. It tought (sic) students home production skills, basic financial skills, basic life skills, and domestic skills. Since schools have gotten rid of (sic) in the name of gender role equity, female marital qualities have worsened."

The case for my field isn't helped by claiming the Senatorial candidate from Tennessee. Her degree in home economics has become the butt of jokes, but it does not warrant such criticism. Whether she herself does is a different question to be answered by voters though I will say I expect she doesn't even know the difference between the Declaration of Independence and the U.S. Constitution.

I would argue that whatever societal problem bothers you most, it would be improved if Home Economics were still a mainstream area of study. Consider the environmental cost of producing one's food. Or those who struggled with their mortgages in the 2008–2009 financial crisis. Or those who don't understand exports and imports and take others' explanations at face value. Or young adults accounting for students' loans as they decide whether to pursue a trade or an academic education.

A New DOR ~ 10/22

Finally, without fanfare, mid-day on this Monday, an announcement was made. Wendell wandered the floor, collecting congratulations from the PhDs and soliciting their thoughts about David's presidency.

Not all PhDs welcomed him. One with wrinkled clothing, mussed hair, and other signs he might have spent the night in his office, snapped back at Wendell that he had a revision due to a journal. The PhD's exceptional record of journal publications had protected such behavior in the past and would going forward if Wendell's submissiveness and apology for the interruption were an indicator.

When Wendell's and Stella's paths crossed late in the day, he was noncommittal when she asked might he and she meet soon.

On his way out, he told Winnie he'd meet with her the next morning at 9:00 a.m. and asked for her help in keeping administrative meetings off his calendar.

Winnie asked which were administrative meetings.

"Well, anything to do with the budget or rules. Stella stuff."

"Are you sure? She said there's a lot coming up."

"For now."

On Tuesday, Winnie was eager and nervous as she finished her coffee, reapplied her lipstick, and moved things on her desk, inch here, inch there. Winnie called Stella at 9:30 a.m. to tell her she'd been stood up and asked should she worry about her job. Stella reminded Winnie of Wendell's penchant for arriving late.

When Wendell rushed in at 9:50 a.m., he invited Winnie to join him in the DOR office. He asked for her usual arrival and departure times, when she checked her Fed Bank iPhone in the evening, and whether she ate lunch at her desk.

Then he abruptly ended the meeting. Winnie was stunned. Back in her cube, she pulled a shoebox from her drawer. She took down the collection of magnetic state souvenirs from a previous boss. A rubber Gumby and a spinner Santa toy joined the magnets in the box. When she heard Wendell's footsteps, she hurriedly put the box back in her drawer.

When he saw her standing, waiting, he tried to appear sheepish. "Can you come back? I needed to get coffee before the cafeteria closed."

"We'll continue our meeting?"

"Oh, yeah. I guess I should explain myself more now that regular people report to me." His eyes held both uncertainty and hope. "So, you'll be my Assistant. Good with that?"

"Thank you. Yes with capital Y. I've enjoyed working for David and Stella. I'm planning to stay seven more years."

Wendell shifted in discomfort in the chair still calibrated for David's shorter height. "We should bring my chair over here. Seven more years puts you at?"

"Sixty-five. Twenty-eight years of service."

Wendell rocked his head to each side in thought as if he were weighing her plans. "Huh. Okay. We might retire around the same time about the same age. I didn't realize you'd been here that long."

"With my prior service, way back before my daughter was born."

"And you're a widow?"

"Yes."

"So what is it you do for Stella exactly?"

"Compensation paperwork, diversity program correspondence, meeting coordination when she chairs System — "

He waved in dismissal. "Why don't you make me a list? What did you do for David?"

"Calendar, travel, organizing FOMC materials — "

"Let's talk about my travel."

Winnie told him how she'd handled David's travel.

"You better not book any FOMC for me without asking. Maybe someone else will go with David." Each Fed Bank President outside of New York was allowed to bring one other person to the FOMC meetings and that person was usually the DOR and usually, the DOR considered it a high priority. Frankly, some of the DORs thought of it as the highlight of their role and even their career. He continued. "Sometimes I'll need you to book my wife's travel too. You know I do it a little differently."

"No worries here. Happy to do it. She called the airlines direct, right? I'll get your travel files."

Wendell smiled at her eagerness and said, "No, not yet. I haven't told anyone I picked you. But I'll give my wife a heads-up she'll hear from you."

Winnie responded, "Work wife, home wife, working together." Naming the role and seeing Wendell puff up with pleasure bolstered Winnie's confidence.

He said, "I like that." He rubbed his hands together in excitement. "Now, my office. How do we get it renovated? Wait. Let's take a ten-minute break."

Wendell knocked softly on his previous Assistant's cube wall when he saw she was on the phone. And sweeping.

Years earlier, when the Fed Bank's travel staff stopped booking staff's families' and own personal travel, Wendell took issue and added it to his Assistant's responsibilities. When on hold with airlines, she'd become a fidgeter and the fidgeting took the form of "sweeping" her desk. The broom pen, along with an index-card rug that read, ironically, "Don't sweep problems under the rug," were trinkets from HR. Whenever she hung up from the airlines, she used the broom to mark off the days to her retirement on her calendar.

"I'm on hold. What do you need?"

He told her she wouldn't be "moving up" with him. When she failed to hide her expression of delight, he sputtered and repeated himself in different words.

"Really, Wendell, I didn't expect to go with you. I'll support whoever replaces you as Group Head if he wants me to — "

He was annoyed when she turned from him to respond to the voice that had come over the phone.

Winnie had printed a floor plan of his office and followed Wendell back into his office.

Though he seemed relieved by her excitement as she explained how she'd organize his office's renovation, he said, "I'll probably want to be involved. Can you just set a meeting up? Maybe later I won't have time, but for now I'll make the choices."

Winnie told him she'd let Stella know for the budget. Wendell told her to keep Stella out of it.

Winnie told him she'd give the Tech staff a heads-up, and Wendell said he'd rather they not know about any changes yet.

Her eagerness evaporated.

After he left for the day, Winnie headed for Stella's office. She took a couple of Silver Tops from the bowl on Stella's table and said, "At least he let me send the invitation to Facilities. I don't think he knows how to use staff."

On Wednesday morning, Stella looked up from her monitor for a few seconds before resuming reading.

Twenty minutes later, Ellen, Stella's executive coach, arrived.

"I'm sorry I'm late, Stella. And I didn't get to your cafeteria for coffee."

Stella offered tea and said, "No worries. But if you'd rather coffee, one of the economists bought extra pods for their cappuccino machine and sells them on an honor system in the kitchen."

Ellen pulled a tea bag from Stella's tea basket. "Probiotic, huh?" She put it back and continued to look. "I'll go for regular old breakfast tea. I'm afraid to touch their cappuccino machine. Heather told me about it. She and Gage were happy their PhDs were invited to join the coffee machine."

Gage's area was a spin-off from the RD. A year earlier, when Frank asked for help from the RD's PhDs to research his and other Fed System Payments function leaders' questions, David declined and reminded Frank that the RD's PhDs research only their own questions.

The rejection might sound odd, but in the Fed System, there's a line of separation between the RDs and the Payments function that retains a kernel of legitimacy. David claimed it and Frank didn't buy it. But in the end, since David, like the DORs in other Fed Banks, reported to the Fed Bank President, while the Payments function, like its counterparts in other Fed Banks, reported to the First VPs, there was no cost for David's snub anyway.

So Frank formed a new group and pulled Gage from the RD to head it. Gage hired Heather. The two used their budget to hire lawyers and PhDs, thinking Frank would come up with more money so they could hire support staff. Frank couldn't but appealed to Stella and her team to support Gage's team as an extra since it was so similar to the RD.

Ellen added, "What happened with the procedures?"

Stella laughed. "Done. But for all the thinking, debating, and surveying they did for those procedures, they could have darn near designed a new tool of monetary policy. Smarts for economics don't transfer, apparently. Wendell said something to Adam about appliances being technology, but the tech staff said no way and I'm supporting them."

Adam was the RD's IT manager and backup for most of Stella's job.

Ellen asked, "How are you getting along with Wendell?"

"Not much occasion to yet. I've asked for time with him, but he says he's not ready. I need to make sure he and I are in sync on an RBOPS memo that came right before David was named President. The Board's implementing budget guidance where there was none so it's a big deal and I don't think he realizes."

"Be careful until you know Wendell. His not making time for something is probably not a sign he won't care deeply about the outcome. I heard about that budget guidance. I spent the last two weeks in Washington at the Board."

"Oh, cool. I didn't know you were working with them. Do they feel like us?"

Ellen was hesitant in answering. "Not much. They're very aware of their accountability to Congress."

Stella said, "I secretly empathize with the Board."

Ellen's laugh rang false and turned to a wince. "Seriously, Stella. Stay in lockstep with Wendell. It's nice to want to help the Board, but your first allegiance is always to this Fed Bank and in particular, to Wendell. What do you think about me talking to him to find out what he thinks about your role? Would that be helpful?"

Stella's eyebrows rose. "I didn't realize allegiance to a Fed Bank existed independent of allegiance to the Board."

Ellen tapped her pen and was quite serious. "Not everyone here is invested the way you are. I think David's term as President is going to surprise a lot of Officers and staff who've been around a long time. Time will tell."

Stella thought Ellen was only blowing smoke and flashed her eyes as if provoked. "A mystery, then. Anyway, maybe in a couple months, I'd appreciate Wendell's feedback on the role. We could talk about that next time we meet?"

Ellen lifted her eyes from her notes. "Sounds good. You know, Stella, about Gage, Heather wondered if you would make a formal complaint to HR."

Gage was increasingly forgetful and had taken to employing chaos to mask it. His resentment of Stella's team's natural tendencies to cut through chaos was too often turning to cruelty, so much that Stella was concerned for her staff.

Stella's eyes narrowed. "I know, Ellen. Heather's approached me directly more than once." Stella shifted back in her chair. "To be honest, I think Heather should take her concerns to Frank. Gage reports to him. Or she could go to David. David oversaw Gage's move out of Research to form his group."

Stella knew Gage and David to be second cousins and close childhood friends. Gage had gone on to fly airplanes while David studied economics, but when Gage became unable to fly planes, he followed in David's steps. When David became a Head about the time Gage began work on his dissertation, he hired Gage.

Stella wisely suspected Heather knew the same. In a culture where facts rule, criticism is direct, and gossip unfamiliar, Heather was artful at gaining her peers' trust by trading some small secret for a bigger secret, eventually ending up with a secret of enough import its sharing benefitted her. Heather wouldn't risk angering David as she intended to succeed Gage.

Stella asked Ellen about her new grandson and after sharing photos, Ellen asked, "Should we plan to meet in three weeks?"

"Let's go out to nine or ten, just before you'd talk to Wendell. I have lots of travel coming up." Stella didn't have lots of travel.

"Nine or ten would be better. Thanks. I'm really not a morning person." Ellen winced.

Stella smiled. "Oh no Ellen, I meant nine or ten weeks. Nine or ten in the morning is fine also though."

"Great. All right. Off to meet Heather."

"Oh, Ellen, could you take Heather's charm?" One of the PhDs had found the tiny silver coffee cup in the seminar room. Though a week had passed since Winnie called Heather to confirm the charm had fallen from Heather's charm necklace, the two inexplicably stood off. When Winnie complained to Stella about Heather's demand Winnie deliver it, Stella offered to drop it off the next time she went to Gage's area.

"Sure." Ellen dangled the charm in the air. "Cute. By the way, we saw this on our competition's site. It's dated but valuable. Any chance my firm could get something similar?"

Ellen handed Stella a screen print of a web page. A previous Fed Bank First VP was quoted, "We are very interested in the development of emerging leaders, and Vantage has played an important role through their coaching and mentoring services. Their support has made a big difference for numerous professionals…"

"Huh. I didn't think we made endorsements. I'm sorry, Ellen. Your best bet is to talk to HR."

On Thursday morning, Winnie, still in her coat, hurried to Stella's office and cursed when she found it empty.

Adam, next door to Stella, heard the curse and offered help.

Winnie said, "Let's go in your office." She pulled the door shut. "Wendell and I are meeting with Facilities. He likes coffee in the morning. I didn't think of it until I was on the train. Should I get a coffee cart?"

"No. Facilities never orders catering for their staff."

Winnie exhaled and thanked him.

"Good luck with the Facilities meeting."

Stella and one of the PhDs were chatting in the elevator bank when the contingent of Facilities staff arrived on the floor. The Facilities executive wore a navy suit and red tie, the other men wore ties, and the women wore skirts. After Stella pointed them in the right direction, the PhD asked her if the visitors were auditors and the RD was in trouble.

The Facilities staff reached Winnie's cube precisely five minutes early. As Winnie showed them into the conference room, the Facilities Officer introduced a newly hired architect.

Ten minutes later, Wendell arrived, shrugging off his coat as he came down the hallway. As Winnie followed him into his office, he admonished her lack of forethought to turn on the lights in his office to mask his tardiness. Winnie carried two notepads and pens and handed him a set as they made a U-turn out the office's door and into the conference room.

With one foot in the conference room, he stopped, pulled a five-dollar bill from his pocket, and gave her a coffee order.

"But I'll miss the meeting." Only rarely had David asked her to secure a beverage and even then, only if she was not otherwise engaged.

While they waited, the Facilities executive whispered to the new architect, "The decisions in the next hour will be the closest we ever get to decisions about interest rates."

Many new employees find inspiration in the relationship of their job to FOMC work. For a long time, it was a norm for management in Central Support to explain how their staff's work tied back to monetary policy. Increasingly, Central Support instead focused on recognition from their own industries instead of digging into the complexity of the Fed System though some of them tried for a happy medium, simplifying the description of their work's link to monetary policy as a need to "keep the PhDs happy," a worrisome goal indeed.

Wendell claimed, "Train delays."

The Facilities Officer stood, hand extended, while his staff smiled in greeting. "Wendell, let me congratulate you again. We're looking forward to getting you settled." When he and Wendell were seated, he continued. "First on our list is to confirm you're staying up here."

"Hmmm. Do you know if any of the Research Directors ever sat on the E-Floor? I might like some space there but as an addition."

"I can investigate."

"I'll let you know. But let's see what are the furniture options for this space. Storage too, I have lots of books."

The Facilities Officer asked, "Let's start in this conference room. Would you tell us about your AV equipment needs?"

"Projector is fine. What we need is an easier way to hook up a laptop. And the kind of keyboard you can hover over." Seeing the looks of confusion, Wendell added, "Adam knows what it is. He said even a ghost could use it."

"Okay, we'll get you some alternatives. We think this furniture is in good shape, if it's in line with your plans?"

Wendell looked around the conference room. "Hmmm. That picture. I'd like to change it."

The Facilities Officer directed Wendell's attention to the Facilities staff. One said, "We have many alternatives in storage and if nothing there appeals to you, we have an artwork budget."

"What would you replace it with from storage?"

"If you could tell me what you like and don't like about it, I can hone in and see what we have. This was chosen by your EAT group, the economist art team who worked with us and local artists during the last renovation."

"Oh, then let's leave it alone. But I'll still need art in my office. What's there were probably David's picks."

"I'll arrange for you to view what we have available. There are some nice pieces, new or historical all the way back to artwork from George Schaller's office. Or, again, we could go outside."

"Who's he?"

"He was Governor of the Bank in the 1930s."

"In D.C.?"

The young man turned red as he explained, "I'm sorry. He was the President of this Bank when the Presidents were called Governors. Before the Governors in Washington were called Governors. They changed the name in his term, so he was called President too."

Wendell said, "Historian on the side? No one knows that stuff." After others laughed uncomfortably, he added, "I think I've seen all the art we've ever had in the Bank, let's jump to experts."

The architect asked, "May I work with Winnie on that?"

"Sure, after we have everything figured out. Let's see if we can find her anyway to take notes."

Winnie's boots pounded the floor as she hurried over, his coffee in hand. "I'm here."

He took the coffee and said, "Here, sit by me." He pushed over her notepad and pen.

The Facilities Officer said, "We're just getting to furniture, Winnie."

As the discussion continued, the Facilities staff's faces showed increasing concern. Wendell requested a meeting table with chairs, a wardrobe, a buffet-height table, two extra guest chairs for the desk, a small table that could sit under the desk and hold his printer, and a bench on which he could set his backpack. His self-satisfied expression turned to displeasure when he looked up from the floor plan and saw the confusion on the others' faces.

It was as if Wendell wanted to prove something, to himself and the others, because what other sense could be made of his next words.

"I'd like a couch too. It doesn't have to be big or leather. The E-Floor folks have them, right?"

The new architect, earnest and sincere in her desire to be helpful, said, "This office may be a foot or two shorter than those on the E-Floor. We could help you prioritize that list before we identify specific pieces."

Wendell's eyes sharpened at words he took as a challenge. "If a couch can't fit the way it is, how about we break through the wall and combine these spaces." He sat back and pulled at the collar of his sweater. "Hey, what's up with the heat over here? Let's fix that too."

The Facilities Officer caught the eyes of one of his staff who was nearest to Wendell, but she subtly shrugged one shoulder and tilted her hand upwards. "Well, Wendell, let's see what we can figure out. We have a rule prohibiting corner offices, but I'm certain we'll get you in an office that will meet your needs."

"We broke your rule on putting offices on the east and west sides of the building." Wendell sounded petulant.

"Stella could tell you about the case she prepared to get all of your PhDs in window offices. That was a pretty big deal and a rare exception. We don't put offices on the corners for security reasons." He laughed. "Even Stella couldn't get us to give on that."

"David's office is on a corner."

The Facilities executive was serious once more. "Right. His and Frank's are the only corner offices in the Bank. Let's see what we have in surplus for furniture, and otherwise, what's out in the marketplace. We'll superimpose your choices on a floor plan to make sure you'll have adequate open floor space and we meet fire codes. Rest assured our job is to give you what's needed for your work, and it sounds like it's a little different than when Michael and David were in here, but we are up to that. We want to do the best job possible to support you and get you the right space for those highbrow discussions about monetary policy."

Wendell wasn't ready for the meeting to end. "When you gather up your artists, look for the art that won't depreciate. I want to be able to say I increased the money supply when I chose my art." Wendell smiled at the Facilities staff's interest and missed the Facilities Officer's wince. "I could explain that if you wanted."

The Facilities Officer read Wendell right when instead of claiming rightful authorship of the example, he asked, "How does that work?"

Wendell's stance and tone became professorial as he walked to the whiteboard and explained how the Fed System pays for assets, such as artwork, by increasing the amount of dollars in the art dealer's commercial bank's account at a Fed Bank, creating dollars that didn't exist anywhere before that entry.

He concluded, "But artwork isn't really going to matter for the money supply. For the real deal, the New York guys buy securities, in much bigger amounts. That's called open market operations."

When the Facilities Officer originally gave the presentation at an Officers' forum, some of the Fed Bank's jokesters offered to redecorate their departments to goose the economy. He'd made the presentation to increase awareness during a time when Congress was questioning the size of the lobby in one of the other Fed Bank's new buildings and included a reminder that all spending should be evaluated in light of its potential to draw the scrutiny of Congress.

Wendell turned back toward the table but bumped into a wooden three-legged stool. Unlike the rest of the furniture, the stool was well-used and nicked, its green paint chipped.

He asked, "Where'd it come from anyway? It's not real Fed furniture."

"No. We had it on the surplus floor and Stella asked for it. You had a presenter who needed to elevate his leg."

"Huh. Get rid of it. We advocate for stumps rather than three-legged stools anyway." At the others' looks of confusion, he continued. "Three-legged stool, represents the stability the Fed brings to the economy? Depends on three legs, Payments, S&R, and Research. Versus just a Research stump?"

The Facilities Officer told his staff, "Just FYI, 'Payments' and 'Financial Services' are used interchangeably."

Wendell sensed he might get drawn into a conversation that wouldn't aid his renovation and hurriedly reclaimed the conversation. "Toss this. I think we can afford something real. Anyway, what's the usual spend for E-Floor offices?"

The Facilities Officer said, "There's no established dollar amount, it varies by need. We'll get this office fixed up for you."

Wendell extended his hand to the Facilities executive. He said, "Don't forget about bringing down the wall here."

The Facilities Officer picked up the stool with one hand, and seeing Wendell was occupied with rolling up his shirt sleeves and fanning himself, turned toward Stella's office.

She looked up when he stepped in. "Hi."

He whispered, "Wendell wants it trashed."

"I'll keep it in here?" He nodded. "It's come in handy. Thank you."

After checking both ways, he left her office.

Stella tucked the stool into a small space between a filing cabinet and her office's windows. Though hidden from Wendell, it might give staff at the commercial bank across the street pause as the days got shorter. Inevitably, staff here and there check the always-changing weather before they leave at the end of the day and can't resist the ease with which they see into one another's buildings when office lights shine in the dark winter sky.

I perched on the stool in Stella's office for the rest of the day. In the 1970s, this Fed Bank opened a Regional Check Processing Center in Des Moines, Iowa, to shorten the distance some checks had to travel before they cleared the check writer's checking account. The Officer responsible for the Des Moines Center had brought this stool from his farm for a skit at one of the Fed Bank's staff holiday parties and left it behind. He's long since retired.

I'd liked it in the DOR's conference room since I spend most of my time there. As furniture does, it retained some essence of where it had been, even the tree from which it'd been made. And because it has a heart carved on its underside.

Winnie took advantage of Wendell's 4:00 p.m. departure to visit Stella. She asked first about the soup restaurant where Stella had met a friend for lunch.

Stella said, "They didn't have plain old tomato soup, but they had some rattlesnake stew stuff. Not my kind of place. Otherwise, it had a nice atmosphere. Even their vegetable soup was over the top."

Winnie was not swayed. "I can't wait to go there. I have a business question now. In this meeting we had with Facilities, what did they mean when they said buying artwork is monetary policy?"

"Yikes, who said that?"

After Winnie gave Stella the context, Stella explained the same as Wendell had earlier in the day, but also used the artwork metaphor to explain the other side — when the FOMC drained dollars from the economy. Stella said, "And poof, it's gone," and added, "I have to caveat this. I don't think we, a Federal Reserve Bank, are allowed to sell art but I'm not sure. For sure, the Board of Governors may not buy or sell art, though they've amassed quite the collection through donations. Artwork's just an example of how money is poofed into and out of the economy. People use it because there's nothing intuitive about money creation or elimination and artwork's at least a familiar asset. Too few understand the poofing, even among us here."

Winnie nodded. "But the buyer paid for the painting."

"If they bought it from anyone else, say Joe somebody, the money would still exist because Joe would have it in his bank account and could buy a car or something with it. But if they bought it from us, it affected our dollar liabilities, you know, how each dollar says it's an obligation of the Federal Reserve? The electronic dollars are our dollars in the same way. Our liability, our obligation. If someone gives us some back because they owe us for something, it just cancels out the obligation we had on those dollars."

Winnie looked confused and Stella was thoughtful as she continued. "Maybe this way will make more sense. There was an article one time about the artwork Bernanke selected to go above the fireplace in his office when he was Chair. If the fireplace was still in use and the art fell into it, the artwork would be gone. No change in the amount of dollars, the money supply." Stella stopped for a beat and said with care, "But if the Board was allowed to sell it and they did, the artwork is gone from the Board, but the Fed gets dollars back so there are less dollars floating around in the economy. And when there are less dollars, rates go up absent other stuff going on. Like when there's a shortage of strawberries, the price goes up so long as nothing else is going on."

"I don't know."

"I don't blame you. One more if you can stand it. Completely different example but same idea. Your peanut butter cookies, Winnie, the best ever. Say I wanted some and I said in exchange I would," Stella's mouth twisted in thought, "yikes, I can't think of anything I can do other than this job."

"Help with taxes?"

"Yes, with help from TurboTax. So. You bring me the cookies tomorrow morning, hint, hint." Stella and Winnie shared a comfortable laugh. "When I take the plate, I will have an obligation to do your taxes come tax time. Say, uh, one of Wolf's hairs was in the cookies, and I give them back. You would give me back my promise to do your taxes. I would just extinguish the promise. Does that help? Do you really want to know this?"

"I think so, let me think about it. I think Wendell thinks I understand more than I do, and I don't want to disappoint him. Maybe I'll bring the peanut butter cookies in exchange for the lecture. You know, I do worry a lot about Wolf's hair. I thought one of the E-Floor Assistants found one in the oatmeal cookies I brought last week for our Executive Assistants' meeting. But it was red, her own, not Wolf's. Which reminds me, time to get home and let Wolf out to roll around in the dirt and get rid of that hair."

When the floor was empty, I left the stool and returned to the conference room. Though the room has a formal name, the staff call it as the DOR's, now Wendell's, but I will always think of it as my corner. I prayed all night that it wouldn't become part of Wendell's office.

Winnie dropped her coat at her cube on Friday morning, and coffee in hand, went to Stella's office. "Hi, Wendell's not here yet so I came over to ask another question."

"Of course. How are you?"

"Okay. Say Wolf's hair was all over the peanut butter cookies, but you threw them away and didn't tell me. Then you would still have the liability to do my taxes, right?"

Stella's smile grew. "Yes."

Winnie held up her finger and continued. "But if you find the hair and return them, poof, there goes your obligation."

A rare dimple showed from Stella's smile. "Beautiful. I was afraid you might have run out of here screaming after we talked."

"No. But then it's a good thing you're so polite and would never reject the cookies to my face, yes?"

Stella laughed and then, seriously, said, "Win, I don't even know what the economists really think any more about how the Fed affects markets. So that, what we went through, it's a textbook example. But New York does lots of other stuff too. But this stuff with the cookies, it is the textbook example of how the Fed affects the economy."

In a turn of conversation, Winnie said, "I finally looked at apartments over the weekend, just for the next few years, to see what it's like to live in the city, you know. Then I'll go back to the suburbs. I didn't know kitchens could be so tiny."

"What an adventure for you. I know about the kitchens, especially in the high-rises. Most people don't cook often. Where I live, almost everyone in my building's elevator after work is carrying their dinner."

"Do you ever cook?"

"No. I did when I was younger but forgot it all, and there's so many places with takeout. One of my later-in-life plans is to have a bigger kitchen and have my mom and my sister visit and re-teach me our recipes. They are exceptional cooks. And bakers. Moving in the city will probably be pretty cool for you, Win. You'd love the Lakefront path."

Stella walked along the Lakefront regularly, including to and from work on most days. Winnie is a jogger.

"I can't wait. I think I'm going to do it. I think Wolf will like the Lakefront too."

"I'm sure."

"Why don't you get a dog, Stella? Don't you ever get lonely?"

"What a question. No. I'm happy living alone. And am blessed with enough family and friends that I don't have to wait long if I want someone around. Are you worried about that?"

"Not really. My daughter said she'll go places with me."

"It's not too hard to meet people with common interests, maybe a running club?"

Eventually, their conversation turned to Stella's calendar and a project of Winnie's. After Stella suggested weekly meetings with Wendell, Winnie became vague.

At precisely five minutes before 10:00 a.m., the Facilities Officer, architect, and planner arrived for their follow-up meeting with

Wendell and Winnie. The Facilities Officer explained why the wall between the DOR office and the conference room could not be removed, and when he saw Wendell preparing to bluster, added that he'd consulted Frank.

"Then I'd like a door between my conference room and my office." Even Wendell looked surprised at his words as all eyes went to the existing door. Both Wendell's office and the conference room were rectangular and exited into the hallway near their dividing wall. Moving between rooms is a U-turn. "I'll be able to move around without getting pulled into any hallway conversations."

The Facilities Officer asked, "Where would you propose a door?"

Wendell pointed.

"We'd have to take away some of the whiteboard wallpaper, would you be able to live without that?"

"Hmmm. Could the door be flush with the wall, without a frame, and covered in the whiteboard so I don't lose that space? A hidden door?"

The Facilities Officer grimaced, a show of emotion unusual for him. "We can't hide ways of egress."

"Okay. But keep it as unobtrusive as possible. It's really hot over here."

"I'll talk to the HVAC folks. Regarding the sofa, would you like to join us at a display floor to make a selection or might Winnie do that for you?"

"No, I don't want to go anywhere. Just start with something that's comfortable. You'll get some in here to try out, right? Maroon. I have to go."

A Rabbit Hole:
Three-legged Stools

Folks here have a long history with the three-legged stool metaphor.

In the Philadelphia Fed Bank's 2012 Annual Report, their then First VP framed his letter with the metaphor. He described each leg in turn – Financial Services, Bank Supervision, and Monetary Policy. For the latter, he reported his Fed Bank's economists' "role in contributing to monetary policy through analysis of regional and national conditions," and claimed, "Our research publications and analyses are delivered to business and academic forums everywhere and are archived on our website to inform consumers, businesses, and academics."

And five years before, in the St. Louis Fed Bank's 2007 strategic plan, their then President proposed a five-legged stool for the St. Louis Fed Bank. A fourth leg would represent the Fed System's "performing effectively as the fiscal agent of the U.S. Treasury." The fifth would represent his Fed Bank's "providing regional economic research, community development programs and economic education." He explained, "It is not often that you'll see a Reserve Bank tinker with its mission statement. We felt, however, that adding a couple of new legs to the Federal Reserve stool would make that stool sturdier." Since neither of those new legs represented new efforts, it was unclear whether he proposed to reattach shavings left from whittling the original three legs.

Even Stella would have put someone milking a cow on the ground when she once described a stool with three legs, but one leg is made up of thirteen cuts, each maintained by a different builder who chooses how much paint and glue is needed and if more wood is attached to support the original piece. These pieces might twist as if trying to choke off the others and some stick out. She added a ring between all of the legs, the kind you put your foot on when you sit on a barstool. Stella likens the ring to the Support and Overhead structure as it forms a mantle of governance in the Fed System because it pushes so hard into the business lines and might well eventually crack them.

And regarding Wendell's reference of a stump, it is not original, and it ironically surfaced for the first time around the time as a presentation at an agricultural economics conference that included a picture of a modern one-legged stool for milking a cow. Attached to the farmer with a belt, it was a relatively small single round post upon which she might sit.

Truth be told, I wouldn't trust anyone here to build a stable stool.

I had a three-legged stool. In my childhood, I used it to milk cows and as a tic-tac-toe board. My friend Everett carved the board after the rain washed away the one we'd drawn in the dirt.

I sat upon the stool one morning, reciting times tables in the quiet while milking my favorite cow, Milkshake, named so because of her walk. Milkshake and I were surprised when out from behind the barn door came my friend Everett, unsuccessfully pulling his younger brother, Craig, by the hand.

When Everett told me they were there for a loan, I remembered my parents' conversation about Everett's mother's struggles to keep his uncle from taking over their farm. Everett's father had died a year before.

Everett knew about my piggy bank. A gift from my grandparents, the bank came with a lecture on why granddaughters must be as money smart as grandsons. I'd taken the words to heart and entered into savings competitions with my brothers. Though I'd been ashamed of bragging about my wins to Everett after I overheard my parents, I was grateful he knew to come to me for a loan.

Everett said how another of our neighbors gave his mother a dress pattern and fabric and how his mother warned Craig to stay far from the dining room where'd she laid it out. But Craig didn't and tripped and spilt tea on the pattern. It shredded when he tried to wipe it dry.

When Craig finally came out from behind the door, he was terribly upset, his face blotchy after crying. Everett handed me the envelope of a Butterick pattern that sold for fifteen cents and told me Craig would return the fifteen cents and one cent interest. They'd been in such bad straits since their father died that both boys had been helping at other farms, but I knew those wages went to their mother.

I was fortunate that I didn't need the coins and, of course, made the loan.

Craig told me then "Everett's good with the knife. He won't break the piggy bank. He's going to be a banker someday."

I must have made a face because Craig's words just tumbled out about how Everett knew angles and put the knife in the coin slot so the coins came at the right angle to fall out and their mother didn't realize when they'd emptied their pigs.

In the couple minutes it took me to get the piggy bank, they had finished my milking chores, hung the three-legged stool on its hook, and delivered the milk to the icehouse.

Everett had the coins for fifteen cents out in a flash, piggy bank intact, as promised. Everett handed Craig his poke and told him to put the coins in it and not to worry. Craig's little shoulders fell in relief and Everett was just so kind to him. And considering the penny interest plus the milking they did, I earned a usurious rate of interest for making the loan. I loved Everett then, and the next morning, when I swung the stool over to the cow and saw he'd lightly carved, "note 16 c due," on the stool's underside.

Over the years, Everett continued to carve on it as a record of our relationship. It had long been retired from its barn duties when I brought it to Chicago in 1914.

And in July 1915, when we packed to return to Iowa to make our home and await our baby's birth in August, we treated the stool as carefully as if it was fine china. But we didn't unpack it in Iowa.

We accepted the midwife's recommendation to wait to travel until the baby was born. Since our apartment was already let for August, we gratefully accepted my Aunt Edna's and Uncle Louis' offer of their guest room. Their lovely home was near the Financial District, where Uncle Louis worked. We'd spent many evenings there while we'd been in Chicago.

The guest room was up at the top of their entryway staircase. Decorated with a nod to Uncle Louis' hobby, birds were perched on tree branches scattered across the wallpaper and carved into the room's furniture. Though we left most of what we'd move home to Iowa in our trunks, Everett had secretly unpacked the stool and surprised me with a newly carved tiny bird sitting atop her nest.

I wonder what happened to my stool.

I wonder who carved the heart on this stool.

WEEK ONE ~ 10/29

The culture of the RD is cast in a cloak of gravitas during FOMC Briefing Weeks. Intellect, curiosity, wonkishness, and capacity for laser-focus are evident, and egos are mostly set aside as critical feedback is sought and addressed.

The Business Economists supplement a myriad of statistics with anecdotal stories from their regional contacts and enjoy an increased standing during Briefing Weeks, even among the few PhDs who otherwise disparage them as PhD-wannabes.

Most PhDs deeply respect the reach of the FOMC's role and offer up their expertise. A few forecast specific sectors of the U.S. economy, such as construction or leisure and hospitality, noting novelty in the numbers.

The Research Assistants revel in the rigor required to run the forecasts and many take pride in the real-world application of their work.

Dawn, an Administrative Assistant, distributes the briefing materials in accordance with the BOG's *Program for Security of FOMC Information* (Program).

The others – Stella, her team, and the remaining Administrative Assistants – take care to insulate those who work on FOMC. Central IT might be asked to delay software changes. Facilities might be asked to reschedule noisy construction on an adjacent floor. Adam had once even asked for rescheduling of an evacuation drill.

Stella and Adam spearheaded this defense when she moved to the RD, just after her transfer from one of the "umbrella areas." Umbrella areas are usually less than fifty staff who fit within the scope of monetary policy but don't fit in the academic culture of the RD. They include Public Affairs, Libraries, and Community Affairs, and rotate in and out of the DOR's scope of responsibility as if on a carousel.

Stella's umbrella area shared the floor with the RD. A then-new PhD blamed the sound of the umbrella area's printer for an incomplete FOMC memo and enlisted a helper to move the umbrella area's copier out to a back hallway. The melted-down PhD refused to apologize.

One attempt to calm the ensuing drama was a get-to-know-one-another happy hour. When it came time for an ice breaker, Stella, one of the few staff comfortable in both the umbrella area and the RD, was paired with that PhD. In the end, Adam oversaw a build-out of walls to create a sound barrier between the two areas. That umbrella area was soon after booted from the floor.

Wendell is the only one who still speaks of that drama, his memory of it retrieved from his mental notebook of tales of conflicts. His favorite and most-cited memory is one from a conference where an economist from a think-tank and another from academia almost "came to blows." Knowledge of that mental notebook is what causes Stella and Adam to keep their defensive efforts secret from Wendell.

As intense as a Briefing Week is here, it is more so at the New York Fed Bank and the BOG. In New York, in addition to briefing their President, staff also monitor financial markets, including those in which they would later conduct open market operations on the FOMC's behalf. And BOG staff prepare briefing materials for each Governor and for all FOMC members.

And there, in Washington, staff carry the weight of the FOMC's relationship with elected officials. The relationship is managed with the precision of a tuning fork, one prong to represent the BOG staff's responsibility to preserve the independence of monetary policy, the other to represent the FOMC's accountability to Congress for maximum employment and stable prices.

The stakes of moving outside a desired frequency were high under then U.S. President Trump as he used social media to exploit gaps in his supporters' knowledge and foment confusion. If he could get them to expect inflation, they would act accordingly and unwittingly create it, reducing the cost of his debt.

Though he wasn't the first U.S. President to prioritize his own interests over the independence of the FOMC, his willingness to bully and discredit the FOMC using words such as "wild," "crazy," and "loco," signaled his desperation. No matter to him when he was reminded he nominated J. Powell as Chair of the BOG and the FOMC or when he learned that across the globe, economic leaders were defending the FOMC and Chair Powell and cited their need for independence.

Here, on Monday morning of this Briefing Week, Stella jumped when Adam materialized in her doorway. Laughing at herself, she said, "Geez, Adam."

After three decades in the RD's IT team, Adam had mastered invisibility. It was a survival tactic, without which he would spend his days cornered in the RD's hallways by those PhDs compelled to complain about the rules and constraints that come with using the Fed System's technology.

He apologized and asked about her weekend.

"It was nice, quiet. I'm taking a half-day Wednesday, by the way. I'm hoping to see my great-nephews in their Halloween costumes."

"That should be fun. Sally says I should ask if you've ever had trick-or-treaters in a high-rise. I've been told I should get candy just in case, but I know we'll end up eating it." Adam and his wife Sally had moved from the suburbs to a city high-rise a few months earlier.

Stella shook her head. "Not for thirty-whatever years. Not even when I had the tiny studio in the Goldcoast building where people actually raised kids."

"Sally's really missing suburban Halloween stuff. Anyway." He exhaled. "I just delivered the new iPad to Wendell."

"That reminds me. Are we in trouble for Luigi? I saw the email about the iPhone. That's five in three months?"

"Ugh. Yes, we are in trouble. They said being an airhead professor is not an excuse. I knew Wendell would be pissed, but I asked him to talk to Luigi." Luigi was a member of the group Wendell headed before his promotion.

Stella's mouth was twisted in concern. "He's joked about Luigi's forgetfulness, even told us at a Heads meeting how when Luigi was leaving his university, younger professors bid on his unclaimed travel reimbursements. Luigi apparently wasn't motivated by the money. Wendell said the high bidder paid Luigi something like ten thousand, did the reimbursement paperwork, got twenty-five thousand. I wish Wendell wasn't so impressed by grand gestures of noncompliance." Stella looked serious. "He's got to understand Central IT will penalize the whole RD if we keep replacing Luigi's phones."

"They said no other department would tolerate this. Central IT asked if he might be selling the lost phones on the side." Adam's face was hangdog.

Stella looked as if she felt pain. "If they only knew his salary. I'm sorry you have to deal with this but am grateful you talked to Wendell. Let me know if you want me involved."

"Defend me if Wendell complains." There was an edge of fear in Adam's voice.

"Always. Though I've yet to meet with him and now it's Briefing Week. Things aren't going to go smooth, are they?"

His laugh was harsh. "I told you. David made a mistake, not that anybody wants my opinion."

"Imagine a world where a recruiter would ask a candidate's IT person for input. Your team knows how people treat support staff and how they treat their devices. You could tell so much about a person with just that."

Adam and his team did their best to manage the inherent contradiction in the needs of the PhDs. On one hand, the PhDs' independent research calls for the most sophisticated computing equipment and loads of data that may be shared with peers in universities throughout the world. On the other hand, their classified FOMC work requires a tightly controlled computing environment. His team is often in the line of fire between the PhDs and the Fed Bank's Central IT and are master negotiators. In a similar line of fire at the Fed System level, Adam is joined by his counterparts to negotiate with System Central IT. Wendell refers to these negotiations as "fighting the good fight."

Even though Adam had closed Stella's door when he entered, his voice dropped to a whisper. "I came to warn you. Wendell's using that damn couch. He said it's here on spec. We sat on it. Together." He shuddered.

Adam and Stella knew one another well enough to appreciate the other's discomfort at sitting on a deep-cushioned love-seat-sized sofa with a coworker.

At noon, Winnie told Stella that Wendell would finally meet with her. "At one. He needs an excuse to get out of a briefing meeting."

Stella pulled in her lips as one eyebrow rose. She nodded.

At a few minutes after 1:00 p.m., Stella sat in one of the chairs between Winnie's cube and Wendell's office. The chairs were red, described as comfy by Stella, but a source of angst to Winnie who felt watched when the chairs were in use. Since David asked for them, Winnie never told him, but had no qualms asking Wendell didn't he think they were in the way of entry to his office. Wendell didn't, and to Winnie's dismay, proposed adding a side table.

Winnie returned at 1:07 p.m. and checked her email. "He'll be right back, he said. He sent that at, let's see, 11:57. Do you want to go to your office and I'll call you?"

"No, I have stuff to read. Thanks."

When Stella followed Wendell into his office at 1:10 p.m., she grimaced in surprise. She was lucky his back was turned to her as he hung his coat behind his door.

"I need to run down the hall, why don't you wait outside by Winnie again?"

When she followed him in for the second time, she walked to his table. "It looks nice in here, Wendell. Were you able to get everything you wanted?"

He sat on the couch. "Let's sit here. We're testing this one out."

"Oh, shoot. I've got a bunch of papers to show you. Could we sit over here?" She pulled out a chair at the table.

"Okay. Before your list, I wanted to talk about Adam. He brought an iPad over this morning but didn't know how to use it. How's he doing these days?"

"Very well. It's to his credit you're probably the only one in the Bank with the new iPad."

"We'll see. Sometimes, I think he's a bit lazy."

Stella's head shifted back and tilted. "I don't see it. He gets great feedback. Do you have an example?"

He said, "Let me think on it. So you have a list."

"Yes. One. May I ask Winnie to schedule weekly meetings for us, except during Briefing and FOMC Weeks, until we're in sync on all things administrative?"

"Well, something like that is probably appropriate. I need your help this week. I want to get Joe $45,000. His girlfriend just had a baby, and they are getting married. Melissa said you'd know how to get around the restrictions from the System joining the government pay freeze." Melissa was HR's liaison to the RD's Officers.

Stella nodded. "We need to write a memo to justify the increase since it's over ten percent and puts him above others. HR might recommend an incentive agreement or retention agreement rather than adding to his base since he's only been here a few months and is a brand-new PhD."

"Don't go down that road. Just give it to him in salary. I don't have time to write a memo. Will you tell them I'll get it to them after FOMC but go ahead with the increase now?"

"Salary changes are bi-monthly so it can't go into effect that quickly anyway. And I write those memos, if you'll share a couple of reasons for the increase."

"Good. He might have interviewed at another Fed and we want to keep him."

"We try to offer certain specifics and avoid asking for salary bumps to compete with other Federal Reserve Banks or the Board of Governors. On principle. Did he have that interview?"

Wendell scowled and in a louder voice said, "Then just say he got an offer and had an interview at a university."

Stella's willingness to accept an obviously stretched truth was uncharacteristic. "Okay. Do we really believe he's a flight risk?"

Wendell's volume returned to normal. "Not really."

"I'll draft a letter and check in with HR and update you." Stella's sigh was barely noticeable. "Two. I sent you an email about this. My System committee, RAOC, wants to establish a direct relationship with RBOPS. We've prepared a letter to Carolyn and thought it would be best received if it comes from a Director of Research. Since I'm chair of RAOC, precedent is that you, as my Director, send the letter."

"RBOPS?"

"Reserve Bank Operations and Payments Systems. We, RAOC, care about the part of RBOPS who oversee the Fed Banks. They've historically interacted with Central Support areas in the Bank, but the Research Departments are getting information secondhand at best and after the door is closed to input. We want to establish ourselves as a System body with whom RBOPS may communicate proactively on all things related to the Research Departments."

"I don't know if I want to get involved in this."

"I know you're busy. And it's not great timing. I thought you might enjoy the opportunity to introduce yourself in that environment. If not, a few of my counterparts are happy to solicit their Research Director."

His voice rose again. "Again, I don't even know if I want you to be involved in this. I don't think we get much bang for our buck for all the System work you and Adam do. Why would I even want a relationship with them?"

Stella drew down her eyebrows and forced a neutral expression. "They've got the Governors' ears. They drove the target budget guidance letter and got the Governors' support."

"I doubt they're really that powerful. What's the name of that woman who runs RBOPS?"

"Carolyn. She is that powerful though. And has a strong network. The dynamic of Board oversight of us has changed as support operations centralized. In the old days, Central Support used to side with us when RBOPS came after the Bank. Now, they side with RBOPS."

"I'm not sure any of the Research Directors should be doing this, let alone me. You'll have to convince me. Another time though. I have two immediate concerns. I think you are claiming you have some open positions in your group. I need to see a case for hiring."

Stella's face showed confusion. "Nothing new after the cases I brought to the Heads meeting. You all agreed I would replace a Budget Analyst and hire a Manager for the Admin Assistants."

"I didn't read the cases then." His voice held pride.

Her eyes narrowed. For not having read the cases, he'd certainly been a vocal critic.

He asked her for a quick summary. As she sat forward, he sat back.

After Stella described the skills of the person who'd been offered the Budget Analyst job, he asked, "Was she the blond?"

"Oh, that's right. We saw you by the elevators. Her hair is blond."

"Okay, but if she turns the offer down, come back to talk to me."

Stella reminded herself to choose her battles. "And the other job is the Admin Manager job."

It took nine hours of team leader discussion over a three-month period, thirty-one charts, and twelve single-spaced pages of written explanations to gain support for a new position to manage the Administrative Assistants. Instead of each economics group housing one Assistant, the Assistants would make up their own team reporting to a Manager while continuing to each support an economics team. The job was posted and interviews were scheduled.

"Why are you doing that again?"

"When the Macro Admin Assistant position was open and Gage said Hill was backup but didn't have time, Dawn stepped in on FOMC support even though she already supports her own economists and is backup for conferences. FOMC was supposed to be temporary, but she's gotten stuck because Macro trusts her. They don't trust their new Assistant yet. So we've already broken the one-to-one relationship between Assistants and Heads. Also, the Assistants are beginning to pull rank on one another, trying to boss one another around just because their Head bosses the other Heads. There's no incentive to back one another up since the Heads don't care. Bringing them together creates same meaningful incentives and promotes sharing knowledge among themselves and gaining recognition for their expertise. Remember the discussion about what you called pats on the head when we all agreed they need legitimate recognition and respect. Everyone supported it."

He shrugged. "That was then. This is now."

"But why?" Stella squinted with sincere confusion.

"Just don't move quickly."

"There's some urgency because we need all hands-on board for upcoming conferences."

Wendell said, "I'm sure the girls'll work it out in their own way. Doesn't seem like we need to spend more dollars for someone to check in on them. You can move ahead but don't move too fast."

Stella's eye twitched as she reminded him interviews were scheduled.

"Let's move on. David told me to tell you and Adam he wants us to bring Gage's group back into Research. Get a Group Head meeting on the calendar within a week or so to talk about it. Don't tell Adam right away."

"Coming back on our books and/or physically moving back to this floor?" Stella looked confused.

"What does 'back on our books' mean?"

"Grouped in with the economics groups in the Research Department's budget and policies or just coming back physically?"

"Let me see what I can find out. Come back at three."

"Okay."

Wendell closed his door after her and checked his emails. He stood then, and crossed his forearms behind his back, clasping his elbows, and stretched. Then he began shadow-boxing, feet planted behind his desk. He whispered, "Right, left, jab, hook, Frank down," ending by shaking his fists over his head.

Wendell exuded tension when he came to Stella's office at a quarter after three.

"I'm back. Frank said Research may take a budget hit for bringing Gage in. What'd he mean?"

Stella explained the Fed System's expenses are allocated according to PACS, an iterative and complex process to allocate each dollar to the three output areas – Monetary Policy, Supervision and Regulation, and Payments. "Its rules-based nature sometimes gets in the way of sense."

To his credit, Wendell listened to Stella before asking, "Why would I care about that?"

Stella told him about the deal Frank, Gage, and David struck when Gage's group was formed and described how a reversal may work. She even drew pictures of buckets of expenses, but when she saw him lose interest, she said, "Changes to how Gage's group is allocated will impact our ability to meet the RBOPS target budget guidance."

"Oh. Hey, someone told me one time there are a lot of our Police charged to monetary policy."

Stella was startled at the change in conversation. "Well, I know that was true of the Fed Police in the past because monetary policy depends on being trustworthy, so we have to at least be able to protect the cash in the basement. So a big chunk did use to hit us through the iterative process that allocates expenses to the buckets. How much of this do you want to know?"

"Am I paying for dog food? For Bella and Mac?" He snipped off their names in humor. Wendell loved dogs and had three. Though he rarely initiated discussion of his, others learned about them through an HR manager, who, whenever she found herself in meetings with Wendell, brought up whichever was the last dog show where they'd run into one another.

Stella smiled at Wendell's reference to their K-9 coworkers in Law Enforcement. "You know, they're on Twitter now? Ours tweeted today to say hello to their KC counterparts. The KC dogs posted a video talking about their work, checking trucks and packages."

"I'll have to look for it. Let's push budget talk to after FOMC."

On his way out for the day, Wendell stopped at Winnie's cube. "Why is Stella's office over there?" He pointed in the general direction of Stella's office, about a half-block away.

"These are bigger and were used only for Officers with PhDs. And she likes to be by her staff."

"Tell her you want her to move over here."

"I like the exercise, that's no trouble. She's over this way during the day anyway."

Wendell pushed up the strap of his shoulder bag and zipped his coat. "Right. But I can't tell her I want her over here. I'm asking for work-wife help. Gage next to me, then Stella in my old office."

Winnie smiled with pleasure at the reference to work-wife, nodded her head, and wished his back a goodnight.

Winnie went right to Stella's office.

"No thanks, Win."

"Please. Just think about it. I'll come in early and we'll be done by noon. Facilities'll pack your shelves, we'll pack your files, and they'll move everything over."

"I've sat by my team for years, Winnie. I'll come by you more often."

"It's a bigger office, Stella. And I'll be right there and can do a better job managing your calendar."

"Let me talk to my team."

"Do you know why Wendell wants to save an office over there for Gage?"

Stella frowned and shook her head.

In the past, Winnie would have revealed the reason behind Stella's move and asked Stella to pretend to be surprised if needed. In the past, Stella would have revealed Gage's return to the RD but asked Winnie to not tell anyone.

The next morning, Stella told Winnie, "I'd rather not, but I will. I think there's more behind this move than you're saying."

"Nope, I just want to pick my neighbor. Let me go set up the move with Facilities and the IT folks and then I'll come back and pack. Okay if Facilities packs your shelves?"

When Winnie returned, she and Stella loaded a cart with Stella's coat, backpack, tea kettle, laptop, critical files, and tchotchkes, which included the requisite magnetic sculpture, a desk-size labyrinth, a small crystal ball, and a sparkly cupcake topped with clips to hold notes.

In her new office, Stella told Winnie she didn't require any refinishing or painting, but when she opened a drawer that held pretzel crumbs, she asked Winnie to put in a work order for cleaning.

As Winnie walked out, a PhD stopped in the doorway. "Oh no, the dark side, Stella?"

"You're in early."

"New leaf." He laughed. "Nah. Got an FOMC memo due today. You're over here now?"

"Seemed like the right thing to do. I'm surprised one of you didn't snap up this office." The PhD was a Knowledge Leader, an Officer-equivalent job title for PhDs who didn't have staff.

The PhD laughed and made a "pshaw" sound. "No. I try to avoid this corner whenever possible. Randy's here. I get more FOMC work every time I see Randy so out of sight, out of mind. Except for today, I'm on Randy's list with nowhere to hide until my memo for FOMC is done. Good luck over here."

Stella wiped the desktop and credenza, set up her tea kettle, opened her laptop, made tea, and checked emails.

When Wendell arrived, Winnie reported, "Stella's settling in. Check."

"Thanks. You have her calendar too? I should know about where she is."

"Do you want access to it? I can show her how to give it."

"No, that's too much. But when she's out, put a note in mine. Reasons are good too."

"Okay. Stella asked if you would sign this. It's the increase for Joe."

"Okay. Let me get a pen." He looked it over. "It's supposed to be $45,000. Not $4,500." His eyes darkened and his eyebrows pulled down.

Winnie hesitated, shifting her weight from side to side, knowing his reputation for penalizing mistakes. Perhaps that was why, in a firm voice, she said, "Oh, my. I'll talk to Stella."

Winnie went right to Stella's office, closing the door behind her. Clipping her words, she asked, "Is there a typo in Joe's increase? Shouldn't it be $4,500?"

"$45,000. No typo. I think the increases will be larger now, Win. David always thought we piddled when we stuck to the ten percent, but now he's in charge and will probably approve anything Wendell wants." Stella tilted her head. "It does seem ridiculously big though, huh? I can't imagine, honestly. We have to tell the young ones in our families to reach for a PhD in economics. And get a job at the Fed. Thank you for questioning it. Better safe than sorry."

"Oh." Winnie hesitated, tapping her fingers on the page, while Stella waited. "Yes, you should have told me. Okay, let me go and get this done."

When Wendell signed the corrected version, he thanked Winnie for catching the error.

Winnie's mouth worked and she shifted from foot to foot.

When he asked if there was anything more, she turned without saying a word.

On Wednesday, everyone in the RD fed the collective energy reserved for the "Big Group" briefing. All PhDs were expected to attend, and most did. Once they and the Business Economists poured into the elevator lobby, those left in the RD sighed in relief.

Hours later, the PhDs began to trickle back, invigorated from what one Fed Watcher described as a free-for-all nature of briefing debates. One PhD continued to argue points even as the apparent counterpoint holder walked away. Randy and Wendell returned last, talking about the economic forecast David would share at FOMC the next week.

The floor cleared right at 5:00 p.m., except for Randy, Stella, and a couple Business Economists. When darkness fell, only Randy remained. After Housekeeping finished and turned off the floor's lights, he made a particularly poignant picture of a committed public servant.

On Thursday, Wendell arrived at 8:40 a.m., and soon after he, Randy, and four others made their way to the elevators. Gage would join them downstairs. This morning's meeting was the "Small Group" briefing. The Small Group is made up of those who have access to read the Class I, or most secret, FOMC information – the President, sometimes the First VP, and seven others designated by the President. The Small Group would formulate the statements David would make at the FOMC meeting in Washington.

When Wendell returned to the floor at lunchtime, he went right to Stella's office and asked, "What's the deal with the chairs?"

"I'm sorry. Chairs?"

"The ones in David's and Frank's conference rooms. Yesterday, the guys had to take some from Frank's. Today, Frank comes in and throws a hissy fit." Frank's conference room was adjacent to David's on the E-Floor.

Stella said, "Remember about a year ago, that happened right before Frank's meeting with some external folks, and he had to go hunt for replacement chairs. David promised no repeats."

"Well, you should have told me." Wendell had apparently forgotten the Heads' discussion about the chairs. David had reported being taken to task by the previous President and told the Heads to ask an E-Floor Assistant to find chairs and never, ever let the PhDs just "grab the first damn chair they saw."

Stella asked, "Sorry?"

He wrongly took the word as an apology and changed the subject. "What do you know about Goodfriend's nomination?"

"Oh, I thought he didn't clear the Senate hearing."

"Who else has Trump nominated?"

"I'd have to look it up. I think Nellie Liang was nominated. And Michelle Bowman has her hearing next month."

"Nellie is from the Board, right?"

Stella nodded. "Technically retired from Board S&R."

"Would you help Winnie to keep track of this?"

"I could, but I think David's Assistant downstairs already does and probably doesn't rely on *Wall Street Journal* articles, so it'd be better to tap into her effort. Winnie and I could ask her together."

He declined her offer and turned to go.

Stella added, "And Clarida, he's confirmed. I think he'll be at the FOMC meeting next week.

I was saddened though unsurprised that neither Wendell nor Stella was certain about nominations for Governors. That they were not compelled to certainty told about the odd structure of the Fed System and the limit of the Governors' influence in the Fed Banks. On the other hand, it also told about Fed Bank staff's trust that the U.S. President and the Senate mostly choose qualified and appropriate Governors.

The process of appointing a Governor is worlds away from that of appointing a Federal Reserve Bank President. At the BOG, there are no Presidents, First VPs, or BODs. The BOG is led by seven Governors who've been nominated by the U.S. President, approved in a Senate Committee hearing, and confirmed by the full Senate.

The BOG was created after the Great Depression to replace the original Washington, D.C., overseer of the Fed System. Decades after the original Federal Reserve Act passed, Congress ratified the importance of independent monetary policy by setting Governor's terms at fourteen years. The long terms were intended to prevent any one U.S. President and Congress from appointing too many of the Governors or making Governors' reappointments contingent on implementing a political party's policy desires. But increasingly, Governors don't stay their full terms. Though the low pay is surely a factor, I think it is likely outweighed by their hard jobs being made even harder when the Chair of the Senate Committee on Banking, Housing, and Urban Affairs (Senate Banking Committee) prevents filling the vacancies, resulting in seven Governors' work being spread among, for example, two.

And in 2016, as Chair of the Senate Banking Committee, that was just what Senator Richard Shelby did when he refused to hold hearings on then U.S. President Obama's nominations for Governors. Shelby's shenanigans positioned Trump to pack the BOG and by this point in 2018, Trump had nominated candidates to six of the seven Governor spots.

Though I don't often wish my lingering on others, I can't help my hope for an author or signer of the Federal Reserve Act to haunt

Senator Shelby and others of his ilk who set aside their responsibility for oversight of an independent institution in order to extend their party's power beyond their own terms.

On Friday morning, most greetings included a complaint about the slush that fell from the sky onto their shoulders and accumulated on the sidewalk to splash their ankles.

Dawn's greeting didn't. She was energized by the close of a successful Briefing Week, dressed in a comfortable but sophisticated lapis-colored jersey pants and top, ready for the inevitable last-minute documents requiring hand-delivery. She logged her steps and since Monday, she was already at 63,000.

Hilerie, Gage's Administrative Assistant, was chatting with Winnie when Dawn delivered Wendell's FOMC documents.

"Good morning, Hill. Since you're here, let me give you Gage's. His light was off upstairs."

Hill tightened the hands she held at her waist before releasing them to accept the document. As Dawn walked away, Hill pretended to hide a pretend laugh. "Winnie. Her shoes."

Winnie pulled a frown. "Always professional is what I say."

"Same here. At least she could wear clean gym shoes, not something she wore in the slop outside."

Hill envied the power vested in Dawn during Briefing Week even as she'd skirted any suggestion she train as a backup. Unfortunately, Gage aided the skirting without ever giving her the pep talk to build her confidence.

Winnie and Hill were mortified when a smiling Dawn returned to the center of the cube's opening. "I had just run out on an errand when that document came through. I'll thank you to address any concerns about my appearance to my face, though you might want to think before you speak."

Mid-afternoon, Wendell and Randy returned once more from the E-Floor. Still in the hallway outside Wendell's office, Randy reviewed the remaining briefing work. "Okay, so over the weekend, we'll need to continue editing David's statement for the meeting, go back and forth with him."

"The weekend?" Wendell made his fake surprise face.

Randy was annoyed. "Yes. Then David and I leave for FOMC. You're sure you don't want to go to introduce yourself as the DOR?"

"No, no. You like to go."

"So, we have Small Group again Monday, and then David and I fly out, but work on David's statement continues all the way until Wednesday. In the meantime, there's a Presidents' meeting Monday night. The agenda item has to do with control over Districts' budgets. On Tuesday, I join him."

"Wait, what about the budgets?"

"I don't really know. The agenda said something about a Research budget target."

"Huh. So who all goes to the FOMC meeting?"

"The Presidents with a plus one, except the President of the New York Fed who brings half a dozen, and the Chairman, who has twenty to thirty staff. When you go, you'll have a designated seat. Not at the table."

Wendell laughed. "For now."

Randy rolled his eyes. "Day one of FOMC. Meeting preliminaries, coffee. A President might talk on a special topic. Then there are presentations by the New York Fed and BOG staff. New York Markets, Tealbook A, *Financial Stability Report*, projections, Q&A. Then there is the first go-round of participants' views, regional and national. Day two starts with leftovers. Then Tealbook B. A second go-round for views of appropriate policy. Then a vote, well first the Chair summarizes a sense of consensus, the group wordsmiths the statement and communications, then a vote."

"And David is a voter?" Except for New York's, the Fed Bank Presidents vote on a rotation.

Randy said, "Not till next year. All the prep work here will be the same then, David presents just like now, only difference is the formal vote. You should probably keep a vote rotation schedule somewhere so you know."

"Probably. I'll be around after 10:00 a.m. tomorrow."

Once more, the light in Randy's office shone in the dark floor.

WEEK TWO ~ 11/5

Wendell went straight to Randy's office on Monday morning to confirm their Small Group meeting. One side of his mouth pulled up when his eyes lit on Randy's carry-on, and he shrugged, as if assuring himself one last time that it was fine Randy was taking his place as FOMC sidekick.

His next stop was Stella's office.

"Since I'm letting Randy go to FOMC, I thought I should get the Heads' meetings restarted tomorrow."

She reminded him she'd scheduled off.

Wendell appeared genuinely perplexed. "I thought you wanted to get them restarted."

"I do." She glanced at her calendar. "I could come in but need to leave by 10:30."

The corners of his mouth pulled down. "I guess that would work. You've probably left early in the past without making up the time so it'd even out anyway."

Stella's head tilted with uncertainty and caution. Wendell was a bundle of contradictions when it came to HR policies. In meetings with other Officers, he advocated for telecommuting yet when faced with individuals' requests, he brushed them off. And while he considered even an hour of a PhD's work sufficient to claim a day's pay, he'd once added up a non-PhDs' coffee and cigarette breaks and suggested the person ought not claim a day's pay.

Finally, she exhaled and said, "I scheduled a vacation day. I'll keep a half day off." When she saw his eyes begin to narrow, she added, "I'll be in early and will make up any deficit working at home later in the afternoon."

They stared at one another for a beat. Finally, Stella picked up an index card and asked Wendell if he had anything for the Heads' meeting agenda.

"You probably thought you'd still be in charge of the agenda."

Stella reacted to his tone of tolerance and humor. "Wendell, why in the world wouldn't I?"

"Best to ask my thoughts going forward." Extending his arms with magnanimity, he said, "We can fit in one of your items. Maybe two."

Stella opened her mouth just as they heard Randy call out.

Wendell scurried out. "Yes, yes. I'm hurrying. Can't keep the big cheese waiting."

Randy reminded him David would not attend their meeting.

Wendell seemed relieved as he found something to justify his simmering discontent and snapped, "Then why the hell are we going downstairs?"

After Randy and David had left for the airport and Wendell for a lunch walk, Winnie visited Stella. Unwrapping a Silver Top, she said, "Wendell asked why you don't just come back here after your appointment."

"Oh. Why? I mean, why does he care?"

Winnie quickly abandoned an attempted defense of Wendell's inquiry.

Rather than sharing her plans for lunch and a walk through Lincoln Park Zoo with a friend, she asked Winnie, "Is it a problem, Win? The Fed gets its money's worth from me."

"I told him that. I said you're always early and staying late and skipping lunch. I think he just wants you to be available. He relies on you, and I think he doesn't like for you to change your plans for work."

Winnie grabbed a couple more Silver Tops and left.

When Wendell arrived on Tuesday morning, he asked Winnie to collect Stella and then told them he was disinviting the two Heads of umbrella areas from the Heads meeting since, "Neither woman seems to enjoy the meetings and most of our topics are about Research."

When Stella spoke, Wendell stared at her jeans and walking shoes. Though not unusual dress in the RD, it was for Stella. "There's no other channel for them to get and opine on the info you bring back from the Executive Committee."

"I could meet with them separately."

Her sideways nod was noncommittal. "David and I told them in the past that the meetings are optional for them. That's why I get the agenda out early. Or used to. Then they can decide if they'll come."

Wendell extended his hands and pumped them as if to squash Stella's words. "I'm trying to do them a favor."

Stella pulled in her lips.

His last-minute exclusion of the two was made worse by the elaborate scheme he described to Winnie to prevent them from knowing the meeting would go on without them.

Stella asked if she might take back the pages she'd asked Winnie to copy for the meeting, but Winnie refused, reveling in feeling needed.

Stella was first to arrive at Wendell's conference room for the Heads' meeting. As she placed her notebook at her usual seat at one end of the rectangular table and turned to the beverage cart, Wendell cracked the new direct door from his office and asked her to come over.

After an awkward moment before Stella realized he intended for her to exit the conference room and enter his office from the hallway, she joined him.

Meanwhile, others had begun to arrive.

The Head of the Finance Group fixed his coffee, took his seat, and tapped his pencil against the table with increasing force. Wendell, on occasion through the years, challenged the Finance Head to split his PhDs into "traditional," or those who study banking, and "modern," or those who study market pricing, to ensure none in the first group benefitted from the RD matching the competitive salaries of the latter. David, as DOR, allowed Wendell to grouse and the Finance Head to ignore Wendell.

Next to arrive was the Regional Head. Looking toward the tapping, he asked, "Morning going well?" The unlikely pair had already commiserated over Wendell's reign. The Regional Group was made up of both Business Economists and PhDs whose work is largely based on stakeholders' needs with little time for exploration of their own interests. A natural outcome of their work is recognition from District stakeholders. Wendell had, in the past, made clear he thought academic recognition was far more important.

When the Macroeconomics Head arrived, conversation stalled.

The Microeconomics Head arrived precisely at 9:00 a.m., stuffing his hat into a sleeve of his Canada Goose jacket and sliding the bundle under his seat. When he saw Wendell wasn't there, he laughed in relief.

At 9:09 a.m., the topic of weather exhausted, the Regional Head looked toward one end of the table. "No Wendell," and the other end, "No Stella. Might this have been cancelled?"

The others shrugged.

He called a student's wait rule, refilled his coffee, and was leaving when Wendell's direct door clicked.

"We're here."

As Wendell prepared his coffee, he said, "At David's request, Gage et al are returning to Research."

When grousing came from three directions at once, Wendell said it wasn't up for debate. Once seated, he continued. "Payments is tired of having to pay for Gage's area when they don't get anything from it. So, David took a bold step and told Frank we should let another Reserve Bank step up and do research for Payments."

At the first peep, Wendell added, "It's done. Gage'll be Associate Director reporting to me. Other Feds have an Associate Director to take some of the administrative crap load off the Director. It won't really matter to you." Finally seated, he looked around. "Stella. Maybe."

Stella asked, "Maybe?"

The Microeconomics Head distracted Stella from her own question when he asked, "Why can't Stella just ramp up her magic in her unacknowledged Associate Director role?"

Wendell said, "Stella's not a PhD."

The Macroeconomics Head jumped in. "Couldn't they just stay upstairs and Gage report to you? Give Gage that stairway."

Gage's area was located right above the RD, and he'd asked for a buildout of a small atrium and stairway to connect the heart of his area to the heart of the RD, claiming his retention issues would disappear if his PhDs could have constant contact with other PhDs. Though there was a stairwell a few yards outside the entrance to his area, he was adamant.

Gage never grasped the irony of his request despite Frank's multiple reminders that only a few years had passed since the Fed

Bank's outside tenants reached a critical mass and atriums throughout the building were sealed and their stairways removed to improve security.

Frank referred to Gage's request as a "Stairway to Heaven." Staff in Facilities, Central Support, and in Stella's team found Gage's obliviousness either humorous or demoralizing, depending on whether their job was accountable to Gage.

Wendell said, "They come as soon as we get Frannie booted out. She'll get his space upstairs."

The mood turned sharply as with near-giddiness, one Head pumped his fist and another called out, "Why didn't you start there." The economics Heads disliked the umbrella areas, including Frannie's, more than Gage's area.

Stella's eyes shot daggers. "Hey. Frannie doesn't know yet. Be careful, please?"

That Head said, "Well be sure to tell us when we can tell the economists. If Gage tells Heather, she'll leak it."

Soon after, Wendell nodded at Stella, and she told them she was excited to share an idea from the Assistants.

She reminded them about the process for reimbursing PhDs for their own and their colleagues' meals with visitors from academia out at local hot spots. That these meals out are covered was a point of pride for David, who had years before overcome resistance from Stella's predecessor and Central Finance.

Then, just a couple months earlier, a PhD submitted a receipt for his and a visitor's coffee at a nearby Starbucks, citing the reimbursement policy for meals. It was denied by an Admin Assistant and at appeal to Stella. The PhD went to David who took advantage of an elevator ride to gain buy-in from a new Central Finance Officer. David said he hadn't known the issue was already decided. Nevertheless, coffee reimbursement became a new PhD perk.

But then, just a few weeks earlier, System Central Finance had, for the first time, calculated the cost for the Fed Bank to reimburse an employee. The cost was the same to reimburse five or a thousand dollars. Not Stella, nor the Assistants, nor their peers in Central Finance could gloss over the obvious absurdity of the coffee reimbursements.

Stella continued. "In light of the cost of processing a reimbursement, the Assistants ask that the PhDs save up and submit their coffee and taxi receipts after they have reached at least fifty dollars or at the end of the quarter."

After two minutes, Stella cut off the stream of complaints about bureaucracies. She offered, "I have their calculation to share with you." Stella riffled through the copies Winnie had made. "I guess I don't have those copies."

Wendell slapped his hand flat on the table in sudden anger. "I pulled those copies. I don't want my first days in the job tainted by new rules. Can't this wait six months?"

One Head rose to take napkins from the cart to wipe up his and another Head's spilled coffee.

Stella responded after a few seconds. "Risk in delay is that Central Finance folks push back on the coffee reimbursements altogether. I heard their new boss has since learned one of the other Feds doesn't even pay for dinners with visitors and has questioned the extent of our reimbursements."

All eyes turned to Wendell.

Calmer for having let off steam, he said, "The cost of replacing a PhD after he leaves over a three-dollar cup of coffee is a lot more than the cost of reimbursing him." He glanced at everyone but Stella and asked, "What do you guys think?"

After twenty-eight minutes of discussion, including dismissal of the idea a PhD would resign if his coffee wasn't reimbursed, the Regional Head jumped in and said, "Maybe it will work if the Assistants keep track of this for the PhDs. And let the PhDs know they need to be grateful. Might find they like the fifty-cent vending machine coffee just fine if they buy their own."

Another Head asked Stella if the cost of processing a reimbursement was fixed or variable.

Before she could answer, Wendell exclaimed, "Gage. Gage's job now. Are we done here?"

The energy of the room fizzled as Wendell refreshed his coffee and exited through his direct door.

A while later, Wendell hollered for Winnie, and after they were seated on his couch, asked whether Stella worked when she telecommuted.

"Of course. She's usually online early and late too."

"Huh. I don't trust people who work that much. I liked that preview of Stella's copies. Keep it up going forward but get her pages the day before the meeting so I can screen them sooner."

Winnie was pleased to share a solution. "She met with David every other week to tell him what was up and to find out whether he needed anything from her. The Heads' meeting agenda was one of the things they talked about. Sometimes they met for two minutes, sometimes an hour."

"Huh. Interesting. I'll see what Gage thinks. What do you know about coffee reimbursements?"

"I wasn't involved in that. I ordered catering if David wanted coffee with a visitor."

"I might take visitors to Starbucks or one of the other places so you might have to find out about reimbursements. And for these Heads' meetings, cut that big bowl of creamers to one or two. They're fattening."

"But the economists come in for the coffee once the meeting is done, some of them use it." Winnie worked her fingers in discomfort but didn't tell him that her post-meeting cleanup included collecting the fancy creamers to store in the refrigerator from where she'd retrieve one each morning. Her comfort with half-truths was new, only since Wendell asked her to lie to Stella about moving offices.

On Wednesday morning, the Regional Head, unable to find Wendell or Winnie, stopped at Stella's office. When he'd returned from vacation the day before, he'd been surprised by a reservation to fly out to this Fed Bank's Branch this afternoon. "Bushwhacked, Stella."

Branches are *of* a Fed Bank, but not all Fed Banks have Branches. Atlanta has five. New York has none. This Fed Bank has one.

Branches have their own Boards of Directors.

Branches played a critical role when paper checks moved about the country, but as fewer checks were written and electronic transmission implemented, their work changed. And their role in cash distribution was simplified by cash outposts. Many Branches were closed as the Fed System collaborated and consolidated.

Branches that remained open may have a Research outpost. The profile of the outpost varies by District.

At this Fed Bank's Branch, there is an administrative staff and a Business Economist or two. The Business Economists collect state and local information for input into FOMC briefing materials and present information about the economy to the Branch's Directors.

The Regional Head said, "I think those two think they'll get information for FOMC, but it's not like that. It's different in the Branch world. Those Directors don't necessarily think about the national economy. And they invited the alumni Directors who are past the non-disclosure stage and have no business in a current policy convo. They're going off half-cocked for some reason. There are ways of doing things that are appropriate for a central bank and this schmoozing ain't it. Do you know what's going on?"

She held in a laugh after seeing his sincerity. "Honestly, shouldn't Directors call us out for bad behavior if we schmooze? I'm sorry you came home from Alaska to this. How was the cruise?"

Wendell interrupted then and the Head followed him back to his office.

They crossed paths with Winnie. She was on her way to tell Stella that Wendell wanted to meet with her at 10:00 a.m. about the "Carolyn deal."

The Head rolled his eyes at Stella as he walked out of Wendell's office at 9:59 a.m.

Wendell asked her to wait while he ran down the hall, and when he returned said, "You know, it's only a two-second walk. You don't have to get out of your chair until the meeting time."

"Got it."

"You schmooze, don't you?" His question might have been a landmine if Stella lacked context.

"Oh. Everybody does sometime, right? I've been trying to schmooze my New York counterpart on making friends with RBOPS at the Board. He's the only holdout."

"He might be the wise one."

"I don't think so, but it's interesting. First time anyone pulled the New-York-is-the-most-important card in RAOC."

"I thought you were all women. What's that acronym?"

"At the beginning. There's two men now. Research Administrative Officers Committee. R. A. O. C. Pronounced 'rake' for ease."

"What does he do with the RBOPS?"

"Same kinds of things I do but just for budget. He doesn't have tech, editing, HR, or umbrella areas that the rest of us do."

He pulled his phone from his pocket to look at the time. "So he has a lesser share but of a more important District. Huh. So why would I want to talk to Carolyn?"

"She's a good person to know. She has the Governors' ears for Reserve Bank matters."

Wendell rolled his eyes.

"And the smoother things flow from Research to the budget overseers in RBOPS, the less administrative burden on you, Frank, even David. Communications from RBOPS mostly come through Central Support areas. They like it that way – it gives them power – but messages get muddled. For example, last year, Congress asked for the amount of money the Research spent on visitors. Finance handled the request using our expenses, keying on the word 'visitor.' Not all visitors were included and not all who were included were who Congress wanted. Similar missteps happened in other Banks. RAOC wasn't told about the request until after the numbers went to Congress so unless some other District overstated, the System would have been understated by the error in our numbers."

Wendell laughed. "Brilliant. We can't even be blamed because it was an honest mistake. What did Congress say when they got the numbers?"

"We never heard."

"Probably because they were understated. Huh. Genius. So we want to be the one the Board asks for the information to get it right?"

Stella nodded.

Wendell chuckled. "I'm not convinced that would produce better outcomes. A little confusion can be good."

"A second example and maybe better example deals with the budget targets in the RBOPS memo."

Wendell was inexplicably defensive as he reported having read the RBOPS memo.

Stella's brow furrowed. "I've mentioned we probably missed an opportunity for input into the target. I found out it's fact. RAOC learned that Finance folks made input based on our strategic plans. Historically, our plans had what we wanted to brag about. Not necessarily what we spend money on. Not knowing our game, our Central Finance lowballed what we needed for a budget."

"Okay, getting us more money is a good reason to have a relationship. But why me?"

"In the RBOPS and Central Finance part of the Fed, people do this stuff formally and match titles or levels so we needed a Director of Research. It came to you because I'm RAOC Chair right now."

"I assume a rotating chair. What's your term?"

"Two years. Till next fall."

"So if I decide to do this, what will it involve?"

"RAOC drafted a letter for you to send to Carolyn. Winnie and Carolyn's Assistant would set up a time for the two of you to talk. We'll give you talking points. Once you and she agree, RAOC takes back over."

Wendell was semi-serious. "Do I have to schmooze Carolyn?"

"No. She strikes me as someone who relies on presentation of facts."

"Let me think about it."

"Carolyn's here next week to talk to folks in the Payments world, so there'd be an opportunity to meet face-to-face."

"That's not a good reason to move so quickly. I'd probably wait until I'm at the Board. If I decide to do it."

Back in her office, Stella unlocked her computer.

Wendell must have started typing before she'd passed through his door. "I'll need to check out how other Research Directors feel about this RBOPS contact. I'm going to call Bill and will let you know but don't count on this."

Bill was a DOR in another Fed Bank.

Her brow again furrowed, Stella closed her door and dialed.

"Veronica, Research Department."

After the two caught up and talked about the upcoming RAOC meeting, Stella said, "I asked my DOR about talking to Carolyn. I wanted to give you a heads-up he's going to ask Bill for advice. He's looking for a reason to kill the initiative. He's a tough one."

"Oh no, Stella. It's hard to know, you know, most of the DORs have presidential aspirations and want their name out to RBOPS in some context other than a Board review finding, but then there are those DORs who'd rather pretend they work at a university."

"I had to ask him, but it was damned if I do, damned if I don't. Sorry to drag RAOC into this with me."

"We've all been there. Bill's out today anyway. I'll send a note and tell him to tell Wendell he should talk to RBOPS. He asked me why SRAC or RAOC didn't have input into the budget target so he's all for us doing this."

SRAC is a committee of the DORs. Its full name is the System Research Advisory Committee.

When Stella hung up, she dialed another number, and asked, "Lunch?" A few seconds later, she wrapped a shawl around her shoulders and left the floor.

When Stella returned to her desk after lunch and began reading emails, she whispered, "Oh fuck no."

From Wendell

Stella, I'm bringing Gage into our discussion because he has experience with Carolyn and I'm heading for the airport. He said she demonstrates a pattern of retaliation with Reserve Banks who don't follow her lead in the Payments arena. Is there someone other than her?

From Gage

You are right to be cautious, Wendell. Carolyn wields her influence like a club. Why would we want to invite a relationship with her? Stella? Board Research has little similarity to Reserve Bank Research.

Stella quickly typed the explanations she'd given Wendell and attached RAOC's charter before she left for her next meeting.

A new string of emails was waiting when she returned.

From Gage

I'm still not certain what gave birth to RAOC. It seems contradictory to the independence of the Federal Reserve Banks. Calling it a "federation" doesn't mask a marginally evil intent.

I agree with Wendell's concerns. Board economists have limited time for their independent research. There's been too much policy work since the '08 financial crisis and it is inhibiting their PhDs from doing research. Someone told Heather there was a post on EJMR taking the issue of policy burden into the public forum. We do not want to draw attention to this Reserve Bank and in particular not for some nice-making with the chief bureaucrat for some administrative benefit. I think that qualifies as the tail wagging the dog.

Stella looked out her window, and asked, "Tail wagging the dog?" She shook her head and continued reading.

From Wendell

I'm at the airport and will lose my connection soon. At the last System Economics meeting, someone from the Board told me he heard we give our researchers 80% time for independent research and require only 20% for policy. Carolyn must know Board economists get nowhere near that. I didn't correct the Board guy because it would be stupid to let them know we shoot for 90% research. Stella, are you or your counterparts the ones behind that gossip? Gage makes a good point though I wouldn't worry too much about EJMR.

From Gage

EJMR has a post comparing the Board and New York to the rest of us. New York's balance is similar to the Board's. I talked to one of their newer PhDs at a conference. He asked about jobs here but his pedigree was not at snuff for us. Let's not get Carolyn pointed in our direction.

Stella: In case you don't know, EJMR is Economics Job Market Rumors, a site on which economists share information about jobs for economics PhDs.

To be clear, this drawing out of Carolyn was our idea, not something forced upon us by dragons under threat of frying in their breath?

I wasn't sure whether Stella's expression of disgust was caused by imagining a fried human or the mention of EJMR.

From Wendell

It sounds like we are converging on an anti-plan. Stella, can you extract your counterparts from this? At a minimum, you should extract yourself.

Stella said aloud, "No." She rose and turned on her tea kettle, tapping a tea bag with one hand on the other. She paced while the water heated and then while the tea steeped. When she sat back at her desk, she said aloud, "Okay."

From Stella

RAOC is made up of my counterparts. Each represents their DOR, their Bank, and System interests. RAOC was born when some Research Directors wanted a say in the way Central Support costs were being allocated. Those Directors foresaw the accountability for our spending that is now coming to fruition as evidenced by the RBOPS memo. There was unanimous approval from SRAC to create RAOC. David was our member then.

Also, several months ago, when RAOC first started to coalesce around the idea of reaching out to Carolyn, David supported our plans.

Our budget, Board review findings, accounting for anything that may or does draw scrutiny from the public and/or from Congress – that all lives at the intersection of the Research departments and RBOPS. We cannot stop the evolution in the rest of the System and at the Board. Central Support is going to keep consolidating and absent efforts such as reaching out to Carolyn, we are going to be increasingly disadvantaged.

I appreciate Gage's concerns about Carolyn but RAOC knows her to be reasonable and amazingly informed on all things Fed.

Please note this Bank pulling away will not affect RAOC's effort but will likely cause us pain in the long run.

I didn't mean for this to take so much of your time.

From Gage
It is clear the initiation of this RAOC effort was an error. If Carolyn has not yet been contacted, all reason indicates the effort should meet its demise now.

From Wendell
I'll call David and see what he thinks. I don't want the other Research Directors to think I'm uncooperative. Getting ready to take off now.

Stella pinched the space between her thumb and forefinger for a few seconds. When that didn't stop her forming headache, she opened the blinds further and turned off the overhead lights.

Wendell's flight was only an hour long, and he called Stella after he landed. "I just got off the phone. David will talk to Carolyn."

The RD was at ease on Thursday due to Wendell's absence, the end of the FOMC cycle, and the next day's holiday. Since Veterans Day was on Saturday, the Fed Bank was closed on Friday.

Stella checked in with her team to make sure none had deadlines that would keep them late.

When Adam asked her about her plans for the weekend, she offered up just her book club that night.

Adam reported his weekend would be partially inspired by the weekly Bankwide blog. He usually wasn't a fan, but in this week's blog, one of the Law Enforcement Officers, a Veteran, wrote that he would spend the day looking for restaurants that provided free breakfast or coffee to Veterans. Not for the breakfast or coffee, but because it was there he would find Veterans who might need an ear. A Veteran himself, Adam said, "I'm copying. Good use of time off. Otherwise, Sally and I are planning to grocery shop afterwards so we can hibernate if the forecast for freezing rain turns out right."

WEEK FOUR ~ 11/19

Carrie, the RD's Event Coordinator, smiled as she read the tiny card nestled in a burst of Gerbera daisies. She pulled one of the daisies from the vase and went to Stella's office. "I'm back."

Stella jumped up and the two hugged.

"Yay, welcome back, oh Carrie, we've missed you. How are you?" Stella pulled out a chair. "Sit down."

Carrie, returning after a knee replacement, said, "I'm fine. Doc said like new. Here, have back a flower for in here. Thank you for them. I opened the door afraid Gage had moved me out and instead I see bright pink and yellow. They're beautiful."

Stella pulled a bud vase from her shelf. "Perfect. Thanks back. How's your knee?"

"I wish I'd done it years ago. So's my office safe?"

"Yes. Molly and the Editors moved so Gage's folks could be all in a row. I'm hoping Gage recorded that in his dumbass favor bank."

Carrie blushed as she revealed she knew much of what had been going on. "I wanted to know the dirt and the Assistants wanted to complain. Except for Win, of course. They said she barely talks to them anymore now that she's reporting to Wendell. I can't believe we report to Wendell. David must have had a screw loose."

When the two finished catching up, Stella asked, "Are you really ready to be here, Car? You only get one chance to heal right. You could telecommute."

"The doctor's PA told me to come back to work. I was going crazy at home. Are you free for lunch? Jake wouldn't bring me Burger King, not even once."

Jake was Carrie's husband and didn't appreciate the guilty pleasure Carrie and Stella shared.

When the two returned from lunch, Winnie heard their laughter. "Stella, Wendell's waiting for you. Your calendar was clear. What's it like outside?"

"Slushy. Wear boots."

Stella changed back to black pumps and used a napkin to wipe away the slush from the back of her ankles before heading to Wendell's office.

He said, "You were gone quite a while."

"Oh. Sorry. Catching up with Carrie."

He sat back in his chair and held his chin in one hand. "You know. I like her but we did fine without her. Might be a sign we're overstaffed."

"Not at all. Those who covered for her, especially Dawn, stepped up but it's time they get settled back in their steady state workloads."

He abandoned the tack. "Winnie said you see a coach. I'm thinking of getting one. Is it useful?"

"More so than not. Especially at the beginning, mine provided a non-Fed view which was a good reality check of how odd we get."

"Huh. What'd you mean odd?"

"Well." Stella cut herself off and took a few seconds. "No bottom line. Bureaucracy. You had an example you used to offer up – when you were on the awards committee that gave Facilities one award for turning down the temperature one year and another for turning it up the next year."

"That reminds me. I saw your email about bonuses. Did I ever tell you about loss aversion?"

"You did, during last year's bonus meeting, but I wasn't sure how it applied, unless you wanted us to start using prospective incentive agreements instead of the retrospective payouts we do."

Wendell's anger was evident in his tone. "That sounds like a challenge. I'll think on it. I think we're done here."

Stella's expression held surprise and concern. "I don't mean it to be a challenge. I'm not a behavioral economist. From a mechanical view, I just don't see how it could work with retrospective awards."

"Like I said, I'll think on it."

"Did you have any questions about the calendar of deadlines for the bonuses otherwise?"

He calmed as quickly as he'd angered. "No, but what's your coach's name?"

"Ellen."

"HR gave me a few names. Gage found his coach through his wife's volunteer work. I'm not convinced it's not a bunch of hooey but I guess I could see a possibility of benefit since I'm in a job I've never had before."

The subtle insult went over Stella's head.

He asked, "Winnie said you wanted something else for your System friends?"

"Oh. No, we're good. That was a week or so ago."

"Well, what was it?"

"My Board counterpart recommended RAOC keep on hand a list of a couple of the independent research papers that, when first published, appeared to have little to do with monetary policy, but years later, did turn out to be important for monetary policy. Legends, she called them. The list would help us respond consistently when Fed colleagues call out a paper, such as the St. Louis paper on the effects of pregnancy and parenthood on research productivity of academic economists, if we could say, well there was this other paper and it foretold a topic that became super-relevant for monetary policy."

She was unsurprised when he questioned the legitimacy for the list. After a bit of back and forth, she said, "This is another of those things that's left the station. We don't have to use it here if you'd rather not."

"I didn't say that yet. Who here would ask about our research anyway?"

Stella told him about her colleagues from their Fed Bank's S&R.

"I don't think I have to worry too much about that since S&R reports up through David and he'd squash them. I suppose I should help though if it will get people off our backs. What is it again?" He reached to pull a pad of paper from a pile on his desk.

"Okay. Sure. A list of three or four independent research papers that seemed among the least related to monetary policy when published but then a year or five or ten later were resurrected and turned out to be very important to monetary policy."

"Like the ones in the obscure journals?"

"I guess. What exactly does that mean?"

"Intellectual journals. For academics."

The two agreed on a due date, and Stella flipped the cover of her steno pad and slid her pen through the coil in preparation to leave.

"Not yet." Wendell sat up straighter, using both hands to hold his pen horizontally. "Where are you on hiring that boss for the Administrative Assistants?"

"Same as when I emailed you and Gage. Candidate's response on the offer is due by close of business today."

Wendell's pupils darkened and expanded. "I thought I told you to slow this down. Winnie's taking the job."

"Winnie's never had interest in even temporary project-level coordination of other Assistants' work and generally avoids even joint projects. And just to be certain, I asked her two months ago if she might be interested, back when David was still here, just before you all approved hiring. Zero interest." Stella hesitated and her face softened. "She's got a new grandbaby. Which is not a reason not to ask her, of course, but for the first time, she's talking about retirement and wondering if her plate here is too full." Winnie regularly referred to her workload as her plate.

Wendell's breathing became audible, his increasingly loud words bitten off defensively. "She told me about the baby." He wiped sweat from his upper lip.

Stella's nostrils flared in fear and her voice shook as she spoke carefully. "Of course. I just meant that she's less likely to have changed her mind since two months ago. Plus I'd told her if she changed her mind to let me know."

Anger coated Wendell's words. "I told her we'd trade the chicken on her plate for steak and she was happy. Why in the hell wouldn't you support her?" He rolled his chair out from behind his desk.

She pressed back into her chair as if held by a centrifugal force. "To be clear. Were you asking me or telling me Winnie would be the Manager and is she aware of it and agreed to it?"

He rolled forward further around the side of his desk. "Telling you and telling you. Don't interfere with her managing the other women. Now what are you going to do about that offer?"

Stella's face was still, her eyes were flat, her arms crossed over her notebook. In a quiet, too-even voice, she said, "I'll call HR and find out. The candidate was waiting on information about her husband's job."

His rage simmered. "Winnie reports to me. Don't reach around her. You probably had a hand in raising the temperature in here too."

"Pardon?"

"You're always wearing a scarf in here. Did you have the heat turned up?"

"No." She didn't wait for his response. Stella rose and moved toward the door, not turning her back to him until she was at the door.

Once she'd left, Wendell's expression held self-disgust and once his anger had turned sufficiently inward, he released it by cracking the tip off a pencil.

Though not the first time she was faced with a temper, that was the first time I'd ever seen Stella truly afraid. Back at her desk, she tried to read emails, but after a couple minutes, she dialed the phone and asked whoever was on the other end to join her at Starbucks for hot chocolate.

Wendell arrived at her door just as she stood. His rage gone, he spoke in a fake friendly voice through a fake smile.

"Can you schedule one of the pre-meetings you wanted to have before Head meetings? Add Gage. And schedule a Heads meeting for Wednesday."

"I'll ask Winnie to schedule — " Stella froze.

"It's okay to ask her to do her job. Just don't go reaching around her."

"May we also use the Heads' time to talk about bonus information due dates?"

He agreed and asked, "This is the usual process, same as when David was here?"

"Yes."

She gave him time to return to his own office before she hurried down the hall.

The next morning, Winnie arrived earlier than usual. She dropped her coat in her cube and carried her coffee to Stella's office. She shut the door and sat at the table. Stella picked up her mug and joined Winnie.

Winnie took a deep breath but gasped mid-exhale. "Okay, Stella. Here is the thing."

"Good morning. How are you?"

"Fine, fine. I haven't curled my hair yet is all. You know I think that consultant who uses that office where I finish getting ready saw my curling iron. That doesn't matter. I wanted to talk to you first thing. I don't want to manage the girls. All that drama and fights and dealing with the economists. I like my job with just you and Wendell and me in our own world."

"I wondered what was up when he said you wanted to be Manager. Did you tell him you don't?"

"I did not. I can't disappoint him, Stella. Can't you talk to him?"

Stella hesitated, her lips open, as if she'd remembered Wendell's anger. When she finally spoke, she punted, something she almost never did. "No, I'm sorry. Why don't you tell him today?"

"Stella, the man was so excited. I could try. Maybe."

Winnie's resistance grated on Stella.

"Wendell thought you wanted it. Are you sure you don't?"

"Well, it's a promotion. I didn't think I would ever be a Manager, but he said I would do fine. He said he likes to help women get a leg up to a next level, like the old KC Fed President who was in some old *American Banker* for helping women climb the ladder. He said he wants to be in an article like that." Winnie stopped for a beat. "He kept staring at my eye shadow when we were talking, do you think I wear too much?"

"You look beautiful. He stares at my nail polish too. He stares at some other things on other women. I'm not sure he realizes."

"What should I do?"

"I think you should be honest with him. He'll listen, Win."

"What if he gets mad? I heard him yesterday, when you were in there."

Stella watched as Winnie gathered the Silver Tops wrappers before speaking. "He likes you, but this is about what you want. Enjoy the compliment of having been asked to be Manager. Congratulations on that no matter what you decide."

"He's not going to announce it until next Monday so I have the rest of the week. My brother is hosting Thanksgiving so I won't be cleaning up on Friday and can think about it then and email him over the weekend."

Stella started to tell her to keep her day off Fed-free but instead asked if Winnie would see her new grandbaby on Thanksgiving.

The Group Heads greeted one another as they arrived for their Wednesday morning meeting, taking their usual seats. Stella at the foot of the rectangular table and two Heads on each side, leaving the seat in the middle of each side empty and the seat at the head for Wendell.

When Gage arrived, he brushed off the others' greetings and looked around the room and declared, "I should be at Wendell's right."

Thinking Gage was joking, the Macroeconomics Head in that seat laughed.

Wendell entered from through his direct door and stopped at the coffee cart. "Are we oversold?"

When the Macroeconomics Head felt the pull of Gage's hand on the back of his seat, he slid his coffee over to the middle seat, stood, and motioned to Gage with a grand gesture.

Gage swished his rear a bit and announced, "It's warm."

Their meeting finished in record-time when the Heads clammed up rather than engage with Gage.

Wendell said, "Stella should have added another agenda item. Make each meeting the same length." When he saw the others' expressions, he added, "This is good too. Early ending is probably a good precedent."

The usual casual conversation while the Heads refreshed their coffee was absent.

Randy followed Wendell through the direct door. "So you're really using this door."

Wendell told a story of the only FOMC meeting he'd attended. He'd gone with the previous President when David was sick. "I didn't know there was even a door and out comes Bernanke straight from his office. I bumped into him and spilled my coffee. Now I've got a Chair's door."

"Sure you do. Ready for FOMC 101?"

"Let's go back in there by the coffee."

Once settled, Randy slid a four-week calendar across to Wendell.

Wendell said, "Well, I know about the Blackout." FOMC staff are restricted from public speaking around the FOMC meetings. "Hey. It wasn't so warm at the head of the table. Let's move around."

Randy is referred to as the FOMC Czar, but I think of him as the conductor of an orchestra, one with reach to draw any resources into the interlude of FOMC about eight times each year. Once the stage, FOMC lost its place to the RD's independent research.

During the first week of its FOMC cycle, the Fed Bank submits its inputs for the Beige Book to whichever Fed Bank is coordinating on behalf of the Fed System. Formally known as the *Summary of Commentary on Current Economic Conditions by Federal Reserve District,* the Beige Book contains the stories behind economic statistics.

Also in the first week, Randy assigns the work of special memos. Special memos are classified memos that explain timely topics and are designated as "special" because they are on top of the routine briefing materials. Each Fed Bank has its own special memos while the BOG staff prepares a set of special memos that are distributed to all members of FOMC.

Randy referred to the second week of the calendar as ramp up and read, recommending Wendell plan to read the other Fed Banks' submissions and the summary when the Beige Book is published that Wednesday.

And on Friday of the second week, the first briefing meeting is held. The BOG's Tealbook A and special memos are distributed. Tealbook A is "*Economic and Financial Conditions: Current Situation and Outlook.*" Randy warned Wendell he should expect to spend that weekend reading.

In the third week, what is known here as Briefing Week, this Fed Bank's economic forecast is completed, the PhDs' special memos are due, and Tealbook B, officially subtitled "*Monetary Policy: Strategies and Alternatives,*" arrives from the BOG. Meetings are held to brief David on all of that.

The last week of the calendar shows the FOMC meeting that takes place in Washington, D.C.

When Randy dispensed with the calendar entries, he slid over a list of five PhDs and memo topics. "Since we're just a couple days away from assigning our special memos, I brought my thoughts to see what you think."

Wendell's contribution to their conversation was a reminder that one of the five was a procrastinator.

Soon after, they agreed that David would be satisfied with the planned memos.

After Randy left, Wendell bit his nails and seemed lost in thought for a few minutes before he looked for something else to do.

He picked up a can of Sprite from the coffee cart and headed to Stella's office. Just outside her door, he watched for several seconds as she marked up a spreadsheet at her table. When he finally moved and entered her vision, she startled.

Once seated with her at the table, Wendell said, "I shouldn't sneak up, sorry. That's an odd pen."

"Yes." She held it out. "HR gave them out at one of the all-Bank things. I need to get to the supply closet for normal pens."

"Looks like a wizard broom. Can you get me one? My grandson's into Harry Potter."

"I'll ask HR." In flipping the pen back to a writing position, Stella dropped it and instead of catching it, clumsily propelled it toward Wendell's foot.

Stella started to rise, but he reached for the pen. After the awkward moment ended, he lifted his foot to the opposite knee and removed his shoe to massage his foot.

"Did the pen do that?"

"No. My foot is bothering me."

"Ouch, I'm sorry. Did you see a doctor?"

"I'm in PT. The girl might have done something to my foot since it feels worse today."

"Did you let the doctor know?"

"No. What can he do? I don't want any prescriptions. Which reminds me. This isn't why I came over, but did your System buddies talk about that letter from Brown and Donnelly about drugs? The Research Director from Cleveland wants us to have a check-in on whether the System's done enough now that a year has passed since they asked us to do research on opioids."

"We talked about it last year when Yellen got it. We thought it was a big deal because none of us could remember getting a letter like that from Senators before."

"I need to read it." He began searching on his iPad.

"They were asking us to do research on the impact of the opioid epidemic on the economy and for Community Affairs to look for community solutions. Some of my counterparts thought it impinged on independence."

Wendell said, "In one of our Beige Book go-rounds, we got anecdotes about failed drug tests getting in the way of hiring. I don't think we gave anybody any other info."

"No, we didn't."

"How do you know?"

"I kept an eye out. I didn't agree about the letter being an issue for independence, but I didn't see why the Senators thought the Fed was the right place for that research to be done. I looked at some of the stuff the System's done, and though the questions are smart, the answers are based on whatever data the researchers could get. The economists don't consult with any pain professionals either. I read a couple papers that jumped from prescribed opioids to the whole labor market, without consideration of illegal opioids."

Wendell tipped his head in curiosity. "Why did you read all that?"

Stella continued after checking his expression for anger. "My sister has chronic pain and she had to find a new doctor after her old doctor stopped prescribing opioids. The effects of this research have a way more immediate effect than the usual economists' work, and most people wouldn't understand economists' conclusions are based on whatever data they could get. I assume research in healthcare doesn't take whatever data they can get and heap on assumptions the way economists do."

I was surprised Stella said all that and even more surprised Wendell seemed thoughtful and appreciative of her perspective.

He said, "This banker they mention in their letter. Someone said Bowman might have grabbed the Governor spot from her." Michelle Bowman was being sworn in as a BOG Governor the next week.

"The banker who Brown and Donnelly talked with was a President of a community bank on Cape Cod and a prior bigwig of the ABA."

"What's ABA. Not the Bar Association?"

Wendell wasn't bothered when Stella smiled. "No. American Bankers Association. Lobbyists for banks."

Stella rose and riffled through a stack on her desk while Wendell pulled up an article about the Senators' letter on his iPad.

She pulled an article from a file. "You can have this if you want. My St. Louis counterpart was in S&R in 2013 and heard her talk at a Fed conference for bank examiners. When she addressed the group, she made a point of thanking the Fed's 'researchers' – her word – and said she'd been told the Fed was a research organization. But she was talking to only S&R folks."

Wendell leaned back in his chair. "I wonder what the examiners thought when she talked about researchers. Isn't there some to do about not calling ourselves a research organization?"

"It's because our mandate is to be a central bank, not a research organization, and calling ourselves something we are not supposed to be may draw Congressional scrutiny." Stella thought for a few seconds, then continued. "The Cape Cod banker said something like that an issue doesn't exist without research, and she thanked the Fed for making issues a reality. Making societal issues a reality is a leap from managing money and credit in the economy."

Wendell tapped the article Stella had given him. "This must be what Bob meant about Bowman. This article says the woman from Cape Cod might be considered for the community banker spot on the Board, that she sat next to Trump at some small banker dinner at the White House. Where's the date? Oh, that's really old." He looked at his watch and glanced around her office. His tone took on surprise. "This has been useful. You got the pies? For tomorrow?"

Stella looked over at the shopping bag. The Fed Bank's catering took orders from staff for Thanksgiving pies. She'd bought two. "Oh, no. My mom's a baker. One's for a neighbor, one's for my building's doorman. Did you get any?"

"Oh, no. My wife is in charge of pies. Hey, are those Senators involved with the Fed on other issues?"

"Sherrod Brown, yes, I read an article not long ago about his calling for the S&R foks to be careful not to weaken middle class protections from bad big bank practices. Overall, he's pretty active as ranking member of the Senate Banking Committee. I don't see much about the other Senator's positions on the Fed."

"I should probably read the *Wall Street Journal*."

Though the moment wouldn't qualify as a turning point, there'd been no tension between them. Oddly, he'd never said why he'd come over.

Just before three, Wendell sent an email giving permission for staff to leave early. Stella was debating whether she'd leave when Hill knocked. "Are you leaving or do you have a minute?"

"Come on in. Are you all settled here now?"

"Yes. I'm getting caught up on the foreign travel statements so I'm going to stay until five. Thank you for letting me know the economists were complaining."

"Thanks for getting caught up. I know Gage told you the bit about no rush since the economists make so much money, but for the Bank's accounting, the reimbursement should fall somewhere near when the expense was incurred."

Hill pulled at her sleeves before folding her hands at her waist. "We'll see. I have a personal question. You know how you and me are the germaphobes here?"

Stella laughed with embarrassment. "I do."

"Something happened today with someone we both work closely with."

"Do they need help?"

"That's not what I mean. He could contaminate others. The person was touching his feet." Hill's lips curled, her hands tightened, and her shoulders shook in an exaggerated shudder. "We should do something. Would you talk to Wendell? I can't give the name of the person because it's medical, but I thought we should do something."

Stella squinted and her supportive smile was fake. "Huh. Do you think it's really a problem, Hill?"

"I do. Feet carry diseases. Gage is all about being healthy these days."

"He is, isn't he. He commented on my Diet Coke yesterday. Different topic but since he's gotten so committed to his exercise schedule, he cancels meetings at the last minute. Could you put his gym and trainer time on his calendar?"

"His doctor says he must put his exercise program at the top of the list."

"We all should. I'm asking only about blocking Gage's calendar. Back to your concern. This person who's rubbing their foot might just have a cramp. If you think it should be referred to Wendell, please do, Hill. You're comfortable with him."

Hill's smile was crooked and her hands worked together in nervousness. "Well, maybe I will. Thanks, Stella. I'll get back to work now."

This wasn't the first time Hill had tried to trap a coworker by sharing some problem, encouraging complaint, watching as it all backfired on the complainant, and inserting herself as a gracious peacemaker. But it was the first time she'd tried it on Stella.

Though Hill's bad behavior arose mostly from her own insecurities, as is common for many, hers was mildly diabolical. I suspect she was angry over the travel statements and concerned at Winnie's offhand comment about what would happen to her if Gage retired.

Stella was logging out when the Regional Head came by. He'd volunteered to serve as the RD's Officer-in-Charge on Friday, but his plans had changed.

Stella said, "I'm sorry. I'll take the upcoming eves and the week between but not this Friday. Ever since I first moved into the city for college, a childhood friend and I meet up for early-bird Black Friday shopping at Field's-turned-Macy's and lunch at the Palmer House. Well, at first it used to be lunch at McDonald's, but we upgraded over the years."

His words had an uncharacteristic brittle edge. "You know, Administrative Officer Stella, we used to have an Officer-in-Charge here until 5:00 p.m. even when the Director of Research sends everyone home early such as happened today. Isn't it an Administrative Officer's duty to explain these Officer-in-Charge duties to Wendell?"

Stella said, "I did not know that though I remember not being allowed to leave the building. Honestly, I've not seen the official rules in twenty-some years but I think Win still reports who's in charge to the risk office. Other areas treat the responsibility much more seriously than we do. Would you care to ask Winnie to go over the rules with Wendell?"

"I'm just being a curmudgeon. But I need to get out of Friday without an encounter with Wendell. Happy Thanksgiving."

"Good luck. Peaceful Thanksgiving." Many years ago, when she and her sister arrived to collect her grandmother on a Thanksgiving morning, they'd found her dead. Stella hadn't wished anyone a "happy" holiday since, instead wishing others' holidays would be peaceful.

I never knew how they resolved who would be in charge but was grateful it was no one near my corner.

I was able to enjoy my vantage point in quiet, watching the flow of visitors from Union and LaSalle Street Stations that began just before the Thanksgiving Day Parade on State Street and continued through Sunday. Most appeared happy. Though economists would study data about the shopping bags carried back to the trains, they'd be better served wondering what the mood was of the children being carried, pushed, and pulled back to the trains.

My heart fell when a toddler nodded off in his carriage and released his stuffed puppy. Even as I wondered whether I might pass through the window to float to the sidewalk, I felt a strengthening in what tethered me here. I didn't know what I could do once there anyway and was relieved when the toddler's family member turned back against the flow. And grateful for a little girl who pointed the puppy out to her mother and her mother who tucked the puppy into one of the Fed Bank building's alcoves. That the family member's scarf fell from his shoulders unnoticed as he crossed the flow to get to the alcove seemed a small price to pay to recapture the puppy.

As the flow of visitors slowed, I was left to wonder whether my dear baby had loved his first stuffed toy, an Ithaca Kitty. Aunt Edna's daughters had ordered the then-popular pattern from New York, sewn it for him, and claimed to have stuffed it with love. I hoped if he had ever dropped it, there'd been someone to run back for it.

A RABBIT HOLE:
CHOCOLATE

I dwell too much on change. Or lack of, as is in my case. Or change in the speed of change, a concept the PhDs use though they make it unrecognizable with symbols.

The dwelling is less tiresome when on change of chocolate.

A first-year Research Assistant had self-designated herself as a baker for those of her peers who would join her in a Friday-before-Briefing-Week meeting. That her generous cookie commitment ensured her inclusion in others' FOMC Briefing Week plans was lost on most of the other Research Assistants, including a couple of them who I expected thought a young woman who'd bake cookies for others couldn't have an ulterior motive.

In this FOMC cycle, all of her peers joined her, some with milk, some with coffee. They asked about one another's assignments and a couple offered assistance. The offers were motivated by being able to make a claim to a complete understanding of the FOMC forecast when they filled out PhD school applications.

The conversation inevitably turned to inflation, and the baker unintentionally claimed their attention with an emotional outcry. An inflationary deception had ruined her cookies.

Since she hadn't made her grandmother's recipe for chocolate oatmeal cookies since she'd left home for college, she'd relied upon the recipe card. Her grandmother's penmanship was perfect and the list of ingredients precise. Three Baker's chocolate squares, it said. No further description was needed since those squares had been the same size since the 1700s when Mr. James Baker and Mr. John Hannon first produced them.

Or so she'd assumed. The increasingly animated baker described the abomination of a company who shrunk the size of a square. She shared an article written by someone named the Haggler and sputtered in frustration when she noted the company's claim that the change was consumer-driven. And, add insult on top of injury, she said, Baker's kept the number of squares per box the same.

When one of the Research Assistants asked if the change would result in an error in the Consumer Price Index, their conversation went down their own rabbit hole.

Interestingly, their conversation never turned to the Haggler's note that the box of smaller squares sold for $2.89, while the original box of larger squares sold for $3.89, resulting in a 47 percent price increase for the chocolate. I hoped those among the Research Assistants who would someday study consumers might appreciate how the pang of the price increase would outweigh the inconvenience of the change in square size for most.

When their conversation wound down, one Research Assistant stated, "But we got brownies."

Turned out she delivered the cookies to a neighbor she'd thought would be more tolerant of the lack of proper chocolaty-ness. She started anew after she'd found the Palmer House Hilton brownie recipe online. It listed the chocolate in ounces. When she finished baking, she'd created a simple app where she could store her grandmother's recipes with their converted chocolate amounts.

I'm excited to share I knew those brownies.

My grandparents brought me to Chicago in 1902 to visit my aunt, uncle, and cousin Lizzy. We'd ended a wonderful day with dinner at the Palmer House Hotel's restaurant where our waiter recommended the brownies for dessert. Their recipe was born when the Hotel's owner, Bertha Palmer, asked the Pastry Chef to create a dessert suited for the box lunches for ladies visiting the 1893 World's Fair. The brownies were delicious.

And when I arrived in Chicago in the summer of 1914, Aunt Edna and Uncle Louis treated me and my husband, Everett, to lunch at the Palmer House. Of course, we enjoyed the brownies. And given my interest in home economics, my husband's interest in the laws of banking and markets, and my uncle's jobs at the Board of Trade and as an occasional professor at the DePaul University's College of Commerce, our conversation turned to a comparison of the price of the brownie in 1902 versus 1914.

The Palmer House still makes the brownies, or did at least until some years back when, after the Fed Bank's Officers attended an overnight offsite meeting at the Palmer House, one of the RD's Officers who'd had enough team building claimed critical work and returned to the Fed Bank, carrying a take-out container of brownies for his children.

I wished I could ask Stella if she and her friend had them when they met there for lunch. And with my husband and uncle in mind, I wondered if the price has been tracked over all these years.

That night, when I settled in near my baby's commonplace book, I was happy to contemplate how the brownies had persisted but then as bothered as the young baker by the change in the chocolate squares.

My baby's commonplace book was one in a long tradition of my family. The books included recipes, poems, quotations, family trees, charts of planting cycles, ways to manage flowing water, spells, a true wonder of notes.

My baby's included my mother's brownie recipe. Her recipe was a tweaked version of one that was in the Boston Cooking-School Cook Book our neighbor received from her sister in 1907. And now I remembered it called for Baker's chocolate squares.

I've thought with joy and certainty of the day when the commonplace book is found and returned to my family. But now I wonder, what will they think? That we preferred a less chocolaty brownie or were primitive bakers or will they know about Baker's inflationary deception? As I slipped into a meditation which makes for my sleep, I wondered whether the Universe preferred change or persistence and what did that mean for me.

And when the sun broke the next morning, I wondered what it meant for Stella's long tenure of success.

WEEK SEVEN ~ 12/10

On Monday morning, Wendell was a bit giddy when he told Winnie to book his flights for the next week's FOMC meeting.

He talked over her when she began to ask a question. "Since it's my first time attending in my DOR capacity, the stakes are high so I'll need you to make sure I have the right information and whatever else you used to do for David."

Winnie looked at him kindly, as if he'd overcome a fear of FOMC.

That was the only kindly look he'd receive that day. He channeled his excitement into interfering with fine-tuned Briefing Week processes.

At Dawn's cube, he asked for a last-minute change to the distribution of the FOMC documents. When she reminded him with equal parts humor and seriousness that the distribution couldn't be changed willy-nilly, he said a request from a DOR would probably never be rightly classified willy-nilly.

Dawn held firm, citing the BOG's Program which sets forth the eligibility for each of the three classes of FOMC materials – Class I, II, and III – dependent on a PhD's country of origin, immigration status, and so on. Though one might imagine a DOR who would applaud a staff member standing up for what she thought right, that wasn't Wendell.

Dawn wouldn't modify her process without direction from Randy or Stella.

"Well then let's go see them."

Dawn began to turn into Stella's office, but Wendell charged forward down the hall to Randy's.

Wendell told Randy, "If I'm going to FOMC with David, I want to make sure he's got our best expert input. And the expert being from a different country shouldn't preclude that. David knew I was giving him the Class II docs."

Randy asked what Wendell meant by "was."

"I gave the Class II doc to him already and held off on the Class I until Dawn added him to the list."

Dawn said to Randy, "He is not even eligible for Class II according to the chart. His country isn't on the approved countries list." She didn't suppress a side-eye at Wendell before looking back to Randy. "Wendell didn't tell me he'd already shared the document."

Wendell asked Randy, "Isn't there some loophole where someone from a no-no country can sign something promising to apply for citizenship someday and then they get the same access as a citizen?" The no-no countries to which Wendell referred were those not aligned with the U.S. in any defense agreement.

Randy said, "Come on. A loophole? We have rules. If someone plans to apply for citizenship within a specified period of time, we ask them to attest to it, then we bump them up one level of access. Of all the rules in the Fed, these weren't the ones to mess with. If it was that important, we could have asked Board staff for an exception."

Wendell said, "Dawn, get him to attest."

Dawn's confidence was glorious. "Wendell. Our procedure is to ask new PhDs their intent. He already said he has no intent of becoming a U.S. citizen."

Wendell asked Randy, "Can't he just sign the form? No harm, no foul. I trust him."

"Nope. There were already eleven of us who got Class II anyway so even if he was a citizen we'd be in trouble. I need to report the violation to Board staff."

Wendell blew out his breath and pursed his lips. "I'll get it back from him. We still need to fight back on the whole Program."

Randy looked askance at Wendell.

For as long as I remember, there's been restrictions on the number of staff who could see FOMC information. For a long time, those were the only restrictions in this Fed Bank. But the BOG, established as a U.S. government agency, was subject also to restrictions on hiring foreigners.

When, at the turn of this century, it became challenging to find and hire economics PhDs who were U.S. citizens, the Fed Banks hired foreigners as needed while the BOG was unable to maintain a full staff for FOMC.

BOG staff created the Program to gain an exception and allow it to hire foreigners for roles requiring a PhD in economics or a related field, subject to stipulations such as whether a foreigner's country of origin was allied with the U.S. in a defense treaty.

Once approved, the Program went into effect across the Fed System. While the BOG gained freedom to hire foreigners, the Fed Banks lost their freedom to assign any FOMC work to any foreigner. And Wendell was in the middle of making an offer to a foreign PhD and lost the candidate to the BOG. Years later, Wendell continues to behave badly whenever he is reminded of the Program.

Outside of Randy's office, Wendell told Dawn to speak with Winnie about what had happened and Dawn went right to Winnie's cube.

"Winnie, Wendell said I need to talk to you about the Program for FOMC eligibility."

"I don't do that. Let me talk to him."

"Aren't you the backup?"

"No, no. When Macro got their new Assistant, she was supposed to take over FOMC."

"Since you're her Manager, will you tell her it's her job?"

"Let me talk to Wendell."

Wendell brushed off Winnie and told her something had gotten messed up and worried over the RD getting in trouble for something so important as FOMC.

Winnie told Hill she didn't want to press Wendell and asked Hill's advice before she went to Dawn's cube.

Wearing an expression suited to scolding one's dog, she told Dawn, "He just wants to make sure you remember that this is the most important part of your job. He said you messed something up."

Around a lump in her throat, Dawn bit off her words. "Winifred, I did not mess up anything. I wish Stella was here." Stella was on her way to a RAOC meeting in New York. RAOC took advantage of their bosses' involvement in FOMC to meet during Briefing Week.

After a full minute of silence, Winnie said, with a hint of threat, "I may email her. Do you have any questions?"

"Please do email her."

Dawn returned to her cube, deflated and dejected, not unlike a balloon propelled to the ground as its helium escaped.

Randy appeared and asked was she okay.

"Do I report to Winnie for this FOMC work? Or to you and Stella?"

His mouth twisted before he sighed and said, "I guess Winnie. I don't think she knows much about it though, so keep checking with Stella or with me."

"That was wrong."

"It wasn't right. I came to drop off this doc and I have to get back to work. Let's get through this week and then we'll figure out what's going on."

"I'm taking that as a promise."

On Tuesday, Wendell left Dawn alone but asked Winnie to convene the Research Assistants.

They got to the conference room before he did and whispered about whether they'd made a mistake in compiling the forecasts.

When he arrived, he asked they share their "pedigrees." The Research Assistants are a collegial group, often from similar backgrounds and driven by similar life goals, most having come to the Fed Bank right after graduating from a top school with a bachelor's degree in a mathematical field.

Then he asked about their plans for their future, despite knowing they wouldn't have been hired if they hadn't committed to seeking a PhD within two or three years.

After the first dozen responded, others said, "Same."

Wendell became suspicious and warned them not to stray. He described a few Research Assistants who'd left the path for investment banks or hedge funds and suggested they'd be burnt out by the time they were forty. And occasionally, he said, a Research Assistant goes so far off the path they must have gotten scared by the power of economic research.

A couple years earlier, a Research Assistant from the past was interviewed by the *Wall Street Journal* after his promotion to editor of

The Onion, a satirical news source. "'I have zero comedy background and training,' said Mr. Bolton, now 31 years old and the editor of the Onion, in a telephone interview. 'My job wasn't particularly challenging. I had a lot of free time,' he said of his Fed tenure. 'I probably wrote quite a few of my first headlines on the job.'"

Wendell was oblivious to the two Research Assistants who looked as if he'd just lit new paths for them.

On Wednesday, Wendell's voice held relief when he reminded Winnie he'd be in the Big Group briefing all day. "You can hold the fort up here, right? And you got us snacks and lunch for the briefing?"

"Good morning, Wendell. Yes, we can hold the fort and E-Floor Assistants take care of the catering order."

"You don't do that? Huh. Is Dawn doing okay now? I probably should have just let her do her job. She does a good job with FOMC, doesn't she?"

"I don't work with that citizenship stuff. She worked with Stella to set it up."

"Well, why don't you learn about it? I might have made a mistake there with her. Stella should've explained that stuff to me instead of yammering about the budget."

Gage, Randy, and Wendell were last to return from the Big Group briefing.

Wendell seemed hesitant to part as he tossed out questions about the forecast.

Finally, Randy said, "Got work to do," and left.

Gage took a step in the wrong direction, hesitated, turned a half circle, and then moved toward his office with slumped shoulders.

On Thursday, Wendell asked Winnie to verify the catering for that day's briefing and confirm that Stella had returned from her System committee meeting.

Winnie made a face of confusion and looked toward Stella's office, where the light was on and Stella and Adam talked in the doorway.

Wendell's eyes followed Winnie's. "Oh, she's busy."

Soon after, he, Gage, Randy, and four others made their way to the elevators to meet with David for this cycle's first Small Group meeting.

A minute later, Carrie greeted Stella and Adam. "Morning. I saw them walk by. It's like on a plane, when you get to some altitude and the pilot comes on and says you can now move about the cabin."

Stella laughed. "Oh God, it is, isn't it."

Adam agreed and said he'd take advantage of their absence to get some work done.

Carrie asked Stella, "Speaking of flying, how was your meeting?"

"Good. Productive. We talked about you."

"Uh oh."

"No. I think you'll be happy. We talked about how we all use different apps for conference registration. A couple are using Cvent, like us, but some still use homegrown apps and some pay other vendors too much. We think there's savings to be gained by all using Cvent under a System contract."

"I'm happy to share info with anyone."

"I knew you would be. And because you implemented it here and got the Bank to adopt it and trained other Departments, I volunteered you to head up a task force to share information about registration apps and Cvent between the Research Departments." Stella smiled with fake nervousness.

"That would be fun. Thanks. I'm excited."

"Perfect. I wasn't 100 percent sure, but there was no time to ask."

"Oh my, I'll be in charge of conference calls." Carrie looked to the side with a pretense of slyness, drawing a laugh from Stella. Carrie's dislike of conference calls was well-known.

"Yes, all you, in charge. Let me know if I can help. Otherwise, when everything wraps up, you would share outcomes with RAOC. RAOC meets here in March if you'd prefer to report in person. How were things here this week?"

"The drama. The other Assistants are asking why Winnie is a Manager and Winnie tells them because Wendell said so. She calls Hill the Assistant Manager and Hill's at her games. What was Wendell thinking?"

"I don't know what he was thinking nor what to do. He tells me not to reach around Winnie like he's making a threat. He's got to know it was a mistake. I'm sorry. I figured they would drag you in, Car, you're the best listener here."

"Winnie told me three times this week she doesn't want the job. She said he makes a pouty face when she tries to talk to him. What is that? Stella, be careful though. Adam told me not to get involved, but I'm going to tell you anyway. Wendell came in my office on Tuesday and asked about you."

"Why?"

"It was weird, Stella. He was asking all of these questions. Especially about how you get along with everybody. I think he's jealous of you."

"God, why? He works way less hours and makes a hell of a lot more money than me."

"He said he read your old reviews and David praised your treating the Assistants the same way you treat the PhDs. He asked if there's anyone who doesn't like you."

"I could give him a list. What'd you say, Carrie?" She shook her head and added, "I shouldn't ask that."

"I'll answer. I'm afraid for you. I told him you have a low tolerance for bullies and like stuff to be fair. He kept pushing for examples. It was really weird. Plus, like I told you before, he gives me the creeps. He kept staring at my earrings. And what is it with putting his finger in his mouth?"

"I know, I want to offer him floss. Or he'd go to the dentist. Don't worry about me." Stella raised one eyebrow and tipped her head. "My coach is supposed to get feedback from him. I was putting it off until the new year, but I'll send her an email today so I can figure out how to find a productive equilibrium with him. I thought it would just naturally get better over time, but it isn't. And your earrings are lovely and festive."

Carrie held her earlobe and pushed one earring forward. "They're silver and gold Christmas bells."

"They are adorable. I love the sound of bells. That reminds me. I sent you a *Wall Street Journal* article about the gold vault."

"I love the gold. I just told my friend who's going to New York to Christmas shop she should try to see the gold vault. Did you get out to shop?"

"No, I used my free night for dinner with a friend from college and her partner out in the boroughs and then we drove around the bridges. I love New York's bridges. Makes me realize how much younger Chicago is. No shopping. This stuff going on with Wendell has made me think about how financially unprepared I am to lose a job."

Carrie clicked open the link Stella sent. "You won't lose your job. Did your committee do a gold vault tour?"

"Nope. We're all oldies and have already been. Plus, the Richmond member's claustrophobic. It's a treat to see their building anyway. We entered through an entrance I'd never come through before and there was a gorgeous light fixture. Black, ironwork, very gothic, un-Fed-like. I want it."

Carrie's attention lapsed as she glanced at the article. "All these conspiracy theorists should have to come work here for a month. See who we are, how we work. We might be a lot of things, but we've got integrity up the wazoo when it comes to the mission and protecting that gold." Carrie giggled as she added, "Though it's kind of flattering they think we do all that secret stuff on top of our jobs."

"Imagine. They could make intelligent criticisms in way less time than it takes to spin up their conspiracy theories. We're too complicated is the problem and it invites the cons. What's that saying about truth and fiction?"

"Let's go back to talking about shopping."

On Friday, after Wendell and the others left for their Small Group meeting, Winnie entered Stella's office, closing the door behind her. "Good morning. Can I come in? Your calendar was clear. Can you tell me about the country stuff for FOMC?"

"Sure."

The two joined at the table and each reached for a Silver Top.

After about five minutes, Winnie stopped her. "I don't want to learn all that."

"Will you let Wendell know?"

Winnie collected three more Silver Tops and left.

When Wendell returned from the Small Group meeting, Winnie followed him into his office, shut his door, and asked if she could talk to him. He told her not then, he was going for a walk and needed to meet with Stella when he returned.

And he did, surprising Stella when he took a seat at her table and focused on opening his bag of chips.

Stella grabbed a stack of napkins from her drawer on her way to join him. "Hello, Wendell. How's FOMC?"

When he finished crunching, he snapped, "I'm not here to talk about that. I thought about what you said about garbagemen's wages."

A couple weeks earlier, while they worked together on finalizing the annual bonuses, Wendell asked Stella why economists weren't as important as garbagemen and, at her look of confusion, told her about a well-known paper titled, "Why Aren't Economists As Important As Garbagemen?" He'd seemed sincerely concerned about the differential of economists' and garbagemen's compensation in light of garbagemen's responsibility in creating a healthy society but, like the author of the paper, wondered at why economists weren't regarded at least as important as garbagemen. He suggested Stella's job was comparable to a garbageman's and they'd returned to the work at hand.

Now, she said, "I thought I'd get the paper but hit a paywall and haven't gotten over to the Library. I didn't know we were going to talk more about it."

"We should talk about it after you read the paper. But in the meantime, I looked at Officers' bonuses and used them to reward policy work and merits to reward publishing. I tweaked a couple amounts. I left the staff's alone with the extra share they steal from the PhDs. You said that was important."

Ever since bonuses were made part of compensation, the RD thought of its pool of money in aggregate and non-PhDs had benefitted from being part of a pool with the high-paid PhDs. A tiny percentage of the PhDs' share was significant to Stella's team. Though Stella wasn't able to convince Wendell, he went along because the Heads agreed with her.

"We can't do that. The numbers were final last week."

He slid a sheet of paper toward her. "My changes are in the new column. Beth in HR made the changes officially."

"You went around me?"

His voice was impatient as if she'd stated what was obvious. "Well, I think it's really weird you're involved in these bonuses anyway. For sure, you shouldn't have seen yours. I told you they weren't final."

As she looked down the column he'd added to her spreadsheet, she asked, "You took six thousand dollars from me and gave it to Gage?"

"Yes."

"Did you revise the explanations that go to HR?"

"What explanations go to HR?"

Winnie knocked and said Randy really needed Wendell's input on the *Summary of Economic Projections*. BOG staff aggregate the Summary's short- and long-term economic projections before each meeting and release them after each FOMC meeting, including the "dot plot" oft-referenced by the media.

As Wendell walked out, he asked Stella to take care of any paperwork if they really needed to do anything about the explanations.

Stella was angry. She spent ten minutes looking at postings for open jobs in this and other Fed Banks before pulling up her pension estimates.

When Adam stopped by, he asked, "You okay?"

"Yes, sorry, long week."

"I and my staff want to thank you for the generous bonuses. I heard you really went to bat for us."

"The awards are very much deserved. Thank you and thank them for their work, please."

"And when I was helping Gage with some file he couldn't find, he mentioned Wendell gave him some of your bonus. I'm very sorry."

"As am I."

"He sucks."

"Big time."

In Wendell's office, Randy handed him a near-final version of David's input for the *Summary of Economic Projections* for his review.

Wendell handed it back and said, "I trust you."

Randy told Wendell the double-check wasn't about trust, but Wendell didn't budge.

While Randy went to ask the Head of the Macro Group for the double-check, Wendell left for the weekend with a skip in his step.

I've never before been bothered by Randy working through the weekends before the FOMC meeting. In fact, I usually enjoyed at least a bit of time reading along with him. But this weekend, I'd wished there was no one here to remind me that I was.

THE HOLIDAY BREAK

I was more grateful than ever for the holiday break. Even the usual few stragglers were absent, and I attributed that to Wendell's having destroyed the sense of peace the stragglers previously found here at the close of the year.

My spot near the commonplace book felt gentled by the light cast from nearby buildings' holiday decorations.

Directly across is the Chicago Board of Trade's clock, flanked by hooded figures – a Mesopotamian farmer holding a sheaf of wheat and a Native American holding a cornstalk. And flanking those figures were three others, unseen by passersby. I'd always suspected there'd be some like me, given the fortunes made and lost there. One appeared modern and quite sorrowful, perhaps new to this existence. Another was dressed as a farmer, perhaps from about my lived time, though I expect suits were the standard dress there then.

When I was young, I listened to my grandfather describe his visits there to hedge the risk of falling prices for my family's and our neighbors' harvests. He told us that was just one piece of sound farm finances. The other was access to a sound banking system that would provide credit for a new year's seed purchases after a weak harvest. By the time the Federal Reserve Act was passed, I'd learned enough from him to appreciate the necessity of a central bank who could serve as a lender of last resort to that banking system. And when it came time to set up the Fed Banks, I appreciated the inclusion of the Secretary of Agriculture on the three-men Reserve Bank Organizing Committee.

The BOD of each of the Fed Banks are intended to represent a cross-section which includes agriculture. And the U.S. President's appointments to the BOG are to include a fair representation of the interests of agriculture, among others. I've no evidence that has been sustained and though this Regional Group studies agriculture in this region, another Fed Bank claims leadership regarding the national agricultural economy.

When I wonder whether my grandfather or new friend across the way would think the Fed System had lived up to its promise, I remind myself the Fed System has sustained its seasonal lending program in which it lends funds to the commercial banks who lend funds to help farmers plant before harvest profits are got.

I was relieved that finally, at New Year's, I was ready for staff to return. Especially since returning staff mostly excluded PhDs.

I enjoyed their holiday stories, mostly. I was sorry when Molly, the Editorial Manager, and Stella shared their feelings of guilt. The Editorial Manager, because she'd not traveled to her mother's for Christmas, and Stella, for considering a warm coastal vacation even as she should plan to visit her sister. Nora's husband was finishing chemotherapy treatments so they couldn't make the cross-country trip to celebrate Christmas. I wished I could tell them to not give their guilt the opportunity to become a regret.

WEEK ELEVEN ~ 1/7/2019

Business-as-usual resumed this week when the PhDs returned en masse from their annual Allied Social Science Association (ASSA) meetings where they'd enjoyed three days of presentations, receptions, and meals in an economist-type party atmosphere.

When Stella passed by on Monday morning, Carrie called out, "Did you see ASSA made it into regular-people news?"

Stella shook her head and pulled her lips in even as she smiled. "My New Year's resolution is to read more fiction. So today's news is still news to me."

"Why don't you spend your morning at your desk reading news like the other Research Officers? Did I ever tell you — "

"You did, ick. Yay for electronic news." Carrie worked for the Library back in the day when the RD and the umbrella area in which Stella worked shared a single paper copy of the *American Banker.* The RD Head at the top of the routing list enjoyed reading it in the men's room. "What did I miss?"

"An explosion of articles about how economics treats women. Here, I printed this one about hotel room interviews. Heather will probably be mad at you, you know." Carrie giggled.

Stella took the article, quickly read it, and one eyebrow rose. "She probably will, won't she? I'm just glad they're stopping them." The year before, though the meetings had been only a mile from this Fed Bank, Heather conducted interviews for Gage's PhD vacancy in one of the meeting hotel's sleeping rooms.

When Heather submitted the reimbursement, Central Finance took issue with the room not being booked at the Fed rate and called Stella. Heather admitted interviews were scheduled at the last minute and was maddened by Stella's struggle to understand why Heather and Gage's other two PhDs conducted job interviews in a sleeping room.

Carrie said, "Remember, when she complained to me about you and told me how she'd been interviewed that way when she was on the job market as if it was a badge of honor."

"I still don't get it, Carrie. She told me they let the candidate choose where to sit as if it made a difference."

"Seriously though, no told-you-so with Heather. Gage was in here early. He said he's still on some other time zone from his vacation. I guess Heather sent him an email from the meetings complaining that the other Groups' PhDs didn't invite her to hang with them. He said they don't appreciate what she's done for his area and maybe she should get your job and be Associate Director to the Associate Director and then they'd have to be supportive of her. And he told me he brought back a charm from his trip for her necklace. A megaphone to encourage her to speak out. Weird."

"Yes. Gage and his wife take the coolest vacations. When he said he was going on a safari, I joked about his going off to see lions and tigers and bears. He got pretty upset and pulled up a map of Africa to lecture how lions and tigers never coexist." Stella shrugged. "I've never been on a safari nor, sadly, have I seen lions and tigers in the wild."

"Is he still signing emails 'thank you muchly?'"

"I think," she crossed fingers on both hands, "he's finally forgot. I don't know why he just didn't tell me to my face that 'thanks much' had so deeply offended his sense of grammar."

"I think he was trying to make you look bad."

Once Stella was settled at her desk with tea in hand and a cursory check of her inbox complete, she searched the news.

The *New York Times* said the meetings pushed toward a reckoning. "The economics profession is facing a mounting crisis of sexual harassment, discrimination, and bullying that women in the field say has pushed many of them to the sidelines — or out of the field entirely... Leading male economists offered an unprecedented acknowledgment of harassment and discrimination in the field." Ben Bernanke, past Chairman of the BOG, said, "Economics certainly has a problem." The corners of Stella's lips turned up even as her brow furrowed. "Many male economists long dismissed claims of bias and discrimination, arguing that gender disparities must reflect differences in preference or ability. They pointed to theories that predict that, in the simplified world of economic models, discrimination on the basis of characteristics like gender and race would disappear because of competition."

Stella clicked through to links that described how the lack of diversity in the profession fed a lack of diverse representation in content of research studies. At one of the links, economist Julie Nelson, in 2018, wrote in *Gender and Failures of Rationality in Economic Analysis*, "Meta-analyses of this literature reveals how confirmation and publication bias have made the 'findings' of this field unreliable." And, "At the broadest level, our discipline is gender biased in its definition, models, and methods. These favor realms of life and aspects of human behavior that are culturally associated with masculinity, and studiously ignore those traditionally associated with femininity."

I wondered whether the RD would set aside worry over being in the crosshairs to see the value in the turmoil. There's been other inevitable truths surface with the energy of a float cut from its anchor only to bounce around before settling back into the flow.

Otto, one of the PhDs, took a step in Stella's office and asked, "Something wrong?"

"Oh no, my eyes are just irritated from my monitor." She held out the tiny bottle of eyedrops. "Happy New Year. I was going to look for you today."

"Happy New Year to you as well. I wondered if your father liked the books."

"Oh Otto, that is why I was going to look for you. Thank you so much for the recommendations. He's finished one already and told me all about it. So my record is one of eleven for the books I pick out, and yours are six for six."

"I'm glad he enjoyed that one."

"The books you recommend are magical. Not in the sense of the magical realism in the fiction fluff I love, but magical in their appeal. A book enjoyed equally by a PhD researcher and a retired tradesperson must be written with such skill. Someday, when I have more time to read, I'm going to get them from him so I can read them and see how the author does it."

The two finished catching up. Otto's son, at just eight years of age, had decided against a career in economics after being forced to endure a lecture about adopting a puppy as the opportunity cost of adopting a kitten, and vice versa. Especially when, as the eight-year-old told his father, opportunity cost hadn't mattered. Both the kitten and the puppy were enjoying their new home.

Wendell approached Stella's office. As he greeted Otto, Stella closed the articles she'd been reading.

"Good morning. Or I guess I should say Happy New Year." The words were right, but Wendell's smile was insincere.

He pulled out a chair from the table, sat, tipped back onto two legs, and abandoned any show of pleasantries. "Winnie showed me that book you assigned. She thinks you believe in Santa Claus."

One day in December, after Winnie collected Stella's mail, she pulled from it an unsolicited sample pamphlet titled "*The Leadership Secrets of Santa Claus.*" When Winnie asked if she could have it and order another for Hill, Stella agreed.

Stella hadn't given it further thought until last week, when Winnie called her over to see her and Hill's lunchtime haul from the sales on State Street. As Stella "oohed" and "aahed," Hill said she was enjoying the Santa book.

When Stella asked Winnie had she too enjoyed it, Winnie tried to deflect and asked wasn't Hill reading a book about crawdads.

Now, in this conversation with Wendell, Stella laughed. "I kind of do."

He didn't laugh. "Look, I told you not to reach around Winnie." His pupils grew large and dark and his fists clenched.

Stella froze as might a rabbit at the appearance of a predator.

He continued. "Why are you making them read that idiocy? You're making Winnie dislike the job."

Stella snapped back with narrowed eyes, "I didn't, and can't, really, can I, make them read that book. It came free in my mail and Winnie asked for it for herself and another for Hill. I used that company's materials a long time ago for an event in my old department. I offered Winnie a few other choices, but she said they wanted that one."

"Well, next time, tell them to get a recommendation from Gage. He was the one who told them to read a book. You're getting in the way of their success."

"You've asked me to not be involved in Winnie's role as manager and I've not been. Are you saying you think giving Winnie that book is hindering her success?"

He glared at Stella for a full minute.

She matched his gaze, but her fingers were white where they gripped the arms of her chair.

Finally, he said, "Just stay away from them. I was going to ask another question about how the Board allocates the System's Treasury portfolio across the Fed Banks." He sighed in disgust. "I don't know why I think you know stuff about the Bank anyway."

His anger dissipated when he saw hurt flash across Stella's face. Stella took tremendous pride in her reputation as a resource to the RD for information about inner workings of the Fed System.

In an even tone, he continued. "Luckily, you do know how to manage a salary bump program for the PhDs. Put together the usual comparisons and have Winnie put you on my calendar."

Gage, with salad, beans, and a bottle of water, and Wendell, with a small but loaded pizza and a Sprite from across the street, joined in Wendell's conference room.

Gage watched as Wendell shook hot sauce over his pizza, and said, "I don't know how you eat that and stay so thin. I'm on a post-vacation diet."

Wendell asked how things were in Gage's world.

"There's a problem with the far corner conference room. Let's see," Gage set his fork down and stood. He turned one way and another and then in a circle, using the direction of Lake Michigan to figure out the cardinal directions. "The conference room in the northwest corner, yes. The Macro economists like to use the space for their consultant du jour. My staff has a need for business meeting space."

"Consultants have had first claim there since the last renovation. Maybe we can persuade your folks a half-block walk isn't so bad. I meant to bring a floor plan. Hold on."

Alone, Gage formed a grin that reminded me of the Joker on a Batman postcard a long-gone Research Assistant hung when a Batman movie was being filmed in front of the Fed Bank. That Research Assistant and a few others had been quite excited for the filming. Most staff had been annoyed, especially after the Gotham City Police halted their returns from their lunch hours due to filming.

Still grinning when Wendell returned, he said, "Heather reported a few dust-ups so pride's entered into it. Something about her having lost a charm in the room, and the consultant wouldn't let her look for it until he was off the phone. And she and a couple others trying to find space to meet with folks from the Board of Trade weren't allowed to displace the consultant even though she'd stuck a reservation sign on the door the day before. My team has sufficient surplus in our favor bank, wouldn't you say?"

While Wendell drew a line from the corner in question to a nearby conference room, Gage asked what good was a favor bank if the favors weren't called.

Wendell's words came slowly. "Let me talk to the economists over there." His mouth formed speech twice before it emitted the name of one of the female PhDs who sat nearby. "We ought to be careful for a while after the ASSA meetings."

Gage agreed, "Sure, sure." Not knowing the reason to be careful, Gage changed the subject. "Hilerie wants to make sure she has some manager duties, at the same level as Winnie's."

"Wasn't the salary increase enough?"

"The money's sunk. The title, Wendell, would give her the power she needs to be Winnie's sidekick." Again, the grin.

"I wouldn't say the money is sunk."

Gage asked, "Why not? All compensation is sunk here."

This time, it was Wendell who changed the conversation. "Let's talk about Stella. When I listened to the Governors at ASSA, I imagined Stella trying to expand that conversation to women and minorities who support PhD economists. That, combined with her influence, especially in the System, would cause us problems. David thought she used her influence to help the RD, but I don't trust her."

"She is one of the Bank's best bureaucrats. Her eyes practically glow when she mentions the mission." Gage extended his hand and waved it in excitement. "I just remembered. Hilerie says Stella's a witch."

A week before, Hill was struggling to find some paperwork and Stella suggested a location. Though Stella was known for having a mind map of the RD, Hill was flabbergasted to find the paperwork just where Stella said and asked was she a witch. Though Stella laughed, Hill backtracked and asked Stella to please understand the question was because how could anyone have known. Stella wasn't bothered at all until Hill apologized in Gage's presence.

"Probably not a good idea to call women witches, especially now."

"All right but I think there are things Stella is doing that should be in the Associate Director's portfolio."

Wendell complained about warmth just as Gage's hand jerked and sent a cherry tomato flying.

Gage looked at his hand in confusion.

Wendell popped his finger from his mouth and wiped it on his napkin. "Let's wrap this up. Maybe you could work on figuring out how to counter Stella and then we could talk about taking away her work. The biggest problem is probably going to be the Department's dependence on her relationships in the Bank and in the System."

"I could talk to people here. History has shown that most everyone in this Bank will prefer the higher-rank."

"I've got to run."

When Wendell tried to open his direct door and felt resistance, he pushed harder. My energy waned just then, and when the door flew open, he stumbled. I wasn't sorry.

Stella was finishing soup at her desk when Carrie knocked.

"Hi, Stella. Got time to talk about the Sandwich Committee?"

"Of course. This is about the fancy sandwiches they had at ASSA?"

"Really, Stella, big-bucks economists are now going to spend time selecting sandwiches? Heather gave her new permanent visitor or whatever he is a lunch card for his first day, and he asked me where he picks them up going forward so I'm in a bit of a mood."

"I know, Car. I'm sorry about that guy. I asked Heather to talk to him but she says – her words – the other PhDs shit on him so he has to have someone he can shit on. I'll talk to Gage or Wendell."

Stella didn't tell Carrie how Heather reported that her permanent visitor had asked was Carrie "slow." Heather didn't tell Stella her visitor had also asked was Stella "slow." I wondered if Heather realized that he'd probably ask if she, too, was slow. He was a real creep.

Carrie said, "I heard he yelled at the guard downstairs when they asked why he threw away his ID. I wouldn't yell at someone with a gun so I'm thinking he's a little nuts."

"I don't know why Heather hired him. I think she's having a hard time finding anyone. Plus, she said something about him having some data she needed. What you said about the lunch committee. I had to stop myself from calculating how much this will cost us with the PhDs' time, catering staff's time, your time, especially when the PhDs start questioning how the turkeys were raised and what is sufficient crispness for lettuce in a sandwich. But if you feel it gets out of hand, holler."

"The PhDs can't just get their own lunch like the rest of us, pay for it out of their big paychecks?"

"Nope."

"They can't meet at some other time of day?"

"They won't. They claim this is what's done in academia."

"We can't tell them to bring their lunch from home?"

"I know, Carrie."

"I know you know. Do you know how thrilled I'd be with a free turkey sandwich, chips, cookies, and beverage each workday for the rest of my life."

"Me too."

Adam, at the doorway, said, "Me too. I heard. I'm shutting the door."

He joined them at the table, and the three talked about how much money they'd save with free lunches. Their conversation turned to working in such a quirky culture, their ages, and how grateful they were to have pensions on the horizon.

At 3:00 p.m., Stella waited in a comfy chair outside of Winnie's cube after Winnie told her, "At the little boys' room."

When he returned, his manner held no residual of their earlier conversation.

As Stella slid some pages across his table, she said, "Here's a list of current PhD salaries, with last bonus, signing bonus for new hires, retention payments, and notes about leaves. Staff first, then Knowledge Leaders."

He reached over to his desk for a legal pad and then threw away the pages that held the ring of a coffee mug. "Let's dig into it. Why leaves?"

"Personal leaves, when they go to a university for a year, allow the continued accrual of time off, so when the person returns from their leave they get their full annual allotment of time off. And whether they return or not, they get service credit for their time away which feeds into the pension calculation. It's a nice deal and we average two economists on leave each year and more when a married couple goes. So there's all that non-salary compensation. Enough that there's some gaming so I include it as FYI."

"I doubt anyone is gaming it."

"Consider a married couple, they go on leave to a university for a year, they return from the summer, they start a new leave at the end of the summer. Or Gus, who's on leave right now called with questions about getting a withdrawal from his thrift plan to buy a house even though he claims he's returning in May."

"That's just building a career. Explain the service credit though." Stella did.

"What do the other Fed Banks do?"

"There is no System policy about the service credit, and no one else allowed people on leave to accumulate service credit. David and I once talked about limiting leaves, but nothing materialized. When I asked for a version of a leave without the service credit, HR refused to make an exception to the existing policy."

"I'll think about it but that sounds like we're looking for a problem. We should make sure the economists understand it though so they recognize it as a perk."

Stella opened her mouth but closed it without speaking.

Wendell continued. "When David was at the December FOMC, Karl asked him how he was dealing with the drop in salary. Karl's the President of a mid-tier Fed — "

"Yes."

Wendell nodded. "Karl asked David how he was dealing with the cut in pay. Karl made more money as Research Director than as President and assumed David was in the same boat. So now we know we're all underpaid. We the PhDs. He's capped, but HR is figuring out what needs to happen for me, Gage, and Randy. And I'm figuring out what happens for the rest of the economists."

She said they should look at the budget.

"Nope. David's making me talk to Frank and he'll tell me if I have to look at the budget. You won't be involved in that. What I need are charts. Regressions of salary on years since PhD, salary on journal publications, salary on citations, stuff like that. We'll equate Knowledge Leader to a full professor, the senior economist to associate professor, and economist title to an assistant professor. How quickly can I get them? And after I sign off on the first round, go ahead and do a set with logarithms too. If Frank asks too many questions, I'll pull those out to frighten him."

Stella rose to leave, but he continued. "Hey, are we involved in that year-end turning over of the leftovers? Can we keep some of that money to cover these salary increases? Since you're worried about that RBOPS target."

"We are indirectly involved when Finance staff bump into our unclosed items. Hilerie's been working on some reimbursements we never collected after the economists traveled on someone else's dime. But no, we can't keep any of the money that's leftover."

The "leftovers" are derived through the implementation of monetary policy. Though the intent of the FOMC's trading of U.S. Treasury securities is to change the amount of the dollars in the economy to influence interest rates, it is also a source of income. The FOMC is active in other markets as well, especially when responding to crises, and those activities also produce income.

This income is an important contributor to the independence of the Fed System from politicians. It allows the Fed System to decide on how much money is needed for its operations, instead of having to appeal to Congress for funding through the Congressional appropriations process. Most Fed staff are careful custodians of their spending in respect of that independence. What isn't spent is turned over to the U.S. Treasury.

He added, "Gage said he needed to talk to me about Hill. Maybe it was those reimbursements. Don't be so persnickety with nickels and dimes."

Stella said, "I think the RBOPS memo to Banks' Research Departments was the warning. If we don't watch our nickels and dimes, they will. And now we are in the new year, and I expect RBOPS will make sure our spending stays within the budget target so we have to consider tradeoffs."

Wendell's pupils expanded and darkened. "This sounds like Stella's spending rule. I'll worry about the Board." With the force of his index and third finger held tightly together, he tapped the table as he finished, "You get my charts done." When he saw her flinch, he stopped tapping. "What? We're still turning over sixty-five billion. I saw a draft of the number. You think a couple thousand will be noticed?"

As she walked out, he dismissed her with a wave of his hand.

Stella sat at her desk and rubbed her forehead. Then she sighed and reached into her backpack for the front half of a greeting card. The cover scene was a quiet, starry night with sparkly snow and leafless trees. Its greeting was "Peace." On the reverse, she'd written: financial security, health, family, peace. The corners of her lips pulled downwards as she tacked the card on the bulletin board above her credenza, starry side out.

WEEK SIXTEEN ~ 2/11

Ted, the only non-Head PhD with direct reports, was copying a list of his staff's ages, assignments, and "contribution outside of Casework," from the whiteboard wall when Stella entered the conference room. After she warned him some of her team would arrive soon, he snapped a picture with his iPhone.

As they erased the board, he said, "There are so many reasons to hate February."

Stella nodded toward the window. "The weather guy labeled it wintry mix and had sparkly snowflakes. Too pretty for what's really slippery slop."

As Ted was erasing the lines beyond Stella's reach, he said, "Slippery slop describes Wendell's meddling. This stuff that was on the board, it's because it's February and there's no FOMC, no conferences to go to, no visitors will come here. Once he gets his nose in, he won't get it out. Slippery slop on a slippery slope. Doesn't your team have something for him to do to keep him out of my hair?"

"Hah. You know, he's had a beef with Casework for a long time. I wondered why out of the blue last week he asked how well I knew Judith."

Ted stopped erasing and said, "Man, he doesn't like her. And he won't even try to understand why Casework is part of Research. Is something wrong?"

"Yes, my eye started twitching. Ach. Too often lately."

"I had a colleague back at ISU whose eye went crazy. She couldn't stand it. She ended up quitting and it went away the next day."

Stella looked doubtful.

When Adam and Carrie arrived, they laughingly asked if Ted was coming over from the dark side to join their team.

Ted didn't laugh. "Slippery slop and slope and a dark side all before noon on Monday. Good luck."

Molly, the Editorial Manager, and the new Budget Analyst arrived.

Stella asked for their help with a stack of surveys about their expected usage of Central Support.

Just as Adam began to share some intel about System Central IT, the Budget Analyst jumped in and said, "Gage says we shouldn't do these surveys. He said no one ever notices if we skip this kind of stuff."

Carrie watched the interaction, the only one unsurprised. She seemed relieved to call out in the open, "So Gage told me you and he have a standing date at Starbucks?"

Though a flash of embarrassment crossed the Analyst's face, her cockiness remained. "He wanted a younger person's view and I need a mentor."

A shadow passed across Stella's face. "I've been trying to figure out how he got my strategy doc. Did you share it?"

"He asked what I knew. It wasn't a secret, was it?"

Stella told her, "Regarding the surveys. All these requests are important. Of course, someone would notice. We don't ignore them. If we think there's a real problem, we should and do create business cases and propose changes. Let's move on."

When the meeting ended, Molly and Carrie hung back. The two conjectured that Stella may not realize the games that had begun.

In the afternoon, Ken, a colleague from S&R, arrived at Gage's office. Five minutes later, he peaked in Stella's door and asked if she wanted company. "I'm stood up. I had a meeting with Gage."

"He just left for coffee."

Following the 2008-2009 financial crisis, some blamed S&R's focus on the micro, or idiosyncratic, risks of banks. The BOG responded by mandating that the RDs help expand S&R's knowledge of macro prudential, or systemic, risks in the banking industry. Ken and Gage shared responsibility for this Fed Bank's implementation of the almost decade-old mandate.

Ken asked, "Nice. Stella, what's up with Gage? I was going to try to talk with him. We have these regular meetings with him and my team tells him all this stuff and then he regurgitates it at an upstream System committee as if it were his own thoughts. And if he's asked a question, he flip-flops. It's worse than you and I talked about way back when he'd flip like a pancake to the biggest title in the room, now, he just flip-flops for no apparent reason. Something's bad, a minute later, it's good. And if he gets challenged, it's time to end the meeting. Is he healthy?"

Stella's brow wrinkled and she pushed her hair behind her ear. "Some of us here wonder the same. This morning he, Wendell, and I were meeting to plan the RD's version of an Officers' meeting. He tried to cancel it nine times. Not jokingly. He seemed desperate."

Ken's laugh cut off. "I guess it's not funny. When I worked for Frank, we were always at meetings Gage organized, the most useless, time-sucking, politicized, power-playing meetings. At the end of the meeting, he'd provide a favor-bank tally he thought was so clever. I wonder if he still keeps that up."

Stella's face colored with embarrassment. "Yes. When he brought it up last week, I didn't want to deal with it so I said I'd never heard of it. I thought we'd just move along and get done what we were supposed to get done. Instead, he asked had I read Tom Wolfe's *Bonfire of the Vanities* and when I said I had, he told me I should reread it with particular attention to that character who had the favor bank."

They laughed together before shaking their heads.

"How, Stella, how did he ever get up this high? He never really did anything for the Bank other than schedule dumb meetings."

"No idea. Over ten or fifteen years, he finished two papers, with co-authors, and just one got published. He's David's cousin, but I didn't think David was that kind of guy."

"We all are sometimes."

Though Wednesday's clear and bright sunshine was accompanied by biting cold, it bumped everyone's mood. Or almost everyone's.

Winnie, hands tight on her coffee cup, asked Stella to feel how cold were her fingers. When she extended one hand, Stella declined.

Winnie asked if Stella had pages to copy for the Heads' meeting.

"Nope, I'm good. Maybe it's time to fly away to a warm beach?"

Winnie moaned. "Who knows what will happen if I take off. Let me do the copies next time. I want to be able to tell Wendell that you need me and I can't be Manager anymore."

Stella's eyes opened wide. "Win, no. Please don't tell him that. Just tell him you don't want to be a Manager if you don't want to be."

"Wendell said he's never been on a beach vacation. I couldn't believe it. I told him they were the best, that you go too. He said maybe he and his wife will stay on after the spring economics conference. I couldn't remember where the conference was even though I made their flights, but it's at a beach, he said. I can't disappoint him, Stella. He told me not to involve you, but I don't know who else to talk to."

The two looked at each other, Winnie with exhaustion, Stella with fear.

When Stella remained quiet, Winnie straightened her back and rubbed her palms on her thighs. "I did tell him it is too hard working with these women on top of supporting him. He keeps saying they'll come around. He asked if you were losing weight, Stella. That jacket does fit better." Stella wore a black skirt and shell with a teal jacket she'd had for years.

"Hmmph. A little maybe. Anyway, good luck for your talk with Wendell."

"What are you doing? I gained six pounds."

"I guess I don't get out for lunch anymore as much. It takes too long to get through Security."

"I should start running again at lunch. As soon as it's warm out."

Winnie took a couple of Silver Tops and left.

Unused to arriving at the same time for their meeting, the Heads and Stella bumbled around one another at the coffee cart and told one another about their commute. Most lived in either the nearby gentrifying area or the college town a short train ride away.

When Hill escorted Gage in from the hallway, the others greeted her and jokingly asked if she was she joining them. She marked Gage's place with his pen, one reminiscent of those executives used in the 1970s. When she stood back, clasping her hands at her waist, Gage assured her he could fix his own coffee and she was free to leave.

He shook as he approached the cart and didn't notice the others step back to give him space.

Wendell entered through his direct door and with uncharacteristic energy, asked, "Everyone made it in, huh? First fight of the day." He shadow-boxed right and left to punctuate his words.

Gage, focused on pouring cream into his coffee, didn't see the first punches and was startled when Wendell, in response to the Heads' side-eyes, punched a third time.

Stella reached around Gage to toss napkins on his spilled coffee.

Wendell asked, "What? This is dog sled weather. What is it they say? Mush?"

Once all were seated with their coffee, or in Stella's case, tea, the meeting moved at a good clip until Stella handed around a comparison of last year's budget to their final spending and reminded the others of their accountability for the RBOPS budget target.

In a flash, the atmosphere changed. Wendell's pupils darkened as he bit off one syllable at a time. "Maybe you should have told us this before we gave those salary increases. These guys don't need to read that memo but send it back to me. I didn't see anything about a minimum."

While Stella's face crunched in confusion, Wendell continued gaslighting as he looked around the table with an insincere smile and a subtle roll of his eyes, asking the others to interpret Stella's acquiescence as shame.

Finally, she defended herself. "Right. The target is max spending. It doesn't change anything — "

Gage said, "Wendell, don't forget I have that offer out."

The economics Heads perked up at Gage's words and Wendell said, "Offline, Gage."

Gage glanced to Wendell, then to Stella, and then looked around and said, "Eternal vigilance is the price of liberty. Do you know who said this, Stella?"

Stella shook her head. Gage's eyebrows rose as if to match her own.

This wasn't the first time Gage had tossed out a random quotation and one of the Heads tried to redirect. "Yes, eternal vigilance of RBOPs' machinations. Let's move along to talk about planning."

Wendell spoke, "What's next, Stella?"

"The annual strategic planning process begins now. Our draft is due five weeks from today. The template is the same as last year. I'll create a draft." Stella ticked off the order of the others' review of the draft.

Gage interrupted. "Correction. I'll review the economics Heads' work. And, like Wendell, I'll also get the Bank plan back through the Executive Committee."

When Gage reported to Frank, he'd been placed on the Executive Committee. Since he'd been moved back into the RD, HR had asked Stella three times if she'd talk to Wendell about removing Gage. They complained about Gage's annoying questions, his being in the Executive Committee's compensation pools, and the RD getting two votes. Not knowing Stella to punt, HR was surprised when three times she referred them to David and Wendell.

In this meeting, Stella asked Gage if he was trying to change their process.

Gage sat forward, leaning over the table, forcing the Head next to him to lean back. With eyes both vacant and focused, he said, "Why don't I take this over from you? You have a full plate."

When Stella laughed, thinking it was a joke, Gage asked Wendell, "Why not?"

Wendell finally engaged. "Gage, let's shelve that. Stella, move on."

Gage held his hand out and over the table as if to silence the others until he thought of a response.

A Head asked, "Gage, why? It's thankless work. It's a mystery who even reads it. Stella gets sainthood for taking it seriously. Take my role, but don't mess with hers. Or just wait and rewrite it all when you get the consolidated version with your Executive Committee friends."

The other Heads laughed.

Wendell looked at Stella. "I guess I should probably understand who reads it."

"Both Boards. First, our Board of Directors, for their blessing. They sometimes have input, especially for gaps in things common to business, like diversity practices. Then when they are done, it goes to the Board of Governors staff who make sure we're not planning anything controversial and that we justified our budget. Board staff bump it to a Governors' Subcommittee who uses it to meet with our Board of Director's Chair and Vice Chair and David and Frank."

Gage said, "Introduce me to whoever made the request for the information. You've done an outstanding job in the past and your cooperation will be critical to our success this year." There was the Joker smile again.

Stella asked, "Gage, how about if you take over the all-important last leg of review and submitting it to Frank's staff?"

Wendell snapped, "Let this go, Gage."

Gage fisted his hands and moved them to his lap as tears welled.

The others all looked toward Wendell, but he, shocked, was already reaching toward Gage. He touched Gage's arm, and in a soft voice, said, "It's okay, Gage, I didn't mean to yell."

The Heads looked on with embarrassment and wonder.

Gage sniffled as Wendell continued to offer comfort.

Stella broke the quiet. "Last item. It's time to start on consultant renewals. All of last year's info was attached to the agenda for today. We'll need the usual." She rattled off a list of information. "My team'll combine the lists and then we reconvene and do a sanity check on contract terms. Does that work?"

The consultants are PhDs from outside the Fed System who are under contract with this Fed Bank. They may provide feedback on the RD's PhDs' research, co-author research with staff, or help plan a conference. Most of the Fed Bank's consultants come in once a week, find an open office, and work on their own research while being available for any of the RD's PhDs who want to talk.

"That's it for the agenda."

Wendell looked up then from whispering with Gage and nodded.

Only one Head refilled his coffee before leaving the room.

The workday afternoon slump is particularly pronounced in February and during the slump on this Thursday, Stella's team gathered, greeting one another with sincere pleasure and filling the conference room with friendly chatter. These monthly meetings were born after the team's engagement survey results revealed a feeling of isolation.

Twenty-five or so people comprised the RD's embedded support. The lack of overlap in their jobs prevented them from meaningfully commiserating though each sat in a hot seat between the Fed Bank's Central Support staff and the PhDs.

That the team felt isolated had not surprised Stella. The degree of it did though.

The team's first meeting had been scheduled in a conference room that had been co-opted for an informal, unscheduled FOMC debriefing. When the PhDs saw Stella's team waiting, one held a sign of a cross with his fingers and backed away while another asked, "Why the conclave?" Two other PhDs chimed in to ask were they going to make new rules. Once the PhDs were gone, Stella's team quickly dismissed the PhDs' attempt at humor by sharing their experiences of taking the bad with the good in their jobs. The name "Conclave" stuck and that go-round of good and bad became a standing agenda item.

A couple other standing items were added, but the agenda was largely left up to the organizer, a rotating position. Sometimes, the agenda was exhausted in a few minutes, and the team spent the time instead enjoying one another's company.

When everyone was seated, this month's organizer uncovered a pan.

Adam said, "You brought a cake. You win being organizer."

This prompted much laughter and cries of "Not again, Adam." Most of the team were happy for catered snacks, but Adam had tried to convince the others this meeting was of a type that called for home-baked goods. For a while, others complied, but then Stella nixed the requirement and made home-baked or bought goods optional on top of the snack cart. She never explained why, but the change came after she learned one team member spent seventy-seven dollars on cupcakes. On the now rare occasions when home-baked goods appeared, Adam lamented their irregularity with levity and announced a new winner of the meetings.

At the end of this meeting's agenda, Dawn noted the Budget Analyst's absence and asked, "Can we talk about Gage?"

One reported Gage's angry response when she'd offered him help after finding him outside the women's restroom. Another reported Gage's direction that she ought to be ashamed of asking for a receipt to reimburse his parking while another said he no longer drives.

One of the IT staff said, "I wasn't sure what to do with this. Jacob from Central IT had been helping him, and when I went in, he told me Jacob had been there but couldn't remember his name and instead said 'the Black one.' Jacob was still nearby and probably heard."

Stella paled.

Carrie, from her spot next to Stella, said, "Stella, you know his wife calls Hill when Gage leaves home and Hill calls his wife when he gets here and vice versa at night?"

Someone asked, "Maybe it's just a medication? Should we be having this conversation?"

Stella finally spoke up. "I'm sorry the Department is not on top of this. I don't have a solution. I'll talk to Wendell, for sure about what happened with Jacob. If you're concerned Gage needs physical help, give Hill a call. And when he talks about us or any other support staff being ashamed of our work, ignore him, and if you tell me, I'll circle back with him. Each of you and Central Support should take great pride in the work you do for the Bank and your public service. I wish this were different."

They concluded the discussion with a commitment for increased communication among themselves, wishes for good health for Gage, and agreement to escalate any further inappropriate behavior to Stella in real-time. Their disappointment in what didn't sound like a real resolution faded when their conversation turned to discussing upcoming college visits for those with kids that age and spring break escapes for those whose kids were grown.

At the end of each meeting, the coordinator of the next was chosen in a draw from a plastic hat. When that was done, the team dispersed.

Wendell was a few steps behind Stella as she returned to her office and stopped to ask if she'd come from the large conference room and, in an accusatory tone, reported having heard loud laughter. She reminded him about her team's Conclave and invited him to join an upcoming meeting.

He worked his lips in thought, then said, "Maybe. Do you have a minute?"

"Sure."

Wendell pulled out a chair from her table and moved it near where Stella sat behind her desk. "I have this problem. Gage really wants to take over the strategy stuff so I gave in. But I need you to be ready to jump in at any point."

Later on, Gage emailed Stella with a copy to Wendell. "Wendell says you'll work collaboratively with me to ensure a successful on-time completion of this work."

Stella emailed back, asking Gage for a description of her revised responsibilities.

Wendell replied without copying Gage, "Make this work. This is a good example of how you could improve relationships with others."

Stella walked over to his office. "Wendell. Your email. Could you say what relationships you referred to?"

"Well." He drew in his lips and thought for several seconds. "With Gage. I've asked you to be more supportive in his transition off Class I access."

"Oh. I didn't know he was off Class I. Will he spend more time on research or his work with S&R?"

"No. He's already got a head start on our strategy stuff."

After Stella checked her calendar, she entered vacation time for Friday and the following Tuesday. Monday was Presidents Day. She looked at some last-minute flights to Florida and some to Wyoming and emailed Nora to ask about her plans for the weekend. Then she emailed her direct reports and told them she was taking off and hoped their long weekends were peaceful.

RABBIT HOLE: MY FAMILY

Stella never made it out of Chicago due to more wintry mix. She kept her days off though. As I wondered about her life away from the Fed Bank, I began reminiscing about my own.

In the summer of 1915, just before my husband Everett and I were to move to my Aunt Edna and Uncle Louis' home, the midwife asked to inspect our accommodations. I planned to meet the midwife at Aunt Edna's and then Everett and I would stay for dinner with Aunt Edna, Uncle Louis, and their daughters.

The midwife's inspection was brief. When she grumbled a bit upon learning there was no bath near the second-floor guest room, Aunt Edna distracted her with an invitation to join us for tea.

The midwife asked about Violet, Aunt Edna's youngest, whom the midwife helped deliver fourteen years earlier. Aunt Edna told us Violet was with a neighbor's family visiting a new art installation, the Early Explorers Series, in the South Side's Fuller Park. The innocent mention of the South Side ignited the midwife.

Sputtering in frustration, she described a South Side obstetrician who, invited to speak at an important national conference, intended to describe midwifery as a barbaric practice. At her increasingly incensed distraction, I felt a frisson of fear.

I allowed my mind to wander away, looking forward to my mother's arrival from Iowa. I reminded myself that Violet was delivered safely by this very midwife, and that Everett and I had carefully evaluated both midwifery and the new hospital birthing.

I was pulled from my thoughts when Aunt Edna signaled the end of tea by pushing back her chair. "Well. One's own worth ought not stand on destroying another's. If his way is optimal, it will come to light as truth does."

As the midwife pointed in the air to begin again, Aunt Edna, having seen my face, held her arm to usher the midwife to the door, just as Violet came in.

I forgot my concerns as Violet's excitement overtook us. She described each panel of the installation's murals and pleaded with a laughing Aunt Edna for permission to paint their home. "Mother, please," she said, placing her hand on the yellow kitchen wall, "just one panel of flowers, here, and well there, on the cabinet's side."

While Violet continued to make her case, my dear cousin Lizzie sprung through the back entry porch, and seeing us, screeched, "Don't look," as she pulled a Marshall Field's shopping bag from our view and bounced up the back stairs.

Usually, Lizzie was only too anxious to display the spoils of her shopping so long as Uncle Louis was away. He took issue at the speed at which she turned her wages from her new job at Marshall Field's into purchases, and especially when he was off-term from his faculty job at DePaul, directed his lessons toward her. Though Aunt Edna and I always pretended neutrality during these lectures, we secretly shared gratitude for his thinking women ought to know finances. Lizzie didn't respond when I called out to tell her Uncle Louis wasn't yet home from his job at the Chicago Board of Trade.

She returned to the kitchen to help with dinner and Aunt Edna sent me to rest and soon after Uncle Louis arrived home with my Everett in tow.

That night, Aunt Edna's dinner table was as enchanting as ever. I thought her table setting to often be driven by resistance to the farmer's dinner table with which we'd all grown up.

The quiet moment while Violet gave our prayer of thanks gave way to a cacophony.

As our plates were filled, I began to tell Everett about the midwife's visit, but Aunt Edna interrupted. "Lucy, I called your Aunt Merilee and the pharmacist told me that she asked he tell me she will only trek to the drugstore to return calls on Saturdays. Have you heard any news of her from your mother? I worry for her, alone on that farm since Ronald died. Those small Iowa towns must get the telephone lines."

"Mother said Merilee's passed the turn all of a sudden and seems herself again. She'd gone to the banker, you knew him, Aunt Edna? She asked for credit to buy seed for a late planting this year. He told her he wouldn't lend to a widow, and he thinks her harvests last year were mere luck. I am certain if the old banker were still alive he'd sack his son in a flash."

"Lucy, why didn't you tell me that earlier?" Aunt Edna set her spoon down and rubbed her forehead as if trying to draw an idea. "She wants to stay on the farm so badly. Louis could have lent her a sum."

"Aunt Edna, I ought have said the good news before the bad. My father introduced her to the man who is going between Iowa and Chicago to get futures for the farmers. He was happy to pay now for the promise of the October harvest. She bought seed and made payroll and harvest delivery is set." That reminded me. "By the way, Uncle, Mr. Ronald Parker is a crumb. On my last day of work, he'd come to the Fed Bank to meet with Mr. Myer and he asked Mr. Myer, 'Why is the skirt here? Futures are the business of men.' I wasn't sure if he was put out they weren't meeting at the Board of Trade or truly because a woman was present. Mr. Myer defended my presence as stenographer but Mr. Parker insisted I leave."

Uncle turned serious. "Lucy, be careful with Parker. He means no harm with his bluster. Myer has been on a limb, helping hide your marriage and pregnancy. If Parker takes interest and realizes either, he will make trouble for Myer, or even for me. Though I concede he is a challenge. I fear the futures exchange will someday forget its agricultural roots under the care of men like him."

"Yes. I'm more grateful to Mr. Myer than I can say. No matter, my last day is passed. I'll hope not to see Parker again. I'll go back to see Mr. Myer though, just before we leave for Iowa. He's writing a page for the baby's book, to tell what it was like to open the Fed Bank. He's kind, Uncle. He promised the baby would be welcome to come work with him after college. Though it's a long time away, I have to agree with him, a stint at any of the regional Fed Banks will serve a banker well. Everett and I hope our baby will someday take over the bank we'll open."

Everett asked, "Louis, do you think the Federal Reserve will still exist when the baby finishes college?"

"I do, it is important that power is decentralized this time. Spreading it across the country will certainly solve some of the problems that plagued the first two central banks. I'd say the structure of twelve reserve cities is ingenious. And if nothing more, some say third time's a charm. How is your research study proceeding?"

"It is nearly complete and now has a title, *Agricultural Price Volatility*. Though I'm sorry we're not in Iowa, I can't regret having spent the summer on this study. I think the futures market will only become more important to farmers' welfare."

Lizzie joined the conversation. "Perhaps a new suit will help, Everett. I could introduce you to the menswear salesman at Marshall Field's."

I asked, "Lizzie, has anyone made their purchase with notes from the new central bank? Violet, would you please pass the potatoes?"

"We received the loveliest green ribbon for wrapping packages. It's more important to wrap well than to examine bank notes."

"I'll give you the potatoes, but Lizzie said she is afraid that your going-home-to-Iowa present won't fit if you keep eating the way you do."

I turned to Lizzie in excitement. "Oh, Lizzie, was what you hid earlier the rose dress?"

Lizzie placed her hand on Violet's wrist with the slightest sisterly threat and said, "It's a surprise, Lucy. By the way, Violet, did you return my scarf back to my dresser?" The two began to whisper.

Everett said, "I expect the new notes are out in circulation at least here and near the other cities that claim a Federal Reserve Bank."

I asked, "Uncle, have you seen the $10 denomination notes that are circulating? I've heard they are similar to the national bank notes though they say 'Federal Reserve.' Mr. Myer referred to them as elastic."

In a quiet voice, Violet asked Aunt Edna a question about elastic for some pajamas and the two began a conversation of sewing.

Uncle said, "I have seen them. That elasticity is at the core of the creation of the Federal Reserve Banks."

"Well then, the Marshall Field's customers aren't using them then, I would remember stretchy paper."

The laughter that bubbled from me, Everett, and Uncle Louis at Lizzie's words earned one of Aunt Edna's squinty-eyed looks.

I tried to redeem myself. "Lizzie, it's not stretchy paper, though perhaps that would be what most people think, now that you say it. It means that more money can be put into circulation. The total supply of money, everywhere in the economy, can be changed now. That is what is elastic. If something happens, and people need more cash money to do their business, the Federal Reserve will provide it."

Lizzie held out her hands. "But why would people not just go to the bank?"

Uncle appeared pleased that Lizzie made the inquiry. "Lizzie, it would be as when you were an early teen and Violet just born. See, some banks had troubles after the San Francisco earthquake in 1906, and it was as if the earthquake tremors left the ground and went right up to shake the firms who had sold insurance in San Francisco, then shook the banks, and once one bank failed in the face of the devastation, people were frightened and everyone tried to withdraw their deposits from their banks, and when there just was not enough cash money to cover all those withdrawals, people panicked. Mr. J.P. Morgan stepped in, but that was only to fix things that one time. The Federal Reserve System was created as a permanent lender of last resort. That means when there's nowhere else to go, they are ready to lend. If Marshall Field's had no cash to pay its employees and it goes to its bank and its bank has no cash money to give it, then its bank can go to its Federal Reserve Bank." Uncle looked around the table to see who was paying attention and his eyes returned to Lizzie. "The regular banks have accounts at the Federal Reserve, just like I have an account at First National Bank, and they can ask for a loan or make a deposit and the Federal Reserve will never run out of cash money because there is now an elastic money supply."

Aunt Edna, as always, focused on the good in anyone and commented that Mr. Morgan must be a kind person, but Uncle told her, "Not necessarily, Edna. I don't know him or anyone who does so can't say, but I do know a failing banking system causes a failing economy, which would have hurt all of us but especially bankers. One healthy bank in a failing banking system won't be for long."

Lizzie stopped twirling her fork and smiled. "Thank you, Everett. Thank you, Father. Michael said he met Mr. Morgan once. I wish Michael would come home. Mother, Mary Johnson told us her cousin in New York sent her a pair of blue stockings and wrote we'll all be wearing pastels soon. Do you think it too forward to ask Michael to bring some from New York?"

Aunt Edna whispered to me behind her hand, "Are your dresses still comfortable? You've blossomed since you've stopped hiding your pregnancy. I could add a slip of elastic at the waist easy enough."

Through dessert, my family moved in and out of the varied conversations, interpreting the subject of each relative to the information they wanted to give or to get. When we finished, Lizzie rose to clear the dessert dishes. "Sit down, Mother. Come, Lucy."

"Where are we going?" As I pushed the kitchen door with my hip, I heard Everett's voice and stopped. "Thank you again, Edna, for our show tickets. I mentioned in passing to a colleague that we were going to see *Amarilla* at the matinee. He said Midway Gardens is a grand place to spend a Sunday afternoon. I've heard so much about Mr. Frank Lloyd Wright's work."

Aunt Edna was pleased with Everett's words. "Louis and I wanted your first anniversary to be special. I'll look at the schedule for the elevated line, and if Lucy is up to it, we'll lunch at Marshall Field's Walnut Room before we go."

I turned back to the dining room. "From me too, Aunt Edna, thank you." The door swung shut behind me. "I'm here, Lizzie. By the way, if you are interested to know, your Marshall Field & Co. President, Mr. James Simpson, is a member of the Board of Directors of the Federal Reserve Bank of Chicago, to make sure the actions of this Fed Bank are good for retailers, including your store, Lizzie."

"Enough about that. Set the dishes here. Let's go out to the garden. It's nicer now for this afternoon's sprinkle."

Lizzie wiped the garden seats. "Sit down. Cousin, how were you certain Everett was the one? Your waiting for child has put the inkling of grandchildren in Mother's mind and she asked was Michael going to be the one for me."

"When will he return from New York?"

"A fortnight. He says it's necessary for promotion, but sometimes I think he may just be there behaving like a wolf. But how were you sure? I'm twenty-two. I feel I'm old enough to know, but I don't."

"Do you really think Michael a wolf? Remember, I knew Everett as a child. When his parents owned the farm until his mother had to sell it to his uncle. We were ten when his mother moved him and Craig in with her parents."

Lizzie looked thoughtful as she said, "It's good Craig stopped getting so blotchy. Then when did Everett find you?"

"He moved in with his uncle, trading chores for room and board while he was in college. I think I hear Aunt Edna in the kitchen. Let's go start the dishes."

"That's like a fairy tale."

"Applesauce. Likely more helpful to tell you when I wasn't so sure." I held the door for Lizzie as we returned to the kitchen. "Aunt Edna, leave us, we'll wash the dishes."

It took a moment for Aunt Edna to agree, but she did, and I began to tell Lucy when I was uncertain Everett was the one for me. "When Everett first moved in with his uncle and told me about starting the agricultural program at Iowa State, I told him I was starting their home economics program. The first year of the home economic Ladies Course was the same as his agricultural program, but he acted like his program was harder until we started to study together and he saw. Lizzie, where's a clean towel? Then we promised to one another and midway through the second year of school when he decided he would leave at the end of the year and go to Northwestern for law school, he expected I would stop school to go with him and I wouldn't. We were distant then, until the next Christmas when he was back in Iowa and we talked a lot about everything and decided after I finished school, we would marry and I would move to Chicago while he finished his last year of law school, and here we are. I think you already would know if Michael is right."

"Who will I ask such questions of once you are in Iowa? I'll miss you, Lucy."

"And I you. Lizzie, the midwife asked your mother today might you still return to your nursing studies. Do you think you might, yet? It was unfair that you extracted my promise to not ask you about it. Ah Lizzie, you'll be the best nurse. This foray into shopkeeping of yours, you'll have to learn the business finances eventually, is it really what you want?" When I noticed Lizzie's narrowing eyes, I tacked on, "See Lizzie, Everett and I chose you to be the baby's godmother. Will you? You'll have to come to Iowa more often. And how blessed the baby with a godmother who is also a nurse."

Lizzie squealed in delight, causing the others to call to us in worry, and we went to join them in the living room to share the news.

Soon after, Everett and I walked back to our apartment under stars shining in a moonlit sky.

WEEK TWENTY-TWO ~ 3/25

On Monday morning, Hill jumped from the comfy chair when she heard Wendell's footsteps. Locking her clasped hands at her waist, she told him Winnie was in the emergency room with chest pains.

As he hung his coat and turned on his computer, he asked if he should send flowers or a fruit basket. Hill told him no, that Winnie probably wouldn't be there long since the doctor already confirmed it wasn't a heart attack.

Wendell stilled and turned toward Hill. "Was it stress? Did they say it was stress?"

Hill swung her hands downward on the word, "not," when she said Winnie said it was not stress.

"Let me know when she calls again."

"Okay. She asked me to get your conference room ready for your meeting with Finance except I should leave the equations on the board."

"Right." He grimaced. "Barbara's coming. Yes, leave the equations. They scare people. Make sure Stella knows Winnie's out."

Barbara, this Fed Bank's Chief Financial Officer, was an unwelcome guest in the RD. A year earlier, petulant after meeting with David and Stella, she'd stopped in an empty conference room to take a call. When she found a stack of FOMC Class II charts, she took them to the then President. He didn't react as she'd hoped, and in a worst outcome for her, told her to take them to Randy and make sure Randy knew she'd seen the pages.

Regardless, this day's meeting would be in the RD. Not wanting her on the floor was outweighed by Wendell's pleasure with internal meeting dynamics that dictated she come to him for this meeting.

Hill asked if he needed anything else.

"No. Were you here just to wait for me?"

She nodded. "Let me know if there's anything I can do while Winnie's out."

When she released her hands, the blood flowed back into her fingers.

About noon, Hill entered Wendell's conference room. She looked at the table, the seat of each chair, the windowsills, and in each drawer of the credenza. She looked under the tray of markers and behind the erasers on the whiteboard ledge and at the floor under the table. She pulled a cherry tomato from where it was dried and stuck to the carpet.

When she poked her head in Wendell's door to tell him his conference room was clear, he asked if she'd heard from Winnie.

"She'll be home soon. They gave her antacids and she feels better."

"Did the doctor say it was stress?"

"She said it wasn't stress."

"Okay. When you talk to her again, tell her take a couple days off."

"And Wendell, I'll put in a Facilities request. There was a little tomato under the table. They'll clean the carpet."

He brushed off her attempt to show him the picture she'd snapped.

Stella, Barbara, Stella's peer in Barbara's area, and a couple others were waiting when Wendell came through his direct door. Stella laughed and Wendell was confused when their guests startled in surprise. The first minutes of the meeting were given over to Wendell's and Barbara's discussion of the validity of the guests' assumption that the door led to a storage space, because after all, she said, any extra door in any other conference room did.

Though Stella and her peer would soon be on opposing sides of the discussion, they looked at one another in camaraderie. They'd been together in some version of this meeting each year for many seeking an elusive compromise in how the RD would apply PACS, the Fed System's accounting rules.

How close they'd get to a compromise would directly affect the likelihood the RD would stay within the BOG's spending target for Monetary Policy. Because of Gage's staff's occasional service to Payments and because of Casework and other staff whose work helps S&R, the RD is able to offload shares of its expenses to those functions. Though the cross-charging calculations are complex, the offloading would offset some of the unbudgeted PhDs' salary increases.

Twenty minutes in, Stella offered a back-of-the-envelope estimate of the effect of a PACS rule that equally weighted high-paid PhDs who commanded thousands of travel, consultant, conference, data, and other dollars and relatively low-paid staff members who commanded few dollars.

When Barbara said the estimate was irrelevant, Wendell exploded. Anyone with a basic knowledge of math and a rudimentary understanding of the RD could see that weighting by head instead of expenses was an illogical way of allocating expenses, he said.

Barbara's staff looked frightened and Barbara as if she wanted to escape. Stella was relieved that Wendell's temper targeted Barbara, who Stella viewed as a bully in her own right.

A flushed Barbara threatened Frank's involvement.

After the others left, Wendell motioned to Stella to stay.

"Who's in charge of them?"

He listened as Stella explained the roles of the Offices and Officers throughout the Fed System involved in the governance of the Fed System's finances. She generously noted the same staff who so frustrated the RDs with PACS also worked on the Fed System's balance sheet where adherence to rules and precision was critical and asked he not judge the individuals by just their PACS work. She added, "PACS is nuts though."

"Would the relationship with RBOPS help?"

"RBOPS is already helpful. I worked with them to put through some sense-making revisions to PACS a couple years ago. It's mostly the Fed Banks' CFOs whose incentives do not prioritize accuracy over process in PACS."

Meetings such as that have taught me no one can hear me, even when I holler. PACS reeks of high-cost bureaucracy. Though Stella disliked PACS and made small inroads to change, the core of PACS persists. The management of PACS were powerful long-timers who rested on laurels won in the 1980s.

PACS was new when it was discussed at the Subcommittee on Domestic Monetary Policy of the Committee on Banking, Finance and Urban Affairs of the U.S. House of Representatives.

Then BOG Chairman Volcker had gone to the Capitol to address the Subcommittee's questions. Though one Representative admitted to falling asleep halfway through reading the advance written material, he and the others acknowledged PACS' ability to provide honest and transparent information about the Fed System's spending. They revisited the need for the FOMC's budget independence and validated it remained important since they, the politicians themselves, were sufficiently self-aware to admit some in their role would starve the Fed System and let the economy run amok if it would get them reelected.

Also in that hearing, a Subcommittee member brought up the "lot of money" spent on economists and economic data and proposed that "some" might say the Fed System could get along with 90 percent of the economists the Fed System had then but concluded, "They have enormous responsibility…and we simply can't afford to in any way decrease their ability to do the job that has been assigned to them by the Congress."

The RD's Officers in the 1980s appreciated the Subcommittee's trust. I don't think Wendell, Gage, or even David, have ever once verbalized a need to justify economists' positions by the job assigned to them by Congress. Nor has anyone here referenced any more current presentation of PACS to Congress.

Mid-afternoon, Wendell came to Stella's office. He brought a chair from the table to her desk.

After asking about Winnie, he said, "I talked to your coach."

"Oh good. I wondered when she'd get to it. She's talking or talked to Gage too."

"I told her you do a fine job and gave her a couple of things you should work on. I finally selected my coach."

"Oh, good luck. I hope it works out."

He leaned forward, elbows to knees. "I should have said thank you last week."

Stella's hope and relief were obvious. "You're welcome but why?"

"You worked with Gage after the pre-GAME meeting."

Wendell renamed the Heads meeting to GAME since Group Heads Meeting could be abbreviated as GHME, which sounds like "game." Turned out he'd hated the label, "Heads Meeting," for as long as they'd used it.

He referred to when he, Gage, and Stella had discussed the upcoming Heads' discussion about consultants. Gage had become increasingly distressed each time Wendell referred to the discussion as a "fight" and took comfort from picking on Stella. Once Wendell left, Stella had sat quietly with Gage as he had worked off his distress.

"Looking back," Wendell admitted to Stella, "I know it's hard working with him sometimes. He has ups and downs but we all do. You know, I feel like I owe him. He went along with everything when he came back to Research and I got bumped from SVP to EVP because I had him. The only way to repay that is to keep him happy here. If you would help me do that, I would appreciate it."

A surprised Stella said, without thought, "Sure."

"Anyway, I saw your email and it looks like we're set for the fight."

"Wendell, just so you know, Gage twice more said to cancel the meeting and do it instead by email." She made a motion of uncertainty with her hand. "I told him I couldn't make that decision but he could talk to you, so — "

"I'll figure something out if he comes to me."

On Tuesday, Winnie phoned Stella.

"I wanted to ask if you would tell Hill we always do it that way. I don't mind if she does manager stuff, but the other stuff for Wendell could have waited. Don't let her do anymore of my work, okay?"

Stella assured Winnie there was more than enough work to go around.

Winnie continued. "One more thing. I want to know if you could meet tomorrow. Right at eight."

"Yes, eight works. Or 8:30, if you want to walk slower from the train. But relax the rest of today, will you please?"

"We'll see."

"Not we'll see. Go relax. Bye now."

Mid-day, Stella opened an email. Gage had written, "I read the materials you sent. My area doesn't hire consultants. Frankly, I know little to nothing that would prepare me. I plan on winging it.

I presume if my input is needed that someone will ask me questions and I will answer. Is there more to things than that?"

One of the documents in the meeting materials he referenced was a policy about consultants, written five years earlier by a team of four PhDs he led.

Stella's eyes softened and she shrugged. Finally, she typed, "Sounds good. Thank you."

On his way out for the evening, Wendell poked his head in Stella's office. "Hilerie said Winnie called. How is she?"

"She was worrying about stuff here. We didn't talk long. She asked to meet in the morning."

"Well, don't let her do too much."

"She's not doing any work for me this month. But yes, her health first." When Stella noticed Wendell's eyes were drawn to the half-eaten Snickers on her desk, she said, "Do as I say not as I do," and shrugged.

There were a few seconds beat after he said, "Okay," before he said, "Good night," as if saying the latter felt unfamiliar. He pulled up his hood while he waited for her to reciprocate.

"Yes, good night."

He smiled and nodded and turned.

The next morning, Carrie called out as Stella passed, "Where'd you go? I was in the other security lane and waited by the elevators but you never came."

"Oh, sorry. I'm setting that damn metal detector off again. How was your trip?"

Carrie told Stella about the conference she'd attended and then said, "What went on here? I got seven emails about some ruckus when Hill met with the Assistants."

"Oh, crap. I didn't know about that."

"Hill told them she had talked to Winnie and Gage said if Winnie approved, Hill could be Manager."

"Winnie's back today."

"Dawn's going to Employee Relations. That was the last email."

"I think Wendell and I might have turned a corner and I'm treading carefully so unless someone officially pulls me in, I'm staying out. But will you let me know if Employee Relations can't calm it down? I'm sorry you end up in the middle. It's that reward for being nice — "

"Getting stuck in a big old mess. No worries. And it's not like there's a real solution to Hill's screwing with people anyway so long as David will totally dis anyone who contests her. I'm going to take Friday off."

"Me too. For fun or doctor?"

"Half and half, doctor and shopping. Why you?"

"My sister is back here for a few days. I'm hoping to convince her to come downtown or I'll go out to my mom's to see her."

"Do you think she'll ever move back?"

"She's coming closer. This trip is to close on the sale of the farm they still owned here and then she goes from here to Michigan to look at a couple of cottages for sale. Her husband can't travel yet but she said there's a good deal on a fixer-upper they don't want to miss. It would be great to have them in Michigan."

"What about her shop?"

"She's opening a new one after she moves. She figures there will already be a flower shop and/or gift shop wherever they'd end up so she's focusing on herbal remedies."

"Jake, glass-blower extraordinaire, used up all that burn cream. Whenever, if she sends stuff to you, would you ask her to send more and I'll send her a check?" Carrie's husband's hobby was creating glass beads.

"I keep giving mine away so she's already bringing more. I'll bring you one next week."

At 8:15 a.m., hot coffee in hand, Winnie came to Stella's office. "It did take me a little longer this morning."

Stella carried her tea over and joined Winnie at the table. "How are you feeling?"

Winnie showed Stella where the pain had emerged and told Stella about the handsome young doctor who diagnosed a pinched nerve and gave her a script for physical therapy. Winnie hadn't yet made an appointment and asked hadn't Stella used the place in the basement of the Board of Trade.

After Stella responded, Winnie continued. "Hill said Wendell was really worried and kept asking if it was stress. Do you think he was really worried?"

"We all were, Win. He'll be glad to see you."

"When I told the doctor about my job stress, he asked if I could go back to my old job."

"What did you say?"

"I told him about Wendell and how good he's been to me. I wish I could undo it." Winnie reached for the bowl of Silver Tops.

"Going to the emergency room is always scary."

"Not that. This." She waved her hand toward the Assistants' cube block.

"Wendell will understand. Look at the positive. He believed in you and you've been doing the job now for months. That's great, Win. No job is forever. Wanting to instead focus on the job you had before is just a choice." Winnie was unwrapping the chocolates and didn't see Stella wince at her own words.

"Maybe. Thank you for the Fannie Mae and the coaster."

Stella laughed. "Oh, Win, not a coaster. It's a little labyrinth. It's supposed to help you relax. Here, I have one." Stella brought hers to the table. "With the stylus, enter the labyrinth and move through to the center. Hold it there and take deep breaths, then back out. There was a little instruction booklet. I swear it reduces stress."

"We'll see."

Wendell got the fight he wanted at the GAME meeting. The Macro Head said his consultants should get bigger contracts because they research monetary policy. Even as the Micro Head stressed the dependence of macroeconomics on microeconomics, he dismissed altogether the need for consultants who studied regional issues such as the economic effects of local weather disasters. The Finance Head asked Wendell was there a point to defending Finance consultants, and wanting to draw others into his pain, brought up the HuffPo article.

The HuffPo article, first published in 2009 and last revised in 2013, is a bit of a legend in this RD. The article claims the Fed System controls the economics profession through various relationships in order to prevent criticism, such as of when it failed to see the housing bubble. And, "The Fed also doles out millions of dollars in contracts to economists for consulting assignments, papers, presentations, workshops, and that plum gig known as a 'visiting scholarship.'"

In response, Wendell surprised everyone by proposing a discussion about the rates.

Stella rose and headed to the whiteboard to write the three-tier rate structure he suggested. The highest rates would go to the "consiglieri." Stella smiled at her uncertainty of the spelling. Wendell told her to sound it out and then did so.

His rudeness served as a signal to the others and their contributions to the conversation stalled while he continued. Consultants in the middle would be given a "good lieutenant" rate. Finally, the bottom tier would be given the "new guy" rate. Stella wrote "new" and stopped. Wendell asked had the marker dried. She wrote "guy."

The requirements of the consultants were reviewed in light of the new rate structure. The consiglieri merely needed to show up. Wendell said they couldn't pay them enough. Good lieutenants should be an important colleague to at least one of the RD's PhDs. The new guys were made up of some early-career academics and a few others who were mid- or late-career but whose research was not of interest to Wendell or David. The PhDs would ask the new guys for effort on a one-off basis.

When the room went quiet, Gage asked if anyone knew which consultants had consulting contracts with other Fed Banks. Wendell brushed off the question and instead reminisced.

Once, in a December, a local academic who'd not used any of the days of his annual contract came into the Fed Bank, each weekday, through December 31. Afterward, he'd confessed to having needed a place to avoid his in-laws while his school repainted its Economics Department and his office. That most of the PhDs with whom he usually talked were out on vacation while he was paid to be present had become an example, one Wendell said the Heads should make sure didn't get repeated. Stella confirmed the contracts now required consulting days to be spread throughout the contract period.

The newest Head asked, "But we paid him?"

Wendell shrugged. "What else could we have done?"

Stella said, "And with that, I think we are done."

Wendell nodded.

Gage followed Wendell through the direct door and asked, "I think that went well. Is there anything else that you would like from me?"

"No, no."

Months later, Gage's year-end bonus would be topped-up for his work leading the consultant process.

On Thursday, David stopped to say hello to Stella while she was talking with Adam. When he asked how things were going, Stella told him fine but Adam asked how'd he think things were going to go.

Both Stella and Adam were surprised when David said, "Everybody gets a chance. Hey, that reminds me. Do you know anything about some warm spot between his office and the conference room? Do you remember anything from the old renovations?"

Adam said, "I couldn't feel anything but who knows what's in these walls."

David left them to join the PhDs in a conference room to debrief the FOMC cycle just ended.

When the debriefing ended, the conversation turned to the nationwide *Fed Listens* initiative, a listening tour conducted as part of a *Review of Monetary Policy Strategy, Tools, and Communications*. Listening sessions had begun in February and a *Conference on Monetary Policy Strategy, Tools, and Communications Practices* was planned for June at this Fed Bank.

David said he'd talked with a few of the RD's long-time consultants about a conference panel that would discuss how individual communities' experience nationwide full employment. Though there's lots of evidence that some communities continue to struggle despite the strong statistics, the consultants had been surprised to learn about the disconnect.

One PhD said, "Come on. We live the disconnect. Someone could walk out of here, get on any CTA bus or train, and within a half hour have traversed the disconnect."

Most excused the consultants' ignorance saying things such as, "They don't research low-income areas."

One asked, "How are they supposed to have known?"

When David's coffee spilled, it splashed both him and the PhD sitting next to him, the one who'd just spoken.

I'd only meant to bump into the PhD's arm to interrupt him but enjoyed the dirty look he got from David.

WEEK TWENTY-FOUR ~ 4/8

Stella and Carrie's Monday morning catch-up meandered from how many April showers were required for May flowers to how much of the increased daylight was caught in the layer of rain clouds.

Finally, Carrie said, "You know?" Ron, the Head of the Finance Group, had told her about Wendell's decision to discontinue the banking conference.

"Wendell mentioned it, but I thought he was just blowing smoke so I'd let increases in consultant spending fly. They really did it?"

"Yup. Ron's pissed he had to write a seventy-page case for Wendell when Wendell knew all along he was killing it. Wendell said he wasn't comfortable with a conference that influenced laws and regulations. And he told Ron about some big deal RBOPS memo that had a footnote about public events."

"There was no footnote about public events in the only big deal RBOPS memo I know about. Wendell's been such a weasel with that memo. Dismisses it whenever I bring it up as a constraint then recalls it like it's written on stone tablets whenever he wants to cut something. It's too bad S&R couldn't have taken Ron's conference."

"Ron asked but Wendell wouldn't consider it. He thinks Wendell can't stand the Bank being known for a banking conference. I wondered what that means for my job. I wasn't going to tell you, but Raj called and offered me a job." Raj worked in the RD when he was young, left for a long career at Goldman Sachs, and recently took a faculty job at a local university. "They need an event person."

Stella's brow furrowed. "Oh. Other events will fill up your time or projects so there's no concern with your job. But Raj, huh?"

"I'm not going, just made me think."

Stella's brow was still furrowed though she said, "It's nice to be asked."

"He called you when he first went to Goldman, didn't he?"

"Yeah, like thirty years ago. Back when I couldn't imagine ever leaving the Fed."

At 9:00 a.m., Ellen arrived for Stella's coaching appointment, a bag of blueberries in hand. "One lonely stall braving the dampness at the farmer's market. Should we talk over blueberries?" She held up a plastic bag from which small clods of dirt fell to the floor.

"Thank you but I brought berries from home. A new grocery store opened by me yesterday. Their produce was stunning, nine hundred, ninety-eight different kinds, they claimed. Fabulous colors and smells, even at 6:30 at night. I got a bunch of stuff. Any other day I'd have jumped for fresh blueberries."

"I think we are getting one of those stores, too, up in that food desert where my husband and I live."

"Community Affairs just wrote an article on the impact of the food deserts in the city. It's sad, it seems so fixable. I thought you lived in Old Town."

"We do. It's not really a food desert. I shouldn't call it that. Let's get to your feedback. Wendell or Gage?"

Stella sat up straight, picked up her pen, and chose Gage.

As she pulled a pair of flowered readers from her bag, Ellen asked Stella if she had completed a subordinate survey for Wendell's 360 review.

Stella hadn't known he was doing a 360 but told Ellen good for him.

"He really should have asked you. Back to your feedback. Gage says you're very smart and do a good job keeping all of the balls in the air that need to be kept there and dropping those that should be dropped. He thinks you do an excellent job keeping Central Support hounds at bay. He's especially grateful you fought HR to get Vance's, Vance is a new economist?" Stella nodded and Ellen continued. "Vance's full relocation benefits paid out before he moved."

"What an odd thing to mention. The Bank wasted a boatload of time on Vance's ploys to capture every possible dollar from the relo menu. HR was pretty upset. Vance's Head thought it was funny, said economists are trained to be maximizers. We're probably just going to give unconditional pots of money going forward. Did Gage say what he'd like to see done differently?"

"Yes." Ellen became serious. "He said you hung on too tightly when he needed to get involved with some strategy document. And he worries about you on a personal level. He asked if you were happy. He thinks you might be a lesbian and wishes you felt comfortable talking about it."

Ellen described the struggles her daughter, as a lesbian, faced in her workplace.

"I'm sorry for what your daughter deals with. My niece deals with some of the same. It's unfair. Are you sanctioning what Gage said?"

Ellen set down her pen and crossed her hands in her lap, holding the readers. "You are right, he was inappropriate. I wanted you to know though because it came from a good place in his heart. I think if you made a point to talk to him, and show him that you're happy, not about your sexuality, just let him know that you're happy. When you told me about the produce section, you came alive, tell him things like that."

"He makes my staff sweat and stutter and tells them to tell Central Support staff that they should be ashamed of their work. I'm disgusted that he behaves the way he does, that David and Wendell don't deal with it, and that I won't risk my pension to jump out and call it crazy. I'm not a Susie Sunshine at the best of times and am not going to pretend I'm happy when he puts down my staff. I don't think telling him about asparagus will help." Stella tipped her head. "Really, Ellen?"

"You can't change this, Stella. Don't be too cavalier. Focus on you and the overall message was good. He did want to talk about your relationship with Hilerie, but he ran out of time. I'll give him a call this week."

Stella's smile was weak and fake. "Okay. Wendell's."

"Now, Wendell's. Don't be so negative, Stella, he has no issue with your work. Wendell thinks you do a good job with your staff, that you represent their interests in the GAME. That's your executives' meetings?" Stella nodded, and Ellen continued. "In the GAMEs, then. You are helping him to keep Gage happy and that's important to him. That you are able to move a lot of work through the Heads despite their resistance and occasional overdone analyses. He mentioned something about shredded cheese at his quarterly luncheons for all his staff. Did I get that right?"

"Yep. Forty-five minutes the Heads spent talking about cheese for a taco bar. Then when I finally got them to stop and leave it up to Carrie, she said two of them stopped by her."

"He thought you handled it well. He gets good feedback from the Bank areas you work with. He said he gave you a salary bump because David said your salary was out of whack, but he didn't know why it was so important to you because – I wrote this down – 'she isn't raising kids or supporting a spouse.'"

"He didn't give me a salary bump. But yes, my salary is out of whack. I jumped the usual ladder of promotions and salary increases right to Officer pretty early and then Officers get frozen whenever government staff salaries get frozen. When we talked about it, David recommended I get some job offers. I didn't. Did you tell Wendell that last bit was illegal?"

Ellen squirmed in her seat, flipped her notes, and finally looked up and over her readers. "Stella, I may have misstated about the bump, it looks like he said you'd asked David for a bump. I apologize." Elbows on the table, she swung her readers and said in a defensive tone, "Of course I did not criticize him. He is who he is in the position he is in and he isn't going anywhere, and you, via me, asked for his feedback. He was being transparent."

"He's going to get the Bank in trouble. Will you tell HR?"

"Here's the rest." As she finished, she glanced up over her readers though her eyebrows remained pulled tightly together and said, "I think you'll just have to keep being careful around him. He doesn't have any problems with you and thinks you do a great deal to make the department work well which allows the PhDs to be highly productive. He isn't concerned that the two of you bump heads. In fact, he said, let's see here, 'she never wants to fight and he thinks a good fight now and again would be helpful.'"

"He really does mean fight. It's how he releases aggression. He's not looking for the back and forth that gets to better solutions. Makes me truly uncomfortable. I don't like when people raise their voices."

"He does tend to be domineering. It's a shame he didn't ask for your input on his 360. We can work on bolstering your willingness to fight back."

Ellen began collecting her papers, using the tabletop to line up the edges, dropping them five times on the horizontal side, five on the vertical.

Stella asked, "Time's up?"

"Yes. I have to run. I'm meeting with Heather. We should talk again soon after you process the feedback. How about three weeks, same day, same time?"

"I may take a week off. How about mid-May?"

After Ellen left, Stella went back to her desk and was soon lost in thought, her head tilted and expression confused.

When Ellen reached in for the blueberries she'd left behind, she scolded, "Don't frown like that, Stella. It's unbecoming. They said positive things. Don't focus on the negative."

Stella exaggerated a frown after Ellen turned away.

On her way to Heather's office, Ellen saw her colleague sitting in the comfy chairs. "Who are you waiting for?"

Her colleague told her, "This guy."

After Wendell ushered his coach into his office, he returned to Winnie's cube. He pulled a frown when she told him it was too late to order a coffee cart for his session with his coach and pushed up a smile when she offered to retrieve the beverage cart from the meeting he'd just left. "But clean it up first, okay? Sometimes the economists leave a mess."

Rob was the seventeenth coach Wendell interviewed, chosen because he'd studied economics before psychology.

At their first session, Rob was dismayed to find out Wendell had never received 360-degree feedback, except of course, for feedback on his research. And during their second meeting, Wendell offered excuses and bit his nails but finally agreed he "should probably have a 360." Now, a month later, the feedback was ready.

Rob slid a copy of the RD's org chart to the center of the table. "I want to take a minute to revisit the people you selected to be surveyed and acknowledge the inevitable information gaps. First, remember the group of subordinates was limited to male staff who hold PhDs, except for Winifred."

Wendell shrugged.

"Despite the bias, there's useful information." Rob pulled the org chart back and pushed forward a bound booklet. He explained the layout of the competency ratings.

Wendell asked questions about the validation of the survey instrument, the significance level for coefficient acceptance, and so on, until Rob moved them along.

Seeing his strengths included technical proficiency, an ease with his scope of authority, and a willingness to dig into details and set aside rules and boundaries, Wendell said, "This isn't so bad."

"Try not to think of it as bad or good. Just information. Let's move to opportunities." Rob took a sip of his coffee.

Wendell adopted an expression of fake humility. "I have a sort of plan. By a year out, I'd like to be in candidate pools for Federal Reserve Bank President."

The simultaneity of Rob's hard swallow and suppressed guffaw could only have come from practice. "Ah, your assumption wasn't wrong, but HR tends to sugarcoat and uses 'opportunities' to describe behaviors to improve." Seeing Wendell's face fall, Rob continued. "Each of us has flaws, strengths, weaknesses, and so on. Doesn't mean we are strong or weak people, just that we're human. Having the privilege of knowing our strengths and weaknesses carries an obligation to improve on them, be a better leader."

Wendell's pupils had begun to darken and he sat forward, uncrossed his legs and squared his shoulders, and said in a mocking tone, "Well, let's see these opportunities."

Wendell was quiet through the first couple competencies, but when Rob got to empathy, Wendell got defensive. "It's not that I don't know how to be empathetic. We don't have that culture here, we're facts and analysis."

Rob rubbed his chin. "Those aren't mutually exclusive. There are many studies that make a case for empathy in leaders in technical fields. I can send some over."

"Wasn't there some guy who said empathy was bad for society?"

"Yes. Bloom. Claims empathy requires placing the interest of one over the interests of the many."

"He's at Yale."

Rob steered the conversation, "Look, context is helpful. Let's tackle this from a different direction. Do you have any examples where you thought you could have been more empathetic?"

During the silence, Wendell tapped his pen on the edge of the table, until he missed the table and the pen flew. When he returned to his seat, he set the pen down, and sighed. "Here. Winnie might not like her manager role. I put her in it." Though his lips were poised to speak, he hesitated before continuing. "I might have disadvantaged Winnie when I told Stella, my Administrative Officer, to stay out of Winnie's business."

"Winnie's managing staff for the first time? And I don't think you've mentioned Stella."

Wendell nodded and showed Rob where Stella was in the org chart.

"Huh. Would you be able to jot down a couple impediments to Winnie's success?"

"I can do that." Wendell scribbled a note. "Looks like time's up."

Rob looked at his watch and said, "We've got a minute. There's one last piece of the results on this page. For each competency, your score is the dark blue dot. This light blue bar is the range of all of the executives here."

"Was the printer running out of ink?"

Rob smiled. "The width of the line represents the number of people at each point."

"Huh. So the thin line connecting my dot means I'm an outlier?"

Rob nodded.

The graphical representation had more impact than words. Wendell said, "I guess I might have some work to do."

"Even if you subscribe to Bloom's work, I can create a case to show empathetic-like behaviors are a neat counter to a tendency for authority."

"I guess. Send over some stuff. I have to run but Winnie can give you some open dates from my calendar. Give me a month for that list." As Rob placed his hand on the door handle, Wendell added, "Hey, you don't give HR this info, do you?"

"We give a copy to HR to share with whoever completes the survey as Boss. For you, David."

Wendell's pupils darkened and his fingers curled around the pen as he told Rob, "Well, don't."

Rob seemed as if he would say something, but instead he gave a noncommittal nod and continued out the door.

This time, the pen flew intentionally.

Stella arrived on Tuesday without her usual bracelets. Her jewelry was limited to tiny diamond solitaires and a watch. Her morning greetings lacked any invitation for conversation, and she closed her door as soon as she entered her office.

Seconds later, Heather knocked once and opened the door.

"Hi. Thanks for passing on Ellen's blueberries yesterday. I planned to grab breakfast from the conference, but it was plated so I was starving by the time I saw her." As Heather spoke, she twisted her charm necklace tight to her neck, usually a tell of discomfort. When she released the necklace to spin free, a charm caught on her sweater.

Though Stella saw the charm pull at a thread, she didn't tell Heather. Instead, she said, "Nice of her to offer them. Glad it worked out." Stella looked toward her door then, one of her tells.

Heather sat on the edge of a guest chair. "She said it was a rough time?"

"Sorry?"

"Ellen. Your feedback, rough. She said you might need some support."

Stella's laugh of surprise was harsh. "I guess it's fine she told you. It wasn't rough so much as wrong. Did she tell you Gage asked was I a lesbian and Wendell asked why I want more money since I don't have kids?"

That Heather was working up a lie was evident in her face. "Oh, wow, no. I'm sorry, Stella. Wendell can be insensitive. I told you that time he said your dedication to your job was," she made air quotes, "'a little nuts.' I think Gage has a lot of respect for you but wonders why you aren't married. They wonder the same about Frannie."

"Do you tell them that's out of line?"

Heather, using more air quotes, said, "I try to stay within the 'annoying but overall helpful' categorization. I think it's kind of nice they care, but they do go too far sometimes." She made the Cheshire cat smile she thinks is comforting and asked, "What will you do?"

Desperate for a path back to normalcy, Stella's guard came down. "What would you do?"

Heather answered the question with a question. "Wendell can be a tough one. Would you consider legal action?"

Stella looked tense and tired though it was the start of the day. "I spent most of my life protecting the Fed from having its dirty laundry aired in the public arena."

"Here. You'll appreciate this. He's gotten criticism for how he handled gender in some papers. Which is bad, but he also did some research one time that dealt with homemaker versus work outside the home. He split women into something like married women, divorced women, and widows, without ever addressing unmarried women, and then he tried to argue they were unimportant. The research died. You know if you don't do anything, he'll keep at it. And Gage we've talked about."

In the few seconds of silence, Heather realized her necklace was caught.

Stella finally asked, "Oh, no, I have a seam ripper if it would help?"

"I tell my husband to ask the salesperson whether a charm will catch before buying it, but he doesn't." She untangled a musical note. "There."

"Heather, don't tell anyone. I shouldn't have said anything but since you and I share Ellen."

"I just want to be helpful. Us PhDs can be a challenge sometimes."

Heather left with sufficient information to twist a tale. First, under a guise of concern for the Fed Bank's reputation, she asked Andrea, the new head of HR, for guidance on talking to Stella about legal action. Next, Heather caught Wendell in his office and warned him he'd gone too far in his feedback, speaking in a carefully collegial, we're-on-the-same-side way. When she assured him she'd handle it, he snapped at her and so she moved on. She shared the whole story with one of the Heads and asked if he would support her in preventing Stella from suing.

Heather was pleased at how she'd centered herself in the trouble she'd brewed.

On Thursday, Carrie came to Stella's office mid-morning. "You got by my office this morning without me seeing you."

"Not intentionally. How are you?"

"Befuddled? Lost? Gage asked me for my thoughts on promoting Hilerie to comanage with Win. I told him Hill doesn't really do anything for me so I shouldn't have a say. Stella, he accused me of downplaying what she does for me. He listed off a bunch of made-up tasks she told him she does. She's totally taking advantage of him being in LaLa Land. He said maybe if I thought, I'd remember. If he promotes Hill to manager, it's going to kill — Hi Winnie."

Winnie had come right into Stella's office, closing the door behind her. She was shaking and Carrie pulled out a chair for her as Stella joined them at the table.

Winnie asked, "Can I talk to you? I just got my hand slapped. Wendell's furious."

Though Stella's eyebrows pulled into one another with tension, her voice was gentle. "Win, just metaphorically, your hand?"

"It would have been better if he really did it. He didn't want his wife to know about one of his trips and I didn't know. Then I forgot to call Facilities. He keeps saying there's a hot spot in his conference room and sometimes in his office, but I don't know what he's talking about."

Stella reassured her. "He thinks the world of you. He'll get over it."

"He's really mad. Like this." She rose from the table, grabbed the ruler from Stella's desk, and slapped it on the edge of the table, three times. "I told him I deserved it, and he could keep this year's bonus pay if he wanted. And I told him Hill wants to be the Manager, and I wouldn't have made the mistake with his wife if I wasn't doing two jobs."

Carrie and Stella shared a look and Carrie pushed the bowl of Silver Tops toward Winnie and said, "His temper is his problem, Win, not yours."

Winnie picked up the ruler again. "I'd better get back out there."

Carrie said, "She took your ruler."

"I'll get it back. I've had it since the day I joined the Fed. Cause it's wood without the metal strip and doesn't scrape or smear when I use Flairs. Best ruler ever."

"Hill cannot get the Manager job. I know I said I didn't want it, but I want things to go back to the way they were before Wendell stuck his nose in. So, I am officially asking if I can be the Manager. Without the banking conference, I have free time. Dawn wants to take on other events and Macro promised she'll be released from FOMC within two more cycles. I was a Manager, way back."

"We'd be very lucky to have you in the Manager role here. Gosh, Car, do you remember back then, you reported to Crystal when she was the first woman in charge of Facilities?"

The two reminisced about earlier years in the Fed Bank.

Wendell knocked on Stella's door. As soon as Carrie turned the handle to open it, he pushed through. His tone was urgent. "I was just at David and Frank's meeting with the BAC, and they think we might have gone too far looking for savings when we squashed the banking conference. I'm supposed to meet with David in an hour. Do we have some data that will make the case without showing any reallocation to consultants?"

The BAC is the Committee on Federal Reserve Bank Affairs, a three-member Subcommittee of the BOG.

Carrie told him she'd send him what she'd given him before and didn't know anything about consultants.

Wendell nodded at Carrie and looked to Stella. "I got the agenda for your meeting this afternoon."

"Yes, the Conclave. Will you join us?"

"Probably. I might have free time. And do either of you know anything about Herman Cain tweets?"

Both Carrie and Stella did, so Wendell took the seat Winnie had vacated.

Carrie told him, "Someone from Bloomberg posted the Fed Governor nomination. Someone else responded that, I think it was from '89 to '91, Cain was Chair at Kansas City's Omaha Branch's Board of Directors, then starting in '92, he was Deputy Chair of Kansas City Bank's Board of Directors for a couple years, then took over as Chair of their Board for a couple years. So, Cain's defenders claimed he was a perfect fit for a Governor spot because he already did the job in KC, without realizing Governors and Directors have wildly different roles. Then one Cain defender called Krugman a dipshit because Krugman said Cain has no relevant experience. Some PhD, Justin Wolfers?"

Wendell nodded.

Carrie continued. "He was trying to explain that Cain's experience isn't what people think it is when they claim it is relevant to being a Fed Board Governor in D.C., but Cain's defenders couldn't comprehend how being on a Reserve Bank Board of Directors is in no way an indication of qualifications for being a Governor. Wolfers really tried. As far as I know, Fed Twitter stayed out of it."

Wendell said, "People should know there's a difference between Governors and Directors even if they don't know what the difference is."

Stella said, "The *Journal* had a decent article about Cain. They asked him about whether he is staying in the process. He did a good job describing the mess of paperwork needed for the Governor confirmation process and told the reporter he'd respect Powell. And he wants the Fed to link interest rate policy to commodity prices." When Stella saw Wendell's interest, she noted, "He's out though. Rejected the nomination. Claimed pay was too low."

"Huh. And there's another guy, Stephen something?"

Carrie looked at Stella and shrugged. "I only knew about the pizza guy."

Stella said, "Stephen Moore. He really wants to be a Governor I guess, but he didn't even know what the Fed was or did. And he's got a bad track record with women."

Wendell looked confused and opened his mouth.

"Mistreating women in professional settings."

"But he's still in?"

"Yep. I don't think he's got Senate support, but we'll see."

"Let me know if anything blows up on Twitter about him."

Stella and Carrie agreed.

Wendell nodded his head and looked at Carrie, then Stella. "This was helpful. I'll come to your Concave or whatever it is meeting later."

Wendell detected the damping of energy at the Conclave when he entered. He kept silent while votes for an annual training excursion were counted. Surprised a writing class beat out paintball, he shared his grandson's paintball experience.

At ten minutes before the end, the team moved to the successes and challenges go-round.

When Wendell's turn came, he claimed a meeting with the BAC was both a success and a challenge. He explained the BAC as "the couple Governors who keep an eye on the Reserve Banks."

Wendell followed Stella into her office. "Are you free right now? That was a good meeting. Different. How often is it?"

"Monthly."

"Where were Winnie and Hilerie?"

"Oh. They don't come. I invited them way back. Winnie's said she's not part of the team. Gage and Hill told me Hill was uninterested."

"Invite them again. I'll talk to Winnie."

"Will do."

"Would you put together a couple reasons why this Manager assignment didn't work for Winnie? Just the big ones."

"Yes."

"And Winnie's not having any luck finding the source of that heat by me. Do you have any ideas?"

"I'm sure she's doing everything, but I'll ask if she needs help."

"Last, I have some other news. Effective on the sixteenth of this month, your salary is increased by fifteen thousand dollars. For good work defending us from System people."

Stella tilted her head as if she was clearing water from her ear. "Thank you, Wendell. I really appreciate that."

"And Winnie said you're off tomorrow?" After she nodded, he asked, "If anything comes up with the BAC, will you be doing something we could interrupt?"

"Yes. Except for an hour."

He waited for more but she only reiterated her gratitude for the salary increase.

What she didn't tell him was she taken off to see a psychologist. Fidgety and miserable when she made the appointment, she'd explained her struggles when she failed her employer's security screening most days.

Week Twenty-nine ~ 5/13

Stella's path to her office on Monday morning was uninterrupted. Once inside, she left her light off and curled into her chair with her eyes closed, whispering over and over, "Isnotthesame." When she finally opened her eyes, she tapped the space in between just as Carrie knocked.

"Good morning. Were you sitting in the dark already? This should help." Carrie was returning from a trip to her parents' home in Florida.

Stella unwrapped a desk-size Zen garden with seashells. "I love this. Did you get your parents moved?"

Carrie described her parents' new place as Stella emptied the bag of tiny shells onto the sand. When Stella's expression turned wistful, Carrie asked, "Aren't you overdue for a real vacation?"

"Maybe Martha's Vineyard after Labor Day when rates drop. By the way, thank you for telling me to go to that pension session. I never realized what we had. I just have to be here two more years. Every time I pass the homeless on Lower Wacker Drive, I think of how quickly everything can change and am beyond grateful for the pension."

"Yes. Jake and I were talking and I think I'm going at fifty-five, but I worry about inflation, knowing who's responsible for managing it. Maybe we can find jobs together somewhere else. Wendell can make you miserable but I don't think HR would let him get rid of you."

Stella shrugged.

Carrie continued. "You reminded me. I replaced a quilt in our guest room. Are you still dropping stuff off for your homeless neighbors?"

Stella's apartment was at the intersection of the Chicago River and Lake Michigan where luxury high-rises sit next to homeless communities. "I will. I'd stopped a month or so ago. I'd been dropping a bag of food on Saturdays when I cut through to where I get my nails done and a guy started to wait for me. He wasn't coming near, but still. I'm just on edge these days and got afraid. But a book club friend was doing the same so we're going to start going together on Sunday morning. I might hang on to the quilt until September so whoever gets it doesn't have to find a place to stash it for the summer."

Carrie asked, "I'll bring it then. The big question. What the hell did Hill do? I had thirteen emails."

"The Board asked for some information and Win was off so Wendell told Gage ask Hill. When she gave the info to Wendell, he asked me to look at it. There was a problem with the columns in the spreadsheet. So Hill met on her own with the admins and blamed them for her mistake and went off about 'you guys' should have known, 'you guys this,' 'you guys that.' Even when they asked Hill to stop blaming them and Dawn asked Hill to use their names and stop referring to them as 'you guys,' Hill kept at it. Dawn went to Wendell and told him 'you guys' is racist which bothered him. Or scared him."

Carrie's nose crunched and her lips curled in disgust. "Damn it, why does Hill mess with people. She didn't used to do it."

"When Hill found out Dawn had complained to Wendell, I think she got afraid and she ran to Gage. So Gage starts making fun. Standing in the hallway with Hill and using 'you guys' and Hill pretending to cry. In the hall with Heather and Heather says 'boo hoo' and they can't do their research because he called them 'you guys.' Stunningly unprofessional. Then Gage blames it all on me for being picky about the list. So Wendell and I talked. I think he gets that even if 'you guys' is not always associated with racism, that Hill's use could reasonably have been perceived as racist, and even if she didn't mean it as racist, it was still wrong because it was being used as a divisive put-down. He said he'd talk to Gage and I talked to Dawn and now he and I are going to talk in a little while. And I'm glad you are back. Gage and Hill probably would have complained to you and you could have talked them down." Stella closed her eyes for a few seconds. "I'm grateful that Wendell didn't blow off Dawn."

"I'll avoid Hill for now. Has Wendell said anything more about me taking over?"

"Yes. Just waiting for you to get back. I'll check with him today. There's no reason to wait. You're sure?"

"Yes."

The conversation with Carrie had snapped Stella from her earlier mood. While her tea steeped, she pulled her jewelry and belt from her backpack and finished dressing.

Wendell came by mid-morning. "I'm early, is that okay? Winnie's finally got Facilities to come figure out what makes it so hot over there. You said you have some intel about 'you guys' for me? Did you talk to Dawn? I didn't get a chance yet to talk too much to Gage. It makes the most sense I talk to you first anyway."

Stella's eyes over-widened when she halted their involuntary narrowing. "Yes. Dawn and I talked on Friday. She said 'you guys' was probably the way a master would have talked to slaves, similar to 'boy,' but she also said that she didn't say it came from *Roots* and asked where you heard that. She and the others are concerned with Hill's behavior and what is Hill's official role."

Wendell nodded his head left and right, weighing the words.

Stella continued. "Here's an article from *The Washington Post*. More about 'guys' on its own, but the word's origins are derogatory. But for our purposes, 'you guys' itself is just a symptom. Dawn does about ten times the work Hill does, ten times better, makes about twenty percent less, and then Hill blamed Dawn and the others for her own weaknesses and gave feedback in a harassing manner."

Wendell stopped the nodding and looked at Stella, one side of his mouth and one eyebrow raised in doubt.

Stella continued. "And Dawn asked why we'd want her to bring her work down to Hill's level. I think she's had it and I think there's real risk to the Bank if we don't get this cleaned up."

Though Wendell wasn't at all angry, Stella shifted back when he sat forward.

"Well, we can't really control what Hilerie does. Let's talk about Winnie when we're done with the 'you guys.'"

Stella took a breath and straightened her spine. "Will you put aside the issues you have with me for a minute? I'm not going around Winnie. This thing with Hill and the other Admins could get very bad very fast. Hill's not a Manager, but Winnie was and she didn't prevent or stop a behavior perceived as discriminatory and harassing that certainly sounded like it was in fact harassing. And not only did she not stop it, she provided a forum for it. You told me I can't get involved, and I'm not, but we need to get to some fair resolution. If Dawn sues, which she well may, we have no defense. We already play with fire when expectations for Hill are so different than those for the other Assistants."

If only Stella would defend herself from Wendell the way she was defending Dawn from Hill and the organization from the risk of legal action.

Wendell's temper remained in check and his worry was sincere. "That inconsistency isn't really our problem. It's been Bankwide for a long time. Suing seems like an overreaction. She wouldn't win?"

"Gage devotes a nontrivial chunk of his workday to mocking Dawn. It's great he wants to defend Hill, but he's a Senior VP. I hear him in the hallway, his loud laugh, telling anyone who will listen how Dawn claimed 'you guys' is discrimination. I told you about Heather responding to him with the 'boo hoo' nonsense, and then just a couple minutes ago, when Heather brought over a foreign trip plan for him to sign, he says, 'you guys ask for too much,' and she said, 'you can't call me you guys, where's HR.' That two Officers are feeding off each other is absurd. If I hear it in my office, Dawn hears it in her cube. You tied my hands on dealing with Winnie, but someone's got to shut this down. And none of this touches the gender issue with the word, 'guys.'" Stella's eyes pleaded, "Will you instruct Gage to dial it back?"

After a silence, Wendell's face contorted, as if his words drew physical pain. "Gage is always loud. He just feels bad for the spot Dawn put Hilerie in. I still think Dawn might've made a big deal from nothing, and I doubt Winnie did anything out of line." Once more, his eyebrow and one side of his mouth drew up in skepticism.

When Stella failed to legitimize his statement, he continued. "So you're not going to let me off the hook. Why don't you talk to Winifred and Hilerie to explain your concerns? Not too complicated, though. And work up some proposals for getting Winnie out of that job? I'll catch up with Gage."

"Remember we talked about Carrie stepping in. She is ready right now."

"Okay. I'll talk to her."

"And Wendell, when we talked about Herman Cain, you asked me to let you know when Moore's fate was figured. I guess he was still saying he was going to get the nomination after the Senate pushback, but then Trump tweeted that Moore withdrew. And called Moore a fine person and said he'd find something else for Moore to do. I guess he was one of Trump's, and Cain's for that matter, campaign advisors. I read Moore had some pretty backward ideas, like getting rid of child-labor laws. The Library's news brief lists some articles."

"Sounds like a screwball. So Trump's only added just the S&R guy, Bowman, and Clarida?"

"Quarles is the S&R guy. Yes, plus Trump kept Powell on. So four of the five existing Governors were nominated by Trump and there are still two vacancies."

"I thought you said you didn't keep track."

"I always try to know who Governors are."

After he left, she set up a breakfast date with Winnie and Hill.

A few minutes before the breakfast date on Tuesday morning, Winnie asked Stella to reschedule to lunch because Hill was waiting on a call from Gage's wife. Winnie asked could they still go to the same restaurant. Across the street, it was a long-time outpost for many staff conversations.

At 11:45 a.m., after Winnie told Hill where they were going, Hill unwrapped her hands from her waist, extended them straight, and exclaimed, "Oh, I hate that place."

It was a hard place to hate and though Stella seemed to suspect that Hill was playing a game, she agreed when Winnie and Hill decided on McDonald's.

Turned out McDonald's had no open seats and their revised plan to eat in a nearby plaza was thwarted. When they entered Wendell's conference room, their shoulders were dotted with the unpredicted raindrops.

Once settled, Stella began, "So Wendell asked me to meet with you about last week's admin staff meetings. I understand the phrase 'you guys' was being used to address — "

"I talked to Wendell and Hill talked to Gage. The women are being too sensitive. They should worry so much about their jobs."

Hill followed, "Bah. Gage says they are being ridiculous."

Stella explained management's responsibility to prevent even the appearance of harassment. She explained why the use of the term was concerning and gave five examples, two humorous and three serious, of ways 'you guys' may offend others.

Finally, Hill said, "I say 'you guys' all the time to my daughters. There's nothing wrong with it." Hill set down her burger and crossed her arms. "Pshaw, I can't stop saying it. Gage said it's harassment to tell me what to say."

"But if something alienates a coworker, why not skip it?" Stella was losing her patience.

Hill continued. "I'm not their coworker."

Stella seemed to give up on coercing Hill when she declared, "But we all work for Wendell and he's saying stop using 'you guys.'"

As they left the room, Hill rolled her eyes at Winnie and Winnie shook her head. Away from Stella, Winnie said, "Hilerie, they mean it. Just don't say it."

Hill flicked one eyebrow in response. "We'll see."

On Wednesday morning, Ellen told Stella she'd returned from another trip to the BOG. "My husband just realized who I'm working with and is impressed. He's a neurologist. He knew I had government clients, but he didn't know you are the Fed with capital letters."

Stella rose to pull a couple pages from a stack on her desk. I was surprised when instead of reminding Ellen the Fed Bank was not a government organization, she said, "Hey. I have a question for you about the Board. In Michelle Bowman's welcome for a *Fed Listens* event, she explains why the Fed is doing the listening tours and said, 'For many decades there was a sense at the Board that the public wasn't interested or even willing to dive into the complexities of monetary policy. That view has changed in a fundamental way especially in the aftermath of the financial crisis when it was urgently important that the public understand what we were doing. So we began explaining as accessibly and as clearly as we could what we were doing and why. Now we are listening carefully.' Ellen, does Board staff ever talk about using 'Board' versus 'Fed System.' I thought her attributing the 'sense' to just the Board was odd."

"I don't know, is she in RBOPS?"

"She's the community bank Governor."

"I probably shouldn't reveal their secrets. And we need to talk about you. I tried to get the rest of the feedback from Gage but he said you'd be leaving soon. He's excited that you're looking at opportunities in S&R. Why didn't you tell me?"

"Pardon?"

"He said you have some exciting opportunities in Supervision and Regulation."

"No. Back after the Great Financial Crisis, I was asked if I was interested but I stayed here. I'll have to ask him what he's thinking."

Ellen made a note. "Let me talk to him. Have you thought more about the original feedback from Wendell and Gage?"

"Not really. I'm committed to the work of the Bank and the System. Engaging with them on whether I'm a lesbian and why I've not borne children would be an energy-sucking endeavor. They have the power, I get that. I just want to be fairly compensated and do right by the Fed and you said they are happy with my work."

"Lesbian, who said you were a lesbian?" Ellen looked as if Stella had asked if she salted her granddaughter before she ate her for breakfast. "I never said anything about anyone asking if you were a lesbian. I said Gage asked were you happy. Happy. Happy is what I said."

Stella's expression turned cold, her eyes like flint. "Ellen, you said Gage asked was I a lesbian, and we talked about my niece and your daughter and their struggles in the workplace."

"We were only talking about our families. Heather mentioned you told her something about being a lesbian after the two of you argued about a summer fellows program."

"Interesting. I made a mistake when I was upset and shared the feedback from you with her but I didn't know we argued. She took over selecting fellows from the women and minority programs the Fed works with. I would really like for them to offer at least one of each year's summer fellow spots to a Black American PhD student. That's what she talked to you about?"

Ellen began to fidget, opening and closing her notebook, capping and uncapping a pen. "Yes. About you bringing up the fellows. She said they hired minorities whose work aligned with staff. She wasn't sure why you keep bringing it up."

"If none of our staff's work aligns with areas of interest to Black students, there's probably something bigger wrong. Ellen, I'm sorry. Could we end early? I'm not feeling well. I'll send you an email to set up our next meeting."

After Ellen left, Stella pulled a small bag of oyster crackers and a can of Coke from her desk drawer as the gravity of the gaslighting settled in her stomach.

On Thursday, when Stella arrived for their meeting, Wendell finished chewing his lunch as he motioned toward his table with one hand and slid his sandwich tray to the trash with the other.

She asked, "Did they fix the temperature?"

"Nope. They're going to take the door off and look at air vents. Before we talk about Winnie, what the hell happened at ILC?"

The ILC was made up of administrative executives from across the Fed Bank and was formed years earlier to assume some of the Fed Bank's Executive Committee's tasks. Stella was a founding member.

That morning, its agenda included an annual review of the Fed Bank's quarterly performance metrics. Though the individual areas' metrics were as dissimilar as their work, committee members were expected to opine on each area's metrics and the scorecard as a whole.

Measuring the performance of a Fed Bank, or of any or all the entities of the Fed System, is quite complex and there are many expert works which study the topic and make recommendations.

I'd say the last time this Fed Bank successfully measured its performance was when we opened it according to a directive from then U.S. Treasury Secretary William McAdoo. "Buy a few chairs and pine-top tables. Hire some clerks and stenographers, paint 'Federal Reserve Bank' on your office door and open up."

That it's not been successfully measured since is not the fault of Stella and her colleagues, but a function of the complex nature of a Fed Bank. Nevertheless, they try.

For this Fed Bank's scorecard, Payments staff measured the level of payments processed, related revenue, and progress on initiatives to update the U.S. payments infrastructure. S&R reported the number of exams in which its staff participated and the number of new regulations it implemented. Central Support areas accounted for the time spent on Systemwide initiatives. Only the RD was not represented, though it once was.

Fifteen or so years earlier, before Stella was in the RD, she was tasked with identifying and implementing metrics for the RD and its umbrella areas, after the then DOR asked for her help when the RD's own executives resisted any role. At its debut, the Fed Bank's scorecard received great fanfare and included three metrics from the RD.

The first measured the RD's support for the President's role in FOMC. Each quarter, the President would check a box, "yes" or "no." But the then President quickly tired of the form and questioned its value since any complaints about FOMC would have been made and resolved in real-time. The metric was eliminated after two quarters.

The second metric intended to capture the success of the RD's conference program. But revenue had no relevance for the RD, where even cost-recovery was rare. Nor did attendance, when many events were exclusive, invitation-only. Stella and the then DOR settled on adding a question to the existing post-attendance conference survey. "Was the conference a worthwhile use of your time?"

When the question was introduced to the RD's executives, Wendell laughed heartily. "Who in their right mind would not rather be at a conference eating a fancy lunch than at their job? What wrong-headed bone-headed strategy person came up with that?" Each time he said "head," he'd jabbed his own head forward. Neither Stella nor the then DOR acknowledged his criticism. Wendell didn't know Stella well back then, or he would have guessed the question to be her creation and their current conflict might have been foretold. Responses to the survey question were used until David prohibited attendee surveys altogether.

Finally, a third metric measured the success of the PhDs' independent research. It was the only one ever of interest to the Heads. The measure aggregated the number of times each PhD's research was cited by a high-quality PhD colleague in a top-tier economics journal.

Much time was given over to whether the metric should cover all papers of current staff or all papers ever published in the Fed Bank's working paper series, or whether it should be in the form of an absolute change or a moving average or a ratio based on the number of PhDs, and how high-quality colleagues and top-tier journals would be defined. The debates became tiresome and finally, just a few years earlier, Stella suggested the measure be dropped since it wasn't a factor in any decisions.

The ILC's members didn't think the RD's lack of measures was a battle to pick. Except for the member from S&R. Each year, when the ILC discussed the metrics, he asked why the RD was excluded. While he couldn't prevent the RD from siphoning dollars from his area's budget by claiming the RD's independent research would benefit S&R, he could and did try to make the RD more accountable. And each year, Stella explained the cost of preparing the metric exceeded any benefit. Once the exchange was had, Stella and her S&R peer put their difference aside.

Were you to think monetary policy lacked any accountability, I'll note that the success of monetary policy is judged formally semi-annually when the BOG Chair provides testimony and written reports to both the Senate Committee on Banking, Housing, and Urban Affairs and the House Committee on Financial Services. And informally whenever elected officials take an interest, either as a representative of you or for their own interests. Its accountability ultimately is to you though.

The ILC met in the BOD's room, one of the quietest places in the Fed Bank. Quite posh, with its marble-topped table, deep carpet, fancy artwork, leather chairs, and state of art technology.

At this ILC meeting's start, David announced Gage was the new in-meeting advisor from the Executive Committee. Gage pulled an empty chair around the table to join the ILC's Chair on a short end of the table. David, catching Stella's eyes, told the group Gage was not representing the RD and they should continue to rely on Stella for all things RD.

Gage mostly remained silent and was mostly ignored by the others up until Stella began to respond to her S&R colleague about the RD's lack of metrics.

Gage cut her off and said, "Since I'm here, that should be directed at me. But first, would someone explain the existence of that elephant?" A stuffed elephant sat in the center of the table.

Members from Central Support tripped over one another to answer in an inevitable dynamic of having an Executive Committee member in the room.

Reference to an elephant in the room was common in the Fed System, but unfamiliar to Gage. The HR executive, Andrea, told her Central Support colleagues she'd take over. "Okay, Gage. See, you all have these issues that are big and you all ignore them. You talk about all the insignificant stuff but not the big stuff. I'll come right out and say this. The elephant at this moment is the Research Department's exclusivity and claims on resources. See, I understand what you all are doing up there with that research and why you get special treatment, but not everyone here does. So the elephant is here to remind us to talk about the big, complicated stuff, like why Research is living a different life spending their big dollars without ever accounting for what they do with them." Though new to the Fed Bank, Andrea already appreciated the stature of the RD.

Gage responded by giving "an account of one of my many travel adventures." He, his wife, and his son had ridden elephants on one of their trips.

Finally, his tale ended, and the Chair reminded him of the metric for independent research.

Gage said, "Of course we should be represented. As Andrea said and Stella should have, monetary policy is the most important task of a Fed Bank. Here, let me have your elephant. I'll call it out." He wrote, "indie research metric," on the side of the elephant with his pen.

The others, except Andrea, looked to Stella with eyebrows raised. She offered the slightest shrug, before reiterating why the RD would not submit a metric.

Gage cut her off once more, "I probably know more about research-y things than Stella. Of course, we'll want our rightful place on the dashboard."

The Chair thanked Gage for his contribution, the act of obeisance an artifact of the culture. The Chair also said, "Stella will follow up and report back."

When the ILC meeting had ended, Gage sped to Wendell to complain about Stella. Wendell was much less concerned with Stella than the prospect of the restored metric. He quickly emailed David, copying Gage and Stella, and received David's blessing to inform the ILC Chair that no metric from the RD would be forthcoming.

When she saw the email flurry, Stella responded, "Took care of it already."

Since Gage had scurried upstairs to tattle, he'd not heard the conversation that erupted. The S&R executive joked about it being his role on the committee to raise the issue, but the discussion was more important than having an actual metric. Others asked Stella for "the deal" with Gage. When she had asked to be left off the hook for the metric, she was, and Andrea committed to putting the elephant through the laundry.

After telling Wendell a bit of that, she finished, "Lots of time wasted on this. Gage probably needs some time to get used to the group, and the group to him. It might be helpful if there were a few sentences to formalize the intent of his advisory capacity. For him, me, and the others."

"Okay, maybe. Thank you for watching out for us today."

Winnie knocked then. "Wendell, David wants you downstairs."

He told Stella, "I think I know what this is about, If I'm not back quickly, we'll have to wait to talk about Winnie when I get back after Memorial Day. But Carrie can take over now. But don't mess with her. Let her figure it out."

He was gone before Stella could speak.

A RABBIT HOLE: THE RIVER

Two Business Economists from Regional discussed the newly opened Riverwalk East, a section connecting the Riverwalk at Michigan Avenue to the Lakefront. One lived in Stella's neighborhood, and he'd attended the dedication of the section's memorial for the WWII submariners who'd traversed the river.

He drew Stella into their conversation when she passed by. They talked about the building rising adjacent to the memorial. It would be the third tallest in Chicago. Stella blamed its weight for her shattered floor-to-ceiling window. They wondered, knowing the neighborhood was built on waste, including radioactive waste from the Lindsay Light Co. of my time, whether the Lake will eventually reclaim their neighborhood.

While the three concluded the Riverwalk was a wonderful new feature for tourists and residents alike, they wouldn't ever eat at its cafes. Their reason was the same as why the Chicago River to me remains the place of horror it was in July 1915.

Drizzle fell from a grey sky when Everett and I woke the morning after dinner at Aunt Edna's and added to the tiredness I felt from my approaching due date.

Kellogg's 40 percent Bran Flakes had just been introduced, and the sample boxes we had received seemed a perfect breakfast for the sluggish morning until we tried them.

We dressed to search for a heartier breakfast that would complement the weather, and as we walked away from the apartment, we made plans to finish our packing that afternoon.

As we neared the Clark Street Bridge, I called out, "Look Everett, a boating party. I wonder what they celebrate."

A gentleman who heard me told us it was a work outing for the employees of the Western Electric Company's Hawthorne Works factory. "The employees' families, also, of course. My son, his wife, and my grandchildren are on the boat, and they'll picnic down the shore. Twenty-five hundred she can hold. We've come to see them off."

Together, we watched the gangway taken up to the cheers of the partygoers and cheered when a man successfully jumped to the boat after the gangway had been taken up. His landing is seared into my mind and reminds me a joy or sorrow is only true after it's happened.

The sounds of the party vanished when the ship's rocking sent everything up top sliding from side to side and the partygoers sought a stronghold. As we and the informative gentleman and his wife looked on in horror, the rocking stopped and the ship leaned until it lay on its side. Some partygoers slid right off into the water while others trapped inside screamed in terror.

I placed my hands on my belly as if I could cover the baby's ears and extended my fingers to curl around the jacket and hat Everett pushed at me. When he bent to remove his shoes, I said, "No, Everett, the baby. Please stay here. We'll help them when they come from the river."

"I must, Lucy." He held my face in my hands and my eyes with his own. "Stay here, please Lucy, no closer? The baby shouldn't be any closer to that water."

The malevolence of the river's fetid air was tangible. I brought my hands from my belly up to quell the nausea of fear, so different from the nausea of pregnancy. "Be careful. Come back to me."

He moved rapidly down the riverbank and called to a young woman who was flailing in the water mere feet from the dock. "Here, I'll help you here." As she paddled toward him, her mouth opening and closing in silent calls for help, he kneeled and stretched as far over the side of the dock as possible. "Catch my arms."

Finally, with their arms interlocked, he began to draw her onto the dock. But a man, conspicuous for the hat still on his head, swam up behind her and grasped the peplum of her dress. It seemed he would create a train but instead he pushed the woman down to lever himself up toward my husband.

My husband's body was so tense he was barely able to bite off words to admonish the man. "Let loose of her, sir. You are next."

The man's head was above water because he had rested it on the woman even as her grasp on my husband loosened.

At my husband's words, the man's eyebrows first shot up in surprise but then quickly pulled down in anger. "Just woman. I am Manager."

By then, one of my husband's knees overhung the dock. When the man gripped the woman's shoulder to push her down once more to gain the counterforce to reach my husband's shoulder, he instead pulled my husband into the slimy water. The man began hollering anew. My husband tried to reach the woman as she floated away.

Other men had come down to the dock to help, and with Everett's help from the water, the men pulled out the unconscious woman. They helped Everett next, but when they saw Everett walk in my direction, one of them yelled, in a harsh voice. "Stop. Don't touch her."

When Everett turned back in fright, the man's voice gentled. "It's the river water. Bathe in the hottest water possible, use as much soap as you own. Touch no one, especially not her with the babe. Go now. And burn your clothes if they can be spared."

My husband thanked the man, and we turned from the tragedy toward our apartment. I'm not sure which of us began, but we prayed out loud together the whole way because what else could we do.

The next morning, Uncle heard the Department of Health warned anyone who had contact with the river water to get a preventative anti-typhoid treatment. He took Everett to get it and afterwards, though Everett claimed health, Uncle was concerned and enlisted his and Aunt Edna's neighbors to move us that afternoon. Once we were settled in their home, Aunt Edna placed us in front of the fireplace, served us soup, and brought our books, though we set them aside when Everett sought my listening ear.

He tried to find meaning in the horror. Seeking to help someone, he saved no one, yet required assistance himself. We talked about the man, the Manager who had interrupted, and wondered did he really think his job gave him such privilege. We talked about what work would move a person to the front of any line. Everett slept then but woke ill at midnight and was soon after admitted to the hospital.

The following morning, Everett was weak and pale though the doctor knew not what was wrong. Everett borrowed hospital stationary to write an essay for our baby's commonplace book. The desperation with which his pen flew frightened me, and my worry increased when his words rang false as he told me how we, together, would paste the page in the book. The Eastland Disaster's cost of lives was so great, he said, because the regulation on the lifeboats was not well written, and there was a great lesson to learn and apply in any work our baby would someday choose but especially banking as the new Fed System created new regulations.

My grief at Everett's death had no bounds and likely hastened baby Everett's arrival just days later. Sorrow and joy fought to occupy my mind as I held our son in my arms.

A couple days later, my father escorted Everett's body back to Iowa. That night, baby Everett and I snuggled in the circus animal patterned quilt Aunt Edna made for him. As we rocked, I knew my husband was there as sure I knew his dead body was on its way to Iowa. At one point, baby Everett looked across the room and after a few seconds, his eyes grew round in surprise and their outer corners crinkled as if he were trying to form a smile. I was certain that Everett's spirit had joined us in the quiet of the night to say hello to his son and good-bye to me.

WEEK THIRTY-ONE ~ 5/27

On Tuesday morning, Adam told Stella he'd been in over the Memorial Day weekend to help a PhD who'd come in to run some programs.

She said, "I'm sorry he yelled at you. Should we remind the economists to let you know when they plan critical work on a weekend, especially a holiday weekend?"

"Wasn't critical. He was making changes on a paper that had been conditionally accepted five months ago." Adam rolled his eyes. "Five months. Did you make it out for your cousin's Memorial Day party?"

Before Adam and Sally, his wife, moved into the city, they lived in the same suburb as Stella's cousin. Her cousin threw an annual Memorial Day party, which often ended with the town's fireworks where Stella had run into Adam a couple times over the years.

"I didn't this year, I'm sorry to say. I stayed home and went for long walks and read the new Stephen King. Did you make it out to the Lakefront for Chicago's fireworks?"

"We did. They really do a nice job. I got his book but haven't read it. I have an idea for him." Adam's excitement was contagious and Stella smiled as she listened. "I came up with it while I was stuck here this weekend. Labor economist writes a paper about how people behave after they lose their job. He can't take criticism of the paper. So he finds a job where he can make people lose their jobs and finagles it so their behavior supports the conclusions in his paper. Then he can tell the criticizers — "

Stella smile turned businesslike when she said, "Good morning, Wendell."

Wendell said to Adam, "Sounded like something fun going on."

Adam shrugged.

Wendell continued on his way.

Adam poked his head out the door to be sure Wendell was gone before their laughter broke out.

Adam said, "Shit. At least he's not a labor economist."

"I get it. That's a fabulous idea for a horror story. I think you should write it."

"One of us. Reminds me. Last week, when I ran into Wendell he asked about why you and I didn't finish our PhDs. He can be a real creep — "

Wendell had returned, "Winnie's sending you an invitation for that meeting that got delayed. Bring that list."

Stella said, "Of course."

When he was sure Wendell was gone, Adam said, "Shit. Twice. I'm out of here. Catch you later."

While Stella waited at Wendell's door, the Micro Head came up behind her.

Wendell explained, "I asked him to stop over too so we can wrap up that mess with HR."

The week before, Stella had asked HR to extend a PhD job offer for the Micro Group. HR requires a couple-day window to process PhD offers. Since salaries offered to PhDs are always above the midpoint of the job's salary range, they must be explained and compared to incumbents. Signing bonuses require justification. Non-standard relocation packages, as most are for the PhDs, require explanation. Some offers are accompanied by an incentive agreement promising extra dollars if the PhD completes some specific work timely. Some include a retention agreement, promising a payment after the PhD has kept his seat warm for a specified period of time. When a candidate is concerned that monetary policy work will impinge on his time for independent research, the offer might include a commitment to restrict monetary policy work. And in cases of simultaneous offers to spouses, offers are reconciled. Some offer terms require the BOG's approval.

The week before, an offer was delayed after Andrea, HR's Officer, restructured the recruiting group on the fly, terminating the RD's usual recruiter. When Wendell found out, he sent Andrea an email ripping HR.

This morning, Wendell asked, "Is the one who got fired the one who came up with all the rules?"

Stella said, "Not at all. The rules come from FRAM." Around in some form since the creation of the Fed System, the Federal Reserve Administration Manual (FRAM) serves as a fabric over the support areas for which the BOG holds the warp, the Fed Banks the weft, and Stella and her counterparts work the loose threads.

Wendell said, "I want to talk about that FRAM in a minute. So has that offer gone out?"

The Head said, "Yup."

"Well, good. And I'll take credit for lighting a fire under HR with my semi-obnoxious email." Wendell puffed up with pride.

When Stella hesitated to respond to Wendell's claim, the Head turned to Wendell and said, "I don't know. Stella'll probably have to mop up."

Wendell puffed up more. "Not at all. Andrea called on Friday. Said she was treating my complaint like a 'hair on fire' moment and asked me to be her mentor so she can learn more about us."

The Head said, "Huh. Good call on her part. I've got a coffee date if we're done here."

After the Head left, Wendell's demeanor shifted from defensive to offensive. "That FRAM you mentioned. I heard your System buddies are shaking the dust off some old language. Why would anyone want to do that?"

"It hasn't been updated since the 1940s and charges SRAC with some coordination SRAC doesn't do nor wants to do. I'll send over the language if you're interested."

"SRAC's my counterparts."

"Yes. When David was our SRAC member, SRAC unanimously adopted a policy of bouncing anything FRAM-related down to my committee."

"You're not in charge of this update?"

"I am. It's interesting. No one owns FRAM. Board said Reserve Banks. Reserve Banks said the Board. Finally found someone at the Board who's supposed to help navigate."

"That's not really what I was looking for. We might talk more about it later. Send me that wording you're messing with. Let's talk about Winnie. Oh wait, one more thing first. Molly. I'm not one hundred percent sure how I feel about this yet but Molly reviewed my economic letter last week. She suggested nontrivial changes." Wendell saw Stella check her watch. "This will be quick."

Most Fed Banks publish at least one brief economic letter on a regular schedule. Sometimes the letters explain a current issue or a technical aspect of the Fed System, sometimes they are simplified, low or no math summaries of PhDs' work.

Stella treaded carefully in response to the whine that had entered Wendell's voice. "Did you disagree with her changes?"

Wendell expression held disdain. "The changes were unnecessary. And she's using outdated software. A Research Assistant who co-authored with me used software he'd used at school. Molly never heard of it. She's been at this a long time and might be getting too comfortable."

Stella continued to tread carefully. "She asked Adam about pricing for the Research Assistant's software and they'll share that with you. A couple folks had a trial a couple years ago and didn't recommend it. In the meantime, we couldn't publish charts made with software running on an employee's expired student license." Though Wendell's pupils darkened with anger, she continued. "We get complimentary feedback about Molly and the other editors all the time. For the Bank's pubs and for editing the economists' independent research. May I talk to her and get back with you?"

He restated his complaint in different words, and Stella shared Molly's outstanding reputation and role among the Fed System editors' community.

Though Wendell calmed down as he tapped his pen, his disdain grew. "Her System friends aren't particularly important to what we do here."

Stella's mouth pulled in worry as she sought an end to his complaints. "It's been a while since Molly's come to a Heads meeting. May I invite her for the next GAME and we could level-set on editorial service expectations?"

"That's a time waster. But ask her to prepare a comparison of software and explain her choices. I'll study that and decide if I need to grill her. I am not completely convinced that she does a good job. I might talk to Adam since he got himself involved."

Stella scratched a note to hide her reaction to the use of the word "grill."

"And one more, before we talk about Winnie, you told me you knew Judith, didn't you?"

"Most of us who've been around a long time do, plus I used to provide her with commercial banks' branch deposit holdings in one of my first jobs."

"Did people like her?"

"Sure."

Judith, as Manager, and Eliza made up a two-person team who conducted the analysis of banking markets referred to as Casework. If a commercial bank in this Fed Bank's District proposed to merge with another, Judith and Eliza studied the markets in which the banks operated to determine if the merged institution would reduce competition and hurt consumers.

When David became DOR, he'd established a "nuisance" category of work, which included the small team. Wendell formally defined nuisance work as any that carried direct accountability to the BOG. Since Casework was conducted under authority delegated by the BOG, the line of accountability was as direct as could be.

Wendell said, "I'm going to test my authority over the nuisance work. We need a new home for the FAC work. If Carrie and/or Dawn take over their meeting support, Judith and Eliza can do the analytical tasks."

Though I used all my force, he barely noticed my kick. I detested his use of that term.

When I worked here, I assisted with communications related to the newly formed Federal Advisory Council (FAC). The FAC was the first of the Fed System's advisory councils, established in the original Federal Reserve Act as an early and strong acknowledgment that the Fed System, by its nature, would need practical information from outside its walls.

This Fed Bank sent Mr. James Forgan, then President of the First National Bank of Chicago, as its representative at the FAC's first meeting in December 1914, where Mr. J.P. Morgan Jr. from the New York District nominated Mr. Forgan for FAC President.

Mr. Forgan had visited Mr. Myers in 1916 and shared his appointment to lead the Illinois' St. Andrew Society. Dating back to 1846, the Society celebrated St. Andrew's Day. Women were joining the dinner for the first time in 1916. He didn't say whether he was specifically responsible, but I hoped so.

When Mr. Forgan moved on, the FAC stopped electing a President and instead relied on a Secretary to coordinate its meetings.

A long-time incumbent in the role of Permanent Secretary was from this District and he'd asked the BOG for help with arranging the FAC's meetings and preparing economic reports.

The BOG asked that this Fed Bank provide the support and it fell to the RD. When then DOR Michael shared the decision with the Heads in the RD, they debated the reasons why any Fed Bank would want involvement beyond naming its FAC member and also whether the BOG still needed the FAC. Finally, when the complaining went on too long, an irritated Michael told them they were becoming too distant from the very essence of the Fed System that employed them. There was pouting. Honestly. Then there were fights amongst the RD Heads about which of their Groups would designate a Research Assistant to provide the support. Eventually, after an assignment was made, the work became routine, and the FAC fell from attention. Until now.

Stella told Wendell, "I'll ask Dawn and Carrie, but once FOMC has been lifted from Dawn and Carrie's settled as Manager, I think they'll be happy to provide support."

Wendell said, "Don't tell anybody yet. I need to talk to Ted and make sure he gets Judith on board with taking on the analytics part." He congratulated himself. "Lumping Casework and FAC analytics makes sense."

Stella said, "Judith may want to keep Eliza as Casework and have the new person for FAC. Casework is under Board governance and this FAC work is accountable to a Secretary who's not a Fed employee."

Wendell laughed. "Interesting. You'd sort by governance. I'll sort by nuisance level. And she doesn't get a new person. That spot is going back to support PhDs like it did before the work got dumped here." He picked up his coffee cup as if he might return to his desk but settled back. "Let's get to this bit about Winnie before I have to go."

Stella spoke carefully. "First, I want to say it's pretty cool that you were able to build up her confidence and convince her she could be a Manager and then gave her the opportunity. She'll always have that, and the confidence that she could do it if she wanted. So I don't think she failed, I think she just wasn't set up for success."

Wendell nodded.

Stella continued. "I think there are two main reasons why it went wrong. One, she never really wanted to do the work of a Manager or deal with the Assistants. Sometimes new Managers get a new perspective or boost that gets them started off right, but she skipped out on training, she never met with the outside mentor we got her, so there was nothing to push through her discomfort in the role. So I think we got to this point because she decided having a Manager title wasn't worth that much change."

He tilted his head in partial agreement. "Okay. Two?"

"Win doesn't have a lot of empathy for her staff and empathy's key to managing."

Wendell jumped forward in his seat, overcome by sudden anger, his pupils dilated and his breathing sped up. He held his arms away from his body and sat up tall, making himself larger. Then he picked up a pen the way one picks up an icepick and stabbed his stack of paper as he made points. "Empathy? You have an empathy problem, but you're an Officer. People complain about you — "

Stella straightened her shoulders and the furrow between her brows deepened as she looked at her notes. "Could we finish talking about Winnie? I did not say she is a bad person or unsympathetic. She and I have worked together for years and were friends until all this weirdness where you put rules around how she and I interact. She gets no enjoyment or satisfaction from being a Manager. She can be judgy and it prevents her from meeting the Assistants where they are. I think you've heard her make fun of Joanie for her doctor appointments." When he didn't respond, she looked up. "That's it. If we're talking about me now, I don't know who you are talking about when you say people complain about me. Would you please provide some examples?"

Wendell's pupils were a void as he slammed a fist on the table so hard his coffee swished over the side of his mug onto his legal pad. Even louder than before, he said, "You don't know anything about Winifred." When she didn't respond, he continued. "I think you're judging. Always sticking your nose in. Have you ever even worked with Assistants before? What the hell?"

Cowering with fear, Stella failed to appreciate he'd accused her of his actions. She pushed back as far as she could in her chair as she drew her papers to her chest and picked up her mug.

When he saw that she was preparing to leave, he stopped for a beat then said, "We'll have to finish this later. I've got to go."

She opened her mouth, but no words came out.

Winnie was standing outside of her cube, her brow furrowed, holding her elbows. "I could hear him. Are you okay?"

Stella ignored her.

Later in the afternoon, Stella caught up with Molly, and in a voice full of apology, asked Molly to prepare the comparison Wendell had requested.

"Stella, really, don't worry, his issues with Editorial have been going on since he came here. He picks at Editorial and before you were here, before I was Manager, even tried to fire an Editor. He's the worst kind of perfectionist." Molly laughed. "He doesn't even want his typos corrected. I'm surprised he's ever published anything. This bullshit about software is nothing new, it's just payback for editing. Pay no mind. I can update a table we shared with the System."

An hour after Molly submitted the comparison, Wendell, calmed and carrying an open bag of chips, came to Stella's office to report

that "grilling was mandatory," and asked her to set up a meeting with
Molly for yet this day or the next.

Stella's fear was no less than when in his office.

A short while later, Wendell stepped into the conference room
to pick up a copy of a research paper he'd left earlier. When he felt
warmth, he moved his hand along the wall and looked around the
room with suspicion.

He hollered for Winnie and told her to place her hand on the wall.

Though obvious she didn't feel any warmth, she noted a possibility
of a draft. "I think they are changing to air conditioning. It's such an
old building, Wendell."

He wiped at the beads of sweat on his upper lip before placing
his hand on the wall once more only to yank it back. "Call Facilities
again. Ask them if I have to call them to get this wall opened up to
see what's in there. Maybe it's a pipe getting ready to blow. And while
they are here, have them put in one of those buttons that calls Law
Enforcement."

"You mean 911?"

"No, our Fed Police. In case someone comes in here and threatens
me."

Winnie didn't hide her confusion. "Threatens you?"

Wendell's tone was insulting. "Yes. Like when there's a threat. You
press the button and the guns come running. Andrea told me her old
company had someone come back with a gun. Haven't you ever seen
them?"

"We have the secure doors in the hall so we could take away
door access if you're worried about someone. I could send an email
tonight." She was pleased at the ready solution.

"Anyone could snap. Judith, Stella, Frannie. We can't lock them
out. Yet." He thought for a moment on how to get Winnie on board.
"You could use the button too."

Winnie said, "Me? I'd run."

David popped his head in the conference room. He'd been on the floor visiting Randy.

"Winnie, how are you?"

She answered quickly and then left.

Wendell asked, "So David, how goes it?"

"You know Wendell, all these months and now I understand Payments and S&R and Central Support, but I still don't care. Especially Support. Why do I have to understand anything more about the budget than how much I can spend? I asked them to talk to Stella about her way of presenting it. She always got right to the point."

"David, come here. Don't you feel like there's some heat over here?"

Instead, David focused on the direct doorway. "Is this supposed to be like the Chair's door? Randy told me about it. A little over the top, huh?"

Wendell's breathing was heavy when he told David he had to go.

Before Wendell left that evening, he looked in the wardrobe in his office and double-checked his door locks.

That Wendell listed Stella as someone who might sneak a weapon through Security was painfully ironic on Friday morning when she hurried from the elevator to her office only to sit in the dark, rocking, repeating "Isnotthesame."

When her breath slowed and deepened, she touched her chair, desk, the buttons on her sweater, and looked at her Fed Bank ID. She pulled jewelry from the pocket of her jacket and set it on her desk. After she scraped her hair into a plain ponytail, using one of the ten-for-a-dollar emergency ponytailers she kept in her desk drawer, she tied a heavy black shawl around her shoulders.

She ignored the first knock at the door but answered one a half hour later.

Adam said, "Call HR. I couldn't stand that every day."

Her voice was shaky. "You were there?" On routine mornings, Adam entered the Fed Bank a few minutes later than Stella. This wasn't the first time he'd been behind her in the security line and told her to call HR.

"Yes. That's not right, Stella. You're just trying to come to work. And it's what, the third time this week?"

"Yes. Silver lining is I'm saving a bunch of money. I don't go outside during the day anymore. Not even to Starbucks for hot chocolate."

He ignored her attempt at humor. "It's relatively new though. Is it all the new guards they hired?"

"I think the new guards aren't helping, but they're just doing their job. I have titanium surgical clips in my pelvis. They aren't supposed to set it off." She lightened her tone. "But I lost about fifteen pounds and maybe the clips are closer to the surface now. Vicious circle. If I can't get to Starbucks for hot chocolate, I lose weight, making me more likely to set off the detector and less likely to ever leave the building for hot chocolate."

"Call HR."

"Yeah. I really can't go through that every morning. And I'm not yet at the magic age."

"Call HR."

"Thank you. Did your daughter get that role?" Adam's twins were studying film in college and his daughter had gone on an audition.

"She did. We're so proud. Her mother's influence clearly."

Stella kept the shawl tied over her shoulders though she looked uncomfortable when she and Molly joined Wendell for the grilling. That Randy passed by as Wendell began was serendipitous.

From the hallway, he asked, "Uh oh. No one in Editorial is resigning, are they?"

Wendell responded, "No, I'm just curious to learn about my people. Well, and my friend Larry was telling me about the editorial business at his bank. Just comparing public to private."

Randy could see there was tension and half-joked, "We can't get better. Let's leave our guys alone."

Wendell relaxed a little and shrugged. "Join us."

"Can't. System call. I wanted to make sure you saw the special memo assignments."

Wendell said he had and Molly thanked Randy for his kind words.

Stella relaxed when Wendell said to Randy, "One meeting and I'll get back out of their way. A little grilling doesn't hurt."

Wendell was sincerely curious and Molly her super-competent self. The meeting ended when he said, "Well, seems on track but keep me informed. I'll keep checking in from time to time. We need a GAME discussion about our in-house pubs soon and maybe you'll have some input."

Stella asked Molly might she buy her coffee and the two went to the cafeteria.

After she returned, Stella seemed more herself than she'd been all morning. She dialed into a RAOC conference call. One agenda item was the update to FRAM.

The section Stella told Wendell hadn't been touched since 1945 noted the establishment of SRAC in 1944 as a "medium through which the research work of the System could be integrated into a System program in the interest of more comprehensive and vigorous research work and unity of action in the discharge of the System's responsibilities as a national organization." It also noted a need for SRAC to "be kept informed of the principal research activities of the Board and the Federal Reserve Banks, and to that end it has been suggested that, whenever any Reserve Bank contemplates undertaking a project that is more than regional in its scope or a project that will utilize services outside of those of its regular staff, the matter be brought to the attention of the chairman of the System Reserve Advisory Committee before the work is undertaken or any commitments are made with respect to the employment for this purpose of additional research personnel."

Decades have passed since this or other Fed Banks considered or adhered to such a requirement. Stella and her colleagues noted the symmetry of FRAM, with its current, specific rules for Fed Banks' HR departments and relics of a long-ago past for Fed Banks' RDs to the BOG's current lines of sight into the Fed Banks' HRs and RDs. Stella and a few of her peers who'd also been around a very long time laughed uncomfortably when they wondered were there other relics that might be used someday by the BOG to curtail their independence.

Week Thirty-seven ~ 7/8

I'd last passed through the Great Hall over one hundred years ago. My desperation to know if my husband was stuck the way I was but in the hospital room where he'd died released me from what holds me here. Not having been in this form for long, I'd forgotten and worried over streetcar fare as I left the building. That was the last time I forgot.

There were many like me there in the hospital. I'm grateful he wasn't one. I hurried back here, drawn by my baby's commonplace book.

On this Monday, I was driven through the Great Hall to the Fed Bank's entrance by concern for Stella.

I paused at the E-Floor. Its plush carpet, elegant seating areas, and fresh flowers create an atmosphere unlike anywhere else in the Fed Bank, but it is the four-story atrium that causes most staff to adopt a hushed tone. The Fed Bank's original marble columns extend upward to a space lit by chandeliers and bordered in gold-tone embellishment, reminding me of the commercial bankers who saw the same when they carried hope and desperation to the teller window in 1914. But when I looked down to the dark marble in the renovated Great Hall, I was reminded of the choices people make when they are allowed to choose change for change's sake over change for either form or function.

As I approached the automated revolving doors that divided the Great Hall from the vestibule, they turned. A nearby Law Enforcement Officer, seeing no person, frowned in surprise.

The vestibule is covered in the same dark marble as the Great Hall.

The outermost revolving doors turned manually at a steady pace as they emptied staff into the lobby. Some staff stopped at a station to empty their pockets into plastic trays while others continued on to what looked like the starting gates of a horse track.

The bright blue of Stella's belted linen shift dress was a surprise after years of black or grey dresses, skirts, or pants. Later, when Molly complimented the dress, Stella would say it was old, from a long time ago, pulled from the back of her closet because it had no buttons or zippers that might set off the metal detector.

Stella placed her backpack on a conveyor belt, held her Fed Bank ID up to a square plate on the gate frame, and stepped into a gate. When a tone sounded and a light above her flashed, she froze.

The Law Enforcement Officer who blocked the gate picked up a billy club and held it horizontally, pushing it to the side. "Over there."

Her inhales and exhales were too even and her eyes were unfocused as if she was willing herself away.

He asked if she had a phone.

He pointed the stick toward her bracelet, an elasticized strand of chunky turquoise. She told him it had no metal and he said didn't matter. She pulled it off and handed it to him.

Next came the barrette that secured her hair in a twist. She told him she had metal inside her and removing her barrette wouldn't help. He said they'd have to see. While most of her hair fell down, the sides stayed in place where she'd sprayed wisps.

He looked at the gate and she passed through it in reverse.

After a second's hesitation, she stepped forward. His eyes moved between her chest and the light above her and when it flashed, he motioned her to the side space.

"Arms out." He drew the stick from her neck to her knees, moving it in and out along her profile. When he swirled the stick, she turned and stood, arms raised and legs spread. Her eyebrows pulled together creating a single, deep furrow, and her eyes emptied as if she'd vacated her body.

"Okay. Off to work."

She moved to the end of the conveyor belt and startled when the guard stepped around her to give her the bracelet and barrette. In an unfamiliar voice, she thanked him.

Those who had been behind her in the screening line had moved to a different gate and already returned to pick up their belongings from the conveyor belt, pushing her bag into a corner when they pulled their bags over hers. When she grabbed hers, its shoulder strap caught in the rollers, and when she yanked it, the strap tore.

She entered the Great Hall hanging on to her backpack and bracelet with one hand, her barrette and belt with the other. She bore little resemblance to the confident woman who'd walked through the columns just minutes before.

Adam waited at Stella's office. "Did you ever talk to HR?"

"I did not. I hadn't set it off for a few weeks and thought they fixed the settings or something. Taking off jewelry and stuff is nuts."

"I forgot my keys in my pocket this morning and that didn't set it off. You should get an ADA exemption."

She sighed. "Your words, HR's ears. I'll call. Thank you."

"Don't thank me, just call. It's traumatizing me to see you go through that to come to work."

After Stella logged in, she opened a meeting invitation and typed a message to Sarah, an Employee Relations Specialist.

Stella neither heard the faint knock nor saw her door open just enough to fit Winnie's face. But she jumped at Winnie's whisper. "Adam said you are busy. Are you on the phone?"

Before Stella could form words, Winnie sat at the table. "Wendell's got ideas again."

From behind her desk, Stella asked, "What ideas, Win?"

Winnie told Stella how Wendell had offered her help to David's new Assistant. "I didn't spend that much time on being a Manager and my plate is already full. He doesn't realize I help Hill when I have time."

Stella shook her head. "How's this gone so wrong, Win?"

Confused, Winnie didn't respond.

Stella was firm but gentle. "Win, I can't help you with this. Plus I need to look at Gage's presentation right now."

"Oh, okay." Winnie took two Silver Tops and left.

Wendell asked Stella to join him in Gage's office.

He rubbed his hands together in a scheming fashion. "So, are we all set?" He referred to their annual strategy session with Frank. Each summer, each Executive Committee member met with Frank to review their current year's budget, spending, and performance and next year's budget and plans. Stella and Gage would join Wendell for their meeting later this morning.

For as long as Stella had been in her current job, she'd prepared the RD's presentation, using a template provided by Marilyn, the long-time coordinator of the sessions. Until this year, when Wendell reassigned it after Gage claimed the presentation was follow-on to the work he'd already taken from Stella.

She reminded Wendell and seemed to be searching for words to tell him more but stopped at his look of disgust.

Marilyn had called Stella the week before in frustration and Stella provided an ear for Marilyn and Marilyn comic relief for Stella. Marilyn knew her role critical to the annual rounding of the Fed Bank, including the RD, back into the Fed System, but Gage tried to convince her to embrace her shame.

Trying to extract the presentation from Gage had made Marilyn sentimental for the pissing contests, when David, as DOR, grew resentful of the annual moment when he was accountable to Frank and Frank lost patience with David's unwillingness to cooperate.

But this year, Marilyn told Stella, was unhinged. Gage refused to use the template and challenged the need for the meeting.

Stella didn't tell Wendell any of that, but her eyebrows rose when Gage told Wendell they were all set. She rattled off several items excluded from his presentation. She was most concerned that Gage excluded any mention of the likelihood the RD would exceed the RBOPS target.

Wendell asked Stella if she'd use the time until the meeting to write up what she'd just said on an index card.

When they rejoined fifteen minutes later and Stella handed Wendell three index cards, Gage tried to reassert his ownership of the process.

"Well, Stella, make sure you add a card stating that morning pleasantries are the core of a functioning society."

Though sadness flashed across Stella's face, she said, "Nope."

Ninety minutes later, the three returned. Wendell went right to Ted's office and then he and Ted went to Judith's. They didn't apologize for catching her mid-bite but waited while she closed her salad container and moved it aside.

Wendell reported Frank's concerns about a phone call from one of this Fed Bank's Class A Directors. Class A Directors represent commercial banks and are elected to the Fed Bank's BOD by a subset of their commercial bank peers. This particular Director headed a mid-size commercial bank whose recent application to merge with one of its competitors had been denied after Judith's and Eliza's analysis had shown the effects of the merger might reduce competition. Without competition, the merged bank might pay a lower interest rate on deposits or charge a higher interest rate on loans.

The Director had questioned the analysis on which the denial was based though he'd assured Frank he was concerned only for the accuracy of the work and had no wish to influence the outcome.

When Wendell finished, Judith said, "It's just a new tack in trying to get it overturned. He's already acknowledged his conflict of interest."

Wendell said, "Frank wants some talking points to get him off our back."

"We can't do that. This isn't the first time a Director failed to respect his conflict of interest. Ted, you know that."

Ted saw Wendell's expression and added, "But we could put together a general primer for Wendell, right Judith?"

"Yes."

Wendell said, "Work out a time with Winnie. I need to get lunch."

Staff came through the revolving doors wet and grumbly on Tuesday morning.

Stella stopped at a bench just inside the door to roll up her wet jacket and tuck it into a pocket on her backpack. A colleague stopped and asked, "Ah. Zipper? I quit wearing one of my jackets here because the zipper set off that contraption." The two walked together toward the gates and the colleague said she'd catch up with Stella on the other side.

Stella wore black leggings and a soft pink tunic, an outfit previously reserved for days before holidays when the building was half-empty though she usually dressed it up with a pink and black tourmaline bracelet and matching earrings. The set had been a gift from her sister who claimed it had calming powers. But on this day, her only jewelry was a pair of tiny onyx studs.

Nevertheless, the tone sounded. Her face crumpled. Without jewelry, a barrette, or a belt to remove, the screening was no less devastating as the guard required her to lift her tunic after the wand flashed near her pelvis.

As Stella struggled to answer her colleague's questions as they walked through the Great Hall, Randy walked up behind them, complaining at how the weather forecasts for the next few days had fallen from sunshine to storms like dominos.

Within the Fed Bank, Randy, as FOMC Czar, was a celebrity. Her colleague, to Stella's relief, addressed Randy. "Can't stop myself. Why did God create economists?"

Randy fake laughed but was saved from answering when a PhD joined them and said, in a flat tone, "To make meteorologists look good. Hardy har har."

In the crowded elevator, Stella seemed to be reorienting herself.

At the RD stop, the PhD went one way, Stella and Randy the other. Randy fretted that the non-local members of the Academic Advisory Council (AAC) would have troubled travel the next day.

"I hope Winifred and Hilerie are early birds today. We're probably going to have to set up some remote links."

The AAC was relatively new, formed to gain academics' insights on monetary policy and other economic issues. Meetings were semi-annual, beginning with an informal dinner at a local restaurant on a

Wednesday evening and concluding the next day after about four hours of presentations and discussions.

At 1:00 p.m., Randy went to Stella's office and handed her a note with contact information for a local AAC member's Assistant. Winnie had called in a personal day and though Hill gave him hourly updates, finally left a message that she couldn't get in either but confessed she'd been taking direction from an AAC member's Assistant who'd inexplicably ended up in charge of organizing the dinner and signed a contract committing the Fed Bank to a guaranteed minimum.

Already, three of the non-local AAC members' flights were cancelled with little hope of rebooking since they were only a state away and flew here on small planes.

"I wanted Win and Hill to cancel this dinner. How do we fix this, Stella?"

"Did Hill say if the guarantee went through our Contracts or maybe the University holds the guarantee?"

"I don't know."

"Okay. If your folks do show up, catering can prepare a dinner in one of our dining rooms." Stella had, in the past, unsuccessfully tried to convince Randy to hold the AAC dinners in-house so she now waited with one eyebrow raised. After he nodded, she continued. "So I'm going to boot this over to Dawn and Carrie for that and to get us out of the guarantee. They'll know what to do."

Randy asked Stella several versions of how they might get out of the guarantee. Though she appreciated his recognition of the risk the public would find out if the Fed Bank had to make good on the guarantee, she said, "Let me get this to them and we can dissect afterwards."

On Wednesday morning, Randy arrived at 7:30 a.m. and went to Stella's office. First, he ranted about the plastic bags that Facilities insisted he use to cover his umbrella. He and other environmentalists in the Fed Bank acknowledged the risk of the Great Hall becoming a slip and slide but preferred Facilities resume laying a rug. Second, he asked about the restaurant guarantee.

"Dawn and Carrie have it under control. I'll let Carrie know you're here. Dawn was able to trade the guarantee for a commitment to send over a couple visitors' dinners."

He exhaled and the furrow of his brow cleared. "How'd she do it?"

"Magic. She'll fill you in. Randy, would you please let Dawn and Carrie take over the AAC meetings going forward?"

"Winnie did them when David was here and when Gage came back, Wendell said Hilerie should help Winnie. Let me talk to him. Can Carrie and Dawn help me today to find out who's still coming?"

"Here they are."

In the quiet of the morning, Dawn had heard Randy's voice and picked up Carrie along the way. Randy waved his thanks to Stella as the three headed to his office.

When Hill arrived and checked-in with Gage, she learned Wendell had scolded Gage and reminded him how important were the AAC meetings. On the defensive, she caught up with Carrie and soon after, told Gage that Dawn and Carrie had taken credit for her work. Gage's nervousness jumped right to Hill, and the two agreed Stella must be behind the trouble.

On the offensive, Hill circled back with Winnie and the two invited Stella to discuss "the advisory council" at 4:00 p.m.

Though Winnie sat at Stella's table, Hill stood with her hands clasped at her waist. Hill warned Stella she had "tough" questions and then asked why their salary bands were lower than Eliza's.

Stella motioned toward the table. "Sit down please. I'm confused. I thought this was about the dinner?"

"No, you guys made a big deal out of nothing. The guarantee was just $500. Gage said we could have easily covered it." Hill pulled her hands away from one another while keeping them clasped.

"That wasn't the point. Is Gage available?"

"No, he had a session with his trainer."

"I still don't understand your question."

Winnie munched on Silver Tops while Hill explained how disappointed she was to find out her AAC work was reassigned to Dawn and how Gage assured her that her salary would be comparable with anyone supporting advisory committees.

"Since you were not here to complete urgent work, Dawn stepped in. That's a good thing. As was your calling Randy with the details. Without knowing precisely what you and Gage discussed, I'll defer discussions about salaries."

Hill added, "Gage mentioned Eliza is going to be working with an advisory committee. I'm not even in her pay band."

"Comparisons to Eliza's work or salary band don't make sense. I don't know what Gage is thinking." Stella quickly explained the FAC was the BOG's advisory council, the AAC the Fed Bank's. The former required preparation of various economic charts, the latter did not.

Hill blushed.

Winnie said, "I told you they were different, Hill."

Hill's glance at Winnie was ferocious.

Stella looked confused but tried to diffuse the anger rolling from Hill. "Even here in the Bank, hardly anyone knows about the FAC and AAC. How could you have?"

Hill recovered quickly and redirected the conversation when she saw straw peeking out from a steno pad. "Is that HR's broom pen?"

When Gage returned, Hill followed him into his office and stood at his desk, hands loosely clasped. She asked about his workout as he worked to control the shaking in his hands so he could change his shoes. He was glad Hill's day had improved though the two worried over Stella's unwillingness to assess the common elements of Hill's and Eliza's work.

Hill's confidence was restored after she'd established he'd forgotten about the AAC dinner. With a sort-of laugh, she reminded Gage she suspected Stella to be part-witch. Smiling at the fear that entered Gage's eyes, her voice was like that of a small child holding a flashlight under her chin. "That pen she uses. She'll command it to grow when it's time for her to fly home."

Gage was tired, confused, and suddenly frightened.

When Hill added, "Just joking," he didn't believe her.

The sun returned on Thursday and all of the local and most of the non-local AAC members made it to the Fed Bank for the formal part of the meeting. Dawn and Carrie kept an eye on the meeting but were happy when it came time to send the in-person attendees on their way and join their team for a Conclave.

Nudging one another, they stopped at the cart where Stella was pouring water over a tea bag and asked her, "She did it again?"

Stella pushed up a smile and nodded. When Winnie and Hill had attended their first Conclave the month before, Hill's name was drawn from the hat to lead this day's meeting. It was no surprise when Hill called in ill and was so sorry, she'd said in her message, she couldn't get to the draft agenda on her computer.

Stella took the rotating spot.

The agenda was barebones with the usual round of successes and challenges, a grammar tip, an IT tip, and news from other meetings. Stella's grammar tip explained whether, weather, and wether and she admitted to having relied on autocorrect to fix "wether" when she meant "whether" and since learned "wether" was a real word. Its definition turned the conversation first to farming, then to the best booths at the nearby farmers' market, then to how the days already felt shorter, and finally, summer vacations.

On Friday morning, Wendell stopped at Winnie's cube to say good morning. When she reminded him Judith and Ted would arrive in twelve minutes, he instead said, "Shit."

He hurried to get coffee and was two minutes late for the meeting. He didn't see Judith's upper lip curl and glance at her watch.

Judith slid a binder to Wendell and explained the tabbed sections, including a history of Casework in the Fed System, staff resources and the number of mergers analyzed for the last twenty years, and annual feedback letters from the BOG. She relaxed as his eyes grew large and round and his eyebrows rose with what she assumed interest.

When she finished, he closed the binder, tapped it, and said, "You must have a lot of time on your hands to have put this together."

With narrowed eyes, she explained she maintained the binder since she'd trained two past Presidents of this Fed Bank, staff at other Fed Banks, and her own staff.

Wendell said, "That good reputation creates a perfect place to tuck the FAC work."

Judith slid a page to each of Wendell and Ted. "I've shown Eliza and I are fully utilized. Slack is unpredictable and fully offset by our extra hours of work when mergers overlap. Also, I created this table showing the lack of connections, even conflicts, between governance of Casework and the governance of the FAC."

Wendell asked, "Hmmm. FAC is monetary policy. If there's no connection of Casework to monetary policy, how did you end up here anyway?"

Though Ted remained silent, he sat up straighter.

Judith's eyes were sharp as she rattled off reasons why Casework was located in the RD.

"That probably made sense ten years ago. Or thirty," Wendell rose and tossed his empty coffee cup into the trash. "I had a meeting with Frank this week. He might want us to get S&R involved with Casework. I don't want us to have any more to do with the Board of Directors than we have to for FOMC."

Before Judith could utter another word, Ted waved his hand and extended his arm showing her out.

She turned to Ted. "What's your role in this?"

A few doors down, Stella answered her phone. Sarah from Employee Relations apologized for cancelling their meeting and asked if Stella wanted to come to HR then.

Stella's words tumbled out. "I can tell you over the phone. I've got this problem with Security."

While Stella shut her door, Sarah said, "I know. There are a lot of people who hate it. I'm disappointed Andrea's such a fan."

"I can't do it anymore. I was assaulted when I was seventeen, and after decades without thinking of it, now I have flashbacks every time I'm double-screened, which is a lot because of some surgical clips. It's really hard for me and a horrible way to start a workday. And there's a new guard that makes it worse. He exaggerates the shape of a woman with the wand, like the shape of women in the old pin-up calendars. I can't see doing this indefinitely and I do not think I should have to leave the Bank because of this but I'm seeing a doctor and he doesn't think the flashbacks will stop unless the screening stops."

Sarah's voice held surprise and great compassion. "Oh, Stella. We can fix this. Is it just the screening or your belongings too?"

"Just my body." Stella sounded so vulnerable.

"I'll call Law Enforcement right now. Do I have your permission to tell them why you need an exemption? They'll keep it confidential."

"Yes."

"Could you bring a note in from the doctor? Just to have some documentation in place in case other staff ask why you're not screened. We wouldn't show anyone the documentation, but we'd be covered."

"Is next week soon enough?"

"Yes. Is there anything else?"

Stella's expression held wonder and her eyes shone with tears. "No, thank you. I wish I had called sooner."

Sarah's words were sincere. "I'm just glad you called before you quit."

Stella took a deep breath. In an unfamiliar voice, she said, "Oh God, thank you. It's over."

At 12:59 p.m., Andrea crossed the RD with energy and confidence in a colorful suit and high heels, a contrast to the casual Friday dress and waning Friday afternoon energy levels of the Research Assistants and PhDs.

"Greetings mentor." She went right into Wendell's office and moved a stack of papers from and took a seat on the sofa. She wasn't bothered as her skirt's fabric hiked above its lining when she crossed her legs.

As a conversation about their dogs began to idle, Wendell asked, "So what fights are on the front?"

"I'm a lover, not a fighter. Well, usually." Andrea became serious. "I'm not sure I should ask you about this. One of our long-time executives reached out to Employee Relations because of some emotional problems she attributes to our security screening. I'll probably put it on an Exec Committee's agenda, but am talking to a couple of you now and you're first since you're my mentor," she nodded her head and they exchanged smiles. "I'm feeling disadvantaged, never having worked in a company with its own police ops. I love it, but wasn't here for y'all's discussions about beefing it up for risks from staff." Something in Wendell's expression caused Andrea to hesitate, but only for a few seconds. "The complainant claims the screening gives her flashbacks of a teenage rape. It caught us off-guard."

He asked, "Pun intended?"

They laughed.

She continued. "So my staff gave her an exemption because of her long service and blah, blah, blah. Others have complained about the screening so now everybody'll be claiming they were raped. I'll back up my staff since they did what they did, but I would not have offered an exemption. If in my shoes, what would you do?"

"Did the employee prove anything?" His expression held both concentration and titillation.

Andrea shifted a little and pulled her skirt down. "We weren't planning to go there. Assume we believe her. I hoped you'd help me figure out how we'll handle the staff who see her walk right through and ask about it."

"Well, it should be all or none for screening, I think. You said long-term, but if she's still worried about something from when she was a teenager, she can't be very old."

"We have legal responsibilities under ADA. I think you'll be unhappy if she up and quits, which is what Employee Relations suspected would happen." Andrea hadn't yet had occasion to look at the demographics of the RD to see a long-term female executive of his concern could only be Stella.

Wendell made fists around the arms of his chair and stretched back into the chair. "Huh. I don't know, it's hard to say, we want to keep the building safe. Let me think on it. I'm for letting people who threaten to quit do it. Except for the PhDs who just do it when they want more money."

They were interrupted by a knock on the door.

Andrea leaned across the arm of the couch to open the door.

Winnie told Wendell he was needed in David's office.

"Got to go when Davie calls. Let's pick this up later."

As Andrea left the floor, her shoulders were slumped and her steps less confident.

The RD was three-quarters empty when Wendell returned from what turned out to be a meeting with both David and Frank. After he found Ted's office empty, he seemed happy to find Stella at her desk. After asking had she a few minutes, he pulled a chair around to her side of her desk as if they would look together on her monitor.

"Did you want me to pull something up on the computer?"

"Oh, no."

Stella suppressed her look of confusion but scooted her rear to the far side of her chair and rolled her chair until her legs were tight against the far side of the desk kneehole.

He pushed back a couple inches. "We had another meeting with Judith. She really is nuts. Do you know if this has been her only job?"

"She is not nuts. I think she was a Business Economist for the PhDs who studied banking back when understanding banking was critical to understanding how monetary policy is transmitted. Then she stood up the Casework function. She cares a lot about her work. That's all. There are others in the Bank who would be super-excited to do the FAC work. They might need training, but what a great way to make use of an econ undergrad or an MBA."

Wendell was pensive for a minute and then with a hint of surprise said, "You just gave me an idea. She threatened to retire. Thanks."

Before Stella could process what he'd said, he asked, "How do you feel about the security downstairs?"

"Same as always. We need an employee entrance."

He asked the question nine different ways, each more invasively, until her face betrayed her. Though he didn't say he knew about her exemption from screening, and she didn't say she had an exemption, it was clear he needed for her to know he knew.

"Last thing. Gage thought you might have been reaching around Hilerie and Winnie again."

"Wendell, if you mean the AAC dinner, talk to Randy. Also, I wanted to let you know that I finally asked HR about your claim that people were complaining about me. They said they don't know what you are talking about."

"What about Jessie?"

"That was twenty years ago and I'm happy to share the backstory."

"You're not happy here anyway. Figure on two more years. I'm sure there are any number of jobs. Gage is interested in pulling up a good amount of your work to put his title behind it. He's said you're talking to S&R about jobs again."

"No. That's not true. What does 'two more years' mean?" Her eyes were icy and her tone cold and flat.

He was slightly flustered. "I didn't plan on talking about this today." He hesitated, but Stella remained silent. "I did want to know if you ever had a 360."

"Of course. Lots of times, the ones we've all done and a couple for leadership conferences."

"When was the last one?"

"Oh. When we did it as a group of Research executives, what was that, five years ago?"

"I was on leave then. What did those 360s say?"

Stella steepled her fingers. "I'm not perfect, but there was never anything horrible. I have a file somewhere I'm happy to share."

Wendell was firm. "No, no, that was just a side question. Gage thinks if you are unhappy you'd be better off elsewhere in the Bank. Two years should be long enough for you to find something."

Stella's brow furrowed and her eyes cast down for just long enough to calculate that two years would get her to fifty-five and eligibility for retirement benefits. "There's a lot of that I don't understand. To the extent I portray unhappiness, it is because you are always so suspicious and critical of me and have on many occasions diminished my contributions."

Wendell fidgeted at her icy tone and sweat beaded on his upper lip. "I need to get to a dinner. We can talk more next week." When he turned back at the door, distrust replaced his discomfort.

"What happened in here? Did you get the temperature turned up in here too?"

"No."

Her exhale was audible as she pulled at her hair. "You son of a bitch."

Soon after, Adam came by to tell Stella about a Fed System IT audit.

"Thanks. It's a year out so I'll still be here. I should tell you, Wendell just put me on a two-year plan."

After Adam's shock abated, he said, "He's such an ass. I'm so sorry. Does two years get you to fifty-five?"

"It does. I shouldn't have mentioned it. I was just thinking about what will happen when we start discussing events outside of my time but he can't really put me out."

"Everybody's off their rocker. I just saw Trump is nominating Judy Shelton for Governor and at least one reporter thinks he'll give her Powell's Chair spot. I never really thought Trump would blow up the Fed until now. God only knows where any of us will be in two years."

"Thank God Trump's first picks were somewhat qualified so there weren't as many spots left after he jumped the shark."

"He said he's going to nominate Christopher Waller too. Waller might be the first Research Director to get a Governor nomination."

"Not that I think it's a good idea, but wouldn't that be great if Trump would take Wendell too. Though I don't know whether Wendell's a hawk or dove or whatever on inflation."

Adam laughed. "My God, I don't either. After all these years. None of his research dealt with inflation."

Stella had opened a search window while they talked. "This says Trump said about Powell. 'Here's a guy - nobody ever heard of him before, and now, I made him, and he wants to show how tough he is.' Trump must not remember Obama put Powell on the Board."

Adam said, "You're right. Replacing Powell with Shelton would be beyond scary. I don't get the gold standard. If we're all starving, why would I give up my last loaf of bread for some gold?"

"I don't understand that either. And why gold? Why not Jack's beanstalk seeds."

"You know, I don't even think Wendell will be here in two years. You're safe."

"I hope so. I can work with two years though. I always wanted to do something different, not that soon, but I can make that work."

Stella looked quickly through job postings in the Fed System before leaving for the weekend.

WEEK FORTY-TWO ~ 8/12

The message light on Stella's desk phone was blinking when she walked in Monday morning. As she listened, the phone rang.

When Stella heard her sister's voice, she asked Nora what was wrong. Stella rarely got calls from family and friends at work.

"Nothing. What's wrong with you?"

"Nothing. I just got the saddest voice mail though. My boss is transferring a coworker to a crappy job right when she's in the middle of a bunch of stuff at home. How are you?"

"Well, I'm worried about you. And our parents are worried. You don't answer your home phone. Mom said to call you at work from the shop so you wouldn't recognize the number."

"I knew the shop number, so there. Are you sure nothing's wrong? It's really early there." Her sister lived in the Northwest.

"Are you sick or something?"

"No. Hold on." Stella closed her door. "Nothing is wrong with me. It's just a really bad time at work."

"How can you have problems at work? Don't you run that place by now?"

"Ha, ha. Somehow everything's gone to hell. Everything I do gets criticized, spaces on a slide, columns on a table, how I greet someone, what book I have sitting on my desk. And the criticizer boss has told me if I don't find a new job, I'll be out in a little less than two years. I'm just too tired when I get home."

"Is it that guy you told me about?"

"Yeah. He's back from vacation today."

"Can you retire in two years?"

"Yes. I'll need to work somewhere else, but I'll have a pension. And I'm finally paying off debt and saving like I should have been all along."

"You'll figure this out. If they don't care about all those years, then don't you either. Why don't you just get a night job cleaning desks to get away from him now?"

"Bank contracts out for housekeeping. How are you?"

Nora said, "We bought the cottage in Michigan. I'm looking for shop space now."

In her excitement for her sister, Stella set aside the beginning of the conversation and asked was the cottage near the water, how big was it, and when her sister said it was a fixer-upper, did it have indoor plumbing.

Finally, Stella said she had to go but promised to call Nora that weekend.

Winnie, coffee and iPad in hand, came over when saw the light on Stella's phone line go off.

Stella oohed and aahed over pictures of the fall flower garden Winnie planted while she was on vacation.

But then Winnie closed the iPad cover and smoothed a Post-it. "Down to work. Wendell is back from vacation today too and wants you to explain why you got involved in the Casework business."

At the designated time, Stella waited while Wendell stood at Winnie's cube, flicking his fingers, shifting from foot to foot, almost as if he was trying to calm himself. He'd just learned that while he was away, Facilities had come to open the suspect wall, but they'd left when Hill wasn't able to reach Winnie to get permission to move the boxes blocking the wall.

He asked Winnie what flowers did one plant in the fall anyway.

All three, even Winnie, were surprised when Winnie asked Wendell what did he think Facilities would find anyway. Her spunk quickly expelled, she added, "Because their temperature monitor was there for a full seven days and didn't show anything. That's all I meant. I wasn't sure you knew."

Stella asked Wendell was there a better time for them to catch up. "No."

Stella looked as if she was being taken behind a woodshed as she followed him into his office.

Wendell wore cargo pants, a new look for him, and pulled a note from his pocket. He asked Stella to clarify the policy on reimbursing combined business and personal travel.

She reminded him Winnie had gotten an exception approval for his trip and, in a friendly tone, asked about his vacation.

He brushed off her question. "Let's start here. Somehow, you got yourself embroiled in the Casework and FAC transfer."

A month earlier, when Wendell and Ted told Judith that she and Eliza would take over the FAC support, Judith retired on the spot.

Caught off-guard and embarrassed after having told others Judith's threat was "not credible," Wendell asked S&R to absorb both Casework and FAC support. They didn't agree until David intervened, but once they did, Wendell pushed for an immediate transfer.

He claimed concerns of Judith's position being vacant even as he as cornered Ted, Eliza, Carrie, and others with his macabre fascination at how someone with Judith's background had beat him at his own game. When Carrie asked how Judith might feel, Wendell claimed she'd been planning to leave anyway.

Nikki, the S&R Officer taking over Casework, thinking David had interest in a successful outcome, was aggressive and showy in creating urgency and worried to anyone who would listen how the RD may botch the transfer of custody of files. Her behavior was unproductive though her worry was justified.

Eliza's heart broke a bit at senior management's callous treatment of the function, though she was pleased with Nikki's promises of an office and promotion to Manager.

Eliza carried the load of the transfer on top of both her and Judith's analysis for a merger application. But Eliza's quiet competence didn't produce sweat, and Nikki was the type of boss who measured effort by visible sweat.

Last week, after a day of Nikki's bullying, Eliza went to Stella's office. "I don't know what to do. Ted's out. Wendell's out. I can't talk to Nikki."

As soon as she sat at Stella's table, Eliza burst into tears. She'd been working against doctor's orders to finish the case analysis but scheduled time off right after. Nikki cancelled Eliza's days off, insisting Eliza "keep up the good work," just until the files were transferred.

Stella steered the conversation when Eliza tried to reconcile her personal sacrifice for her work in light of the Officer-created chaos and finally convinced Eliza her responsibility to the Fed System started only after she'd met her responsibility to her own health.

Stella whispered a prayer of thanks after Eliza agreed to text her husband to ask him to pick her up.

And now, in this meeting with Wendell, Stella seemed to be replaying her and Eliza's conversation in her head, though she didn't share it. "Since Ted was out, Eliza came to me. She needed to be off. So that could happen, I called S&R. Then Judith called me after she talked to Eliza who told Judith that Nikki was calling her at home. She asked me to stop Nikki. So I got that assurance from Nikki. Nikki was worried about the Casework files so we asked Legal to give Adam temporary S&R credentials and me backup temporary credentials so he could pack them and transfer custody and I could help if needed."

"You could have sent Eliza to Heather."

"Wendell, I try to tread carefully around you. Especially since you've told me I only have a job here for two years. Now minus a month. But I won't ignore a coworker in crisis. This whole thing has been so unfair to Eliza."

Wendell brushed sweat away from his upper lip. "Yeah, I might have mishandled this. Are you still talking to Judith?"

"No. I had a message from Eliza when I got in this morning. She won't be back this week. I'll relay that to Nikki."

"I should probably sic Nikki on that Director who started all this with his complaints. Frank asked for an update while I was away and I sent him to Nikki. None of this would have happened if that Director hadn't gone to Frank. When's Ted back?"

Stella's lips clamped shut and her eyebrows drew to center. She didn't remind him that "this" happened because he tried to push the FAC work onto Judith and Eliza to gain Research Assistant time for the PhDs. "Ted's been back since last week and asked I see it out since he'd not been involved."

"Tell Eliza she can call me if she wants."

Wendell's next stop was Gage's office. After Wendell reminded Gage it was his first day back from vacation, they caught up and then Wendell groused about the Casework changes and Stella's involvement. Gage said, "Stella's too smart to be doing support work anyway. Why don't you expand the Casework deal and offer Stella up to S&R too? I think giving her two years was overly generous."

"Maybe it was."

That Stella was only mildly concerned about Wendell's having set an end date on her employment was entirely due to that end occurring after she turned fifty-five. I was devastated for her at Wendell's agreement with Gage and prayed Wendell was just talking to talk.

On Thursday morning, Carrie told Stella how Gage's casual stopping by her office had evolved to regular Tuesday and Thursday chats. Though he said it was because she was now Manager of the Administrative Assistants, he asked a lot of questions about Stella. "Will you forgive me for talking about you with him? I've never bucked a Senior VP in all the years I've been here. I can't do it now."

"No worries. I get it. Luckily, there's been no Seniors like him before and probably never will be again."

"He seems to really want your job. He says Associate Directors of Research in other Banks have your work."

"That's not true."

When Wendell got in, Winnie followed him into his office to review his calendar for the day and reminded him she'd be away for a while in the afternoon for "that Conclave meeting." Her unhappiness with her turn as meeting leader was evident when she reminded Wendell, "I'm only going because you said I had to."

"Well maybe you could have a presentation by another department or skip the goofy grammar stuff. Keep it businesslike. Slip some changes in that nutty agenda. And let me know how it goes." As she turned to go, he offered, "We can go over your agenda together."

"Let me get it."

"Wait, come back after I see Gage."

Gage said, "Well, Wendell, Stella breached again. She made those commitments to talk to high schools, which I have kindly taken over from her. She's told me, an economist with a PhD, that I can't use a finlit paper in my presentation to the attendees. If we're continuing on this way, I'd ask again she report to me so I can control these absurdities."

"Huh. Why'd she say that, Gage? She'd spend all her time making high schoolers financially literate if we let her."

"Well, I'd say she lacks capacity to understand the research in the paper."

"Ask her to enumerate her concerns in an email."

As Wendell walked out, Gage tossed out a final question about whether they'd need him for Class I FOMC meetings in the next go-round.

"We'll find you work to do. When do you talk to the high school kids?"

Gage flipped his paper calendar and pointed to a date in early September.

Later in the afternoon, Winnie waved in the team for the Conclave. "Hurry up. Get in, get out."

Once they were all seated, she said she'd begin with grammar and went on to tell them she was trying something "fresh" for the grammar tip and handed around a quiz she'd found online. She'd brought a box of pencils if anyone needed one.

Being corrected and improving one's grammar was a feature of the RD's culture and, until this moment, team members were comfortable acknowledging their grammar weaknesses and amenable to spending a minute or two each month thinking about their own or others' challenges.

Winnie instructed, "There are fifteen questions. Take your test on your own for the next fifteen minutes. If you finish early, turn over your paper. No cheating. Wendell gave me tips for tests and warned me what to look for."

Most looked to either their Manager or Stella.

Molly asked, "Winnie, let's do these together. Will you lead us?"

"No. I don't want to do that."

Harry, an Editor, stood and walked to the front of the room. "I'll lead us."

Finally, it was time for the go-round of successes and challenges. Winnie said, "Just successes today. Leave the negative out." She waved her hand as if dispelling something odorous.

Adam went first. "I have a success and a challenge." All the others except Winnie followed with successes and challenges.

After the meeting ended, Stella turned to Winnie. "What was that about? I understand if you don't want to come. I know it's important for you and Hill to not be seen as a part of our team. Just let Wendell know. But Winnie, why did you do the meeting so differently?"

Winnie was rattled. "Well, Stella. You said I had to be the leader."

Minutes later, Winnie basked in Wendell's praise.

"Good job. Thanks. Did you get it renamed to Cabal? Or Calamity? It's such a stupid meeting. Chuckleheads?" She laughed with him.

An hour later, Stella went by Carrie's office. "Hi, Carrie."

"Why didn't you say you wanted to discontinue Conclave?"

"Oh, gosh no. It's up to all of you, but I enjoy them. Except for today."

"Then why did Winnie say…"

Carrie turned her monitor and Stella read, "We'll be changing Conclave to CONCAVE because it is less religious and is an economics term. From now on, speakers will be arranged from other areas of the Federal Reserve Bank."

"Concave? What the fuck. Car, Gage and Wendell talk to you. Do you know why, or whether this is about the team or just me?"

"Right after Wendell came that one time, he told me he thought it was a little too fun for the Fed. He made air quotes when he said 'fun.' He didn't like when I told him it was perfect and said he'd talk to a couple others, but he didn't tell me anything more."

Stella returned to her office and typed an email telling her team to ignore Winnie's email in its entirety. There were no changes to the Conclave, but Winnie might create a separate meeting series with optional attendance. She apologized for the confusion and then reminded them if any team member wanted changes to the Conclave, they were always welcome to talk to her.

Though Stella gazed out the window at a familiar view, she looked lost.

On Friday morning, Facilities entered the RD, the Officer with a blueprint and his staff with tools. The Officer confirmed the area Wendell suspected and kept Wendell at hand to reconfirm once the carpenter's cutting lines were drawn.

The lines were drawn on the outside wall to either side of the interior wall that divided Wendell's office and conference room. Though the carpenters removed the unnecessary door, the Facilities

Officer said that they were trying to avoid opening the interior wall to simplify restoration.

No one laughed when Wendell joked about cutting pipes by accident. Frankly, the carpenters looked at Wendell as if he might be out of his mind.

Wendell said, "It's about time, though, huh. What if the heat was from a bomb."

The Facilities Officer sighed as he pulled his phone from his pocket, telling Wendell that there was a rule about claims of a bomb and he'd need to involve Law Enforcement.

In just under two minutes, one K-9 and two human Law Enforcement Officers entered the RD.

The two human LEOs were less concerned with Wendell's mentioning a bomb than his claiming mysterious temperature changes.

When their investigation was complete, Bella's eyes gentled and a low greeting rumbled in her throat. Her handler, uncertain of her what drew her reaction, instructed her to check the perimeter of Wendell's office. She finished her check and approached Wendell's desk.

Of course, he didn't know it was me that attracted her as he told her to get away and hurriedly pulled his backpack from the desk and zipped it.

I scratched Bella's ears and so enjoyed the weight of the pup resting against my leg. That I felt her and she me wasn't so surprising. When I'd lived, I'd thought our animals in Iowa had a special sight.

When her handler called her away, she hesitated. I thanked her.

"All right. Let's get back to getting this wall opened," said the Facilities Officer.

The carpenters made quick work of the wall after Wendell left his office.

The Facilities Officer noted the fireplace shaft in the conference room and the adjacent cavity that extended into Wendell's office and held a flashlight while one of the carpenters reached in. His hand was open upwards when he touched a corner of my commonplace book. Though he grimaced when the book dropped into his hand, he held on. I knew it had been slipping ever so slowly since I'd tucked it against the outermost panel and was grateful it didn't slip right by him.

There it was, and it's blue-green color hadn't even faded. I was overjoyed thinking it might make its way back to where it belonged, with my family. The Facilities Officer looked around then. "Maybe he wasn't completely off. There is something different in the air."

One of the carpenters said, "It's not hot though and there was no airflow at all in there."

The Facilities Officer placed the book on top of the most level pile on Wendell's desk, asked Winnie to find Wendell, and went over to Stella's office while the carpenters discussed insulating the cavity.

Stella asked, "He got you to open it finally, huh? Find any heat-generating ghosts in there?"

"Not unless they're living in a book. Its cover says it's a commonplace book."

"Oh, wow. Whose?"

"So you know what a commonplace book is?"

"I had a professor in college who gave us a choice of some readings and I read this thing by the father of the author of *Little Women*. It said authors were indebted to their commonplace books. Of course, I wasn't going to be an author, but I loved the idea. When I started interning here that summer and so loved the Fed, I started a commonplace book about the Fed. I think it got lost in a move. My great-niece told me there's a commonplace book in *Lemony Snicket* too. It's just a bunch of miscellany, quotes and notes and drawings and whatever. Kind of a scrapbook. I can't wait to see this one."

"You're welcome to take a peek. I came over to ask if you'd let Tim know so he could pick it up." Tim was the Fed Bank's archivist.

The two went to Wendell's office, and Stella said, "Oh, wow. I've never seen an embroidered book cover. Beautiful. I don't know if we need gloves to touch it."

"Hi, Tim, we have a surprise for you." Stella told him about the book.

"I thought the building had given up all its surprises. I'll come up when someone gets back from lunch to cover the circulation desk." The archival function in this Fed Bank was part of its Library.

"It's in Wendell's office."

Winnie found Wendell in Randy's office and Wendell invited Randy to join him.

The Facilities Officer said, "It's not heat generating, but we did find something pretty surprising."

"How? Doesn't look like it's been opened." Wendell pointed.

The Facilities Officer explained they had to close the hole right back up but would come back to restore the drywall.

"I told Winnie there was something there. Where is it then?"

The Facilities Officer pointed at Wendell's desk.

To say Wendell was unhappy when he saw the book was an understatement. "*A Commonplace Book for Our Child*. Is that a joke?" He callously flipped through a few pages with a mix of relief there'd been something that didn't belong and disgust that it couldn't be the cause of the warmth, even as his rough handling drew greater warmth. "Jesus. It's like a sauna."

Randy said, "Be more careful with that. Huh. We should get Tim up here. Someone's going to want that."

The Facilities Officer said, "In process."

Wendell was dripping after he called it a "dumb, old book." He looked at it as if he could make it spontaneously combust.

In that moment, I understood clearly why Wendell felt the warmth. I'd suspected I generated warmth whenever he threatened the book or my usual spot. But it wasn't just the physical threat. Since he'd become DOR, there a spiritual threat too. My wish for so long was to see the book find its way to my family and for me to move on. But lately, I'd relaxed the first part of my wish in light of desperation for the second. If he'd only step away from the book, especially before any drops of sweat fell on it, he'd feel better.

Wendell claimed a meeting and told the Facilities Officer to schedule a return when they would come back to double-check the wall and close it up.

Wendell didn't bother greeting Tim before he said, "There wouldn't be a book if I hadn't asked them to look and I'm not sure we should spend money and time on what's obviously a personal book. We don't even know if this was connected to the Fed. Just leave it here and I'll let you know what to do with it on Monday." Warm again, Wendell pulled at his collar and added, "Anything else? I've got work to do here."

Tim left, disgusted with Wendell's sweating and behavior.

Tim returned to his desk and called Stella to meet at Starbucks to discuss a way to get the book off Wendell's desk. "He had a full Starbucks so he won't be going there. I don't want to run into him."

Wendell closed his door and fanned himself for a minute before he turned the book's pages.

His eyes stuck on a page of quotations and narrowed as he read Henry David Thoreau's aloud in a mocking voice.

"There are nowadays professors of philosophy, but not philosophers."

"We do not learn by inference and deduction, and the application of mathematics to philosophy, but by direct intercourse and sympathy."

"Could a greater miracle take place than for us to look through each other's eyes for an instant?"

I wasn't able to counter the strength with which he tore out the page nor bat the crumpled page away from the trash. But when he pulled the trash can closer and began to slide Everett's book from the pile-top into the trash, I was able to make him drop the trash can. It was as if he knew when he grabbed it back and slid the book right in. As I tried with everything I had to tip the trash can, my energy ran right through it and instead hammered Wendell's shin. I focused on that.

With stained armpits and limping, he complained to Winnie about the continued warmth and left for home.

Hill sat in Winnie's cube. "He looked sick. Is Stella going to stop having those cave meetings now? Was Wendell happy?"

"I don't know why Stella can't be nicer to him."

"I couldn't do what you did to her. Her group likes those meetings. What's the difference to Wendell anyway?"

"He just doesn't like her. Thinks she's weird because of how hard she works. She doesn't even try to fix things with him."

"I really was sick on my day last month, but I didn't want to do what he and Gage asked us to do. I don't know, Winnie. What if Stella loses her job because of all this? Gage's email said they'd given her two years."

When Stella passed Winnie's cube on her way to the supply closet to finally get a new box of pens, she called to them, "Time to start the weekend. See you Monday."

With that blessing, though it was a little early, the two left.

When all the conversations ended, the floor quieted, and even Randy was gone, I was devastated. When I finally left Wendell's office, I was so relieved to see Stella's light and hear her tell someone over the phone that she was staying late on a hunch.

When the Housekeeping staff began to arrive, I heard Stella pack up, but she stayed on and my hope soared.

Stella was the Housekeepers' favorite. When she worked late, she made a point of gathering her trash for their regular pass regardless of how late she planned to work so they wouldn't fail their Manager's check for empty trash cans. She treated them with respect and gratitude. Honestly, the bar for being their favorite among the RD's staff was pretty low.

Stella didn't ask to enter Wendell's office. Instead, she waited until they'd collected both his trash and hers and then asked if she might look for something. There was the book and right below it, thank goodness, the crumpled page. I was grateful for the choice I made so long ago to use a sand colored paper that now stood out among Wendell's other crumpled pages.

When the Housekeeper saw Stella had retrieved my book and page, she winked. "I don't know why, but I'm glad you take it. It didn't want to be in the trash."

A Rabbit Hole: Oz

The memories of my lived life feel quite different than the observations, learning, even imaginings that came after my death. That one of those memories has been tarnished saddens me.

The memory is from the summer of 1902. My grandparents convinced my parents to excuse me from my farm chores and brought me to Chicago where we stayed with my Aunt Edna and Uncle Louis. My cousin Lizzie and I were both nine that summer, and we shared a favorite storybook, Mr. Frank Baum's *The Wonderful Wizard of Oz*.

My grandparents treated us to its first-ever performance at Chicago's Grand Opera House. I rode an elevator for the first time ever when we made our way to our second-balcony seats from where Lizzie and I could see all around the theatre. And from the moment the curtains opened to reveal the stage, we were in a state of wonder at the beloved story being brought to life.

After the matinee, we dined at the Palmer House with the previously mentioned brownies for dessert.

For days after that, Lizzie and I conducted a criticism of liberties taken by the producers. My favorite character, the Cowardly Lion, had been relegated to a non-speaking animal role, despite the talents of the actor who'd played him. Though we enjoyed meeting Imogene the cow, we thought her impractical and missed Toto greatly. Lizzie thought Toto's replacement justified only if Imogene the cow was brought on in an attempt to right the great wrong to cows cast by the reporter who blamed Daisy, poor Mrs. O'Leary's cow, for the Great Fire.

And then, in 1910, as young women, our criticism began anew after we saw the silent film version of *Wizard of Oz*. We remained respectful of Imogene though we committed to telling the story with Toto when it came time for the children we'd have to embrace Oz.

We weren't alone in finding the story eminently criticizable. In 1964, high school teacher Henry M. Littlefield published a paper, *The Wizard of Oz: Parable on Populism*, settling each character and place into the features of a political allegory. Dorothy's silver shoes represented the silver standard for the dollar, the yellow brick road the gold standard, the Emerald City the national keeper of the "greenbacks," and so on, all representative of the monetary issues in Mr. Baum's time.

I learned of Mr. Littlefield's translation when a PhD here researched it for use in teaching the gold standard to his students at a local university. And when the *Journal of Political Economy*, a "top" journal, published a paper, *The "Wizard of Oz" as a Monetary Allegory*. And again, when another of the PhDs wrote an article, reporting, "The yellow brick road is the gold standard, whose fallacy is exposed by Dorothy's triumphant return home borne by the silver shoes."

Though I've never seen the movie, I learned Dorothy's silver shoes had been colored red so they'd show up.

It is my understanding that Mr. Frank Baum never claimed to have written anything more than a fairy tale, and I hope that's never been refuted though one can't blame economists for wishing the magic of such artistry owed a debt to debates over monetary regimes. If only they would use the magic and artistry without ascribing their interpretation as a truth of the author.

None of that did the tarnishing. What did was Trump's nomination of Judy Shelton to the BOG. She'd served as advisor to Trump's campaign and her ideas of returning to a gold standard, closing the Fed System, and getting rid of deposit insurance were oft-called "fringe." And when asked about holding an international monetary conference to gather support for a return to the gold standard at Trump's Mar-a-Lago, she claimed, "would be great." Reasons not to support her nomination snowballed, until even Senator John Kennedy, a Republican, said, "Nobody wants anybody on the Federal Reserve that has a fatal attraction to nutty ideas. Now I'm not saying that's the case here, but that was sort of the dialectic going on."

I sometimes think of my own situation in the context of the Wizard of Oz, especially that I might someday click my heels, such as they are, and be taken to where I belong, which can't be here. But I am no longer able to remember the yellow brick road without Shelton sitting on it.

WEEK FORTY-SIX ~ 9/9

Randy was first in on Monday morning, not so long since he'd left Sunday night. Though he, like most of the staff, rarely expressed partisan ideas, he cared deeply about policy issues and Trump's tweets were beginning to take their toll.

There've been other U.S. Presidents who tried to force the FOMC into actions that would improve their re-election prospects regardless of the effects on the long-term economy, but Trump stood out. His willingness to harm the credibility of the U.S. as a borrower and cause long-term inflation all to lower the real cost of his personal debt was exceptional. Projecting, as was his norm, he called the FOMC "boneheads."

When the FOMC continued to focus on doing their best according to their Congressional mandate, Trump focused on trying to discredit Powell personally, going so far as to call him an enemy of the people. Though most Fed Bank staff have no contact with the Chair, many feel an emotional connection with anyone who chooses to join their "Fed family" and were pained by Trump's words, regardless of their political beliefs.

The pang of that pain was somewhat eased by news that even Trump's allies turned away from his attacks. Senator Kevin Cramer came right to Powell's and the FOMC's defense. "This is an area where I frankly disagree with the president. He's forever attacking the Federal Reserve and particularly Jay Powell...They are independent

of politics, and they ought to remain independent of politics."
And specifically in support of Powell, Cramer said, "In my view I
am amazed he can restrain himself from responding both in words
and frankly in policy. He has done a great job of maintaining the
independence of the federal reserve against a lot of political pressure,
and Donald Trump and Jay Powell have two very different jobs."

When Powell was told of the support, he responded, "Terrific," a
sentiment shared by most staff.

Even Shelby came to the FOMC's defense when he said, "All
presidents whether it's Republican or Democrat, you look back in
history, they all like low interest rates because they help fuel the
economy. The Fed overall, I believe, is doing a good job. They might
not please me day-to-day, but their independence is important."
Of course, he was saying that not long after he'd blocked Obama's
nominations for Governors.

In the end, the impact of Trump's attacks was to validate the work
of those politicians, bankers, and other members of the public who
contributed to the passing to the Federal Reserve Act in 1913 and to
remind the Fed System's Public Affairs staff of the need to help the
public understand the FOMC.

As Wendell unlocked his office, Randy was returning from an
impromptu meeting with one of the other Small Group members.
When Randy asked had Wendell finished reading the Tealbook Part
A and the BOG staff's special memos, both of which were distributed
the preceding Friday, Wendell said, "Let me get coffee. And I need to
talk to Stella."

When Winnie told Stella, she asked, "Really? I thought he'd be
busy with FOMC. Should I go over now?" She'd been rubbing hand
lotion into her hands.

Stella took her place at the comfy chairs. Wendell's return was heralded by the scents of coffee and Tabasco sauce. He motioned with his shoulder for her to follow.

He opened his container of eggs on his way to join her at his table. Her body's rejection of the scent of eggs and Tabasco is so great that she is usually forthcoming, but this time, she didn't say anything and instead just sat as far back in her seat as possible and raised a hand near her face to overlay the food scents with that of hand cream. Still, Wendell saw the involuntary wrinkle of her nose.

"Oh, sorry. My son hates it too." He picked up the container and ate quickly in the hall outside his office.

When he tossed the container in the trash, Stella apologized and thanked him though she kept her hand near her nose since the smell of the trash was no less than of what it contained.

He said, "Gage said you put the kibosh on the research paper he picked for one of those groups you signed us up for."

Stella flipped her steno pad to the inside of the back cover, where she'd stuck a Post-it. Under "In trouble for," she'd written, "Casework," "Winnie," and now added, "Gage - Finlit paper." She answered, "Gage asked me to review his slides. One was a placeholder for when he planned to read the conclusion of a research paper to the kids."

Wendell said, "I asked him to run the slides by you. The paper was about high school kids. What could you possibly have objected to?"

Stella's eyes held a plea he wouldn't get angry. "I'm sure it's been peer-reviewed and is a fine paper for its intended audience, but it doesn't make sense in the context of a presentation to high schoolers."

"Why would you have opined on anything. Papers are out of your wheelhouse."

"Meeting with high schoolers is not. My work being reassigned to Gage doesn't change that."

"I'll give you the benefit of the doubt. He said the paper is about high schoolers. What could be better?"

As she started to speak, she scribbled a few notes. "So it was trying to answer whether personal finance class requirements in high school were good policy. They used data for people something like born between 1946 and 1965 who got their first personal finance class in high school between 1957 and 1982. They ran a regression and concluded high schools should dump personal finance classes. Then they used different but similarly old data and concluded adding a math class is more important. That paper was published in 2015."

"I'd have thought you'd have known we deal with data limitations all the time in research but I guess not."

"I might have been in that personal finance sample. We learned to write checks in social studies class at my high school. There were a thousand more important things in my life that impacted my future investment income, which is how they measured the results of high school. Say like going to college. That's not normal data limitations."

"I'm sure they made an assumption for college."

"Regardless, high school kids aren't going to find inspiration in having this paper read to them."

Wendell smirked. "You may have a point but Gage has a PhD and you wanted the PhDs involved in your diversity project."

A few seconds passed before Stella responded. "I offered Gage an alternative to the paper – a video segment from Squawk Box. Their consumer finance reporter talked to high school kids who had asked for and driven the addition of well-thought-out finlit classes. It was inspiring. Would you like the link?" Stella's eyebrows remained elevated as she waited for his answer.

"Why'd you read the paper anyway?"

She rubbed one eyebrow with two fingers. "A couple months back, an old friend posted about it on LinkedIn. The header was something like 'Should High Schools Be Required to Teach Financial Literacy?' The post went viral, a couple hundred thousand likes and a couple thousand comments, but it didn't look like any of the likers and commenters read the linked article about the paper or the paper.

Most responses were super supportive of finlit in high school. There were some truly insightful, heart-felt comments that would have way better informed policy than that paper."

Wendell stroked his chin. "That's pretty funny. The opposite of the conclusion, huh?"

"Yes. How about since I made the commitment to this school, may I please do this presentation?"

He released his chin, exhaled, and said, "There's probably some truth in what you're saying. But Gage is reporting at Executive Committee next week on how he's taken over the diversity stuff." He straightened in his seat and put his hands on his knees. "You've got other stuff to do anyway. We think you should move on within six months. Gage is talking to S&R to see if they have something. When he told me about the paper, he said you got emotional. Employee Relations said the same when they told me people complained about you."

Stella's expression was one of disbelief. "Regarding the complaints, you said that before, about Employee Relations getting complaints. I asked Sarah and she said they got nothing. She asked Andrea and the other Officers and they don't know what you are talking about. And what is Gage calling emotional?"

"I don't have my notes handy. But plan on six months. I've got to go."

Her glare was fierce as she followed him out.

In her own office, she heated water and pulled a cinnamon black tea bag from a drawer. While the tea steeped, she held her mug close to her face and inhaled the strong scent of cinnamon. Then she typed an email to a colleague at the Boston Fed Bank. She referenced their conversation from a few months earlier in which the colleague asked might Stella consider relocating and asked if that or a similar position was open.

Next, she left a message for Sarah, recounting the conversation with Wendell and asking her rights. Sarah knocked on Stella's door ten minutes later. She came in, closed the door, and sat in a guest chair at Stella's desk.

"Did HR know he was going to do this? I hadn't even gotten a chance to ask for my rights since he told me I had two years."

Sarah referred to a notepad. "The Bank can move you wherever it feels you would be best used. Normally, Andrea would deal with Officer transfers, but as Wendell's mentee, she has a conflict of interest. What do you think about retirement?"

"I will not retire before I turn fifty-five and planned to stay to sixty. I'm not sure why you allow Wendell to claim I'd be best used in S&R. Would they waive their requirement that Officers be commissioned bank examiners?"

"Wendell's convinced this is best. You had asked about complaints. He asked if I'd talk to you about this. He said there are two themes to the feedback. First, your staff complain they don't understand how you make decisions."

"That was the budget analyst who's been here less than a year. Gage told her she could be a Manager. She complained because I won't give her a direct report. She referred to a coworker as a 'good tool' who lived a 'white-trash' life. She talked about her cat named Honky and her dog named Spook in a staff meeting once. When I asked her about it, she got angry. A day later, she said the cat is named after a trip to Hong Kong and the dog was adopted on Halloween. She said she never knew there were other meanings of the words. I asked she choose training or read a couple books to gain perspective. She told me Gage told her name her pets whatever she wants. I planned to ask your advice this week. Nor was there any business reason to reassess her role or add another person to work on budget."

Sympathy flashed in Sarah's eyes. "He didn't tell me who said it, so it might have been from someone other than her. The second theme was around talking to staff harshly. A staff member was using some phrase and you scolded them."

"Right, that's Hill. The phrase was 'you guys.'"

"He didn't say it was Hilerie. He told me he promised to keep the identity of the person who raised the issue confidential."

"He can't do that."

"I told him that and got a commitment he'd come to the next class on law for managers."

"What are my rights?"

"Employment is at-will, but he wants to find you a spot. S&R is open to considering a path for you to get back to an executive level."

"HR finds my being demoted acceptable?"

"Gage is still talking to S&R. "

"Is Andrea involved at all?"

"Yes."

"So her conflict of interest only limits her ability to speak to me?"

"Yes."

Stella's tone was without emotion. "Sarah, I told you what he said about the relationship of compensation and kids and what Gage said about being an unhappy lesbian. I'd like to protect the Bank from the position in which it's putting itself."

At that moment, Sarah's expression made clear that Stella had become someone from whom the Fed Bank would be protected.

I was sad when Stella did what she always does when overwhelmed and immersed herself in work. Every so often, she'd look up, and out, and tears would form.

On Tuesday morning, Carrie told Stella, "I hate him. How are you?"

"You know?" Stella was cautious.

"I do. He came by this morning. I don't know where he gets this stuff. He said something about how you said Winnie didn't have empathy and he asked what I thought. I told him maybe the Winnie thing would have worked some other time."

Surprise and disgust crossed Stella's face before she said, "Good answer. I bet he liked that. I should have learned to give answers like that."

"He's jealous of you, Stella. He said he knew Winnie kept asking you for advice."

"What a mess."

"Would you go to another Bank? Stay in the Fed family?" Carrie smiled in the way one covers uncertainty with a smile when one does it badly.

"I remember the letter I got when I became an Officer, not only was I in the Fed family, the First VP welcomed me into the Fed Officer family."

"I've heard two of the Presidents won't use the term anymore. Maybe you could transfer to their Banks."

"I don't know. Nora brought my brother-in-law's ashes back this past weekend. We had the memorial and buried him here, so she is going to sell their ranch and maybe get a place here. It'd be a bad time for me to up and move away. She asked why I didn't just get a job cleaning desks at night to get away from Wendell."

Carrie laughed. "You can't clean desks. Look at your own office. Who would hire you to clean desks? Seriously, I'm sure you'll be fine and if not, sue. Did she sell the cottage?"

"No. She's keeping it but put fixing it up on hold till she's settled here."

Carrie asked again about going to another Fed Bank.

"I'll do what's needed to get me to fifty-five."

There was a pause in their conversation. Carrie's insistence was unusual. I thought, and Stella probably thought, Carrie was asking on Wendell's behalf. Why else wouldn't Stella have mentioned Boston.

"I told him you had your System meeting this week and he said he'd leave you alone for a couple days."

"Woohoo. I'm heading to the cafeteria. Need anything?"

"I'll come with you. Then I need to get help for Dawn. Since she's got the conference, Hill was supposed to help with FOMC because special memos are due today. But, surprise surprise, Hill called in. I'm so tired of Gage praising Hill to the heavens and bashing Dawn."

Carrie stopped at Stella's office in the afternoon. "Stella?"

Stella bumped her head as she stood up behind her desk. "Ow, damn it. I wanted these for my System meeting." She held up the shoes she'd retrieved from a corner of her desk's closed kneehole. "I meant to ask you if you were going to join us."

"In the morning, for a while. Are you all going out to dinner tonight?"

"We are. At their hotel though, because of the rain in the forecast."

"That's right." Carrie laughed. "You made them get wet last time they were here."

"I felt horrible. I promised my stash of umbrellas and didn't take them when the forecast said no rain and then it poured. Ugh. How's Dawn's day going?"

"Briefing memos all in, done, no drama. She's the best. Do you need help with RAOC in the morning?"

"Nope. Dawn's got registrations on the first floor. Try to come down for lunch."

The semi-annual meeting of Stella's counterparts started the next day and followed the usual schedule for the assembly of Fed System staff. One full day, ending with a reception and sometimes dinner, plus one-half day. Their committee's intent was increasingly uncommon among Fed System committees as they truly sought to balance the wishes of their respective RDs, the needs of monetary policy, and their role as custodians of public funds. Their efforts were reminiscent of the Fed Banks' original administrators, such as my boss and I were.

"I wanted to tell you Wendell brought up Mercy. He's still bothered she took a demotion to get out of Research." Mercy was one of Stella's predecessors and took a demotion to get out of the RD seventeen years earlier.

"He's brought her up to me too. He should just call and ask her why. He says she thought they were crazy. I'm so glad she finally got promoted back to Officer."

The next morning, Stella was logging in to print a last-minute request from one of her RAOC counterparts when Gail, a counterpart, came to her door.

"Are you harboring contraband?"

"Oh Gail, hello." Stella came from behind her desk and the two hugged hello. "I was sorry to hear about your flight but am happy to see you."

"How was dinner?"

The two laughed about Stella's inability to control the weather and concluded their meetings should cycle between the Miami and New Orleans Branches of the Atlanta Fed Bank.

Stella asked, "Contraband?"

Gail told Stella she'd been behind her at Security. Stella brushed off Gail's question about why she'd been made to stand and wait. The Law Enforcement Officers were still learning about her accommodation, and when she told them she had one, they treated her with suspicion and held her while they sought confirmation.

Gail reminded Stella how they'd marveled at the inconsistencies when they once stood together outside the BOG Chair's office without having been physically screened.

Stella asked, "We were trusted. What a feeling. Speaking of Chairs. I'm excited for your term to begin."

"I have a day and a half yet. That's why I came up here. I've never been Chair of anything and I'm getting cold feet."

Stella convinced Gail to stick with their plan.

Gail tipped her head in thought. "Okay, but will you promise to stick around for my term in case I need help?"

Stella turned away as her eyes flash-filled. She blinked away the wetness as she collected her files.

Their first agenda item was a check-in on how each was using an application intended to track FOMC access. It had been implemented in 2018, in response to the most recent major FOMC leak.

Since the newest members hadn't known about the leak, one of Stella's counterparts offered a recap she'd given when they'd created the specs for the app.

"Okay. I haven't looked at this in a while, of course, so if something is wrong or completely outdated, holler. Here goes. The minutes of the September 2012 FOMC meeting were released on October 4, 2012. But in September 2012, Hilsenrath, a reporter, publishes an article in the *Wall Street Journal* that seems to have classified info from the September FOMC. He talks to a lot of Fed folks so medium concern to the Board. Then on October 3, Medley Financial sends out a newsletter to clients that has certain claims of what FOMC is going to do. Bigger concern than the *Journal* because the info went to private investors. The information that was in Hilsenrath's article and the Medley newsletter was information that the Board didn't share with the public until it released the minutes of the September meeting on October 4, 2012."

One of the new members held out her hand and shrugged. "Why was one release worse than the other?"

While the speaker took a sip of water, Gail jumped in. "Because the Medley letter went to its subscribers, who are private investors who can pay a boatload a year for a newsletter, making them a pretty exclusive group. They were given market-moving information. Anticipating the market reaction that would occur once the minutes were released on October 4, their subscribers could position themselves to make money. Insider trading."

The speaker began again. "After the *Journal* article, Bernanke sent a note to the FOMC. Then on October 4, still 2012, he asked the FOMC Secretary and Board Legal to do an investigation. Then in March 2013, the Inspector General says they are investigating Medley and the FOMC Secretary and Board Legal reports out they didn't identify the source of the leak. Then at the end of 2014, the Inspector General closes its investigation, without identifying a source."

After answering a couple more questions, she continued. "Then in February 2015, Elizabeth Warren and Elijah Cummings sent a letter asking for a briefing about the leak and noting the public's right to know. So did others from the Senate Banking Committee. Orrin Hatch asked for a briefing. Then the Inspector General got an anonymous letter naming a name and involved the FBI and reopened their investigation in March 2015. By then, Hensarling and Duffy called out Yellen for what they said was a lack of response. Hateful letter. We don't do stuff like they accuse us of."

A new member joked, "Are you sure?"

The others didn't laugh. Such criticisms of the Fed System as were levied in that letter bothered most of them.

"Finally, in April 2017, Jeffrey Lacker, then President of the Richmond Fed Bank, resigned and said that while he did not leak the information to Medley several years earlier, he had unwittingly confirmed it. The original source remains unidentified. So it's a mystery. But we were charged with figuring out how to track everyone who touches FOMC material and a year ago started to use this app and now we are checking in."

Another member asked, "So seven years passed since that leak?"

Soon after, they resumed their agenda.

At a quarter before five, Winnie slipped quietly into the room and crouched behind Stella's chair. "Wendell wants to talk with you about the accounting for the Casework. He said it's not an emergency."

Stella held her agenda up for Winnie. "We go to reception right afterwards."

Winnie seemed relieved to report, "He thought of that. He said you could be a little bit late since it's just a reception."

Stella did not respond.

"See you at five-oh-two."

On the elevator, Stella's serious expression gave way to a sincere smile when the elevator opened and she greeted Randy and a few of the business economists who were returning from the E-Floor.

She asked, "Long day, huh?"

Each offered a smile or a "yes but good" or something similar, sounding both tired and exhilarated. Randy took over, "David had a big stash of questions this go-round. Tough economy to understand. But you're not supposed to be going this way either."

When the elevator doors opened in the RD, they traded places with PhDs heading home.

When Stella got to Wendell's office, he said, "Tell Winnie to get Gage."

Hill's whispers with Winnie ended abruptly when Stella appeared. When Hill returned from Gage's office, she finished telling Winnie how Gage's wife had been unhappy Hill couldn't stay until Gage was finished.

Wendell asked, "How's your meeting? Any secrets about independent research?"

Stella's eyebrow rose and one side of her mouth lifted with humor, until she realized he wasn't joking. "I'll send a meeting summary but most Directors aren't involved in RAOC business."

He repeated, "Well, don't get involved with other Districts or do anything to make the Board happy."

"Let's go to my conference room." He motioned toward his direct door, but Gage wasn't able to open it. "Then come the long way. Something got out of whack when they opened the wall for that silly book."

Nothing got out of whack. It was me. I didn't want them in my room.

They took their seats, and without looking up from his legal pad, Gage read a single forty-seven-word question, which referenced "Stella's witchy accounting."

Stella ignored Gage when she told Wendell, "Our allocations to monetary policy, S&R, or payments are based on our number of staff, not their cost. Casework staff are not PhDs and so cost less than average." She provided a simplified explanation.

Gage said, "You want to look at underruns to determine an overrun? That's double-witch accounting."

Stella asked, "I think Wendell is good with this?" Wendell nodded. Stella told Gage he could enlist the Budget Analyst's help if needed, and as Gage opened his mouth, she asked, "May I go?"

When she got to the door, Stella looked back. "Would either of you like to join us for the reception?" Wendell looked as if Stella had asked might she twist off his nose and Gage began a long-winded explanation.

Stella cut him off. "No worries. See you tomorrow."

Whatever had fueled Gage's late-in-the-day feistiness evaporated. Wendell pointed him in the direction of his office.

Gage's wife stayed on speakerphone while Gage packed up and reminded him she'd sent a car service who was waiting to pull up in front of the building.

On Friday of this week, finally, after three weeks of travel and vacation conflicts, Stella and Tim were going to look at baby Everett's commonplace book. Stella had stored it in an empty drawer while Tim, without telling the BOG they had it, had tried to suss out an answer from them about the book's ownership.

He and Stella would decide whether they ought to search out my descendants without offering the book to the BOG. Their concern wasn't that the BOG wouldn't return it to my family eventually, but that Wendell would find out the book had not been destroyed in the trash. Though Stella had little left to lose, Tim did.

At the last minute on Friday morning, Wendell decided not to attend the Small Group meeting and Tim didn't want to risk getting caught by him in the RD. Though Stella offered to bring the book to Tim, he said he'd wait until Monday to see if Wendell had gone to FOMC. He told Stella to go ahead if she'd like to take a peek.

She asked if she should come pick up gloves, but he told her clean hands were preferable.

"How did that page he crumpled do?" At his recommendation, Stella had placed the page under a small stack of books.

"A page of wonderful quotes by Thoreau. I'd love to have met her. Why'd he wreck her book."

She removed the candy dish and notepad from her table and wiped it clean. When she returned from washing her hands, she closed and locked her door. She laid blank paper down on the table and placed the book on top of it. She hesitantly touched the embroidered cover and opened it gently.

It was as if she were transported from the Fed Bank to a different world. She smiled as she read and look bemused when she finished.

"Well hello. This is lovely. It's nice to meet you, Lucy. You've reminded me why I stayed here so long. I wonder how you and Mr. Myers would think we were doing at fulfilling our promise in 2019. But you also reminded me I really need to get a life."

I answered Stella. She didn't hear me.

Week Forty-nine ~ 9/30

Instead of calling out to Stella as was their usual pattern of morning greeting, Carrie came to her doorway. "I saw it. How are you?"

In the face of Carrie's distress, Stella's eyebrows twisted up and her mouth widened. "Oh, no. Something to see already? It's only Monday morning."

"Your job, it's posted."

Stella's distress turned to confusion. "My job?"

"There's a big notice on the home page. You didn't know?"

"A notice?"

"Like they do for Officer jobs. Says blah, blah, how good to be in Research and links to the posting. You didn't know?"

Stella sat down, still in her jacket, pulling her backpack on to her lap as if it would hide her. "He said I had six months. Damn him. They don't need more than a month to hire a replacement. I started looking and have a meeting with the First VP at Boston Friday. I don't even know what happens if I end up with a break in service this close to fifty-five." She stopped and took a deep breath. "Sorry, Carrie. I'm going to start over. Thank you for the information. I'll deal with it on my own in a minute. Good morning, how was your weekend?"

"Oh, stop it. This sucks. None of us can believe he's doing this. Adam said all of us oldies are probably in trouble. We're not sure if we should pretend to kiss his and Gage's asses. Wendell can't feel good about doing this. Gage can't feel anything anymore."

"I found out Wendell told three people in S&R that I was in charge of Eliza's transition which isn't going well. HR will let him do whatever he wants. I don't know why he has to bash my reputation. There's a way to do this stuff but this ain't it. Anyway. I think you all will be fine. If you weren't so good, he couldn't put me out. Let me get settled and I'll ask him to meet with all of you to explain."

"We have Conclave at ten because of that Bankwide football party on Thursday."

"Okay, that will probably work out perfect. Who's leading though? I don't want to clobber their agenda."

"Hah. It's my turn. Truly, no worries. This is more important. I'll change my grammar tip to the alternative spellings of fuckhead." Stella looked confused. "*W-e-n-*"

Stella laughed. "Oh, thank you for that. Didn't see it coming. If you want, you can have the meeting after Wendell is done and I've left to start figuring out what the hell I'm going to do."

"Who would be in a mood for a meeting when our team is being ripped apart." Seeing Stella's expression, Carrie added, "Well. She's sure got a lot done on her coffee dates with Gage."

"Thanks, Carrie. I appreciate you." Stella made prayer hands and dipped her head. "The thing is I don't want to stay any more, the nonstop haranguing is changing me. I just needed time. I love Boston and that may turn out well. I'll do what I have to do to get to fifty-five though." She put her hand on her stomach. "I'm nauseous and the day's not even started. I'm going to get a Coke. No one died and I have to stop treating this like the end of some great life purpose."

"We're so weird. No one's in the middle. Either we treat this place like a calling or mock it."

Stella stopped at the door and looked over at one of Carrie's affirmations. "Ah Carrie, I do love your office."

"I'll go downstairs with you. Come by and get me."

In her office, Stella listened to three of seventeen voice mails. Two were from people who had been wanting an Officer-level position for a while.

"Congrats, Stella. It's Bob. I can't wait to hear about where you're going. I wondered if I could talk to you about how hiring for the posting will go."

"Congratulations, Stella, I'm so glad you are getting away from him. Call me."

"Hello Stella, this is Emily Caster. I am a manager in the Cash department. I am interested in your job and was just calling to ask what kinds of skills might be important to have. I'd appreciate if you would call me at..."

She blinked back tears as she deleted the messages and logged in to her computer. Incoming chat messages popped like popcorn. Stella ignored them.

When she saw an abundance of emails with "Congratulations" in the subject field, she ignored those too.

Carrie came then and the two went to the cafeteria.

On her way back, Stella stopped at Winnie's cube. "Good morning. Hey, Win. Do you know about the posting?"

"I do. I'm sorry, Stella. Wendell says the writing was on the wall. I have to send him a screen print."

"What does that mean, Win, about writing on the wall?"

"Oh Stella, I don't know. I'm just glad I still have a job."

"Can I talk to him first thing and does he have time at ten to talk to my team about what's going on?"

"He's out and said to refer questions to Gage."

When Stella heard Gage arrive, she exhaled. She was two steps behind him when he unlocked his door. "Good morning. Wendell is out and I've been told to talk to you."

"Sure, sure. Come in."

"Is it truly intended that my job is posted on the Bank's internal home page?"

"No reason to worry. As I think Wendell told you, we're just helping advance your conversations with S&R. You're very smart. If I were you, I'd want to use my intellect there rather than waste it on Fed bureaucracy."

"As you know, it was after the financial crisis that I talked to S&R, many years ago now. My question is why is my job posted today." Stella held a pen and pad, ready to record his words.

"S&R's HR area is already identifying a job for you."

Stella's voice was clipped and crisp but distant with wonder. "But I do not have another Fed job lined up yet. Why is mine posted now, Gage?"

"S&R will probably place you within a few weeks but you can hang out here in an advisory capacity for up to a year." Stella didn't process his words.

I wished so badly Gage would slip and tell her that Wendell wanted someone else in the job more than he wanted her out, and the someone he wanted in had pushed him to move quickly so she could reveal she'd been dating one of her subordinates. Stella wasn't processing though and missed an opportunity to "hang out." "Hanging out" wasn't unfamiliar to the RD but, up till now, had only been offered to economists.

"Are you free this morning to explain to my staff what's going on and how this will affect them?"

"Yes. Wendell texted my Fed phone and said that I should make this my priority."

"At ten."

"Yes. Also, Wendell asked that I get you going on a list of all of your current work, divided into work for Research versus work for the Board or the Bank, or anything related to diversity you might have withheld from me."

Stella looked as if she might ask a question but walked out without speaking.

Once back in her office, Stella dug up a peppermint tea bag from the bottom of her tea basket. She only drank it when Coke failed to stop her nausea. She spent a few minutes looking for a way to silence the incoming chat requests before she found the computer's mute button.

Then she sent a meeting invitation to Sarah in Employee Relations and picked up the phone when it rang a minute after.

"Hi. I'm in Minneapolis but saw your invitation."

"Sarah. So I arrived this morning and found my job posted. I told you how Wendell had given me six months. I've been given no justification why this is sped up. You said you all in HR were fine with him telling me I had six months to get a new job. Is HR on board with this?"

"S&R is going to find you a place."

"At the same salary and benefits? Without being a commissioned examiner?"

"Gage is talking to Sylvia. How's it going with Security downstairs?"

"Fine. Thank you."

"I'm here if you need anything else."

A look of disbelief froze on Stella's face.

At two minutes before ten, Carrie came by Stella's office. "Ready?"

"Oh. Thanks, Carrie. Hey, Carrie, did you leave a Louisa May Alcott essay on my desk?"

"Oh, not me. What did she write?"

"*Little Women*. But this is an essay about a job."

"No bells. Stella, Gage came over. He asked if I know why you are so upset."

"Let's go."

When the two reached the conference room and Stella heard the chatter, it was as if a windshield wiper passed over her face and wiped away her frown. The chatter quieted when she and Carrie took their seats.

Gage arrived with Winnie and Hill in tow.

Stella started the meeting. "Some of us were surprised this morning to see my job posted and I've invited Gage to tell us what's going on and verify that the changes he and Wendell are making won't affect your jobs."

Sticking to a story of Stella wanting to leave the RD, Gage described his and Wendell's desire to help her. "She wanted to explore new options and Wendell wanted to give her this opportunity though we'll miss her. We have to thank her for the heroic work she's done for us for years. Since she's leaving big shoes to fill, we wanted to get a head start on the hiring process."

He asked for questions and the room remained silent. Stella's neutral expression didn't falter. Finally, the silence broke when Adam popped a tab on a soda can.

Hill took the opportunity to say, "Congratulations. How exciting for you. S&R must be very happy."

Stella masked her disbelief at the question, and answered, "Well Hill, I don't have a job and have been told S&R doesn't actually have a job that is a good fit for me."

Hill asked if Gage and Wendell were considering external candidates and whether members of the team might post.

Gage answered "no" and "yes" respectively.

Hill asked how Gage would know that the new person would know "how special the PhDs are."

Most of the others rolled their eyes.

After Gage answered a few questions about whether there were plans for any other involuntary reassignments, Stella ended the meeting.

Hill reminded Gage of the coffee cart and while the two prepared their coffee, Molly and Stella waited behind them. Molly stuck her tongue out at Gage's back.

Stella's smile was sincere.

She followed Molly out and asked her about the Alcott essay.

"*How I Went Out to Service*? Oh, it is fitting, huh. It wasn't me although I should've thought of it. She was my favorite. Had a role in my becoming an editor."

Back in her office, Stella read the essay. While she planned to set it back on her desk, I was able to create an air current. When it fell atop her bag, she slipped it in. I didn't want her to keep asking others from where it had come. I'd spent all night learning to print.

Stella kept a lunch-time appointment to donate blood. When she returned and passed by Carrie's office, Carrie called out, "Wait. I have something for you. Is it nice out?" She held out a file.

"Yup. Sun's out. Best September day. I don't know if I'm supposed to take anything. Gage told me send all work to him."

"It's not work. I printed some lawyers' info and a couple articles about wrongful termination. I know you won't want to sue but at least look, Stella. This is wrong and Legal knows it and they'll settle before you'd even get started."

"You're wonderful. I just can't make sense of the big rush to hire a replacement."

"I told you, he's jealous."

"He's got a title I can't ever have, makes over three times the money."

"Everyone likes you. He hates that."

Stella laughed. "Not everyone. Too many years, too much history."

Carrie laughed, too, and shrugged in agreement. "Still. He's clueless. And none of us are safe."

"You'll be safe, Car. Wendell likes you. And you're Gage's confidante. You're way better at managing up then me."

"Take the folder."

"Thank you. The thought is much appreciated." Stella rose. "I need to go call my parents. I got this weird feeling. I never call them from here and didn't plan to talk to them until the upset over my job was gone from my voice, but a feeling's a feeling."

"Eeew. I hate those feelings."

"I know, right?" Stella held up the file and thanked Carrie again. "Read it."

At her desk, Stella stared at the phone, crunched the onion rings she'd brought back with her and sipped a Diet Coke. When she finally dialed, she told herself, "Happy happy voice."

A blast of noise came through the phone when the call connected.

"Hi Dad. Is that the TV? It's loud."

"No, that's your mom. They found Nora dead."

"What?"

He repeated it.

"Oh."

"Bye."

Stella's sobs were harsh as she crossed her arms over her stomach and vomited in the trash. Ten minutes later, she turned back to her desk and dialed the phone.

"Carrie, could you come over and help me? Don't knock, just come in."

She logged off her computer and tossed things in her backpack. She was still seated at her desk, pouring water from a bottle on to a tissue and wiping away mascara when Carrie knocked once and opened Stella's door.

As soon as Carrie saw Stella's face and the stains of mascara-laden tears on her ivory sweater, she rushed through her words. "You'll be all right, Stella. You're smart. Absolute worst is you spend nineteen months in a crap job in Sup and Reg and then you're out of here with a pension."

Stella struggled to speak. "Nora died. My sister."

Carrie quickly moved over to hug Stella. As Stella cried, Carrie told her, "Let it out." Their friendship was solid, but was one of coworkers and an awkwardness grew between the one desperate in sorrow and the other desperate to help.

Stella patted Carrie's back and reassured her, "I just need out of here. Would you let whoever should know that I'm out and will be back when I'm back?"

Carrie nodded, and when Stella sighed, looking around her office as she may never return, Carrie asked, "You ready?"

"Carrie?"

"Anything."

"What if God did this because I treated losing this job like the worst tragedy? What if God did this to her to show me?"

Carrie wiped away her tears. "Not the way it works, Stella. Come. Let's get you in a taxi."

Carrie notified Gage and Gage notified Wendell. Gage asked Carrie to be in contact with someone in S&R who had planned some training for Stella.

Most of Stella's team came together in the conference room and as people do when hard things double down, they debated why. They talked about the changes in the Fed Bank and in the RD and Wendell's lack of leadership skills and Gage's illness. Carrie shared Stella's question of whether God felt a need to use a hammer to correct her over-prioritization of the Fed System and they debated why there's an overzealousness in public service. All agreed it was increasingly hard to feel like public servants as the RD's goal turned to competing as a top academic economics department.

In the afternoon, Winnie entered Carrie's office in a rush. "Oh, you're here. Stay here. Wendell's on the phone."

Carrie made a face before she picked up the phone. "Hello."

"Hello. I'm very sorry."

"Oh. I didn't lose my sister."

"No. I knew that. But you were with Stella when she got the news."

"Whatever." Carrie looked up in surprise at what she'd said.

"I wanted to catch you before you told others. Gage said there was some confusion this morning about the posting. It makes the most sense to keep Stella's private news private until she returns."

Carrie sat up straighter, looking at an affirmation on her wall. "I told our team and gave Winnie an email draft to send to the department."

Wendell said, "Transfer me back to her now. Thanks."

Reconnected to Winnie, Wendell asked about the email. Winnie responded with the firmness she emits when reporting successfully completed work and told him she'd sent an email to the RD and umbrella areas and placed a card in the usual place on top of the files outside her cube.

His tone was urgent as he told her to retrieve the card and recall the email while he waited.

She did as he asked but assured him the card would have been safe since it was near her.

He said only, "Keep it locked up. Stella's very private. I'll tell you if there's anything to do."

When Winnie entered Hill's cube, Hill said, "I heard. I think he knows people are going to be mad at him about Stella's job being posted."

The two concluded they would tread cautiously around anything involving Stella.

When Winnie returned to her cube, she saw in Wendell's mail an email to Stella. After fidgeting for a few seconds, she opened it, and read, "Dear Stella, Gage told me about your family's tragedy. I'm very sorry. S&R knows you have a long record of excellent service, and you don't need to feel any pressure to jump up to speed in your new job. Take as much time as you need."

When Wendell returned the next morning, his discomfort manifested in snapping at Winnie. When she asked could she send the email since Heads were looking for Stella, his temper roared.

As the week progressed, Gage visited Carrie each day, reporting with pride on the progress to replace Stella.

Since there was a scheduled Heads meeting on Thursday, Wendell used the time to talk with them about the burden of the Fed Bank's publications on the PhDs.

As they settled in the meeting room, Randy asked Wendell when Stella would return. Wendell mumbled an answer. One of the Heads asked where Stella was moving to and Wendell told him she'd been in contact with S&R for a while.

Gage, invigorated by the power he'd wielded that week, said, "Let's just get rid of these publications. Do we even know who reads this stuff?" He pretended to elbow the Head next to him and laughed as he asked, "Or do we care?" The Head took his elbow from the table and otherwise ignored Gage.

A Head who was last to arrive asked, "How's Stella? Winnie said there's no sympathy card for Stella. Are we doing something else?"

The question brought out the truth though a dismayed Wendell once more began telling lies, sputtering about Stella not wanting others to be notified of her sister's death.

Randy had already known, and said, "Her whole team knows. They're pretty upset. I don't think they know anything about keeping it quiet. Jasmine was down yesterday and she even knew." Jasmine was an auditor working with Randy, Stella, and Dawn on the RD's progress to expand tracking of FOMC access.

Wendell said, "Stella was upset and probably told different people different things. Let's get back on track. Point here is to figure out how to lessen the burden on the PhDs. When Beth returned and negotiated away her and Jack's obligation for writing Fed pubs, word spread quickly and one wisecracker asked if he had to go on a leave first to get his exemption. So we need a way to get modified forms of the PhDs' work out to interested non-PhDs without the PhDs having to do anything." Beth and Jack were married and recently returned after a one-year leave at a university.

The Heads discussed the rare PhDs who didn't mind writing for the in-house publications and proposed a special pull-out from the annual bonus pool to reward writing for the pubs. But the idea was dismissed a few minutes later because, after one asked, "why incentivize any of them to do work that is not at the PhD level." So Wendell proposed hiring a Business Economist who would "digest" and "dumb down" the PhDs' research. A few minutes later, Randy called out the wrongness of referring to writing for CEOs and Adjunct Faculty as "dumbing it down," and after ten minutes of discussion to arrive at the expression, "create applied derivations," they decided to conduct a review of the existing burden on the PhDs.

They adjourned thirty minutes later. No decisions were made.

Wendell told Winnie to take the tea off the Heads' beverage cart order.

On Friday, Winnie reported to Wendell that, despite her repeated emails, Stella had not submitted the obituary he'd requested. Winnie didn't tell him that Stella said the obituary was delayed due to an ongoing criminal investigation as is required when there's no cause of death in the relatively young. She and Hill had decided Stella wouldn't want Wendell to know of the criminal investigation.

Wendell told Winnie he'd have to think on whether he'd send the RD a notification and whether bereavement leave was appropriate if Stella was hiding something.

Winnie stopped at Hill's cube to ask Hill what would happen if Stella returned and the others didn't know. Hill asked Gage the same, Gage talked to Wendell, and Wendell responded, "All the more reason to get this transfer to S&R done quickly."

A Rabbit Hole: My Last Moments

Stella's sorrow drew me back to wonder how my dear cousin Lizzie reacted when she'd come here to collect me only to discover my death.

I believe the dead who'd earned it are at peace without guilt or regret or wondering why. I'm not there yet of course but am certain I will be. In the meantime, I can't shake a bit of ridiculous guilt for what I'm sure was a shock to Lizzie after her time so near my grief for Everett and joy for baby Everett.

In the morning of the day before I died, my mother, Lizzie, and I finalized our travel to Iowa the day after the next.

Lizzie reveled in her role as baby Everett's godmother and would stay with us in Iowa for one month and then return to Chicago to rejoin her nursing program. Everett's sudden death had resurrected her commitment to serve the ill.

In that afternoon, I'd laid out my and baby Everett's travel clothes and my mother was helping me pack. When she asked ought she pack baby Everett's commonplace book, I reminded her I needed yet to paste two pages.

One was Everett's essay on the Eastland Disaster. Thank goodness Aunt Edna thought to visit the hospital the day after his death. Luckily, a kind nurse had found the page and kept it, in case. The nurse thought it must be important because of its title, "Lesson for Regulators and Regulated from the Eastland Disaster." When Aunt Edna brought it here, she'd slipped it into her silver drawer for safekeeping. I planned to paste it this evening.

The second was the page promised by Mr. Myer. Lizzie and I planned to venture out the next day. She to retrieve her final paycheck from Marshall Field's and I to see the Fed Bank's new headquarters and pick up Mr. Myer's page.

After my mother set the commonplace book on the table near the fireplace, she said we'd sit there for our tea since Aunt Edna and her daughters were out.

As we sipped our tea, my mother held baby Everett and set his book on the arm of the chair, turning the pages, alternating between questions for me and descriptions for baby Everett. He kicked his legs in excitement when she tickled his belly and read him the lyrics of "Sky, Sky, Open Up," our version of "Rain, Rain, Go Away" written during a dry planting season. He giggled as she crept her fingers up her arm while she read how to repel bugs from tomato plants and told him he'd sneak into the tomato patch for an afternoon snack.

When Aunt Edna returned, my mother retrieved Everett's essay, but baby Everett and I had fallen into our nap. And after dinner, rather than pasting, I rocked the baby and we fell to sleep.

The next morning, Lizzie distracted me from my worry at leaving baby Everett, though he was sure to enjoy himself with my mother and Aunt Edna.

When Lizzie left me in front of the Fed Bank's new building and I passed between the columns, my vacillations between grief and joy stopped for a moment, as if the new central bank's mission was so exalted it might bound any personal devastation and elation of those going to do business inside.

The building was much more than I imagined when it was described in Mr. Myer's and my meetings with the construction firm. It truly lived up to a description from the news, "the impression of dignity and strength, in harmony with the power and purpose of the institution."

Mr. Myer was a long-time friend of Aunt Edna and Uncle Louis. I met him at dinner at their home and when he learned I sought a way to use my Home Economics degree while I waited for Everett to finish law school, he'd offered employment, contingent on my hiding my marital status, and when I became pregnant, that too. The hiding of either hadn't been a challenge since Mr. Myer's office was isolated in an annex to the main temporary space while this permanent space had been under construction.

Though I didn't know the others in the elevator, I enjoyed listening to their conversation.

I found Mr. Myer's office easily, despite the pockets of continuing construction. I was reminded of all that had passed in my life when a tear appeared in his eye upon seeing me and was glad for a distraction.

"Mr. Myer, what's happened to your wall?"

"Oh dear, the fireplace. In final construction, some noted the location of this fireplace above the cash vault so it can't go here and there is now some debate about retaining the mantel and placing a stove but for my purposes, I wish they would close the wall and be done. Sit here, to avoid the draft from it."

He told me that Mr. and Mrs. McAdoo, the Secretary of the Treasury and his wife, were planning a visit to the Fed Bank, and we talked about how some parts of the Fed System were changing even before they were implemented.

Once we were caught up, I said, "I've brought my darling baby's commonplace book to show you. I'll be quite grateful for your page. With a job offer, no less. My dear boy was born into such a cataclysm, I think the book will be of even more value to him when he grows old enough to wonder at his first days as I am already willing away memories of these weeks."

He slid the book around on his desk. "Oh, my dear, just lovely. Even your uncle has written a page, explaining the times in the stock market, and look here, he explains the value of the futures market to your aunt's farm in Iowa. And my, what a beautiful poem. And this, well, oh, a spell?" When I didn't answer, caught off-guard by his taking the time to look at each page, he went ahead and turned the pages until he got to a blank. "And this is the page for my letter?"

"Yours will go on the right. The left is for an essay my Everett wrote while in hospital. Despite good intent, I didn't get it pasted last night."

He reached into a desk drawer for a jar of paste. "Tell me about the essay."

"My Everett drew a caution about bank regulation from the Eastland's implementation of their lifeboat regulation. You know, it was meant to hold just six lifeboats but got many more when 'lifeboats-for-all' was implemented. He wondered if that was what caused it to tip."

"That's what I've been hearing. I understand the urgency of the addition of lifeboats after the tragedy of the *Titanic*, but even as the addition was being regulated, some noted all ships were not the same. I heard the Eastland ignored the Detroit & Cleveland Navigation Company's warning that some of these Great Lakes vessels would turn turtle if too many lifeboats were added up top."

I felt tears form. "To imagine if one good ear might have heeded the warning given. He tells our baby the best-intended rules may go afoul if not well-thought or the fit is wrong, in banking too."

"My colleagues might benefit from your Everett's essay as well. Here, dear, why don't you paste this while you're here."

I twisted the lid off the paste to stir.

"When is your return to Iowa?"

"Tomorrow. Though the baby is just two weeks old, I'm anxious to settle."

Mr. Myer looked up sharply at the staccato sound of his colleague steps. "Oh my, there is the troublemaker." Most of those involved in standing up the Fed Bank took the mission to heart, but some who had been in opposition joined only to try yet to end it before too much time had passed. The colleague was in the latter group. "We'd better hide your baby's commonplace book. You know, he is the one who claimed there was nepotism and continues to look for failings among all of us so it is better we not invite his curiosity." He placed the page he wrote atop the book and looked for a hiding place.

I told him, "You go to the door, I'll hide it." Finding his desk locked, I slipped the book in the open cavity intended for the mantel just as his colleague's shadow appeared in the door's frosted glass window.

"Mr. Myer, are you there?"

Mr. Myer looked over his shoulder to confirm I was seated before he opened the door.

"Well, you have company. When you return to working — "

"Lucy has returned to see our new quarters."

At that moment, I began to feel ill. While my body fell from the chair to the floor, my mind was filled with a feeling stronger than the strongest craving that ever was and the force of it drew me to my baby's commonplace book, as if I could reach him through it. But I watched as Mr. Myer picked up my body and ran out, yelling for help.

And then I watched as his colleague replaced the lid on the paste, looked around, and muttered about the waste of the paste having been open when there was nothing to paste.

And I remained here, perched on my baby's book as it slipped down into the cavity in tiny increments. Drawn later by noise, I realized I could shift and flit through the wall to see the source. A pale, red-eyed Mr. Myer had returned to collect his case after he talked to Lizzie.

I don't think too many days passed between my death and when my mother and father arrived at Mr. Myer's office.

My mother recounted the afternoon we'd spent looking at and talking about the pages of the commonplace book and told Mr. Myer she'd recreated all she remembered. When she told him she'd still had Everett's essay since I'd not gotten to pasting it in, I was grateful with the kind of gratitude that is a shock of sorts, when something important and good happens only because one failed in their own best intents.

Mr. Myer was teary-eyed, as were my parents, when he said, "I've rewritten my page for the book so you'll have that, but please know we will continue to look here for the book."

My father said, "It will be recovered when it is supposed to be, I imagine. We have an appointment now with the futures man. I'm turning over the planting of twenty percent of the fields for a few years to make time for little Everett. Won't need the contracts on that."

After talking about that year's harvest and the crops of the next, my father and mother left.

They'd not mentioned Lizzie.

WEEK FIFTY-ONE ~ 10/14

Stella returned this Monday. Word of her loss had spread through the Fed Bank and much of her day was taken up with accepting condolences, though in the RD, condolences were peppered with questions about her vacation. By afternoon, Carrie and Adam were fielding PhDs' questions about Stella.

Carrie, annoyed, asked if any of their PhD programs had required even a single course in leadership or human behavior. One who'd joined the RD after being denied tenure at a top school told her how Wendell too, years before, was denied tenure there and his reaction had become legend. The PhD suspected Wendell was driven to build an academic economics department that would rival that school's and saw Stella's concern for the mission as an obstacle.

Just as Stella finished catching up on emails on Tuesday morning, one from Gage arrived. As she scanned it, the sorrow in her eyes gave way to disgust, the disgust to hurt, and the hurt to flint. An attachment was signed by Gage, Wendell, their counterparts in S&R, and the Manager to whom Stella would report. Stella's demotion would be effective at the start of the next quarter and she would be evaluated for return to Officer one year later. Winnie and Hill would help her to clear her office. Her assistance in the transition was critical to its success.

Gage showed up several times at her door in the hours after he sent the email. When he insisted she confirm she'd read the email, she said, "My sister just died. I'm sure you can understand I'll not be able to move out of this office next week. Please correct the memo. I'll email you the same request."

Gage went straight to Wendell.

Wendell hemmed and hawed but said Gage should delay the date, but "Damn it, don't give her anything else in writing."

David visited on Wednesday. With the fake-sad face and tone he adopted when dealing with staff's personal lives, he said, "Hi, Stella. I heard."

Stella's raised eyebrow was a sign of her willful misunderstanding of his words. "I figured you'd hear. I was going to check in with you to see if you thought it acceptable."

"Gage has said they've set you up for success."

"That isn't true. You know I'm being demoted."

"Wendell gave you a year."

"I don't know what that means."

David was at a loss, and in the fake-sad tone once more, "I'm so sorry about your sister."

Stella thanked him.

He didn't hide his relief in escaping.

Her eyes filled.

Winnie and Hill came together a couple times to tell Stella they'd like to help, but their bosses needed them.

Dawn was a godsend for Stella. Without asking, she entered Stella's office, picked up a file, read the label, and in a matter-of-fact voice asked, "Garbage, shred, or S&R?"

Stella's eyes filled again then, but in gratitude.

Twice Stella said something should go into the RD's official files but the third time cut herself off. "Oh shit, toss it. I offered Randy stuff yesterday from old Congressional requests and he said toss them."

"That's right. Look forward."

When Winnie asked Wendell what she should do with the envelope and collection that she'd held back, his attention was drawn to an email from David.

It read, "You didn't pick up your phone. Get this shit with Stella figured out before something blows up. And if there's anyone else you don't like, live with it."

Wendell told Winnie to wait while he closed and deleted the email. "Well, what did we say? Stella was too private. How much is in there?"

Winnie watched while he looked at the card and counted the money.

He said, "Maybe you could return the money."

"I told her I had the card."

"Oh. There's that damn heat again." Sweat broke out on his upper lip. "Just give it to her. Let's get this done." Wendell's collar and armpits were damp.

When Winnie went to give the card to Stella, she hesitated in the doorway.

Stella asked, "Kisses? Go ahead." Wendell happened to be passing and looked in with confusion. He turned toward Stella's door, but when he saw the card in Winnie's hand, he scurried away.

Winnie closed the door and took a seat at the table, fidgeting.

"What's up, Win?"

"I have the card."

"Oh, I got them." Stella's team gave her a card, as had the umbrella areas and many individuals.

"The one from the Department. The donation card."

Stella waited.

"There's not much."

"That isn't important, Win. But I would like to thank people for their thought."

"Well, here." Winnie slid the card across the table and took two Silver Tops.

When Stella saw only eight names on the card, she looked at Winnie in question.

Several expressions crossed Winnie's face as she left.

I'd forgotten Silver Tops became Kisses.

Though the Kisses name was born when I was still alive, my family never used it. What we knew as "kisses" were my mother's butterscotch treats. Mr. Milton Hershey had co-opted the name from its common usage even though his chocolate drops were already well-established as Silver Tops.

My grandfather told us Mr. Hershey had co-opted the shape as well, from Wilbur Buds, using chocolate-making equipment he'd bought at the close of the Chicago World's Fair. A chocolate maker from Germany had sold the equipment rather than transport it back to Germany.

Mr. Hershey's new equipment dropped the chocolate into its shape while Wilbur Buds filled drop-shape forms. My grandfather thought the copying was fair, but I'd disagreed. Should I have the pleasure of seeing my grandfather again, I will be happy to report Wilbur Buds has enjoyed longevity despite the competition.

Adam brought some back once after his System committee's meeting at the Philadelphia Fed Bank and hosted an informal taste test of Wilbur Buds and Silver Tops. Being who they are here, the discussion turned to the importance of the chocolate economy.

At that time, both Wilbur Buds' and Hershey's headquarters were in the Philadelphia District and the then Deputy Chair of the Philadelphia Fed Bank's BOD was simultaneously the then Chairman of the Board of Directors at the Hershey Company.

Wendell must certainly have seen the dish of Kisses on Stella's table. It'd been there since she moved here, always full.

Stella mostly adhered to a rule that she couldn't eat the Silver Tops. Her argument was M&Ms at her desk had a natural limit while the dish of Kisses did not. But today, as she sat with the card, she broke her rule five times before Dawn knocked.

"Ready?" She noticed the card. "You know what he did, don't you? It was on the cabinet by her cube for maximum two hours."

"I figured."

On Thursday, Wendell stopped in Carrie's office on his way back from breakfast. "I wouldn't have let Gage post the job if I'd known about her sister. I don't know why everyone is so mad at me."

Carrie attempted to placate him by asking how anyone could have known.

When Carrie told Dawn and Stella what he'd said, Stella was bemused. "What does that even mean?"

Late in the day, Eliza came to Stella's office. "I'm so sorry about your sister, Stella."

As it turned out, S&R broke each of its commitments to Eliza as soon as the in-flight merger case was closed. They'd demoted her over concerns that Casework had been "Research-idized," but were sure she'd get promoted back in time.

"I quit. They took my computer and I have to call someone to let me back in to get my coat and bag from my cube, but I wanted to say thank you and bye."

"Don't thank me. I'm starting to think about my role in creating this Bank, how it allowed what happened to you, what's happening to me. I'm sorry for me you won't be in S&R but am glad for you and your new start. I pray you've got wonderful things ahead. May we go for coffee?"

Stella returned alone a half hour later. She sighed often during the remainder of the day.

By Friday, Stella seemed to have made some peace with her situation.

When Dawn arrived, they tossed and packed and talked about the Fed Bank.

Stella told Dawn she wondered how the outcome of S&R's big exams, such as stress testing commercial banks' balance sheets, fit with monetary policy and how the BOG prevented conflicts of interest. "Such an odd thing is the Fed."

Dawn asked Stella, "Do you regret ever coming here, now that you see how it's going to end?"

"I don't think so. No matter what job I had, even when I didn't like something, I was proud of my contributions. My System work was important. I just let the Fed become too much of who I was. This has been a wicked lesson."

"My niece just graduated in Finance and asked if she should apply here. I told her it's changing, but I don't know anymore, Stella. This place isn't the same."

"I met a couple of examiners this week who came from private-sector banks. My age. They'd made their big money and think the Fed will give them work-life balance and a claim to public service. Maybe that's the smart order to do things. When I got promoted to Officer, I was so young, and Ruth, my boss then, told me she worried since I'd skipped whole job ladders of increases. I should have been worried too but was so proud to be an Officer. But if not for Wendell, I'd have retired happy and proud at sixty. What about you, Dawn? You've had ups and downs."

"Overall, it's good. I told my niece that. I enjoy the conference work and helping people. I wouldn't even be thinking of retiring if they weren't still sticking me with FOMC. And David's probably going to be around for a while. You weren't here last week, but everyone could tell he couldn't wait to get out of the Town Hall meeting. He doesn't care about the Bank." She looked at her watch. "What time will we meet with Tim? I'm excited to see this book from 1915. It had me thinking about my grandma. I have her quilt. We don't have commonplace books, we have quilts. My other niece, the one you met, she's making me a quilt and she wove in a dollar bill because of all the time I spent here."

"I'd love to see a picture of the quilt. How wonderful." Stella rose. "Let me get the book. I'm sorry I wasn't thinking. You did all the work to find out about Lucy's family and found her great-grandson and never even got to see the book."

"Sit down. I'll wait for this afternoon. You know you should sue, right?"

At lunchtime, Stella was comforted by communications from colleagues in the Fed System. One colleague noted the similarity in what had happened to her and what was happening to Stella. They typed back and forth and reminded one another how few recovered from such takedowns. They wondered if their colleagues closed ranks to prevent laying any fault on the perpetrator that might become known publicly and harm the Fed System's reputation.

Though Stella had cancelled the job interview in Boston, her Boston colleague emailed to ask if Stella might have reconsidered. Stella called her colleague and her eyes filled as she explained how her sister had died alone in a faraway state and she couldn't make her parents fear the same for her.

"I understand, Stella. We might come up with something yet though. Just hang on."

"Okay. I'm being optimistic."

Just before two, Stella cleared and cleaned her office table.

She welcomed Dawn and Tim, and the three joined around my book with anticipation.

They guessed that commonplace books of such a type had become the baby books they grew up with. They wondered what had become of my son Everett. As they turned pages of farming rules, they wondered what those farming in 1915 would think of the current farming industry. They thought the recipes practical, especially etsaput, which made use of early and late harvest surprises. Tim quickly copied it down for his wife. Dawn snapped a picture of the brownie recipe. All three laughed at the spell, and Stella was near-serious when she wondered if it worked. They enjoyed the several pages of quotations and were saddened as they imagined what drove Wendell to tear out a page. When they laughed at instructions on darning socks, Dawn admitted to having darned her husband's.

When they came to the information about commercial banking and the birth of the Fed System, they shook their heads. Stella recalled one of the Fed scholars who questioned the need to maintain the regional independence. Tim marveled at the decline of Congress' knowledge since the Federal Reserve Act passed in 1913. Dawn wondered why Public Affairs didn't work harder to educate people and stop the conspiracy lies. All three wondered what Mr. Myer and I would think of the Fed Bank today and then their conversation turned.

Dawn asked, "Will you sue, Stella?"

"I'm going to try to make the best of the time. A year and however many months as a bank examiner will probably give me a ticket into a commercial bank."

Tim said, "But Stella — "

"If I need to, I will sue. It will break my heart, but I'll do it."

Tim recommended a storage bag and box and Stella ordered it.

For now, the commonplace book would be returned to the safety of Stella's drawer. S&R had required Stella collect her office's back-up keys from Winnie before they'd let her keep any of their paperwork in her RD office. An unintended consequence of their demand was that no one in the RD could snoop and find the commonplace book.

Dawn joked that if Winnie got near the drawer when it was open, Stella should say she was glad Winnie finally came to help clean out the office. Dawn was sure Winnie would scoot right out.

The three took a last minute to make peace with not telling the BOG about the book.

Wendell carried a cookie when he returned after four from the Small Group meeting and stopped at Stella's office. "Making progress?"

Her lips tight and her eyebrows raised, she asked, "Yes?"

First, he shared his thought she was too nice to the PhDs.

She asked for an example.

He responded with an accusation she'd reached around Winnie and contributed to Winnie's downfall.

She asked for specifics in a tone more of a witness than a victim. She pointed to him and to herself when she said, "You know, I know,

HR has embraced personality difference as a legal justification and is not requiring you to find fault with me. But you seem to feel an obligation. It's a hard time for me with my sister's death and these criticisms without examples are — " She searched for a word.

Sweat appeared on his upper lip. He bit a nail for a few seconds, then wiped his hand on his pants before he pulled at his hair. "I'm trying to help you. We're going to depend on you a little longer. A replacement won't be here before bonus work starts. I'll need you to get Gage started."

"Do I have an extension to be out of this office then?"

"That's the same. We want you to get a good start in S&R. We'll email about it. Gage is going to send you a draft of the Bankwide announcement."

She remained still and silent.

He finished chewing, turned, and left.

She stopped tossing without thought when she pulled a tube from her cabinet. I remembered the long-gone staff who'd drawn the chart of commercial banks' assets during the Fed Bank's first decades. I was relieved when she emailed Tim to let him know about it and set it aside.

After the announcement about Stella was emailed to Fed Bank staff, Wendell forwarded it to the RD since the PhDs rarely read Bankwide communications.

He added a note on top of the forwarded email, "Stella has begun working in S&R. All of us, and most especially I, owe Stella a great deal for what she has done to make the department work well over the years. She really made my life easier at the same time she's allowed us all to be highly productive. If you see her, be sure to say thanks."

This time, angry tears overflowed her eyes.

Dawn opened the door without knocking. "Don't let him take away all you've done for the Bank, Stella. I think he just doesn't understand the Fed is something bigger than him."

Stella nodded and smiled. "Everything for a reason, right. I'll be fine, really. I'm just tired. I can't ever thank you enough."

WEEK FIFTY-TWO ~ 10/21

On Monday morning, Stella opened an email from Gage labeled "Communique 2." He directed her to split her days between S&R and the RD. And she should return her computer to Adam and take receipt of a shell computer from S&R. And her subscriptions to the WSJ and other media would be discontinued since S&R does not provide that benefit for staff.

Stella, dressed casually for office cleaning, carried a lidded teacup and a notepad to a meeting with her new Manager in S&R.

Her new manager's first words were, "I'll do you a favor right off. I keep a black or grey skirt and an examiner-appropriate jacket in my wardrobe in my office. I'd recommend you do something similar in the hanging space in your cube. You never know when you'll be called to a last-minute meeting with a banker."

Stella was genuinely curious as the Manager explained the work, so much I felt an inkling of hope for her, but it didn't last. One might think Stella's errant laugh upon learning she'd been assigned an online training titled, "New to the Fed," would have been forgiven, but the Manager flicked her eyebrow in judgement and attempted to justify the assignment.

When S&R's moving specialist arrived to show Stella to her cube, they greeted one another in the way as do all of the staff who've been around for decades and complained about the weather on elevators and chatted about news in a line in the cafeteria but never knew one another's name.

Stella asked her if Facilities might clean the cube. One cabinet was covered with thirty-nine automobile and fourteen automobile accessory stickers. A congealed substance was caked under a keyboard table.

"We don't do that fancy stuff like you folks in Research. You are on your own. The good thing is every re-org has musical chairs so you won't be here long. I wouldn't even unpack all those books Winnie showed me. Facilities will bring up to four moving cases on Wednesday. On your own for anything more than that."

"Winnie?"

"Yes, she showed me your office."

"I'm not physically able to carry boxes or stacks of books."

"Try and find a coworker then."

After the moving specialist left, Stella worked on the online training.

A few hours later, she stopped at the Manager's cube to let her know the training was complete and she'd be back the next day.

The manager invited her to sit.

"This is a draft of your performance expectations based on the agreement all the bigwigs made regarding your transfer."

Stella read through the list without expression but looked up sharply at the last sentences. "Stella has come to S&R from Research. Her EVP, Wendell, called me and told me Stella lacks leadership skills and empathy. He is concerned with her capacity to interact with coworkers and bankers. This is communicated to Stella for accountability."

She asked, "Do I need to leave this with you?"

"No, we'll sign it today and I'll send you a copy."

"I'd like a copy of the signed version to take with me."

With the copy in hand a few minutes later, Stella prepared to leave.

"Wait. Stella. I'll deny saying this, but I recognize you've been dumped here because you pissed someone off. My wife and I have, unfortunately, been in similar situations. That page is a gift. But don't think for a minute I'll let you knock me out of the line for the next Officer promotion."

Still without expression, Stella said, "Thank you for the honesty."

Back in her office in the RD, Stella was lost. Luckily, Dawn came by. The two made short work of two more file drawers and Dawn served as a confidante, providing comfort and logic to Stella's skewed and new view of the Fed Bank.

When they finished and Dawn left her, Stella checked her email, hesitating over one from Wendell before she deleted it. Out loud, she said, "Felt good there." Then she restored it.

She squinted as she read it a second time. "Dear Stella. What I meant to say on Friday was thanks especially for your care in crafting a plan that will keep the department running smoothly as you transition. Gage has run into some problems with tasks we didn't know about. Are there files you can share or something? 1. A regional economic association had asked us to fund one of its receptions. They specifically asked about whether we still have a max on alcohol. I guess we can't just cut a check. 2. Since Tom's on his second leave, System benefits folks called to make sure we knew about the cost of benefits for highly-paid staff. What had we been telling them? 3. Winnie said you were keeping a table on where we stood against that RBOPS memo. The Board is looking for an estimate of our year-end position. Would you send it to her ASAP?"

Out loud, she said, "Nope."

She closed the email and opened a drawer with pantyhose, sewing kits, eyeglass cleaner, and other junk, splitting the items up between her backpack, a transfer case to go to S&R, and the trash. Her eyes filled when she pulled out the paperweight given to staff after the Great Hall's original marble was removed.

She debated whether it would go to her backpack or the trash. I expect it made it to the backpack only because Dawn and Carrie distracted her. They'd come bearing peppermint hot chocolate.

"Thank you. You are the best of the best of the best."

Dawn said, "We're going to FedEx your books and anything else you want to your apartment. Don't tell S&R."

They reminisced about the Fed Bank and decided their love–hate relationships with it were inevitable.

Carrie said, "But we've never gone off the rails before. I fear it's David. He never wanted to run the Bank. He just wanted to be on FOMC. And Frank could step in, but David and Wendell won't let him near Research."

Dawn said, "I've been here through four Presidents. For good and bad. The bad ones make us draw closer. But we are always up in one another's business when our own lives are bad anyway. Like — "

Stella's face squinched. "Don't say it."

Dawn continued. "Like a family."

Carrie said, "Even if we weren't family, we had a spirit, you know? I think because of the mission."

Dawn turned the conversation, "While we're here, I need some ideas for this year's fashion show."

For years, Dawn had organized an annual fashion show for her church's fundraising arm and this year's was the first Sunday in November. Since Stella admitted she was a bad source for fashion ideas and Carrie admitted she'd not bought full-price in at least twenty years, their conversation turned to some of Dawn's new designs.

Their conversation ended on a positive note about finding their passion in life outside the Fed Bank. After they left, Stella's own spirit seemed somewhat restored.

She returned to Wendell's email and typed, "Recall I was directed to trade my laptop and so no longer have access to files that may have been helpful. Dawn, Carrie, Mark, and Molly are your best points of contact."

On Wednesday, I watched the sun rise above the buildings that blocked the horizon. My anticipation turned to a glorious excitement a few hours later when Dawn confirmed that Everett, my great-grandson, would visit at lunchtime.

Stella, too, seemed genuinely excited. "That's terrific, Dawn. I can't wait to meet him. I think I will like him because I like Lucy so much. Her book's had me thinking about all sorts of things. You said he doesn't live here though?"

"He's visiting his daughter. She lives here and he needed to drop off a painting. His wife painted it before she died and he offered it to his daughter since he's downsizing and moving to Michigan."

"You guys really talked. He must be friendly."

"He was. I think he was so thrilled about the book."

"Is our plan still that I'll get him and bring him up so he can look at the book just to make sure, then he and I will come back downstairs and meet you and Tim across the street for lunch?"

"Yes. I know Wendell's at the FOMC briefing but I don't want any risk of him asking me who's Everett. I still can't believe he threw the book away like it was a newspaper."

Stella winced. "I know. If he asks who is Everett, I'll just say he's an S&R colleague."

The few hours of the morning moved slower than any since I died, but finally, I accompanied Stella to the first floor.

I knew my great-grandson as soon as my eyes set on his dark hair and eyes and too-big ears, but Stella had to ask the Law Enforcement Officer who was Everett. He looked about Stella's age.

The two shook hands and Everett apologized for his early arrival. He hadn't realized the Law Enforcement Officer would call Stella and thought he could just sit and read without bothering her. While she collected his visitor badge, she asked what book he was reading and the two talked books for that moment.

At the gates, she explained the security process, and he told her he hedged corn contracts through the Board of Trade, which had its own version of entry security. How proud my Everett would have been of our great-grandson protecting the finances of farmers.

Stella told the Law Enforcement Officer she'd not left the building and was relieved to walk right through. I was relieved too. I didn't want her to vacate these moments the way she usually did when she walked through the screening.

There was an ease between Stella and Everett and within her as they crossed the Great Hall and talked about the current economy and the real risk of inflation and the Fed's independence. While I was enchanted by Everett, I was captivated by Stella.

I'd spent at least some time in her presence most weekdays since she was in her early twenties. She'd not been this version of herself for so, so long. At least not in the Fed Bank.

Everett said, "Stella, these photos, and that painting up there of the Lake Michigan rocks in, Evanston?"

"Yes."

"From an Iowan's perspective, I have to ask, why is all the art of Chicago and its suburbs? We wonder sometimes in Iowa where we fall out in this Fed District. We had that banking family who held a seat on your Board of Directors for quite a while."

Stella thought for a few seconds. "I'm a little embarrassed. I've seen photos of barns and fields here but am only ninety-nine percent sure they are in our Conference Center. Since we have extra time, I'd love to show you if I can find them."

In the elevator, they were crowded back to a corner as a group of students joined them.

They enjoyed their walk through the Conference Center. As they came to the last couple of photos, Everett said, "These are gorgeous. But where's the one of the horse running off after the barn door's been left open?" He didn't wait to see if she got his joke before he added, "Inflation. We were talking about inflation being on the run."

While they shared a laugh, Stella glanced, seemingly, at me.

She told him, "I got the joke. That would have been wonderful. The painting you noticed above the entry to the vestibule, of the rocks by Lake Michigan, the artist hid Alan Greenspan's initials on a rock. It could have been an insiders' thing like that plus it would have given people walking out of serious meetings down here something to laugh about. I'm being transferred to another department and an old friend there gave me a copy of his secret cartoon book. Most deal with regulators behaving badly and one makes its case with a horse far off from the open barn door. Funny. I just saw that. Timing."

While they waited for an elevator, they began talking about the commonplace book. He told her he was grateful the Fed Bank hadn't kept it. She didn't tell him the Fed Bank had no say in the decision.

Everett said, "We have what I believe is an almost-duplicate of the commonplace book that you found. There's a letter — "

Everett sensed the change that came over Stella when the elevator doors opened and she saw Wendell.

Wendell nodded at Stella, then, with a question in his eyes, nodded at Everett.

Everett saw Stella's tight, insincere smile and didn't nod back at Wendell but raised his eyebrows at her.

He said, "I'll tell you about the letter upstairs. But the horse and barn door deal — "

Just as the elevator doors opened on the cafeteria floor, Wendell caught Everett's eyes, nodded again, and turned to the corner. Finding his zipper up, he turned back.

Once the newcomers were settled and the elevator doors closed, Wendell bumped Everett's elbow and quietly asked, "It's up?"

Everett looked confused and said, "Good job."

Stella watched the interaction and drew in her lips.

She and Everett made it to her office before they burst out laughing. He asked, "Who is that guy?"

She said, "That's what he gets for eavesdropping."

Their laughs were deep, from their bellies, until they heard Wendell holler for Winnie. He hadn't ventured too far down the hall before getting caught in a sudden pocket of warm air.

Stella and Everett laughed harder as people do when they try to laugh quietly.

Finally, calmed, Stella asked, "Where have you come from? I've not laughed like that for a while. Thank you. Let me get this wonderful book that belonged to your grandfather?"

"Yes, that Everett was my grandfather."

As she sat, she glanced my way again and told Everett, "I think I'm seeing things today. Too much laughing."

As Everett turned the pages, he explained some of the writings and told Stella, "In the commonplace book my grandfather had as his own, there was a note that his grandmother, who would have been Lucy's mother, had recreated it as best she could after the original was lost. My grandfather said the original lacked an important page. My great-grandfather wrote an essay about the Eastland and whether it's roll was caused by a mandated lifeboat installation that wasn't right for the boat. He proposed all regulation, lifeboat, bank, whatever, carries that risk if it's not well-written, well-thought, well-overseen, well-everything. I'll send you a copy. The message isn't so different than your cartoon of the horse running after regulators left the barn door open. My wife was trying to get the essay published after the 2008 crisis, but then she got a cancer diagnosis."

Stella offered her condolences and told him about the Eastland historians who would certainly be interested.

"My daughter would love to talk with them. She's got Everett's commonplace book with the essay here in Chicago. She just moved in August for school."

Stella asked and he told her about my great-great-granddaughter's studies and her brother's career.

He said, "The book my grandfather had didn't have this family tree page with my great-grandparents. I wished I could have known them. They were the first ones to pursue finance instead of farming. Since then, we've split, some finance, mostly from my grandfather's part of the family, and some farming, mostly from my great-uncle Craig and great-aunt Lizzie's children, but none of us does both farming and finance anymore. Craig and Lizzie raised my grandfather after Lucy and Everett were gone. I'm sure none of that makes sense."

Stella's eyes filled. "It does, here they are on the tree. How wonderful they did that for your grandfather." I was sure she was thinking of her sister's family.

When a tear fell between them, an inch from the book, they looked at one another in surprise.

While I hurried away from them, Stella glanced once more in my direction and said, "Something in the ceiling maybe. They were having problems switching to heat for the winter. Here, let's put the book back in the packaging."

He said, "That job offer letter is different than what we have. The one we have is shorter, with a little different tone. I'll send you a copy."

"We'd love that. The archivist you'll meet soon, he did keep a copy of the letter since it was written by an employee but he thinks the original should go with your book. And it's time to go meet him and Dawn, who you've already met over the phone. They are looking forward to meeting you. I have a tote bag if you'd like to bring the book or you are welcome to come back here."

"I'll come back here."

By then, I'd slipped onto the stool hidden by the file cabinets. I wasn't physically present, but I'd formed a shadow. The one Stella kept glancing toward.

From there, I heard Wendell in Gage's office, claiming that Stella might be meeting with a lawyer.

Gage told him, "Just ask the guy what's his business here. He's in our building on your floor."

Luckily, when he and Wendell knocked on Stella's door, she was already gone with Everett.

When Stella and Everett returned, he was describing the area in Michigan near her sister's cottage. Stella's sister had left it to Stella with the condition Stella leave it to her sister's children on her death.

Stella told him, "Let me look up our addresses on a map. It will be wonderful to know someone when I eventually get up there."

"Everyone's wonderful. It's slower there, People are nicer." He pointed at her monitor. "There, we're neighbors. I wasn't sure I'd keep our cottage after my wife died, but it's turned out to be a good place to escape when my kids stayed with their grandparents. Now I'll make that my main home and trade from up there."

Stella tilted her head. "Everett, I'm sorry, I'm distracted. I'm seeing the same feet pass by outside the door."

Everett realized that only the top three-quarters of the door's sidelight panels were frosted. "I've never missed working in an office."

"The clear panels have provided endless humor. We'd never been so aware of shoes before the renovation that got us those windows." Her voice lowered to a whisper. "I think that's the fly-down guy's shoes."

They laughed again.

She handed the commonplace book to him. "Today was wonderfully fun. Thank you."

He said, "I'm here in Chicago for a few more days. Any interest in dinner?"

I suspected that Stella's heart, broken by the double loss of her sister and her job, created a vacuum at just the right moment when Everett told her he'd never been to the Italian Village.

They agreed to meet the next evening.

After he'd left with the commonplace book, I increasingly felt, well, present. Who knew I'd have to return to leave.

THE END

&PILOGUE

November 2019

From Adam

Hi Stella,

Carrie gave me the good news that Payments brought you over as an Officer. Congrats, I think, though you're probably counting days now anyway.

After Wendell made us collect your laptop, he made a big deal of my checking it for nefarious activity before wiping it. I didn't check it but did try to wipe it. The wipe kicked out a file named LucyStory.doc. Not sure why it won't delete.

It looks personal. I attached a couple pages. I can copy the file to a thumb drive and mail it to you unless you'll be in the Bank. No rush since the laptop's going to be destroyed anyway.

P.S. I interviewed for your job. Gage slipped and told me the posting was a sham. Wendell already decided your replacement. The friend Andrea hired for HR Officer was already dating the Recruiting Manager on the sly. When they wanted to get engaged, Andrea asked Wendell to take her friend in Research. He didn't want to add an HR Officer as precedent so he promised your job. I don't think Gage meant to tell me all that. I think he's unhappy he couldn't promote his coffee buddy.

From Stella

Hi Adam,

I'm sorry you didn't get the job.

All that explains why Gage said at one point I could just hang around for a year. I didn't take him seriously but see now Wendell would have done that just to bring up Andrea's friend. She had started blocking promotions for our team and asking tons of questions about Research a couple months before the posting. She must have known. Damn.

But for you, are you OK there or are you looking? I'll keep an eye out in Payments.

Since the Payments team I'm in is all remote, I'm moving to Michigan as soon as work is done on the cottage. I have Sunday dinner with my parents now and was surprised, though more miles, I can get to them quicker from Michigan than from downtown. If you and Sally ever come up this way, let me know.

Regarding the file, this is embarrassing. I have no idea what LucyStory is and if it was anyone other than you telling me about it, I'd be afraid I was being set up. Does it say it was created by me?

From Stella

Hi Adam,

I'm glad you called. After much thought, I'm worried I don't remember it. I never shared my password or allowed anyone to use the laptop. I guess good for me if I found time to write a book. There's a lot I don't remember from recent months.

On the other hand, I'm certain I talked with my sister four days after she died, so I'm open to LucyStory having been authored by a ghost.

I'd like to read the whole thing but are you comfortable if we just sit on it until January?

From Adam

Hi Stella,

Sure. Let me know if you can have lunch before you go fully remote and I'll bring a copy.

February 2020

From Adam

Hi Stella,

So as things turn out, Sally got a grant related to her research. She needs to be in New York for the next year. We found out about the grant on the same day Andrea's friend told me to start tucking in my shirts. So I'm happy to report I'm joining New York IT for the last year or two of my Fed time.

Should I send a copy of the thumb drive to Chicago or Michigan?

Be careful out there.

From Stella

Adam,

Michigan please. Cottage is finally ready and I need to get away from the elevators in my building here. No way can people socially distance in them.

I've been thinking about your idea. Lucy's Story isn't 100% accurate but that probably doesn't matter. I agree it might be interesting to folks who don't read much nonfiction but want to know a bit about the Fed. We couldn't do anything with it until we retire though. Do you think it would still be relevant?

I'm planning to retire at the earliest July 2021.

I'm off work packing in my Chicago apartment today and tomorrow if you'd rather call.

P.S. Lucy's great-grandson Everett sent Tim a copy of the Fed guy's page from their family's version of that commonplace book. Thought you might enjoy it.

Employment offered to Everett, Jr.

We opened on November 16, 1914, as the United States' lender of last resort. Months into it now, and grown beyond our few chairs, we continue to be formed by Treasury Secretary McAdoo's words, "The way to begin is to begin. When you make a start, everything will be smoothed out by practice."

No two days in these months have been alike and each day requires new learning and new processes. I'm particularly proud that we're accounting for our uncertainty without pretense, reporting to news that "various departments are now fully organized and equipped and in readiness for increased activities, whatever they may be."

More important than our daily work plan is the public confidence we've engendered among those in our region, specifically, confidence that we'll lend to a bank when liquidity troubles might otherwise prevent the bank from having cash on hand for a depositor's withdrawal.

The business of banking – borrowing from depositors and lending to borrowers – is important to every individual, even those who do not use a bank, because it is how idle money is moved to productive uses to grow the economy. But the very nature of the business is fragile as even the soundest bank would be troubled by all of its depositors arriving at the same time to withdraw their deposits. Now, the Fed Bank will be there to step in and lend enough to cover the withdrawals when runs arise at a bank.

The public's confidence in that mechanism is important to the monetary stability that's been lacking in our country, but what's most needed is expanding the public's confidence that the Fed Bank's operations can prevent the runs from ever beginning.

To build that confidence, the Fed Banks must inform the public about their existence and responsibilities. It's most gratifying when others assist in this effort, including the member banks themselves. The National Bank of Commerce of St. Louis was just reported in the news for having included in its customers' statements a short digest explaining, "in a simple but an effective manner, the underlying principles of this [Federal Reserve] act so that the ordinary customer can get an idea of its work."

Your great uncle and your father asked if I truly thought the Fed Bank would be here when you are ready to come. I do. Though the first two attempts at installing a central bank in the U.S. are long in the past, their lessons continue to bite and informed the many compromises of the wise men who created the Federal Reserve. There will always be a need to balance public and private power by distinguishing the roles among those *who've been involved in our creation: for the regional commercial banks, such as those Main Street banks who loan for seed purchases in a farming community; for the money center banks, such as those on Wall Street; and for the federal government.*

Regarding the latter, it is widely accepted that responsibility for monetary stability must be insulated from the political cycle on which our government operates. Discussion has been had of how we will respond when the eventual happens and an incumbent politician would direct us to set aside monetary stability so he might spend more to gain favor and aid his bid for re-election or bolster his claim to fostering economic success. It won't happen in my lifetime, and perhaps not yours, but someday, when a politician is unfamiliar with history and doesn't take the time to read up a bit on central banking. For now, it is a lesser concern because the politicians are the very same who created us.

Aside from the independence of the Federal Reserve System from politicians, we were created with an independence within. A geographically decentralized structure is intended to ensure no area of the country goes unrepresented when monetary policy decisions are made. In each of the twelve Federal Reserve Districts, a Fed Bank is operating semi-autonomously and will set the rates it will charge when it makes loans to banks in that District. Each Fed Bank will be owned by its member banks, who, in exchange, will select most of the Directors. Though a Washington, D.C., Federal Reserve office has an oversight role, we here have independence from it. No one is calling it independence, but I expect some day they will. And I'm hopeful no one of our successors here will take advantage of that independence.

It's an important institution, Everett, one that everyone should understand. Even if you plan to return to your family's farm, or to your parents' bank if their dream is realized, a stint here will serve you well. I'll still be here when you are ready. I see no reason I'll leave. I feel privileged to be able to use the skills and knowledge I acquired in my career to now serve the public rather than profits. This salary is enough.

If I've confused you above in reference to banks, I'll apologize. The distinction of the Federal Reserve Banks within the Federal Reserve System is deep. But perhaps they ought not have been called "Banks" in order to avoid confusion with the "banks" for commerce with which we are all already familiar. I expect we'll figure out proper names before too much time has passed.

I'll wish you a joyous childhood and good studies in school with an appropriate amount of fun and look forward to your joining us here. This constitutes an offer of employment.

July 2020

From Adam

Hi Stella:

How's Everett doing? We've so far stayed healthy but Covid is making us rethink our plans for staying in NY. I had an idea for a horror story a long time ago, a sort of Stephen King with economists. Since we've been stuck inside, I've started it.

So I'd love to get my name out there with Lucy's Story. What's your retirement timeline? I'm going one year from now.

From Stella

Hi,

I'm grateful you two are healthy and that I can report Everett's getting better. He's still isolating out of an abundance of caution.

His daughter stayed with me when she came from Chicago to help him and be near during the worst of it. It was great to meet her. She knows a lot about their family's history. She read Lucy's Story while she was here. I was afraid she'd tell me I was too crazy for her father when I said I didn't know where the book came from but she thinks the mystery is fun.

She says there really is a three-legged stool. She's got it in Chicago and an artist friend of hers painted each carving in a different color. Sounds gorgeous. She's sending pics.

I'm grateful you found Lucy's Story. The more I think about it, the more I love it and your idea that we publish it. To the extent Lucy's interests must be considered, Everett and his daughter, as her heirs, also think we should publish it. :)

I'm still targeting July 2021, same as you.

August 2021

From Adam

Hi Stella,

How's retirement?

I was back in Chicago last week and spent some time in the Loop. When I walked by the Bank, I was struck by the columns. Literally struck. After all those years walking between them, they are not familiar. So wide now that someone could hide behind them. Barely any room to squeeze by. The vertical scallops are deeper, enough room for a Starbucks cup. And they thin out at the top. I didn't feel like I belonged.

Time for a Zoom on Friday to talk about how we go about publishing Lucy's Story? I'm attaching my changes on top of your changes. I ran across a letter Toomey and others sent to Powell to warn the Fed off climate change. It was from this past March so I couldn't work it in.

January 2022

From Stella

Hey Adam,

Did you see the articles about Clarida's stock trades right before the Fed jumped into markets at the start of Covid? Clarida on top of the Dallas and the Boston Presidents resigning last September over their trading, though Boston said it was health. This breaks my heart. I thought the Fed was better than that.

From Adam

Wow. When I used to disclose that tiny pension I have from teaching, Legal made me call and confirm it was not invested with a banking concentration. How in the world did Clarida's trades and for that matter the presidents' not get caught? And why in the world did they think what they did was ethical? I do think the Fed is better than that.

Pockets of problems but I still believe in it. It's got a pocket problem.

July 2022

From Adam

Hi Stella,

I saw the new rejection. Let's publish without an agent.

From Stella

Hi Adam,

Sounds good. Zoom call next week?

And did you see the news this morning? There's a Republican report about China's attempt to infiltrate the Fed. I haven't read it yet but gosh. I hope it's not true and if any of it is, I hope the Fed figured it out itself.

I worry a lot about Congress taking up the Fed in session when too many are clueless and partisan and don't focus on solutions. I fear they'd throw the baby out even before the bathwater because it's easier to do that than learn about what the Fed does and why independence matters.

It would be great if Lucy's Story encouraged readers to hold their Congresspersons accountable for understanding the Fed and not using it for their own purposes.

ABOUT THE AUTHOR

Erma Clare was employed by a Federal Reserve Bank for over thirty years and taught about the Federal Reserve System as adjunct faculty of a university for over ten of those years.

ACKNOWLEDGEMENTS

I'm grateful to so many for support, curiosity about what I was doing, instruction, and feedback. A few went far beyond what I could ever have hoped.

My parents gave up much to get me through college and have done more since that led to my claiming a year to write. My mother was unwavering in her willingness to answer innumerable requests to evaluate metaphors, opine on attempts at a friendly explanation of open market operations, find elements for Lucy's commonplace, and believe in ghosts.

Jane Keane painstakingly marked up a nightmarish first version of a first draft of the book, answered many "what if, would you" questions, and graciously held a vision of the book with me ever since.

Maribeth Hnatyk ushered the book around its final turn with multiple rounds of feedback. Sharing her perspective and laughing with me when I began to balk at daring to publish a book about the Fed were gifts without measure.

Cindy Hessling told me she cried when Lucy's Everett died just when I needed to hear I could make someone cry.

My Fed friends taught me so much as we worked together and shared life's joys and sorrows. To those who read this book, I hope you see it as supportive of our shared goal of helping the public to better understand the Fed.

David Groff, upon receipt of a heap of detritus, provided instructions to demarcate the forest, remove dead trees and nourish growing trees, and clear the forest floor. I'm certain there could have been no better editor than David for me and *A Fed Spirit*. Any remaining clumps of twigs and moldy leaves belong wholly to me.

Marcia Bradley at the Sarah Lawrence Writing Institute went far beyond her teaching obligation to find a path for *A Fed Spirit*. Tessa Smith McGovern at Sarah Lawrence Writing Institute and Otis Haschemeyer and Joshua Mohr at Stanford Continuing Studies Writing Program provided feedback that shaped the book.

CPSIA information can be obtained
at www.ICGtesting.com
Printed in the USA
LVHW100900181122
733438LV00002B/12